WITCH
IN
TIME

A WITCH
IN
TIME

CONSTANCE
SAYERS

PIATKUS

PIATKUS

First published in the US in 2020 by Redhook,
an imprint of Orbit, a division of Hachette Book Group, Inc

First published in Great Britain in 2020 by Piatkus
This paperback edition published in 2020 by Piatkus

5 7 9 10 8 6 4

Copyright © 2020 by Constance Sayers

The moral right of the author has been asserted.

A CIP catalogue record for this book
is available from the British Library.

ISBN 978-0-349-42594-8

Printed and bound in Great Britain by Clays Ltd, Elcograf S.p.A.

Papers used by Piatkus are from well-managed forests
and other responsible sources.

Piatkus
An imprint of
Little, Brown Book Group
Carmelite House
50 Victoria Embankment
London EC4Y 0DZ

An Hachette UK Company
www.hachette.co.uk

www.littlebrown.co.uk

To my sister, Lois Sayers

I am hopelessly in love with a memory.
An echo from other time, another place.
—*Michael Faudet*

1

Helen Lambert
Washington, DC, May 24, 2012

Just after my divorce was final, my friend set me up on a blind date. I walked through Le Bar at the Sofitel on 15th Street and asked for the "Varner party." The hostess pointed to a man sitting alone by the window.

Washington is—at its heart—a genteel Southern town with a dress code to match. In a room bursting with navy suits, bow ties, and the occasional summer seersucker, Luke Varner was terribly out of place. Dressed head-to-toe in black, he looked like an art director from Soho who'd taken the Acela the wrong direction at Penn Station only to find himself surrounded by overfed men swirling glasses of bourbon and chewing on unlit cigars.

He looked up, and I could see that he was neither dashing nor smoldering. The man possessed no exotic features; he was, in fact, rather neutral looking, like a favorite pair of khakis. For a moment I wondered what my friend Mickey had been thinking. This man was *not* my type.

"I'm Helen Lambert." I extended my clammy hand, a sign that shouted I hadn't been on a date in nearly ten years. My first thought was that this would be brief—one drink just to be polite. I was getting back out there, and a practice date would do me some good.

"Hello. Luke Varner." He stood, studying me for a moment like he was surprised by what he saw.

Despite my own disappointment in him, I sank a little, wondering if, somehow, I had also fallen short of Mickey's description. Luke took his seat but seemed pensive and quiet, like he was solving a puzzle in his head. After he motioned for me to join him, there was a long, unnerving silence between us.

"Mickey told me all about your house. He says it's lovely." I sat down and started to chat, rambling really, arranging my cloth napkin on my lap, picking it up and putting it down. To my horror, the white threads from the napkin began shedding all over my solid black skirt. I waved the offending napkin at the hostess as though surrendering.

The corner of Luke Varner's mouth turned up in the beginnings of a laugh at my futile attempts to get the attention of our hostess. Suddenly I felt that I was inadvertently hamming it up like a vaudeville actress.

"Well, it's old," said Luke.

"Huh?" I gave him a puzzled look.

"*My house*." He laughed. "You were asking about my house." His voice had a sandpaper texture to it, like he'd enjoyed his share of cigarettes over the years. "I like homes with period details, or 'character' as they call it nowadays."

"Character." I nodded. "Did Mickey tell you that we sometimes work together?"

Luke leaned back in his seat with what seemed like a smirk. "I heard you run a magazine."

"*In Frame*." I straightened. "The name is a take on photography—what's in the shot or 'in the frame'—we're looking at trends, what is next to come into focus whether it's global politics, culture, religion, fashion, lifestyle...we have beats all over the world with our reporters and writers looking at trends bubbling to the surface. We're known for our photography." I was beginning to sound like a brochure, so I stopped myself before adding that *In Frame* had just won the National Magazine Award, and had been described as "one of the most important magazines contributing to not only the national, but global stage."

The hostess finally handed me a new black napkin, and I spread it across my lap. I was nervous and crossed my legs so they'd stop shaking. Why was I so anxious about a man I'd already decided I had no interest in? I chalked it up to nerves in getting back into the dating scene. But there was something else.

"*In Frame*, that's right," he said. "I've seen it on the newsstands."

"It's bigger than most magazines," I offered. "Makes the photos really jump."

He took a deep breath and looked at the table as he spoke. "You haven't changed. I mean you *have* changed...the hair mostly. It is more of a copper color now." He began studying his fork. "I'm sorry," he mumbled.

"Excuse me?" I thought I'd misunderstood him. "We've just met." I laughed and rearranged my own fork and knife.

He flipped open his menu, scanned it, and then slapped it down. His head tilted. "Do I look familiar to you at all?"

I shook my head, suddenly embarrassed. "Have we met before? I have the *worst* memory."

"Nothing? Really?" He leaned in closer, I assumed so I could inspect his face. His small, deep-blue eyes danced above the lit votive on the table. I noticed his face had an unintentional tan, like he worked in a garden, and he had at least a day's worth of blond stubble—or was it gray? At that moment, in the light, something *did* seem familiar. "Nope." But that was a lie.

"I hate this moment." He rubbed his legs, looking nervous. "I go about thirty years hating this moment, and then you call me and we do this all over again." He circled his slender forefinger to illustrate. "I just haven't seen you in a long time."

"I'm sorry...I *call* you?"

"Uh-huh. The first time was 1895 in France." He paused. "Actually, that was your mother, but we don't need to get technical about it."

"My *mother*?" I was envisioning Margie Connor, my mother, who was at this very moment guzzling box wine and gobbling smoked Gouda cheese bits at her book club in Bethesda. This month they were revisiting *The Poisonwood Bible*.

"Then there was Los Angeles in 1935. Last time was Taos in 1970. Honestly, I wish you'd come back in Venice or somewhere a little more interesting. I mean, this Washington place is a swamp." He scowled. "I know you see a resemblance to Paris here, but..." His voice drifted off and he casually settled back into the banquette like he'd just told me about his day at the office.

I exhaled loud enough to inadvertently catch the attention of the man at the next table. "Let me get this clear. I *called* you in 1895?" I placed my napkin on the table and eyed my jacket. Finally, I stood up. "Mr. Varner. I'm sorry. You must have me confused with someone else."

"Helen," he said with an authority that surprised me. "I'm really not good at this, but theatrics are childish. *Sit down*."

"Sit down?" I leaned in, placing my hands on the table. "You're a lunatic, Mr. Varner. I don't know you. I'm thirty-three years old, not a hundred. I've never met you in France...or anywhere else for that matter. And my mother? She works for the National Institutes of Health. She did not...call you in 1895, I assure you."

"Helen." His voice quieted. "*Sit down*."

And for some strange reason I obeyed, lowering myself onto my chair, like a child.

We sat there looking at each other. Throughout the bar, the candles on the tables were like little streetlamps, and I felt something familiar. Then it hit me. *Gaslights?* I shook my head to ward off the clear image of this man's weathered face illuminated under a gaslight. The images in my head moved quickly, like flashes—this man smiling at me while we went down a wide boulevard in a carriage, the sound of purposeful hooves hitting pavement, the lights around us shining, brightening his face in a sepia-toned wash the way a flashlight does when you shine it under the covers. His clothes were strangely out of place—almost like he was wearing a Victorian costume—and the setting was all wrong. I swayed in my chair, gripping the table with both hands, and then turned and looked out the window. Even the trees outside, swaying slightly in the breeze and lined with string lights, were conspiratorially twinkling, making his face glow mysteriously from another time, like a tragic character from a Shelley poem.

He pushed the menu away. "You called me a little while ago and asked me to do something for you and I did it."

I began to protest, but he held up his hand. "Helen, really? We both know what I'm talking about. Don't we?"

And I did.

2

Helen Lambert
Washington, DC, January 2012

At the end of January, Roger, my husband, told me it was over between us. We'd had our lawyers on hold, neither of us making a move toward a divorce despite being separated for a year. We'd tried therapy, living together, living apart, but nothing seemed to fix the broken pieces of us in a way that felt we were a going concern. Mostly, I'd felt abandoned by him for his first love, the Hanover Collection.

Roger was the chief curator and director of the Hanover Collection, a museum that contained more than three thousand French and American paintings, plus one of the largest black-and-white photography collections ever assembled in the US. But that is making the Hanover sound like a building, and it was much more than that. The Hanover Collection was my husband's obsession. No space was good enough to house it, and there weren't enough hours in the day for him to work on it. I'd find sketches of buildings and floor plans of new wings on napkins and errant paper scraps—even in the bathroom. It was difficult to get Roger's full attention for any length of time for mundane things like fixing a broken dishwasher. For three years, Roger led an eighty-five-million-dollar capital campaign to build the perfect home for his collection—the success of this effort due largely to hiring Sara Davidz who was, apparently, a fund-raising phenomenon. Roger had managed to grow the museum's attendance beyond 425,000 visitors, not bad considering the Hanover, a private institution, competed with the free Smithsonian museums scattered all over Washington. In a museum town, Roger Lambert was a king. A wunderkind in the philanthropy world—a mad genius—he was profiled in the *New York Times* and *Washington Post* style sections as well as *The Chronicle of Philanthropy*. He even gave a famous TED Talk on how grassroots organizers could raise money for causes they believed in. Now he'd shocked Washingtonians—arguably some of the greatest creators of museums—by working *not* with an American architect, but with a Japanese firm to build a block-and-glass contraption in the up-and-coming Waterfront area. The move to take the Hanover out of its location in the old Georgian mansion on Reservoir Road in Georgetown to the trendy stretch along Maine Avenue was one that, briefly, turned the museum world against him—the *Washington Post* labeling his treasured museum design as "an expensive travesty resembling stacked ice cubes." As the stately, labyrinthine mansion in upper Georgetown remained empty, kids began to break the windows, forcing the historical society to board up the eyesore. And then Roger Lambert fell further out of favor.

Roger and I were a bit of a fixture in Washington. We were a couple well known for entertaining at our house on Capitol Hill. Each month, we'd host a dinner for someone we'd profiled in the latest issue of *In Frame*—like "bringing an issue to life." Our dining room could fit sixteen people comfortably, so a seat at our monthly gatherings became a coveted invitation. Roger and I were careful with our guest list, mixing painters with politicians; mathematicians with musicians. Once a year, we might do an all-artists dinner or an all-politics dinner, but the fun thing we both enjoyed was curating an eclectic guest list with some tension. The invitation itself was a phone call from Roger or me, and you'd be surprised to find that people flew in from all over the world just to sit around our table. But our process wasn't without problems. A renowned photographer once turned down an invitation by hanging up on me, saying we were "too bourgeois" (we were, a little, but that was part of the fun). Then a famous actor stormed out of our house because we sat him next to a scientist who didn't know who he was. Unfortunately, our Maryland Avenue house wasn't on a frequent cab route so he had to spend ten minutes in a glacial January waiting for a Nigerian cabdriver who also had no idea who he was.

But it all ended abruptly at the end of January when Roger took me to dinner at our favorite Vietnamese restaurant on Connecticut Avenue and told me that he'd fallen in love with Sara. In truth, this news wasn't entirely a surprise. I'd first suspected then *known* about them, but I didn't take her, or their fling, seriously. I thought it was a phase he was going through.

As he explained it, though, his love for Sara was a hopeless, terminal love—the kind he'd never known until she'd walked through the door. I nodded like a dutiful student in the front row of class, spooning my pho while he wore this wild look on his face—a look I hadn't seen in years. I take that back—a look I'd *never* seen.

I'd met Roger at Georgetown University when he sat next to me in a class called American History Since 1865. It was a class no one wanted to take because the professor was famous for never giving out any grade higher than a C. Although a senior, Roger had registered for classes late, so he'd been forced to take it. As a political science major, it was a requirement for me, and I would be awarded the rare A grade.

In those days, I wandered the campus with my red hair up in a high ponytail with Bettie Page bangs and sported a pair of cat's-eye glasses and a thick volume of Robert Caro's *The Path to Power*, one of several books he'd written about Lyndon B. Johnson, always tucked under my arm. At first glance, I found Roger annoying because he was never prepared for class, but he must have sensed I could be wooed by political maneuvering. That fall, he rigged the homecoming queen contest in my favor, feverishly stuffing ballot boxes and getting large droves of students to vote for me. It was such an LBJ move that, honestly, I was flattered. In the end, I was named a respectable second runner-up and Roger was rewarded for his efforts with a date that lasted ten years.

As I closed my eyes, I could still see our life together—the late nights dressed in our formalwear after a gala eating midnight breakfast at Au Pied de Cochon on Wisconsin Avenue; dinners at 2Amys and Pete's in Friendship Heights, where we debated over which restaurant made the best pizza; buying a grand old row house on Capitol Hill that we could barely afford; driving to Charlottesville in Roger's Jeep listening to House of Love's *Babe Rainbow* tape until it wore out; and finally, him nervously proposing to me among the Barboursville Ruins during the intermission at Shakespeare's *Twelfth Night*.

But there were bad times as well. Roger and I tried, and failed, to have a baby for several years. I suppose for me, this became my obsession. The monthly deliveries of Clomid had sat hopefully in the refrigerator next to the eggs. (The irony of that was not lost on me.) Our marriage had been five wonderful years and two not-so-great ones.

But the Hanover Collection and Sara had changed everything. Roger explained that he'd called his lawyer, who'd put in the paperwork to rush our divorce and that he hoped we'd be in court within thirty days to "finalize things." I hugged him goodbye and went back to my own apartment, curled up in my bed, and with a primal, child-like focus wished Sara harm—or dead—I'm not really sure which anymore. I didn't want to finalize things with Roger. I wanted him back. I wanted the gods to even the score. Now I know that I was sloppy with my wish. But we've all wished someone dead at some point, haven't we? We don't really *mean* it.

Two weeks passed before Roger called again. Our talks were purely transactional now, so I assumed he was calling me concerning the court date he'd wanted so badly.

"I can't meet you tomorrow about the house," he said. "Johanna died."

"I'm sorry, Roger." I paused. "Do we know a Johanna?"

"Sara's mother, Johanna," he barked. "Sara's mother is dead."

I realized that *we*, in fact, did not know a Johanna.

When couples separate, you pick up the slightest thing that shows that the distance between you has increased, switching from morning coffee to chai tea, your ex sporting a new T-shirt that you know for certain you've never washed, or peppering a new name in conversation. Roger had an entire new Rolodex of names now that I knew nothing about. Johanna was one of them, and now, apparently, she was dead.

I was just learning to adjust to being without Roger. In my obser-vations of divorce, if there is another party involved—and Sara was, indeed, another party—your friends spill every last detail to you out of loyalty. They aren't sure of the permanence of your marital situa-tion, so, hedging their bets, they dispense information freely—names, places, cars, times they've seen her, exactly what she wears and where she gets her nails done. Then, just as suddenly as it starts, information shuts off. These same friends look away and change the subject at the mention of her, deciding it's time for you to move on and that hiding details will hasten your grieving process along. But what it does, instead, is alienate you from everyone. As Roger rambled on about Johanna, it occurred to me that I felt utterly alone.

The following week, I passed Roger in the hallway of my lawyer's office where he'd stopped by to transfer the car title. I was startled by his appearance. His face seemed to have been dragged over a cheese grater—an old, rusty one at that. With his hands wrapped in several bloody bandages, Roger explained that the window in Sara's house had shattered on him while he was cleaning it. The whole time he was telling me this story, his voice a whisper, he never looked at me. I'm not sure if it was because he was in pain or because he had seen enough of me, but I was unsettled by something I couldn't put my finger on. That afternoon, I called our mutual friend Mickey and asked him what he'd heard. Over lunch at Off the Record at the Hay-Adams Hotel, Mick painted the whole picture for me.

"First"—he leaned in conspiratorially—"Sara's mother died in some freak accident in like *four* feet of water at the YMCA before her aqua aerobics class. Four feet? Who dies in that? I mean, stand up, right?" He shrugged. "Then a grieving Sara begins to clean everything in the entire fucking house including the windows. Yuck, right?" Mickey rolled his eyes. "Apparently, she has floor-to-ceiling windows in the new addition to her midcentury."

I rolled my eyes. "Of course she does."

"Well, one of those fabulous windows shattered on both Roger and her. It could have killed them both." As if I didn't get the gravity of the situation, Mickey drew a dramatic line across his neck. "They don't make windows like they used to, I guess."

Then he lowered his voice and dropped the bomb. "Sara asked him to leave. She thinks it's bad karma over their relationship."

And I had to admit that I agreed with Sara. Something in the universe was swirling, but I couldn't shake the feeling that it had been me who'd done it—first Johanna, then the window. I was probably being delusional and narcissistic. I couldn't control things like that in the universe. Could I?

And then I met *him* and he confirmed everything.

3

Helen Lambert
Washington, DC, May 24, 2012

I was about to speak, but Luke raised his finger to stop me. I turned to see the waiter standing directly behind me.

"We'll have a bottle of the Château Haut-Brion," Luke said in perfect French to the waiter, who scribbled the order down before retreating. "As I was saying, you called me, but then you called it off... changed your mind. Shouldn't surprise me by now, really. You aren't a vengeful creature. You never were."

"What the *fuck* are you talking about?" I hissed.

Luke raised his eyebrow. "Really, Red?" He reached across the small bistro table between us and moved a lock of my hair out of my eye. "I seem to remember you wanting something *pretty* bad, curled up on your bed." Luke took a deep breath. "I was hoping you'd ask me to kill him, but you didn't. I would have enjoyed that. This time around, Roger Lambert is an even bigger asshole than Billy Rapp, more clueless and duller. Why is it always him, Red? Always. I guess you can't help it, though, can you?"

"What on God's earth are you talking about? Who in the hell is Billy Rapp?"

He looked at me as if deciding something. "Never mind."

"*You* drowned Sara's mother." My voice croaked.

"No." He pointed to me. "Technically, you did."

Luke had ordered appetizers, and the pommes frites with Parmesan and truffles arrived. He began chomping on frites like we were having a casual conversation about the band we'd just seen at Rock & Roll Hotel or something and weren't, in fact, having a conversation about killing a woman. He paused until the waiter walked away.

"Seriously, Helen, you could be a bit more careful around the waiters." He pulled another french fry from the silver tray and pointed it at me before dipping it in mayonnaise. "You were sloppy. You said you wanted…let's see…how did you phrase it." He stared up at the ceiling. "'Harm to come to Sara.'"

"I said I wanted her *dead*." Like a pouting child, I took a couple of frites and stuffed them in my mouth. I chewed them slowly, hoping it showed my disgust.

"No." He shook his head. "You most certainly did *not* say that." He took a drink of water. "Had you said that, she'd be dead. End of story. You never remember this stuff, do you? We're *very* specific about these things." He actually shook a fry at me.

"I never said to kill her mother." I sat back and crossed my arms, smug.

"I repeat. You said, 'I want harm to come to Sara.'" He threw up his hands. "Harm can mean anything. You don't want to play with this shit, Red. You should know that on some cellular level, surely." He put his hand out like he was presenting something to me. "You call in a general order for poultry, you might get Cornish hen or you might get Thanksgiving turkey, am I right? Precision is key here." He pointed his fingers in emphasis like a politician—and then just like a lunatic in a bad B movie, Luke Varner changed the subject. "I like this place." His face lit up. "It reminds me of us in 1938."

"You're crazy." I lowered my voice.

He ignored me. "Your name was Nora then. Nora Wheeler."

The name off his lips shook me, like a song that I'd heard a long time ago, one that had been out of reach in my memory but that I'd still longed for. I didn't admit that to him, of course, but the name Nora Wheeler was familiar. I had the strangest urge to correct him and say, *No, you mean Norma.* This whole thing was mad and it was messing with my head. I figured I'd give it another five minutes before making an excuse to go to the bathroom and slipping out the back door. Tomorrow, I'd deal with Mickey for this date from hell.

Luke continued to snack while the waiter opened the wine and poured the Bordeaux into his glass and then mine before setting the bottle between us. "Can I show you something after this?" Luke picked up his glass and drank it without fussing, no spinning it in the glass or sniffing it, as if there was nothing about it that could surprise or delight him.

We ate in silence and then Luke insisted on paying the check. Once outside the Sofitel, we caught a cab, but I stopped before I got inside. "I'll take the next one," I said. The doorman already had a Diamond Cab cued up.

Luke shrugged. "Meet me at Maine Avenue. The Hanover Collection."

"I can't go there. My ex-husband is—"

"Roger Lambert...you think I don't know that?" He shook his head and crawled into the first cab. "Jesus, Red, sometimes..." I could hear him mumbling.

This was my chance to flee. I got into the cab and told the driver to head toward my apartment on East Capitol Street. But as my cab headed down New York Avenue past the Museum of Women in the Arts, my curiosity began to needle at me. If I was honest, Luke had begun to agitate me, like the tingling before an itch. Despite the crazy things he'd said, there was something comforting about him. Since my divorce, it felt like I'd been holding my breath. I found myself exhaling for the first time in a year. I leaned toward the front seat and instructed the driver to change his route. Minutes later, the cab left me at the Maine Avenue entrance, where I found Luke leaning against the wall smoking a cigarette. "I figured it was fifty–fifty you'd show."

"You have fifteen minutes." I folded my hands in front of me. "Impress me."

I expected us to get turned away. It was after hours at the museum, but Luke walked in ahead of me, through the front doors like he worked there—no—like he *owned* the place. The staff greeted him with a too-pleasant "Welcome, Mr. Varner" as we came through the metal detectors. I was shocked because while Roger and I were married, we never came here after hours. In fact, I stopped in the hall and wondered how in the hell we were even let into the museum at this hour, yet the late-night security staff seemed thrilled to help him.

Overlooking the water, the Hanover Collection building spanned a full block and was three stories tall. Usually, I got turned around in the rooms, finding myself lost deep in the Flemish painters' section. Luke Varner didn't need a map to make his way through the rooms, like he was navigating a Ms. Pac-Man game, never turning back once to check if I was behind him. He knew I'd follow.

"I hate this place." I sounded like a child on a forced field trip. I did hate the glass-and-marble contraption.

"Why?" Luke looked down at the slick floors, recently polished, his boots squeaking. His voice echoed in the hall.

Why? It was a question I'd asked myself a thousand times. I guess I blamed the Hanover Collection, more than Sara, more than our infertility issues, for the end of my marriage. The creation and care of this museum had been like a sore festering between Roger and me for years. I'd been against moving the museum here, encouraging Roger to keep the collection in its original home. Roger, on the other hand, thought the old rooms were too small to showcase "his masterpieces" and said that he needed to "reject nostalgia." Soon he became obsessed with the idea of a big, clean museum, wanting the dissonance of old paintings in a new, sterile exhibit space. Roger seemed like a man possessed, saying he needed more room to expand. Once he knew I didn't agree with him, he stopped talking to me about the move or showing me the blueprints. Sara, on the other hand, thought the move to Maine Avenue was brilliant. Her name began to creep into our conversations more regularly. She liked the land they'd secured, then the floor plan and the marble. Soon she was accompanying him on groundbreaking ceremonies and hard-hat walk-throughs. "This museum cost me my marriage," I shouted ahead to him. "It felt like the other woman." I stopped and considered what I'd just admitted aloud. "Until there was another woman, of course."

"Bet that felt worse, huh?" He kept walking, twisting and turning around rooms.

"Asshole," I muttered under my breath, but I ran to catch up.

"Ignoring that," he said.

Roger's crown jewel in the museum was the recently completed Auguste Marchant installation. His was the largest collection of Marchant's paintings in the world—including the artist's own native France. The years I'd known him, Roger had feverishly collected Marchant's paintings, starting early, when the artist's work was held only in second-tier museums and could be snatched up for a pittance. Roger saw something in Marchant's slavish devotion to the female nude that I never did. Marchant's work had a near-photographic quality to it, but his slick renderings were so polished that they were almost devoid of any sexuality. Hell, Roger and I stood in front of these polished nude nymphs thousands of times, and yet I found an Eames chair sexier. Nude nymphs and farm women looked to be carved from stone and transferred directly to the canvas in muted tones of blush, green, and blue. When impressionists like Manet, Matisse, and Degas began using prostitutes and alcoholics as their subjects, the *real* Paris came into display for the first time, making Marchant's technique look even more dated. One particularly harsh rival said Marchant's paintings were as "relevant as the draperies." Of course the fact that Marchant, in his later years, did indeed make a great living designing parlors for his wealthy patrons only seemed to make him more of a relic to his peers. The rare artist who was rich during his lifetime, Marchant was not treated kindly by the history books—hence Roger's ability to pick up his artwork early on for a pittance. I was always skeptical if they were worth much at all. The oversize, hulking frames reminded me of the bland artwork in hotel lobbies. Downstairs, locked in the vault, were Marchant's easels, paints, and brushes—all items that had been sold by the artist's granddaughter because she'd needed the money over the years. These items had been patiently collected by Roger at every chance he could get them.

Luke stopped in front of a large floor-to-ceiling painting that I had never noticed before. Staring at us was a girl no more than sixteen, with long auburn hair, standing on a step. The girl's hair blended with her clothes, which were in shades of muddy greens and browns, most likely from overuse and poor washing. Her feet were bare and her arms were unfolded in front of her, but her skin glowed pink and smooth, like a cherub's. The painting was so realistic that the girl looked like she could step out of the frame and onto the marble floor below her. The model was double-jointed and her elbow was almost twisted inside out. I noticed this detail immediately because my own arms were similarly jointed.

"So?" Luke stood in front of the painting with his hands in his pockets. I noticed that his dark-blond hair had begun to curl in the Washington humidity despite what looked like a hefty use of gel.

"It's nice." I picked at a peeling patch of nail polish.

He laughed and put his hand on his face, exasperated. "*Really?* That's all you have to say about this painting? *This painting?*" He turned and walked to the bench in the center of the room and sat down like a miffed teenager.

I looked up at the girl on the canvas. "I said it's nice but you have to know, Auguste Marchant never impressed me much. It was a sore spot between Roger and me." I shrugged. As I turned to Luke, my boots made a little squealing noise on the marble floor. I had been pleased with my outfit earlier that night—a short black skirt and boots—but now something about it felt like a costume. I could almost feel the soft, worn fabric on the girl's dress, and I wanted to wrap myself in it.

"Oh, that's beautiful, poetic even. Marchant doesn't impress you much. I've waited lifetimes to hear that…lifetimes." He shook his head and raked his hands through his hair, looking like a frustrated teacher with a stupid student. "It's *you*." He pointed to the painting like I was daft. "Don't you see that?"

I wish I'd said something incredibly profound to Luke Varner at that moment, but I didn't. Instead I cocked my head, looked back at the painting, and said, "Huh?" I walked over to the plate with my hands on my hips and read "*Girl on Step (Barefoot), 1896.*" Then I bent down and did something odd—something I'd never done before—something I didn't even know that I knew *how* to do. I looked at the brushstrokes. From my upward angle, I could see the thickness of the paint, the layering, the reduction, and I understood intimately how this painting had been created. As I stood up, I didn't know what had compelled me to study a painting that way. I walked over and sat down next to him on the bench. I leaned over and said in a conspiratorial whisper, "It says it was painted in 1896."

He stood up. Pacing in front of me, he put his finger up to indicate he'd thought of something. He walked over to me and leaned down, his eyes meeting mine. I could smell the wine on his breath, along with something like a vague cologne that pleasantly shocked me. "Actually, it was painted in 1895. The plate isn't accurate. Use your imagination a little, would you? Come on. Look at it! Really look. Try to remember!"

I peered around him from the bench. The girl in the painting stared back at me. She wore her hair in a simple ponytail; wisps had come free and framed her face. She reminded me of myself when I was thirteen, before braces, surgery to fix my broken nose, and the vibrant copper hair color to replace my more natural auburn shade. The girl's hair was magnificent and unruly. As I looked at her, it seemed like I had gone to a lot of trouble to *not* look like this girl. Her eyes were sad and mournful. "She looks very sad."

"You were very sad." Luke seemed resigned to the fact that I didn't believe him.

I stood up and smoothed my skirt. I wanted something to do with my hands so I picked at some imaginary fuzz. "This has been a very interesting date, Mr. Varner. Really interesting." I smiled at him and walked out of the room and then out of the Hanover, the click of my heels echoing down through the empty museum. Luke Varner didn't follow me.

When I got back to my apartment, I realized that some of the things he had said to me had gotten under my skin. It wasn't that I believed him; but I didn't not believe him. The stuff he knew about Sara's mother and Roger had been unsettling. I guess he could have found that out from Mickey, but I didn't think so. This man seemed to know my thoughts intimately.

Sleep came easily that night. My limbs fell heavy and I dreamed of France: fields and countryside, sunflowers and stone homes, wells with buckets and cold limestone floors all in colors of yellow and green that I don't think I have ever seen in my waking life. Deep jeweled greens from the forest, silver blue-greens from the shrubs, and intense Kelly greens from the soft summer grass.

The grass seemed so real, it felt like I could reach out and touch it.

4

The June morning felt surprisingly warm as Juliet set foot onto the stone porch, expecting it to be cool under her feet. Instead it was hot on her toes and she jumped back into the kitchen. Her mother looked up and frowned before returning to scrubbing the pot. "Hurry back. Don't wander."

Juliet stepped lightly onto the porch and found it not so shocking on the second attempt. She glanced at her mother and then ran full speed down off the slab steps and onto the warm wet grass. The rain from last night clung to the grass, and it squeaked under her feet as if she were scrubbing each blade with the shift of her weight. She held her bucket out as she ran, cautious not to drop it. Her path to the well took her past Monsieur Marchant's house. She stopped before the high stone wall and stretched up on her toes. Although she was taller this year, she still couldn't see over the fence. Juliet contemplated the bucket for a moment and then turned it over and stepped on it for a better peek at the property. The door was open and a white curtain blew out onto the small garden. So the rumors were true. Marchant was back.

"Goodness, girl, you'll fall and kill yourself. If you want to come in, simply walk through the gate."

Startled, Juliet lost her balance and stumbled off the pewter bucket.

"I'm sorry, sir." She looked down at her feet. He had drawn them so well last year. She peered up to find him staring at her.

"My...you have grown since last summer."

She bent over quickly, gathering her bucket to run. She didn't understand why she felt like such a stranger to the man who'd been so familiar with her last year, having painted her dozens of times. He was dressed in a crisp white shirt and simple brown pants. These were his country clothes, Juliet thought, not the things he wore in the salons of Paris. She could see him considering her for a moment more. "I just wondered, sir..." She looked up. He'd grown a beard over the winter that was almost entirely gray. The hair on his head, the color of the fallow field beyond the stone wall, had also begun to gray at the temples and fell loose around his face like he had forgotten to cut or comb it. "I just wanted to welcome you back this summer."

"I think you might want to come by tomorrow morning, young Juliet. Tell your mother I will pay her again for your services." He turned and walked toward the gate, and Juliet could see that he was pulling a pipe out of his pant pocket and filling it with tobacco. She looked down at her own cotton dress and considered how dirty it was and how she must look to him. Her hem was caked with mud from chasing the chickens and her budding breasts were popping through the thin cotton with the shamelessness of a child. Juliet folded her arms in front of her. She was about to turn sixteen and was not a child anymore.

Juliet watched him turn the corner and unfasten the gate, puffing on his pipe, never giving her a second glance.

She took the bucket and ran down the soft green hill toward the well. Juliet primed the pump with quick movements. It had taken her years to be able to work the pump without putting the weight of her whole body into it. The water was clear, so Juliet figured one of the

Bussons' servants must have been there earlier and cleared the stale water away. She washed out the bucket and then, after examining it to make sure there was no dirt in it, she filled it to the top. Getting the water was a job that fell to Juliet each morning. At nine, her younger sister Delphine was not yet able to carry the weight of the bucket all the way to the house. The metal of the handle cut into Juliet's hands, so she trotted quickly up the hill switching from the left to the right. She could manage 102 steps before she had to stop and switch hands—this was up from the 54 steps when she'd started counting. Stopping in front of the Marchants' gate, she adjusted her bucket and peered in at the house. She did not see him, but she spied Madame Marchant in a blue cotton dress coming out onto the porch, her belly swollen with pregnancy. Juliet grabbed the handle and trotted off the path toward home.

She gently placed the bucket down on the table, proud that she had not spilled a drop. She pushed back the long auburn locks that were now sweaty around her forehead. She considered her words. Her mother was chopping carrots and leeks.

"Monsieur Marchant is back this summer."

"I heard." Her mother frowned. She brushed away a strand of dark hair with her forearm.

Once, Juliet figured, her mother had been beautiful, but three living children and one dead had taken their toll. The woman's blue eyes were framed with dark pockets of flesh from sleepless nights, and her clothes hung on her skeletal frame. Juliet was surprised to see her mother indoors on a day like today. Normally she was out tending to her large garden that was mostly herbs—rosemary, nutmeg, lavender, basil—but there were other, more exotic herbs, too: acacia, ginseng, hibiscus, elecampane, and mugwort. While her tan fingers were nearly raw from scrubbing, there was a subtle elegance to her that hinted at another time and station. Although she'd never seen one, Juliet imagined that her mother held herself like a grand ballet dancer. There was a backstory between her parents that was now told only in glances and whispers.

During the daylight, Juliet's mother walked the rows of her garden examining the plants, not unlike a farmer. While Juliet's father studied his corn looking for broad problems with the crop like too little water or the subtle signs of infestation, Juliet's mother delicately touched any plant that did not appear to be thriving with the intimacy of a doctor examining a patient.

After drying the herbs with paper for a fortnight, her mother then stored them. Juliet's mother sold some of those herbs as a paste or oil to the town apothecary. In the night, women often arrived at the LaCompte house at all hours, knocking softly on the big wooden door.

During these visits, which usually accompanied the moon at its fullest, Juliet's mother sent Juliet and Delphine upstairs, but they would sit quietly on the stairs and watch as their mother led the visitor into the kitchen, pulling down various bottles of dried herbs and oils and talking in hushed tones. The stories were the same: An old woman sick with grief over a straying husband, a wicked woman, a ruined crop. The younger ones concerned with bleeding—or not bleeding, as the case might be. Always, there was an air of urgency in these night visits, their bodies stinking of sweat and blood with dirty nails and feet. Juliet's mother knew the exact tincture to set things right again with these broken women.

When they went into town, Juliet noticed how women parted for her mother, nodded to her in deference, or presented a basket containing extra vegetables in season. Juliet would see a familiar woman from the evening carry out a rabbit wrapped in paper as an offering of sorts in the daylight. While the farm wasn't as fruitful as it could be, Juliet knew that her mother's night magic kept the family fed, especially during the winters, but there was a risk to it as well. There were places in Challans where her mother didn't shop. More than once Juliet heard the term *la sorcière* hurled at her mother as they walked past. Juliet didn't understand how herbs could be dangerous business in the country, but she'd heard of other *sorcières* who'd been accused of "murder" when spells had failed to help medical ailments. The accused *sorcières* were then dragged into the street and tied to a crude stake and burned.

Once Juliet even overheard her father telling her mother—his voice feverish—of a young witch forced to sit naked on hot coals until the townspeople were sure she wouldn't be able to "fornicate with the devil" again.

With their often delicate financial state, Juliet knew how to proceed. "Marchant said he'll pay you again if I can pose for him."

"Did he?" Her mother wiped her hands on her apron.

"He said that I could come over tomorrow morning." Juliet walked over and picked at the carrot and leek pieces her mother had discarded, hoping to appear helpful.

"I don't think it is appropriate for a girl your age to pose for him anymore. It was one thing when you were a child, but now I don't think it would look good. The Bussons might get the wrong idea."

Juliet shivered at this thought. Over the winter, Juliet's mother and father had settled on the eldest Busson boy, Michel, for Juliet. The boy, seventeen, was thin and pale with red hair. Juliet couldn't imagine a worse match for herself, yet his parents owned the land that Juliet's parents farmed. That the Bussons had even considered this match was surprising given the LaComptes' lower status. Juliet must have made a face because her mother grabbed her chin and directed Juliet's gaze toward her. Her mother's hands were warm and wet.

"It doesn't look right. You're marrying Michel Busson next year." Her mother's chin was firmly set. "Help me scrub the potatoes your father brought in last night."

Juliet looked at the pile of potatoes stacked like stones next to the window. She walked toward them, feeling the breeze blow through her dress and up her legs as she passed by the open door. She grabbed a kitchen rag, poured some water from the bucket into a smaller bowl, and began scrubbing the dirt from the potatoes. She looked back at her mother, her green dress dirty from the garden. Juliet thought of Madame Marchant and her pristine blue dress.

"Have you ever been to Paris?" Out of the corner of her eye she caught her mother turn pale at the question.

"That's an odd thing to ask."

"Why?" Juliet saw the change come over her mother's face at the mention of Paris. Juliet was becoming more and more preoccupied with thoughts of city life. She liked the feel of the earth and grass between her bare toes and the quiet life she had always known here, but she was beginning to feel that she was missing something or was destined for something more than gangly Michel Busson and a life drawing water from a well. Her mother was mysterious about her past before she'd met Juliet's father. While Juliet knew everyone from her father's side of the family—her grandmother who was still alive, and her uncle and cousins—she had no knowledge of any family on her mother's side, living or dead. It was as though her mother emerged from a clamshell like the painting she had seen Marchant paint last summer.

"I lived in Paris a long time ago." Her mother gathered an onion and began slicing it with sweeping strokes.

"You never told me." Juliet had not expected an answer, and she certainly did not expect the answer she got. "Did you like it?"

"No, not really. It is a harsh place. You would not like it there. Trust me. Michel Busson will inherit his father's farm. You will have a good life here, a safe life. You'll never worry about starving or being cold. Paris is a hard place—it's full of tricksters and charlatans. This painter..." Her mother shook her head. "Don't get ideas, Juliet. No good can come of it."

"I don't want a safe life. I want to go to Paris." Juliet was still making circles with the rag in a halfhearted attempt to clean the pot and make sense of what she had just learned from her mother when she heard the knock at the door. Juliet turned to see Auguste Marchant standing in the doorway. He had put on a brown jacket for the occasion.

"That's because you've never known anything *but* a safe life. You can't imagine the suffering." Her mother was about to say more, but she looked up to see Marchant in her doorway. She did not seem surprised.

"Monsieur Marchant." She walked wearily over to the door, wiping her hands on her skirt, and folded her arms. "My husband is out in the field if you need his help. He should be back around sundown." The neighbor women who came to the door in the middle of the night, cloaked, pale, and shivering, waking the entire family—those women had been treated more hospitably than Monsieur Marchant was being treated now.

"May I come in?" Marchant hesitated for a moment but did not wait for Juliet's mother to respond before stepping into the kitchen. "Ah, young Juliet."

Juliet saw her mother frown behind him.

"It occurred to me that I had not been courteous to young Juliet this morning." He looked at the vegetables on the table then glanced back and forth between the two silent women. "I asked her to come over tomorrow morning for a new series I'm doing. I fear it was rude of me not to come over and talk to *you* about it in advance. Highly improper." Marchant was a man who gestured when he talked. Juliet could see the paint stains on his fingers and in his nails.

Juliet turned back toward the window and smiled.

"I appreciate you coming here, Monsieur Marchant, and we admired the beautiful work you did last summer with our Juliet."

"You still have the painting, of course?"

"Yes." Juliet's mother seemed distracted.

Marchant leaned in toward the woman as if in anticipation of the rejection she was about to give his offer.

Juliet's mother cut him off as he was about to speak. "But Juliet is to be married next year when she is seventeen and I would worry about how it would look to the boy's family. You understand, of course."

"Oh certainly, Mrs. LaCompte. I can see how that would look... to *the boy's family*." He put his fingers to his chin and stroked his beard. "You see, my new series is actually featuring children. Young children. If I do recall from last summer, you also had a very young child. An infant." He waited for my mother's response.

"I do. A son. Marcel. He'll be three."

Juliet felt her joy leave her. Monsieur Marchant had not come for her at all. This show was all for Marcel. She was surprised at how disappointed she was as this realization washed over her.

"Splendid." Marchant put his hands in his pockets. "The new series that I'm thinking of is a woman with a young child. Of course, I would pay you for the trouble of *both* of your children. Let's say double last year's price per sitting?"

Her mother seemed speechless at the offer.

"Surely the time of your daughter and your young son together would not be seen as anything *inappropriate*."

"I...I will have to ask my husband, of course."

Juliet knew from last year that the price of one day of service for her was more than her family earned in a week laboring in the fields. The price for she and Marcel together would be too much for her father to turn away. At least she hoped it would be too much. Marchant gave a slight bow and walked out to the front porch. Juliet began to speak, but her mother put her hand up.

"Silence. I do not need your opinion on this matter."

"But it's now a hundred gold francs for each sitting. That's more than you make at the market in a day."

"I am aware of what Monsieur Marchant offered us last year."

"Who knows? Maybe my painting will hang on the walls of one of the salons of Paris."

Juliet's mother appeared stricken by the thought. "I don't want you posing for paintings. I will not have you being seen as . . . an artist's . . ." She let the word drop.

"An artist's what?"

"An artist's *whore*, Juliet." She put her arms on the table and looked down. "You're still quite young, but since you're marrying, it's time you learned these things." Juliet's mother went back to chopping carrots, throwing them into the empty pot. She sighed and looked out the window. "You have no idea. No idea of the cost to us all."

5

Helen Lambert
Washington, DC, May 25, 2012

I woke up satiated, like I'd had sex all night. Had that been a lucid dream? I'd heard about such things, but never had one before. As I looked around my bedroom, I took in my surroundings. From the thick duvet to the cell phone by my bed, I knew I was still in 2012. Yet it was as though the curtain were being pulled back to show me another time. And the girl—she was exactly the girl from Auguste Marchant's painting *Girl on Step*. It had been a dream, surely, but it felt more like a transfer of memories. I wasn't observing this girl, Juliet. No, I had all of her early memories. I knew the sensation of the stone on her knees when she'd fallen at the age of five and cut her leg, the feel of the rope slung over the oak tree in the yard to make a swing. No, I had *become* this girl in that dream. Even now, the idea of Marchant back in the house next door quickened my pulse. I heard the honking of a car out on East Capitol Street and realized this wasn't possible.

As luck would have it, I ran into Mickey at our Georgetown Starbucks on M Street. Mickey was the homes and lifestyle editor of *In Frame*. "You look fantastic," he exclaimed. "So...Luke Varner...isn't he gorgeous in that dull way you like your men? Kind of like if Steve McQueen had been an accountant." Mickey was currently dating a Dwayne "The Rock" Johnson look-alike. Prior to that, he had been in a Benicio del Toro phase. Not that I thought any of these look-alikes actually *looked* like the celebrity in question—they were usually fatter, shorter, or older than their cinematic versions—but Mickey was convinced they did. After the sex wore off, he'd be off on another phase. In the past year, he'd gone through a Baryshnikov phase, a Peter O'Toole as *Lawrence of Arabia* phase, and then a young Roger Moore in *The Saint* phase.

"I got to bed early." I didn't look at Mickey as I poured too much cream in my coffee, turning it a pale caramel.

Mickey sidled up next to me at the coffee fixings station. "Oh," he replied, looking dejected. "You didn't like him?"

"He was *interesting*." I sipped my drink. It was too hot, so I held it like a prop.

"Uh-oh. Interesting is never good." Mickey's longish, angled black bob swept back and then front like a wave settling itself when he shook his head.

"Where'd you meet him? And why is he rich?"

"He's new in town and just bought a house near Foxhall. The house is fabulous from what I hear, although I haven't seen it. I met him at a gallery opening and suggested you might show him around." With that, Mickey chuckled. "If you didn't like him, I thought you could, at least, get a good story out of him for the Fall Homes issue. He's an art dealer, hence the fortune."

"You didn't talk to him about Sara's mother dying and all that?"

Mickey looked puzzled. "Huh? No. Why?"

"No reason," I said. And then I noticed Mickey's blue tie. I reached out and pulled it toward me, dragging him with it. "That is the most vivid blue tie."

"I know." He blushed. "It's Hermès." He fussed at it, pulling it back like a fishing line and straightening it. "Back off, weirdo. You've seen this tie a million times before."

"Have I?" It was different hues of cornflower and straw yellow. "I've never noticed it until now."

"Is something wrong with you?" Mickey wore a puzzled look as he eyed me and opened the door onto M Street. "You aren't *high*, are you? If you are, why aren't you sharing?"

"I'm not high." But I couldn't stop glancing at the tie as we walked down Wisconsin Avenue together. It was so vivid. And it wasn't just the tie. It was as though all the green trees on the Georgetown Waterfront on K Street had been freshly painted for me; even the Potomac River, despite resembling a giant mud puddle after the recent storms, was almost swirling with a soft-blue color. I felt like I was tripping on acid. I'm not a person to notice trees or colors. I walk down the street with my iPhone in my hand most of the time, but this was different. It was as though everything was now in 1960s Technicolor.

As I walked through the glass doors of *In Frame*'s sixth-floor offices, I was overcome by the mossy leaves on the spray of hydrangeas in the waiting room. My assistant, Sharlene, cleared her throat as I was studying each leaf. I saw Mickey shrug and head down the hallway.

"This is *weird*," I said aloud to the floral arrangement.

"They're waiting for you in the conference room to pick the cover image." Sharlene stood there with the arms of a marvelous green cardigan folded tightly over her rather dull shift dress. Like any good assistant, Sharlene had contempt for me, so sure she could run the company better if only I'd get out of the way and let her at it. "And"— she referred to a notebook in her hand—"Virginia Samson needs you to call her immediately."

I knew I'd choose the cover photo of South Island in New Zealand that went with the "World's Best Road Trips" article, so the meeting to choose the cover could wait. But Virginia Samson calling was certainly odd. One of the longest-serving communications directors on the Hill, Virginia was currently working for Asa Heathcote, the charismatic senior senator from Florida and former pro golfer who was reportedly on the short list of candidates for vice president on the Republican ticket. I dialed her number and she picked up immediately.

"I need a favor." She got right to the point, her slight Ohio accent still lingering after twenty-five years in Washington. When I'd been the communications director for the well-known junior Democratic senator from North Carolina, Fletcher "Franz" Bishop, our bosses had co-sponsored several bills together. She'd taught me the ropes and loved to remind me that I owed her.

Forgetting she wasn't talking to her staff, she'd barked her request like a drill sergeant. I held the phone away from my ear. "Can you interview the senator this morning? Let him show you how to swing a golf club or barbecue—two of the things he loves to do. A little light fare. Nothing involving alcohol, though. That won't play well. You have a video crew over there, don't you? I need video."

"It's nine o'clock in the morning, Virginia." I sipped my coffee, playing along. "You want me to barbecue with him?" As she talked, I took the opportunity to slide into my chair and type "Luke Varner" into Google.

"No one has to know it's the morning, for Christ's sake. You have that fabulous balcony at your office. He can make a mean pork rib. Last I remember you couldn't hit a golf ball for shit, either!"

"I'm not the fucking *Today* show, Virginia!"

"And you're not the fucking *New York Times*, either, Helen. Just warm him up. You're good at that…Please."

While most people outside Washington think that Democrats and

Republicans are at war with each other, that isn't the case with the staffers. Careers here are long. Having a friend or two on the other side of the aisle was valuable.

I sighed. Her owing me for a change might be nice. "Unpack this for me a little, will you?" I was enjoying toying with her a bit. It had been a while since Virginia and I had collaborated on anything, but I knew she was hiding something. "Who else are you calling this morning?"

She sighed. "He's got *National Journal* after you, followed by the *Washington Post* and a lunch at the Monocle with *Roll Call*. Happy?"

This was telling. It was commonplace for an aspiring presidential or vice presidential candidate, or even someone contemplating a run for office, to do a series of media tours in the city. *Washington Post*, *Roll Call*, and *National Journal* were the typical media stops, and communications directors had these interviews tightly scheduled and usually topped off with lunch—often held at Charlie Palmer or BLT—where the aspiring candidate could be *seen*. These media stops were a good training ground for higher-profile national outlets as the candidate fleshed out key policy positions. Heathcote's next interview, over at the Watergate offices of *National Journal*, would likely be where he'd talk about platform issues like his stance on taxes, gun control, and abortion. This call was the greatest proof yet that Heathcote was going to be on the ticket. And Virginia knew that I knew it.

"Okay," I said. "Golf swing it is. Does he still drink Tab?"

"Diet Dr Pepper only now, bottles no cans," she said, sounding distracted. "I carry around several bottles if you don't have any in the fridge. We'll be there in thirty minutes. And I need good video of him, Helen."

"Gee, I wonder why?"

She actually hung up on me. I stared at the phone for a minute and then dialed Sharlene. "I need to get my hands on a set of golf clubs within the next half hour. Either that or some pork."

"I've got a set of clubs in my car," she said. "Why?"

"Heathcote is going to do an interview here, then a stunt of some sort, showing us how to either barbecue or hit a golf ball."

"We have a putting green up here on the roof, you know."

"We do?"

She audibly sighed, my question only confirming to her that I had no clue what went on around the office. I returned my attention to the computer screen. My internet search had turned up several interesting hits on a Luke Varner Gallery on Kit Carson Street in Taos, New Mexico. I decided to wait on that while I did some more pressing research on Heathcote.

A striking man and minor celebrity whose second wife was a former Victoria's Secret model, Asa Heathcote came from humble beginnings in Jacksonville, but now was known as a moderate Republican who would occasionally side with equally moderate Democrats. As the GOP headed into the general election, Heathcote's ability to cross the aisle had some appeal. The speculation surrounding his selection was at a fever pitch this week, with every broadcast news program and pundit giving prognostications as to the secret identity of the VP candidate. When asked this week, Heathcote had been coy about whether he'd been approached for the job, saying he'd be interested in taking the job if it was offered to him, but of course his duties in the Senate were his top priority.

From my years as a communications director, I knew his response was code for "I want the job badly." Heathcote would never admit that the job had been offered to him until the most opportune moment for the campaign—which meant as close to the Republican National Convention in Tampa as possible. And since Heathcote was from

Florida, it would be a perfect setting. This press junket was to whet our appetite for Heathcote so that when he was announced, national media would be pulling our carefully crafted lifestyle pieces.

And that's where *In Frame* came in. I also had no illusions about my place on this media roster. This interview with the senator would appear next to the article on "Best Neighborhood Bars of the World." *In Frame* was the first interview of the day—the warm-up act. I was expected to discuss Asa Heathcote the man. "Light fare," as Virginia had described it. As the senator's tour progressed across town, I knew that news reporters would be rolling their eyes when they heard that Heathcote had started his morning with me. *In Frame* still had critics who thought we wrote "fluff," and Virginia was banking on me delivering softball questions. Something about this fact riled me. Like a modern-day Walter Mitty, I imagined myself asking the questions that I knew Virginia wanted me to steer away from.

The rising sound of voices and forced laughter meant that Senator Heathcote had arrived. As if on cue, I saw the entourage, led by Sharlene, amble into the smaller conference room that had been set up for the occasion, including Diet Dr Pepper on ice—procured from an emergency CVS run. Virginia spotted me and waved. A sturdy woman dressed in a beige suit with sensible one-inch heels, Virginia had readers perched on her blond head and a set jaw, making her look tense as she clutched her giant plastic binder.

Heathcote had a reputation for being heavily "handled" by his team. If you spend time with many members of Congress, you'll find that some of the best-known members are the least high-maintenance, driving themselves places—or famously taking the train or Metro to appearances with the latest edition of the *Washington Post* tucked under their arms. I'd often find the Speaker of the House sitting alone in the green room holding a 7-Eleven coffee cup, having arrived early at our events in his 2001 Toyota Camry. Asa Heathcote was *not* this type of senator. His staff treated him as though he were destined for something much bigger and they were going to propel him there. Media were given strict instructions about topics that were—and were not—off limits in interviews. Violations of any of the rules outlined by Virginia or the senator's chief of staff meant you were never granted another interview.

I straightened my dress and headed down the hall toward the conference room. Nearly sixty, Heathcote was good looking and charming with a perpetual tan and a mane of thick silver hair. He was also one of those men who shook your hand and clasped it with his other hand, a fake gesture that, frankly, I hated.

"Hello, Senator." As I held out my hand, the clasp came around, rehearsed like a Broadway dance number.

"Helen Lambert," he smiled. "You look wonderful. Virginia tells me you run the place."

"I do, Senator."

He looked around. "No barbecue?"

"Sorry." I shrugged. "We don't have a grill up here. Fire code and all," I said. "We'll start here with a few questions. Then we'll have a little golf lesson on the roof."

He looked down at my Narciso Rodriguez cream shift dress and bone-colored Louboutins, hardly golf attire. "Uh... okay," he said.

I glared at Virginia for putting me in this spot.

As if on cue, Sharlene pointed the way through the doors and up a set of stairs that led to the expansive balcony, as though she were a *Price Is Right* model. "We have a new putting green on the roof," she chirped.

Cliff, the politics reporter who'd come in to cover the interview, rolled his eyes at me from behind the senator.

"Excellent," Heathcote said. "Reminds me, Helen. I played golf with Bishop last weekend."

"Did he beat you?" I teased, knowing the answer. Heathcote was the best golfer in Washington.

"Almost." Heathcote chuckled. "His short game is still lacking."

This wasn't just a comment about Bishop's golf game and we both knew it. My former boss was facing a stiff challenger in the next election, and the fear was that while he was good on the national stage, he often couldn't get past the challengers in his own state. "He's got a tough election coming up." I shifted my weight, my shoes suddenly uncomfortable. As I did, I noticed the senator's blue eyes—they reminded me of the Van Gogh that hung in the Hanover Collection, one of the color studies for *Starry Night*.

"While I'd love to pick up the seat," Heathcote said, laughing, "I'd sure hate for it to be at the expense of Bishop. He's a good colleague. Reliable." We assembled ourselves in front of the camera while the crew made adjustments to lighting and sound.

"You have the list of questions?" Virginia smiled down at me as I arranged myself in the chair. This was her reminder not to deviate from her questions *one bit*.

"I do." I smiled, holding up her notes. She didn't get a good look at the paper or she'd have seen my own notes as well. Our video producer counted me down.

We started with the usual stuff *In Frame* did well. How had Heathcote moved from professional golfer to the Senate? How much did he still golf and where? How did his passion for adoption happen and why did he feel more attention needed to be paid to getting older children placed in homes? His answers to the questions about adoption were well rehearsed. There was nothing new here. Even I was bored with my own line of questioning.

I looked at my notes. The next question was so bland, I couldn't ask it. I couldn't let *In Frame* be humiliated by not even trying to ask Heathcote a hard question. It was my duty to make the man at least attempt to spin an answer to my question.

"So," I began. "Don't you want to tell us whether the rumors are true about you being slated as the vice presidential nominee? Come on, tell us everything." I laughed, leaning forward and placing my hand on his arm, avoiding Virginia's eyes. "Tell us. You know you want to!" Even as I asked the question, the curious phrasing I'd chosen caused me to look down at my own notes. That wasn't the way I'd planned to ask it.

I was waiting for a clever roundabout non-denial denial. The kind of thing Asa Heathcote was brilliant at. But the room was silent. Heathcote began to speak and then blanched a bit, as if he was arguing with himself. I swear I heard him mumbling, "No. Don't do it." The man's head shook back and forth. So odd was the scene before us that the cameraman made eye contact with me. I saw Virginia move toward Heathcote, but he held her off with the flick of his hand. I'm sure she thought he had this covered. I'd pay later for asking the question, but there was nothing to worry about here. This man was used to deflecting unwanted questions. As we sat there, I began to sense something was seriously wrong. "Senator?" I had considered that he was choking, but he didn't seem to be turning blue.

Heathcote's bottom lip quivered. He began fussing with his hands, clasping one over the other again and again like some strange patty-cake. Next, he struggled with his tongue, stopping and starting to speak. His team stepped closer. For a moment I wondered if he was having a fit or a stroke of some kind. He picked up the glass of Diet Dr Pepper and his hand began to shake violently. I tried to take it from him, but he pushed me away.

"Yes." The answer came out in waves of breath like a panting dog. "I was asked last week and I accepted it. We're announcing next week, and then we'll do a tour of the South." He tried to stop but didn't seem able to control the next wave of words. "Yes, yes. I'm going to be the nominee. Yes. Yes. They asked." I watched Heathcote put his hands to his tan face as if he was feeling his mouth, perhaps hoping to hold it shut. "But they're worried about it coming to light that I got my assistant pregnant and made her put the child up for adoption. They're trying to pay her off." Then he let out a groan. "Oh God. I don't know why I just said that..."

I sputtered for a moment, unsure of my retort, realizing that I'd just been handed the story of the day—no, the story of the week at least, and given what seemed to be the meltdown of a senior senator, possibly the final chapter of this man's career. Not one person in the room seemed to be breathing. The cameraman looked at me, unsure of what to do next, but the red light on the camera was still blinking.

Someone in the room said, "Oh shit," out loud.

The senator's staff rushed to him. Virginia croaked, "Stop the tape." But the political damage to Asa Heathcote had been done.

Heathcote looked at me, almost pleading, unable to speak now. His legislative director bent down asking, "Are you okay, Senator?" Within seconds, the staffer had Heathcote whisked out of the room, looking confused and shaken. Virginia Samson turned to me.

"I never thought he'd answer it," I started, ready to defend myself. The notes in my hand were all balled up and sweaty.

"Given our friendship, you know what I'm going to ask you." Virginia took off her glasses so I could see her eyes. After all the years of serving several different senators, deep lines were carved into her plump face. Now her normally soft brown eyes were not kind. "I have to ask it, Helen. You cannot let that tape out. It will ruin his chances for the nomination. The party will drop him for this. You know that. Given what he just said, it could ruin his career. Possibly his marriage."

"Did you know this, Virginia?"

She didn't answer.

"Okay." Both she and I knew that I couldn't hold back the interview. To do so would be irresponsible. "You know I can't do that Virginia, even if I wanted to. If there was anyone I *would* do it for, it would be you, but—"

"But he just broke news," she added, her face narrowing. "As though *In Frame* is a real news outlet. But then something like this would help you to elevate your magazine, wouldn't it?"

"You had my politics reporter in the room, Virginia. I can't— I won't stop the story. It would be irresponsible and you know it." I gripped the chair in front of me, suddenly feeling dizzy. "Is there something wrong with him? Is he drunk?"

"You know him better than to ask that question," she said. "He never touches the stuff."

True, I knew that Heathcote's wife was a recovering alcoholic and he was a renowned teetotaler, but there had to be some explanation for his strange outburst. "What happened in that chair, Virginia? I don't know if he's unwell or what . . . but he seems unstable certainly."

She shook her head gravely. "No. He's in perfect health."

"Then what? That was a grave error in judgment. He shouldn't even be considered for office with that type of outburst."

"I have no idea what happened." Virginia turned and walked toward the door. I could hear her pantyhose swishing beneath her skirt. She stopped. "How long do we have?"

Even if I had decided to hold the interview, the cameraman, Sharlene, and our political reporter had been in the room to witness the crumbling of the normally cool Senator Heathcote who had confessed not only that he was the VP candidate but also that he'd had a relationship with a staffer ending in pregnancy. "Ten minutes at best," I said. "I won't stop our reporters from posting it."

She nodded and took a deep breath, brushed past Sharlene, and headed down the hallway.

Sharlene looked down at the phone in her hand.

"I guess now we know why he's so passionate about adoption, huh?" I leaned against the chair to steady myself.

She laughed at my lighthearted attempt at a joke. "I just got a text from Josh and Dave. They're asking what to do."

"Tell them to run it."

As Sharlene moved, the room began to rock back and forth like a boat as a wave of nausea gripped me. I had just witnessed a curious thing: the potential demise of a venerable political star, perhaps the end to the long and storied career of a good man. Or had I caused it? I'd been plagued by this nagging feeling before, after the death of Sara's mother, and Luke had confirmed that I'd played a part in it. My head began to pound and I grabbed onto the faux leather chair as I slid down the cold, smooth material and onto the floor. Then everything went black.

6

Juliet LaCompte
Challans, France, 1895

The next morning, Juliet carried Marcel to Marchant's studio at a near run. The hill to the stone house was steep, so she braced herself with the boy's full weight on her hip. The child had tried to run, but he couldn't keep up, so Juliet had scooped him in her arms. She'd chosen her best dress, a brown shift that skimmed her ankles, and a peacock-blue wrap because Marchant liked all the windows to be left open in his studio. Since the studio was on the western side of the house, it didn't see sun until the afternoon. Juliet recalled the floor tiles and the whole studio being cold, so she carried an extra blanket for Marcel to keep him warm.

Juliet gazed up over the field she'd just come from, the green hills giving way to the newly blooming sunflowers. She could hear the chickens in her farm milling about and clucking in chorus. She was about to knock on the wooden door when it opened. Marchant appeared in the doorway, smiling. "Ah, the lovely Juliet." He bent down to look at Marcel, who was hanging heavily off Juliet's arms. "And who do we have here?"

"This is Marcel." Juliet shifted the weight of her hip to hold the boy. Marchant lifted the child easily from her arms, placing him on the floor. Marcel began to toddle around the studio. Marchant turned his attention back to Juliet.

"You have grown since last summer." He gazed the full length of her with what appeared to be an artist's eye.

"I hope that is a good thing, sir." Her eyes met his. He had also changed. Juliet noticed that he'd gotten wider, not fat, but solid like a stone. His eyes were still soft and green with a hint of gray. Juliet remembered that he'd had a dimple on the left side of his face that was now hidden by his new beard.

"It is." He smiled and walked into his studio.

The studio looked the same as last year. Juliet even noticed the same beige cloth draped across the daybed as though it had never been moved, but she knew that couldn't be the case because Marchant had servants who kept the house for him during the winter. Anyone's romantic idea of a working artist was shattered when they walked into Marchant's studio.

He did not sit down at an easel and begin. The process for him was furious and frenetic. At any given time, his studio was littered with charcoal sketches of hands, an eye, a toe. Other smaller pieces of drawings were ripped from larger sheets; the design might feature a study of the hang of a drape or explorations of light on a face. At the end of a day's work, his studio floor was littered with pieces of paper, but the servants were forbidden to clean until a painting was fully completed.

"I thought we would start by doing some sketches in the garden," said Marchant as he wound his wire eyeglasses around his ears and pulled things out of his leather case. "There is a good morning sun over by the fountain. I'll expect you and Marcel here each day at nine. I like to walk in the morning before I begin my work. We'll work until the afternoon. Is that understood?" Marchant studied Juliet over the top of his glasses. Taking a sketchbook from the easel, he tucked it under the arm of his crisp white shirt and walked out the door to the gardens where the sun was shining.

Juliet turned her attention to Marcel, who had sat down on the tiles and was sticking a wet finger in the chipped holes in the floor tiles. She took the boy's wet hand and followed Marchant out into the garden.

Last year, they'd never worked outside the studio, and she was bitterly disappointed by this change in venue. The studio seemed intimate—it was something that belonged to Marchant alone, and a place that he had shared with her last summer. It had become their spot. The garden was public and Madame Marchant and the servants wouldn't think of it as off limits like they did his studio.

Marchant positioned them by the fountain with Juliet seated on the fountain step and Marcel on her lap. Marchant frowned at the blue wrap and leaned down, sliding it off her shoulders. He rearranged the neck of her dress. He touched her as though he were arranging a doll, but something stirred inside Juliet. Marchant next arranged Juliet's hair, and when he leaned in she smelled the lavender soap he'd used that morning.

"These curly pieces of your hair. They are wild, like you." He smiled and met her eyes. He then placed Marcel's chubby, cherubic legs on Juliet's knees. "I want you to have the appearance of a young mother to him. Just hold him there for a moment while I get the basics of the sketch. Can you do that?" He took a few strands of Marcel's hair and curled them around his finger. Marcel's fingers were in his mouth and the child looked up at Marchant with curiosity.

Juliet nodded.

After several minutes, when Marchant had the sketch he wanted, he called for the maid.

"Take the boy," said Marchant. "Give him some milk and a nap."

The maid nodded and plucked the wiggling boy from Juliet's knee, which had gone numb from sitting in one position for so long. Marcel followed the maid in a trot with the promise of candy.

Another hour went on in silence with Marchant sketching Juliet's face while he sat on an iron bench, his one leg crossed over the other. He worked furiously, alternating pencils and rubbing at the paper with his finger. Finally Marchant's strokes softened, and he met Juliet's eyes. "So, your mother says you are to be married?"

"Yes," she frowned. "Next year."

"But you are not happy about this?" His face disappeared behind the easel and he became just a voice.

"He's an awful boy."

Marchant peered around the easel and met her eyes again. He stopped sketching. "We were *all* awful boys once." He put his hands on his knees. "Do you know what it means to be married, Juliet?"

Juliet said nothing.

"I thought as much." He sighed and shook his head. "Women come into marriage very much unprepared, especially here in the country."

"But I don't want to stay in the country." Juliet was surprised at the force with which she said this. "I want to live in Paris."

"Do you now?" Marchant's head disappeared behind the easel. "Tell me. What do you know of Paris?"

"What do I know of anywhere?" said Juliet. "I'm just a silly girl. I just don't want to be here."

Marchant got off the bench and walked over to Juliet, wiping his hands with a rag as he went. As he crouched down in front of her, she could see that charcoal had stained the forearms of his shirt. "You are far from a silly girl, my Juliet." He reached out and touched her cheek. "There is something about you, but you know that, don't you?"

Something fierce inside Juliet burned and she leaned in toward his hand. He stopped stroking her cheek and leaned in so close that she could smell his breath, which still held the hint of tobacco. "Sometimes I see you in my dreams, young Juliet." Marchant smiled sadly. "It's why I paint you." He released his hand and stood, turning his back to her as though he was ashamed of something or he'd said too much. "We're done today. I'll have my servant bring Marcel to the gate for you."

Juliet rearranged her dress that had sagged down over her shoulder and walked to the gate, touching her cheek as she went. Her face was so hot from his touch that she stopped just outside on the stone steps to let the cool breeze hit her.

As the weeks progressed, Marchant transferred his sketches and studies onto a large sheet of paper the same size as the canvas and then transferred a crude outline of her pose by mixing paint onto the back of the sheet and pressing it to the canvas. Marchant then spent time wiping the excess paint off the canvas, which he did in sections, until he was happy. He let Juliet play with this type of transfer, using a small paper sample. Then he took ink and touched up the drawing, applying a finishing varnish to the transfer to hold the lines in place. Only when he was pleased with the outlines of the sketch did his real work at the easel begin with whites and grays and browns, each day layering on, sometimes thickly, and then holding his knife and scraping back the paint until it achieved a finish that to Juliet seemed even more real than the colors around her. He was patient with his paintings at this point, taking his time applying the thick layers of paint and returning to the color studies as guides. Juliet would often find him searching on his hands and knees through scraps of paper looking for the right shade of blue.

Large with child, Marchant's wife had taken to her bed until the local doctor thought it wise that she return to Paris. Marchant, however, seemed unconcerned with this turn of events and had arranged for her to travel with a maid.

Juliet's routine with Marchant continued in the same way. He worked for several minutes with Marcel and Juliet, then sent the child with the maid for a nap, leaving him alone with Juliet. In those weeks, Marchant had finished three solo paintings of her—all by the fountain. When Juliet worked up the nerve to speak to him, usually in the second hour, she asked him to describe his neighborhood in Paris, and his typical days there. He told her of the bookshops and the cafés, of the walks down to Ile Saint-Louis and of the carousel in the Jardin du Luxembourg.

On her sixteenth birthday, the weather was bad and the rain pattered softly in the courtyard, so Marchant shifted the session back into his studio. On the easel, Juliet found a small painting covered with the beige cloth.

"What is it?" Juliet always liked the unveiling of Marchant's paintings of her.

"Go ahead," he said. "It's a birthday gift."

Juliet lifted the cloth and found a painting of a city. She frowned, expecting to see a painting of herself. She cocked her head, confused.

"It's my Paris." Marchant had walked up behind her, his voice quiet in her ear. "I painted it for you." He was standing so close that Juliet felt the fabric of his flowing pants scrape her ankle. His hands came to rest on her shoulders. "It's what I see every day when I'm there. I wanted you to see Paris through my eyes. I don't do landscapes, so my apologies if it isn't as good as what you're used to seeing from me, but I assure you it is a special painting."

Juliet turned and looked up at him. She could feel tears forming in her eyes.

"Do you like it?" he asked. Marchant seemed self-conscious and began cleaning his glasses with a hankie he'd pulled from his pant pocket.

She nodded. He was tall, so she debated for a moment before she looked up at him so close, knowing what it might mean. "No one has ever painted anything for me."

"Oh, come now." He laughed. "I've painted about twenty portraits of you."

Juliet shook her head. "You've never painted anything *for* me and you know it." His gift had emboldened her. She could sense how much he wanted her to like it. By now, Juliet knew that Marchant had two gazes: the artist's gaze that glossed over her like an object, and the gaze of a man. As he looked down at her, this was the latter. The weight of the rain rattled the window. They stood silently, looking at each other, knowing what was about to happen next, but neither making a move toward it.

Then Juliet observed his leg twitch, causing his pant leg to rustle. In one movement, he picked her up and carried her over to the daybed, gently laying her on it and sitting on the edge next to her.

Juliet's body memorized all of the places where their bodies met, her hip, his thigh, his stomach, her rib. He leaned over her, bracing himself up. His hand brushed her breast as his arm moved across her, all decorum about asking to touch her now swept away.

"I've never been kissed," she said, touching his lips with her finger, surprised that she felt entitled to do so. "For my birthday, I might like that."

He leaned down and his lips touched hers. His beard was softer than she'd imagined it would feel against her cheek. The kiss was light and when their lips parted, Juliet looked into his eyes. He drew her face toward his and their kisses began with a soft rhythm that Juliet picked up and matched until his tongue parted her lips and the kisses became deeper. Juliet tugged at his hair and his neck and he at her clothes.

Breathless, he finally pulled away from her. Juliet found herself pulling upward to stay connected to him. "I want you to stand," he commanded.

Juliet shifted her position and stood in front of him, her legs weak and shifting, her torso twisting. Marchant remained seated on the daybed. They touched now at every opportunity, his hand, her leg— the tangle of them, this new, sudden intimacy.

He looked up at her and pulled her toward him. "Do you want this?"

Juliet nodded, but he shook his head.

"No. Tell me," he said. "I need to *hear* that you want this, that you want *me*. Everything changes with this. Do you understand?" His hands held her firmly away from him, as though he might push her off and run free. "Do you understand, Juliet?" He shook her once to get his message across.

Juliet thought Marchant looked wild and tortured, like an animal in a trap.

"I want this." Her voice was clear. "I've never wanted anything more."

"Let me see you," said Marchant, and his gaze shifted to her body. "I need to see you."

She undid the button of her cotton shift and let the dress fall off her shoulders and onto the floor. Under the dress, she was naked. He looked at her and pulled her toward him, his head coming to rest on her stomach. Then Marchant lowered her back onto the daybed. He'd tried to explain to her that everything would change, but neither of them could know how true that prophecy would turn out to be. All

Juliet knew as he entered her again and again was that, there would be no marriage to the Busson boy now, no chopping leeks and feeding chickens. She was ruined for that life now. After a few moments, Marchant collapsed on top of her, and she knew they were bound together, forever.

7

H elen? Helen?"
I heard Sharlene's nasal voice and smelled the rubber of new carpet. As I shook myself, I realized I was facedown on the area rug with a pool of blood underneath me.

"What the...?"

"It's a nosebleed," said Sharlene, efficiently handing me a bunch of scratchy, not-quite-white napkins from the drink station. "I get them all the time. You fainted."

I sat up. My head was pounding. The dream I'd just had was so vivid.

"You need to go home and rest."

"No," I snapped. "I'll be fine. The air in here is dry. I'm sure that's it."

Sharlene frowned. "Your phone has been ringing nonstop. Everyone was looking for you."

"You all weren't looking on the floor then, it seems," I said with a laugh. I'd never had a nosebleed before, so I was a little rattled, but I chalked the whole thing up to seasonal allergies. People fainted. Noses bled. It happened. I was trying to not connect this nosebleed to my recent dreams.

The video, showing the confused senator against the *In Frame* backdrop forever, had gone viral. I spent the rest of the day taking calls and watching cable news light up with the story that Asa Heathcote had "taken ill" during an interview, where he'd admitted to being asked to be on the Republican ticket and to fathering a child with a staffer. He'd checked into George Washington University Hospital, where he was under observation. Virginia was spinning it as a fit of some sort. I knew this gave Heathcote a way to save face to the party. They'd chosen him carefully, but now they'd have to go back to their short list of candidates. And those candidates would now know that they were the second choice to be on the ticket. Heathcote was done as the vice presidential candidate and possibly as a sitting senator. By afternoon, the news that he'd suffered from dehydration from playing golf too rigorously the previous day had begun to circulate. Reporters had also located the former employee and had been camped outside of her house for hours. I wasn't sure what had happened to Asa Heathcote this morning, but I didn't think it was a simple game of golf. This was my doing, even if I had no idea how I was doing it.

I arrived home just as it was starting to get dark. I was contemplating various microwave meals in my freezer when I heard a light rap on my door.

Standing out on my step was Luke Varner, although I knew I hadn't given him my address. It was a warm night on Capitol Hill, and Luke stood at my door facing East Capitol Street with his hands in his pockets. When I turned the door handle, he looked like he was turning to leave.

"Oh. It's you."

"I was just wondering if anything strange happened to you today."

"Such as?"

"Strange things. Things that are strange."

I eyed him suspiciously. "You mean besides *you* on my doorstep?"

He smiled. Originally I had thought he was rather ordinary look-ing, but now I found myself looking at his dark-blue eyes and smirk, which was oddly sexy. Otherwise, I probably would have shut the door.

"I deserve that."

"I will probably regret this," I said as I moved aside. "But come in."

He was growing on me. There *was* something about him, like when a man looks a certain way and you don't know why that look appeals to you so much, until you remember the look is exactly like someone who lived next door to you when you were young. It's as though that type of handsome has left an indelible mark on your tastes, shaping them early. "I have some wine." I walked into the kitchen beyond the foyer.

Luke followed me. "Whatever you have."

"It isn't French," I warned as I poured him a full heaping glass of Cabernet and slid it across the counter. "No one ever asks me about my day anymore. That's one of the things that happens when you get divorced." I poured myself an equally full glass. "It's kind of nice so I'll start at the beginning. Colors."

"Colors?"

"Colors are odd to me today. Particularly greens and blues and yellows."

"Odd how?"

"Like everything with those colors has a fresh coat of wet paint and is surrounded by all of the other dingy colors I'm used to. I feel like I'm tripping on acid."

"Did you dream of France?" He looked at his wineglass. "I'm

assuming that since I got through your front door just now, you must be having some interesting dreams. Last night, you were just sure I was crazy."

When he said it my knees almost buckled, so I leaned on the counter like I was cool—not in order to remain standing upright. "Maybe."

He laughed. "You have to work with me here a little, you know."

"I haven't been to this particular region of France, but yes, it seemed very French and people were speaking...well, they were speaking French."

"So, you know French?" He smiled, already knowing the answer.

"Not exactly."

"But you understood what they were saying?"

I stopped mid-sip. I had. While I hadn't realized it before now, everyone in my dream had, indeed, spoken French, I'd understood every word. My mom, Margie Connor, had insisted that I study Spanish, not French. I don't speak French.

"Could have been Canada, I guess?" He was teasing me. "You'll dream more tonight. Hard to say what will come back next, but usually it comes out in chronological order."

"You're so full of bullshit." I took a deep breath. "This is craziness. I'm just having some weird dreams, that's all. I just got some vitamin B tablets from the farmers market. They're probably laced with some shit, that's all." With that, I took a too-large gulp of wine and held it in my mouth for a moment before swallowing it. "I also fainted today at work."

He looked concerned at this. "Nosebleed, too?"

"Yes." I could hear my voice rising. "How did you—?"

"That happens to you while your memories are coming back to you—or, as you put it, your 'weird dreams.' It's not a natural process you're going through, so it takes a toll on you, physically."

"So I can expect more fainting episodes? I just thought it was from all the excitement today." I took another gulp of wine. "Oh, I had a senator ruin his career in front of me this morning. I don't suppose you're to blame for that?"

"Nope. Not me this time, I'm afraid." he said. "But the fainting episodes are something I do know about." He picked up the top of his wineglass with his fingers and walked into the living room, like the house was his, as he rounded the sofa and sat down. "Let's do a little parlor trick, like the Victorians used to do. Do you want me to tell you about the dreams you're having?"

"Do you have a tarot deck in your pocket?"

"Tarot...please..." He rolled his eyes. "I can do better than that."

"Sure," I said. "It'll take my mind off of Asa Heathcote."

He seemed unconcerned about Heathcote as he settled into my sofa, rearranging my throw pillows around him. "I bet you I can tell you what you were dreaming about."

"Go ahead."

"You were sixteen years old." He looked out my window before he continued. "You lived in the Vendée region of France—a town called Challans. That's a shipping region southwest of Paris, but also thick with forests, lush. Very green. It is also near the ocean. You come from a family of farmers. Your parents raised corn, sunflowers, and chickens."

I swirled my wine. I could envision the scene he was painting for me. I'd just seen it. "So no royalty or wine merchants?" I knew the answer already, but I wanted him to tell me more.

"It wasn't very romantic, but I imagine you've seen it already, haven't you?" He sat on the edge of the sofa and waited for my reply.

I said nothing but joined him on the sofa—the far end away from him.

"You have to understand that at that time, there was a romantic notion of the countryside. The Parisians thought life was simpler in the country, so all of the painters and artists flocked there in the summers."

"And was it? Simpler?"

"Life isn't simple anywhere. At least that has been my experience." He put his hand on his chin, and I noticed the stubble was forming a beard on his face. "In the summers, the region was home to several famous writers and painters. It was a marvelous place. The area was farther away from the ocean with green and yellow fields. Your family wasn't one of the wealthier families. They didn't own a lot of land. Just enough to get by."

The darkness of the room and the light behind him cast deep shadows across Luke Varner's face. He pushed the sleeves of his thin black sweater up to his elbows and rested his forearms on his thighs. He seemed like he wasn't sure he wanted to continue with the story. But I wanted him to.

He looked up. "And you." He inhaled and leaned back into the sofa that seemed to swallow him up. "Well, you saw yourself."

I didn't reply.

He smiled, knowing he was right. "You don't look that different. You had auburn hair then—they call it titian now, I think." He reached over and touched the bottom of a loose strand of hair. It was an intimate gesture, but I let him do it, though I wasn't sure why.

"Titian, in honor of the painter," I said.

He nodded. "Your hair tumbled down your back and half the time you'd knot it up with something, as if the length of it annoyed you. You worked hard. You were up in the fields by early morning and feeding the chickens. You were beautiful, but country life was hard back then. And..." His voice trailed off.

I half expected the doorbell to ring and to find officers standing on my front step to tell me they had come to collect Luke Varner and return him to some mental institution and apologize for any inconvenience his stories had caused me. He knew exactly what was in my thoughts. How was that possible?

"The artist Auguste Marchant and his wife owned the estate that bordered your family's farm. They visited in the summers to escape Paris."

Although Roger had said the name of the artist thousands of times, when Luke spoke the name, "Auguste Marchant," I felt a chill go up my back. How was Luke Varner describing my dream so vividly? And why Auguste Marchant? Roger's obsession with him ruined our marriage. Now I couldn't even get away from Marchant in my dreams. In fact, Roger would probably kill to be having such detailed dreams of the artist.

"You'll find yourself scattered throughout his paintings over the years. Just look at the paintings at the Hanover Collection or go to the Musée d'Orsay. You were Marchant's muse."

"*Girl on Step*?"

"One of my favorites," he said. "I'm glad that painting is here with you now. It should always be with you. Think about it. You probably touched it a hundred times."

"What you're describing," I finally admitted. "I saw this today. It was like a dream. How is this happening?"

"It's like I explained at the Hanover." He shrugged. "You're extraordinary. What's happening to you is extraordinary. More of the story is coming. It just comes out in pieces. It's a bit of a mess really. Your other lives...well...they want to come out. I'm afraid you're not in the driver's seat in this one, Red."

"I dreamed of Marchant."

"Anyone else?" Varner sounded a bit stung, like he was expecting more from me.

"Nope, just Marchant."

"Just Marchant?"

"It's not a *competition*, Luke. I didn't get to you yet, if that's what you're hinting at. My dream is unfolding exactly like you said it would. I'll see you in these dreams soon? Right?" I half choked on those words. I couldn't believe I was allowing myself to get drawn into this story, but the wine helped.

"Your relationship with Marchant is about to change. That will set certain things in motion. I came in later." He glanced out the window again.

"Let me guess," I said. I took a small sip of my wine, remembering the last image of Juliet and Marchant. "Girl on a step . . . took a step too far." The last image I'd had in my dream was of Marchant and Juliet on the daybed.

I had been kidding, but he looked serious. "And it cost her dearly." He seemed to be studying the gray area rug. He was lost in his thoughts, as if he was weighing how much to share with me. "You could say you still pay for it today."

"You can tell that she knows it, too. In the painting, there is great remorse on her face. A loss of innocence. At the time, a stair step was a symbol for loss of innocence, a fallen woman."

Luke nodded. "You were betrothed to a farmer's son at the time. You would have married him when you turned seventeen."

I remembered. Juliet and her mother in the kitchen discussing Michel Busson. I could feel Juliet's dread at marrying him like it was my own. "You still think this girl is me?"

"Don't you?"

I shrugged. "I think it's an interesting story."

"So how do you explain these dreams you're having?"

"I'm not jumping to conclusions that they're other lives just yet, Mr. Varner."

"Oh yes, the farmers market vitamin B. Well then." He stood up rather abruptly. "I guess I should go."

"Go?" I stood up, too. "But you haven't finished."

"Oh, I have for now. Another time perhaps." He collected his jacket and took a last swig of wine. "You're not ready for it."

"Not ready for it?" I couldn't believe this man had shown up at my door and proceeded to tell me a wild story about what he claimed was my life more than a hundred years ago—and just when the story was getting good, he decided to leave. I wondered if I'd offended him, been too glib. "But you haven't told me how we met."

"I think I'd rather *you* tell me how we met." He turned to go. "Concentrate before you go to bed. The rest will follow. It always does."

"You could save us all the trouble and tell me yourself."

"I've tried that before, Red. It's not so good for you when I do that." He stopped and considered something. "One more thing. There is another painting. It is part of a private collection, but photos of it exist. *Juliet* is its name. That's the painting that started it all."

This painting sounded familiar. I recalled Roger attempting to locate a mysterious Marchant painting to no avail—and Roger had been good at locating paintings. I followed Luke into the foyer. The wine had already gone to my head, and I wobbled a little.

"Oh and Red," he said as he opened the door. "You have a birthday coming up in a few weeks?"

I tilted my head in confusion. "At the end of the month." June twenty-second would be my thirty-fourth birthday. He was right. "How did you know—"

"It's not important. But you need to concentrate hard." He put his hands in his pockets and looked down the street. There was a breeze coming down East Capitol Street. The night was cool, and Luke studied the darkness like he was reading something. "Can you do that for me? You don't have a lot of time."

"What do you mean, I don't have a lot of time?"

"Let's just say you were late this time, so you *need* to remember, quickly." With that, he walked out of the door and into the night. I watched him until he turned on Third Street and disappeared from sight.

After he left, I went back into my living room with the one lamp. I grabbed my computer and did another search for "Luke Varner." There was nothing much of interest. The website for the Luke Varner who owned an art gallery in Taos, New Mexico, featured nothing about the man himself. The art connection seemed logical, and he'd mentioned Taos. Other than that, there was nothing about this mysterious man. No photos existed. No press releases.

What was I expecting, though? This man was crazy. This whole thing was crazy. I longed to call Roger and tell him about it all—the dreams, this crazy man insisting I was Marchant's muse—but I knew that Roger would think I was insane or, worse, trying to manufacture some connection to him. After I'd tucked myself into my bed, puffed up my soft, king-size pillow into a ball, and laid my head down, I thought about the last twenty-four hours—I met a madman who'd insisted I was over a hundred years old, I'd ruined the career of a man with one simple interview, and I was inhabiting another woman in my dreams. Sure that I was going to have a restless night ahead of me, I thought I'd just lie there for a moment, but then a heavy wave of sleep overcame me.

8

Juliet LaCompte
Challans, France, 1895

Juliet smelled cinnamon and vanilla cooking on the stove as she entered the kitchen. Her mother stood at the sink firmly grinding a mixture of dried jasmine flowers with rose petals.

"A love potion?" Juliet peered over her mother's shoulder. It was a familiar combination. Juliet was now able to do some of these simple compounds herself.

"I have an order." Her mother was a keeper of secrets, both for her customers and, Juliet suspected, for herself. Juliet was getting more curious about what went on with her mother and these women.

"Who is it for?" Juliet sat on the chair at the table. "Tell me? No, let me guess. The old widower in the valley? The one who is sweet on the girl who is a year older than me?"

Her mother turned to her. "You're quite happy these days."

Juliet was wary. Her mother had a sense of these things. "It is the summer. You know how I love it. Everything is growing and alive."

Her mother turned back to her potion and leaned down to consult the battered recipe book that was open next to her, but Juliet knew she wasn't convinced. The next thing she asked Juliet would reveal her suspicions. "How is the work with Monsieur Marchant going?"

Juliet's face burned. Her mother *was* suspicious. The best defense

Juliet could mount now was to downplay her paintings. "I'm getting bored," Juliet lied. "I just sit there with Marcel while he wiggles and protests. I hear he'll be going back to Paris soon."

"I heard that, too," said her mother. "In fact, I hear he's leaving in a few days."

Juliet felt as thought she'd been slapped. Marchant hadn't told her he was leaving. As they were wrapped in each other's arms every morning, he had ample time to warn her of his departure. Surely her mother was wrong.

After breakfast, Juliet excused herself and ran to the studio. When she arrived, she went in and handed Marcel to the maid. No longer did Marchant go through the motions of drawing her brother. They'd done a series of paintings yesterday of her on the back step, Juliet fidgeting with her arms and bored because she preferred to be inside the studio, away from the prying eyes of the maid. The steps were hot, by midday, and Marchant chastised her for fidgeting.

Today she found him in the studio painting the folds of her dress from yesterday, dress fold sketches littering the area around his feet. He put down the paintbrush somehow sensing she was near and turned, pulling her toward him and kissing her in one swift motion. As was their routine in these few weeks, they moved to the daybed where Marchant removed her dress and unbuttoned his pants. Juliet knew what to do now—how he liked to be touched and handled, the positions he preferred in these moments. She knew the rote ministrations she performed on him every bit as well as she knew how to move during the Sunday services at church. Now Juliet also knew the answer to the question of what it was to be a wife, yet she could not imagine doing these intimate things with the wretched Busson boy. After they had finished, Marchant lit his pipe.

"I hear you are going back to Paris." It was a statement, not a question.

"That is correct." Marchant leaned down and kissed her breasts. "I meant to talk to you about it."

"*Did you?*" Juliet could tell her voice was strained, and she felt Marchant tense when he registered her tone.

He placed his head on her bare stomach. "I'd like to take you with me to Paris. If you'll go?"

Juliet felt herself visibly exhale. This was exactly the response that she wanted to hear from him. "Of course I'll go with you."

Marchant got up and buttoned his shirt and pants. He went to the easel and sat there looking at her.

Juliet reached for her dress, but he said firmly, "No."

While they had done many intimate things together, the idea of Marchant drawing her like this felt too public and forbidden. There could be no record on canvas of what had happened between them. Juliet protested. "We can't."

He turned her, draping her head down over the bed exactly in the pose he wanted. He gazed at her while he sketched, but she never again reached for her dress. It wasn't as though she didn't believe Marchant about taking her to Paris, but there was some part of her that longed for some record of them together as proof they had existed this way. Within the week, the painting that Marchant referred to as *Juliet* was finished. When Marchant finally revealed it to her, there was no mistaking what had transpired between them. The painting had a raw quality to it, not the typical Marchant model with alabaster skin tones. The skin of the *Juliet* in the painting was flushed and the close-up, intimate pose suggested she was spent, left exhausted on the bed. With pigment and paper, he had captured Juliet's hunger for him.

The model gazed at the artist with the full knowledge of him, and the artist had rendered it perfectly. To Juliet, it was the purest look of desire captured on canvas.

As Juliet drank her tea the next morning, she thought she tasted something funny in it. She put the cup to her nose and got the distinctive hint of burnt cinnamon. The potion her mother had been cooking. So the potion had been made for her. She put down the cup and stared at it.

Juliet heard the swish of her mother's full skirt before she saw her. "Drink your tea," instructed her mother as she began chopping potatoes. "You look pale. It will bring color to your cheeks. You aren't outside as often as you usually are in the summers." When she stepped out to toss the potato peelings, Juliet poured the tea down the drain and returned to her seat with the empty cup.

Her mother looked flushed as she fussed around the kitchen. "We are going to the Bussons for dinner tonight. Madame Busson and I thought it would be proper to have a dinner with you and their boy. It is time you both begin to know each other."

Juliet stared down at the empty cup. So there it was. Her mother had hoped the potion would enhance her affections for the Busson boy this evening.

That night at the dinner, Juliet was seated across the table from Michel Busson, who seemed to not understand the transaction that was to take place between them in a year. Instead he spoke of hunting and of the deer he'd killed in the hunt last fall. Proudly displayed around the dining area were the animal heads from Michel's kills, including the head of the particular deer they'd just discussed. As he ate, Michel's thin arms moved coarsely with seemingly no awareness of Juliet at all. Knowing the intimate things she did with Marchant, she almost vomited at the idea that next year she would be expected to marry this boy.

After the dinner, she asked to be excused to take in some air. As she breathed in the smell of blooming lavender from the Bussons' fields, she saw the light on in Marchant's house. Juliet knew that she could never stay in Challans now. She had to run away with Marchant to Paris within the week. She was about to return into the house when she found Michel Busson standing in the doorway watching her. As she attempted to go past him, he blocked her, grabbing a tiny piece of her inner arm and pinching it, pulling her close to him.

"You look down on me, don't you, little girl?" Michel spat at her. "I can see it in your eyes. But it is I who will look down on you. When we are married, I will *own* you."

Juliet's eyes widened.

Sensing her alarm, he smiled. "That *is* the arrangement that your parents have struck between our families, you know." He laughed. "You little fool. Do you know what that means?" He sneered and grabbed her around her waist with his thin but surprisingly strong arms, pulling her close to him. He held her hips for a moment before he whispered into her ear. "You will belong to me. And make no mistake, I will not be kind."

Then he pushed her back, and she fell on the stone step in front of him. He walked past her, stepping over her as he headed back into the house.

Juliet got to her feet, her legs bloody from the fall. She limped and staggered into the house, where she found Michel serenely seated in the parlor with her parents. All eyes turned to her as she entered the room.

"What on earth has happened to you?" Her mother rose from her chair and ran over to Juliet, tugging and patting at her. "I'm so sorry. This is terribly embarrassing."

Michel calmly turned to look at her, defiance in his eyes. "Oh, Juliet, did you fall on that top step outside? It can be tricky."

"Yes," said Juliet's mother. "She must have fallen on the step." Her mother held her firmly by the arm. "Juliet can be so clumsy sometimes." Turning to Juliet's father, she said, "Let's get her home."

Juliet could see a look exchange between her parents. Just then, Madame Busson pushed through the pantry door carrying a tray of cakes and cheese, but she froze when she saw Juliet and her mother. "What on earth?"

"Juliet has stumbled on the top step," said Michel. He never took his pale eyes off Juliet, defying her to tell a different story. "Isn't that right, Juliet?"

"That's terrible," said Madame Busson, shaking her head. "Our youngest daughter falls on that step all the time, doesn't she, Michel?"

"She does indeed, Mother." Michel got up and removed the tray from his mother's hands. "I'll take this back into the kitchen for you."

Juliet looked at the Bussons' youngest daughter, who met her eyes with a doleful stare.

Madame Busson beamed, stroking his hair as he went by. "He's such a thoughtful boy."

"We're going to get her home," interrupted Juliet's mother. "My apologies, Madame Busson."

"No need for apologies, Thérèse. I'll wrap up some cakes for you to take home with you." Madame Busson smiled at Juliet and then noticed her bloody knees. "We should clean Juliet's legs."

"It's not necessary," said Juliet's mother. "I'd hate to be more of a bother. I can do it."

When they'd gotten the box of cakes, Juliet and her parents headed out across the field toward home, Juliet's father steadying her as she limped.

"I think she twisted her ankle," said her father, finally scooping up Juliet in his arms. "You're not as light as you used to be as a young girl." Juliet leaned her head against him, feeling the warmth of him.

"She made us look like fools," spat her mother once they were far enough away from the Bussons' house. "They probably think they're marrying their son off to some half-wit."

"Now—" Juliet's father began, but her mother cut him off.

"We need this marriage, Juliet." Her mother spun ahead of her and her father and faced them both, stopping them on the slope. Her mother's brown hair had come loose from its chignon and wild, gray strands were framing her face. "Do you understand me? You need to marry Michel Busson."

"That's enough, Thérèse." Her father rarely raised his voice to her mother, but something in her demeanor made his arms tense. Juliet leaned against him.

Her mother turned to her father with a contempt Juliet hadn't known the woman was capable of showing. "You know very well why she needs to marry the boy."

Her father pushed on up the hill, ignoring her mother. "I do, but that doesn't mean I have to like it."

Sensing her father was on her side, Juliet was about to erupt with a story of Michel's cruel treatment of her, but she thought better of it. She needed a plan so, instead, she nodded. "I'm sorry, *Maman*."

The next morning, Juliet hobbled downstairs to find the kitchen empty. Happy that she wouldn't need to navigate her mother this morning, she limped up the hill toward Marchant's house. Marchant had money. He would help her family so they wouldn't lose the farm. As she neared the studio door, Juliet heard shouting. The two voices were all too familiar.

"She's a child," her mother wailed. "What have you *done*?"

Marchant's voice was strained in a way that Juliet had never heard before. He was sobbing. "No, please don't take the painting."

"You have *ruined* her. You have no idea what you've done. I want no record of this disgrace you have committed against my daughter. I'll burn it. Do you hear me? Then you'll leave here. Return to Paris today. I want her paintings destroyed. You'll never see her again. Do you understand?"

"Please. I'll do it, but please, please, don't take the painting."

Juliet was standing in the doorway. She could hear the smashing and ripping of canvas. Finally her mother burst through, grasping the nude canvas of her daughter.

"Get out of my way," hissed her mother. She looked at Juliet for a moment before turning her gaze down to her daughter's waist then closing her eyes and whispering, "No. Oh, Juliet. What have you done?" Defeat washed over her mother's face. After appearing to compose herself, the woman brushed past her, struggling with the bulk of the canvas in her hands. Her mother walked down the hill and turned back toward her. "He was *never* taking you to Paris with him," she spat. "Go ahead. Ask him. You were a fool."

Juliet entered the studio to find Marchant sitting on the stone floor in front of the daybed with his head in his hands. Surrounding him were the frames of snapped and torn canvases—all bearing various forms of Juliet's likeness. Her voice was surprisingly calm considering the gravity of the moment. "Is what she says true? Were you never going to take me to Paris with you?"

"That's not true," said Marchant, his face red and swollen. "Your mother is a liar. I was going to take you. I was. I was going to send for you."

To Juliet, he seemed to be trying to convince himself of this statement, trying it on. Oh, how she wanted to believe him.

"You don't understand."

"What don't I understand?"

But he simply put his head in his hands again and shook his head. "Go home, Juliet. Just go home. When the time is right, I will come for you."

9

Helen Lambert
Washington, DC, May 26, 2012

"What the fuck." I bolted upright in bed. My feet hit the floor and I raced out of the bedroom and into the bathroom to study my face in the mirror. I found the distinct copper-red hair with messy ringlets spiraling down my back. Thank goodness I was Helen Lambert again. As the thought occurred to me, I began to laugh and laid my head on the sink to steady myself.

"Maybe you have one of those brain tumors." I stared up at my own reflection. The scene with Marchant still raw in my memory, I called Luke. Finally, I needed to admit that something unnatural was happening to me. These were more than just dreams. I must have sounded shaken because he offered to come over right away.

It was Saturday, so I was glad I didn't have to worry about work. After the Asa Heathcote interview, everyone was clamoring to talk to me. I now had twenty-six voicemail messages that I hadn't listened to. Checking the news briefly, I saw that Heathcote's former staffer who'd given her child up for adoption had finally given a statement asking for privacy, but nothing more. I sighed and turned off both my phone and the television.

Luke drove up in a black Range Rover, art director glasses perched on his nose and two bags of groceries in the backseat. I raised my eyebrow as he came through the door. "You cook, too?"

"I do." Letting himself into the kitchen, he began opening doors, pulling things out of bags, and lining them up on the counter. After he opened a few drawers, he looked puzzled. "Do you have a whisk?"

I was busy reviewing mail. "Sorry," I said. "I lost it in the divorce. Roger has a thing for kitchen tools. Who has a whisk these days anyway?" I reached into the drawer next to me, pulled out a fork, and handed it to him. He hesitated before he took it and studied it in his hand as though it were a primitive tool.

Soon he was chopping and throwing things into a pan that began to smell amazing. "What is that?" I peered into the pan.

"Garlic and white truffle oil." He backed out from the depths of my lower cupboard, his head finally emerging, with another cutting board in hand. He chopped vegetables, tossed them into another pan, and flipped them with the skill of a professional chef.

"Where did you learn to cook?"

He shrugged. "I've always known how. It's one of the few things I enjoy in this world."

"And the other things?"

"Well, that's personal." He flashed me a smile, his teeth perfectly straight and white.

"We *did* go out on a date. Just a tip, cooking is one of those pesky things you discuss on a first date, not killing people and knowing someone for a hundred years."

"You kind of ran out on our first date, if you recall." He shook the hot pan. "Maybe I was just about to start talking about my cooking skills."

"Any other hobbies besides killing people?"

"Things I like," he said, changing the subject. "I like water. The ocean. I'd like to surf one day."

"Boring." I fake-yawned. "Who doesn't like the ocean?"

"Plenty of people," he said.

"I don't know any." I curled my legs under the stool and leaned in. "Try again."

"I like art."

I groaned. "Not you, too."

"I sell it," he said, laughing. "I don't collect it. Well, I don't collect much of it."

I was toying with what to say. He seemed to be reading my thoughts.

"This dream you had?"

"I saw Juliet again."

"And?"

"I think I might be her."

He turned and leaned back on the counter, amused. He was wearing a black T-shirt and some faded jeans. I'd noticed the line of muscles in his arm earlier as he carried the grocery bags.

"Really? No more 'you're fucking crazy, Luke'?"

"Oh, you might be fucking crazy all right." I played with my sock so I wouldn't have to look at him. "But the dream happened just like you said it would. Even I have to admit that something is going on here. This girl in my dream, Juliet. She feels like me."

"You're all of them—they're all unique, different, but all parts of you." He moved effortlessly around the kitchen, returning to the stove and cracking eggs into a bowl before transferring them to the pan. I saw a fresh baguette peeking out of the remaining bag.

"How many of us are there?"

"Well, there is you, of course."

"Of course."

"You'll dream of Nora and Sandra, too."

"Four of us, then?"

He nodded.

"Assuming this isn't crazy ... and that is a big leap for me. Are we all the same?"

He hesitated. I could tell it was a question he didn't want to answer, but I pressed. "When we met that first night at the Sofitel, you said you'd loved Nora best."

"I was just babbling," he said, stopping what he was doing at the stove to consider this. "I get nervous the first time we meet again after a long time. But yes, Nora was very special to me."

"Not Juliet?" I felt a strange closeness to Juliet, having inhabited her in my dreams.

He didn't answer.

"Sandra?"

He considered my questions while he pulled the outer edges of the omelet toward the center with a spatula. He turned to face me across the counter. "I failed Juliet."

"How did you fail her?"

He inched closer and pointed to my forehead. "You, my dear, have the answer to that question in ... your ... head."

"You could save us both the time and trouble."

He looked pained, distracted. "I haven't thought of Sandra in a long time." There was something in his voice when he spoke of her that seemed wistful. "To answer your question, you *are* similar, but each version of you has grown up with a different background, in a different time ..."

"How long has it been?" Even as I spoke the words, I shuddered. How could I really believe this was true?

"This time? Forty-one years."

"That would be—"

"Nineteen seventy-one."

He took one look at me and grabbed a paper towel, held it to my nose, led me into the bedroom, and sat me down on the bed, lifting my chin to keep my nose elevated. "I saw your nose beginning to bleed. You're getting sick," he said. "You need to rest."

"Do I usually get nosebleeds?"

"You have." He looked concerned. "What you're experiencing isn't exactly human, so it's taking its toll. You haven't had to absorb this many lives before in this short amount of time. Usually, you have more time."

"You keep saying that." I tilted my head back. "Will I be all right?"

Luke didn't answer. He smoothed my hair, and I realized that no one had touched me since Roger. He leaned down and kissed my forehead. "Just lie down and rest. I'll bring your breakfast in here."

He came back a few minutes later with a plate of gorgeous food: a Gruyère cheese omelet, watercress salad, and chopped hash brown potatoes.

"Holy shit this looks good."

He sat down on the bed next to me while I ate. "So where did you leave off with Juliet?"

I set my bloody tissue on the nightstand and focused on my plate. I felt like I was recounting the plot of some epic novel. "Juliet's mother found out about Marchant." I looked over at him, and I could see a mixture of worry and familiarity. "Assuming you're not crazy and this whole story is true, how many times have you made me breakfast before?"

"Too many to count."

"And I like this." I looked down at my half-empty plate.

"You do. In all your lives."

He turned to leave and I touched his arm. "Don't go."

"I'm just going to the kitchen," he said. "I'll be right back." Before he left the room, he looked back at me with what seemed like regret.

"What?" I said.

"Nothing." He smiled sadly. "I just never tire of seeing you, that's all."

I heard the boards creak as he walked down the hall. A few minutes later, he returned and sat down heavily on the bed next to me and watched me eat. After, he pulled me close and curled up beside me. I could hear the clock next to my bed ticking, and then the room seemed to blip as though it were a faulty TV channel. And then darkness.

10

Juliet LaCompte
Challans, France, 1895

Juliet had never seen her mother at work in quite the way she was now. Furious from her conversation with Marchant, her mother paced back and forth grabbing bottles from the windowsill.

Sobs erupted from deep inside her belly as Juliet stepped into the kitchen. When her mother saw her, she ran to her and grabbed her by the shoulders. "You will tell no one. Do you hear me?"

"I love him."

Her mother slapped her hard across the face. "You are a fool, child. You need to be smart."

Reeling, Juliet grabbed her cheek, which was hot and stinging as if she'd leaned her cheek over the fire.

Her mother's face was cold, unforgiving. "You have put us all in danger with your foolishness."

"I don't understand..."

She shook her head. "*Non.* I will fix this." In one swift motion, her mother pulled back the rug in the kitchen to reveal a trapdoor that Juliet had never noticed before. "Help me." She motioned to Juliet, who held open the heavy wooden door while her mother lowered herself into the space beneath the floor, returning with three black candles and what looked like jars of blood and meat and a giant leather book.

What Juliet saw hidden under the floor was different from the love potions and herbs above the ground. Below the secret door was a different kind of magic.

"What are you going to do?" Juliet held the jars and candle while her mother lifted herself out from the space.

"I need someone's help." Her mother carried in her hand the book with a battered leather cover—one the girl hadn't seen before. As she peered over her mother's shoulder, Juliet could see drawings of the moon and strange names she didn't recognize. Her mother's finger lingered on one name—exotic—Althacazur. She nodded, satisfied. Working furiously, using the mortar and pestle to grind herbs, she moved around the room, finally pouring the fine mixture into a crystal bowl with water. Chanting lightly, her mother moved the bowl in circles over her head. As the bowl moved, Juliet caught the smell of saffron, cloves, and cinnamon.

Next, her mother placed the black candles each in a small, crystal cup and poured the bloody contents of the jar over the candles. "Give me your hand." Juliet held out her hand for her mother, who took a knife and before Juliet could protest sliced the girl's finger, pouring the blood over each candle. Juliet winced.

"Do you have anything that belongs to him? Anything he's touched?" When Juliet didn't respond, her mother sighed impatiently. "Well, do you?" The older woman's hair had fallen out of its usual neat chignon. Long pieces hung down her back and across her forehead, matted with sweat.

Juliet nodded and went upstairs and brought back Marchant's birthday present, his painting of Paris.

Her mother grabbed the small painting from her and turned it over and over in her hand. "Did he give you this?"

Juliet nodded. "He painted it for my birthday."

Her mother looked at her daughter with an expression of pity. She took a decorative knife out of her pocket, slit the canvas starting where Marchant had signed his name, pulled the paper off, and held it over the candle.

The oils on the paint took to the flame quickly. As the canvas burned, Juliet stared at the ruined depiction of Paris, the landscape buckling and bending as the flame twisted it. It was Marchant's Paris, yet her mother had said he had no intention of ever taking her there. But Juliet felt her mother was wrong. Marchant had loved her. He would come for her.

After night fell and Juliet's father and siblings fell asleep, her mother woke her from a fitful dream and took her by the hand down the stairs to the kitchen. Without the fire, the room was deathly quiet, cold, and damp. To Juliet's surprise, the kitchen had been transformed. The table had been moved aside to the wall and on the floor, in its place, a giant circle had been drawn with chalk. Inside the circle was a star—the lines perfect as though Juliet's mother had traced them with a straightedge—and at the top of the star, the three black candles sat blazing inside the circle, next to the crystal bowl.

In the light, Juliet was startled to see her mother moving around the space dressed in a strange oversize purple robe, her face painted white, like a carnival clown. But this look was not a jovial costume. There was something sinister about the cloak. She wanted to run, tried to turn, but her mother grabbed her arm and held her with a strength Juliet didn't know she had. "You need to witness. He is asking for it."

Juliet did not know who "he" was, but she felt she could not argue. She hoped her father or Delphine would come down the stairs and rescue her from this macabre scene, but her family slept soundly—too soundly—and Juliet wondered if her mother had put something in the tea she'd served at dinner.

"Sit." Her mother pointed inside the chalk circle. Once she stepped over the crude chalk outlines, the circle felt distinctively warmer than the rest of the drafty room. The cool breeze that flowed from under the door seemed to stop at the edge of the circle drawing. To test it, Juliet ran her hand back and forth across the line, feeling the temperature inside the circle change. Her mother tugged at Juliet's nightdress, pulling it down past her shoulders and letting it bunch in a heap beneath her. Then her mother began applying a stinking brown paste to Juliet's face and then her chest, breasts, stomach, and legs, slapping the girl's arms away as she tried to wipe it from her. Juliet gagged as the smell of cloves and earth hit her. Juliet pulled her arms around her in the circle, sitting on her nightdress, wearing nothing but the brown, pungent paste.

"I'm cold," said Juliet.

Ignoring her, Juliet's mother then knelt at the line of the circle, her robe collecting chalk dust as she slid forward on the floor until she was lying facedown on the floorboards, her forehead resting on the wood plank. As her mother chanted softly, Juliet felt a tug at her stomach followed by a stabbing pain, pulsing at first like a heartbeat but then growing harder and stronger. Gasping, she grabbed her stomach; it felt hard and hot. As her mother's chants grew faster, she felt a warm liquid begin to flow down between her legs onto the nightdress bunched beneath her. Blood. She knelt to touch it but pulled her hand back as her mother began to sing in a strange high-pitched voice, almost like a child's. Within minutes, her voice now lurid, the candles began to flicker faster in time with her song, wax melting rapidly down the sides like lava.

Juliet was frightened. This was a macabre scene, and the woman lying on the floor seemed not to be her mother at all. The figure in purple, now facedown like a wooden doll, began jerking violently. Juliet attempted to stand but found her legs wouldn't work and she was unable to move. As if sensing her desire to flee, the older woman's hand reached out to grip Juliet's bare ankle; as it did, the girl's body shook with convulsions. She fell to the floor in a ball beside her mother, rolling out of the circle where the cold air hit her, her body writhing. The pain in her stomach was searing.

Her mother rose from the floor like she was waking from a deep sleep. With a look of disgust, she glanced at the pool of garnet-colored blood around Juliet. "You were with child, his child, but it is gone now."

Juliet cried out and touched her stomach, the thick brown mud paste crumbling as it dried. The pulsing and pain had now stopped, replaced by a dull ache. She sat up, looking down at her ruined nightdress. It looked like she'd been butchered in it.

"We'll burn it," her mother said as if she'd read her thoughts. "Get back in the circle."

Juliet slid her body carefully inside the circle, her legs shaking, and for a moment she felt the pain leave her as she crossed the chalk line. Her mother looked at her with a hollow expression, a look of contempt.

The woman's high singing resumed. Through the kitchen window, Juliet could see the full moon shining, casting light inside the circle. The candles sat burning in bowls filled with blood. When they reached the point where they'd burned to the liquid line, the blood puckered then bubbled and ran onto the wood floor, stopping at the chalk circle line. Juliet's mother cried out just as the door blew open. A dense, wet fog seeped in, but as the haze swirled, it materialized into a form. What Juliet saw next caused her to yelp. It was a jerking skeleton of a horned goat attempting to walk upright on two legs. The grotesque creature materialized and faded as it struggled to find its footing before settling upon Juliet's mother. It planted itself in front of her mother. There seemed to be some conversation going on between her mother and the creature, then some acknowledgment from the woman. There was a snapping sound as her mother's jawbones broke and her mouth opened to an inhumanly large size, allowing the goat skeleton, which now seemed to have become a solid mass, to step into her mother's throat like it was putting on a pair of pants. Juliet felt bile rise in her mouth. Despite the circle, she felt the cold for the first time as a chill seemed to wrap around her like blanket.

With a sudden jerk, her mother sat up on her knees, her jawbones snapping and locking back into place. The woman touched her face as if to make sure everything was still intact. "It is done." The voice, however, was not her mother's. The woman stood up in one swift motion, but then stumbled, as if her body were an ill-fitting suit, walking woodenly to the stairs, her knees swaying and the purple robe dragging on the floor behind her. The creature climbed the stairs, leaving Juliet sitting naked and alone on the floor inside the circle, candles burning and vomit drying on her thighs.

Juliet arose and pulled her blood-soaked nightgown from the floor. She hobbled over to the kitchen sink to try to wash the brown poultice off her body. With a crude scrub, she got most of it off and wrapped the bloody dress around her, the fabric now having a thickness to it and the sopping material cold against her skin. Stopping first at the door to close and latch it, she blew out the candles and stared for a moment at the brown leather book with elaborate gold and purple embossed designs lying on the table. Juliet reached out to touch it, but pulled her hand back abruptly, feeling she should take the book and burn it. What she'd seen her mother do tonight with it had frightened her. That *thing* had frightened her, and she couldn't shake the feeling that it had come from this book. When she looked at the etching on the cover, she saw the symbol of it—the goat creature that had been in the kitchen. She stepped quietly up the stairs to the bedroom, rolling her nightgown into a ball and hiding it behind her side of the bed on the floor while Delphine slept soundly. Shivering, she changed into another nightgown and crawled into the warm bed, but despite the usual heaviness of the blankets, the cold would not leave her and the smell of the cloves and earth still lingered on her body. The pungent smell was the only reminder that what she had seen had been *real*. While she might have wrapped her arms around Delphine for warmth, she did not want to touch her sister. This wasn't a normal chill, and what had happened with her mother in the kitchen had not been normal. *Her mother was not normal.* If Juliet had wondered about her mother's past, she no longer doubted the secrets the woman had kept from the family. The devil himself had been invited into their house that night. Of that, Juliet was sure.

When she woke in the morning, the kitchen was clean and no sign of a chalk circle, leather book, black candle, or blood remained. Juliet's father came through the door with a worried look. He was a kind man with a big face and broad nose, but now his face was flushed. "It's your mother," he said. "She's taken ill."

Following him up to the bedroom, she found her mother lying in her bed. While Juliet had a chill that she could not shake, her mother's clothes were soaked in sweat. The whites of the woman's eyes were bloody red as though they were about to burst. Her mother spied Juliet and smiled.

"The doctor is coming," said her father. "He isn't sure what it is. Thinks it could be the plague and that you children ought not to be in here, but your mother wanted to see you." He turned at the door. "She only asked for you."

Juliet nodded. She felt certain that what had felled her mother was not the plague or any other earthly ailment.

"I'll keep Delphine and Marcel away from here." His steps were heavy down the stairs.

After he'd left the room, Juliet's mother smiled. "It is done."

Juliet could see bruises around the woman's chin from where her jaw had been broken to allow *that thing* to step into her mouth, but otherwise there was no trace of what had happened in the kitchen. Juliet found she could not look at her; the whites of her eyes were now almost purely red. "I know, *Maman*." Juliet began to cry. "But you're sick because of me, aren't you? You're sick because of what we did last night." Juliet had not been sure what her mother had been last night, but the woman now lying in front of her was her mother once again. "It's my fault."

She shook her head. "No. No. I will get better, you'll see. You must listen to me. There isn't time. A letter will arrive for you in a few days. You must do what that letter says. You must do what *he* says. Do you understand me?"

"Who?" Juliet was afraid that the "he" was the thing from the leather book.

"Just listen to him. He will protect you."

"Protect me from what?" Juliet stroked her mother's forehead, but her mother seemed not to register it. "What do I need protection from? I don't understand any of this, *Maman*."

"I can't see you, Juliet. Do you understand me? Say it."

"I understand," Juliet lied. "A letter will arrive," she repeated. "I will do what it says and I will listen to him." Juliet began to sob. "I'm so sorry. I did this to you—to our family."

"*Non*. It wasn't your fault. You couldn't have had the baby, Juliet. It was too dangerous." The woman smiled. "It was all Marchant's fault, but he will pay for it. All this nonsense with the paintings. You wouldn't have been safe anymore." The woman struggled to breathe, but choked out her words, which had become choppy. "I destroyed them all. Do as the man says. I worked so hard for you to be safe."

"But I have been safe, *Maman*."

The woman shook her head. "No. He is so dangerous. So dangerous..."

"I don't understand," Juliet whispered to her mother, but her mother was quiet now. Did she mean Marchant? She held her mother's hand until she heard a groan and a rattle and then nothing but the sound of the wind shaking the shutter at the window.

Because the doctor was not sure it wasn't plague, they burned, then buried her mother's remains the next day. When no one in the LaCompte house came down with anything in a week's time, the doctor let the family leave the farm. Anxious to finally see Marchant, Juliet walked up the hill to his studio, but found it empty—not like before with the drapes still on the daybed—everything had been cleaned out with a finality that frightened her. Juliet entered the courtyard and found the maid who had cared for Marcel sweeping the stones.

"Monsieur Marchant left a week ago for Paris. His wife and baby died together in childbirth. He is selling this house."

"Did he leave anything for me? A letter perhaps?"

The maid shook her head, turned, and walked into the kitchen, shutting the door tightly.

Juliet came back out of the studio and spied the unfinished nude sketches of her in the burn pile. Juliet thought about retrieving them and saving them, but with so much lost, they were too painful to look at, so she left them.

Night had fallen and Juliet realized that her father had not gotten water. She took the bucket and headed to the well. He didn't know that such things were required for the running of the house. The moon was full and illuminated everything. As she walked down to the well, she heard the reassuring sounds of the chickens busy in their yard.

She thought of Marchant and how the feel of his touch still burned on her skin. She felt her legs grow weak and stopped pumping the well. Sobs overtook her. What would her family do now?

It was the sound of sticks cracking as someone stepped on them and the yank of her dress that snapped her back to reality. She was spun and thrown to the ground. Gasping, Juliet looked up to find Michel Busson and another boy standing over her.

"Is this the whore that is to be your wife?" The other boy spat on her.

Michel knelt down and grabbed her hair. "We found your paintings—the ones at the artist's house. The ones the maid was trying to burn, but we pulled them out of the fire. Look!"

Juliet could see the sketches scattered on the ground behind them. They'd been looking at them. The sketches were in various stages of burn, and the thought of Michel viewing a private moment between her and Marchant sickened her. With the moon shining, she could see the pink color that Marchant had chosen for her skin tone. The other boy grunted. "It looks like she likes to have her clothes removed."

Michel snorted and ripped off her dress, holding her down with his other hand. Juliet screamed once, but he stuffed a part of her dress in her mouth and then climbed on top of her. While he unbuttoned his dirty workpants, the other boy came around and held her flailing arms over her head. Michel finished in a few moments and seemed in a hurry to be done with her, as if the act bored him. Juliet was relieved that it had not been worse. She could survive this. She yelped as the other boy slapped her hard across the face. Michel leaned over and held her down while the other boy took his turn with her. The second boy took a long time and seemed to savor hurting her as his thighs slapped hard against her. "Hit her again," the boy said to Michel before he finished. "For humiliating you and your family."

When it was finally finished and the boys had grown bored with their prey, Juliet crumpled into a ball, hoping they would leave her, but she found she could not sob. She felt a warm liquid fall over her legs and head and knew what the boys were doing standing over her. She kept her eyes closed as if seeing the act of them urinating on her would make it more real to her and harder to forget. And she *needed* to forget this night.

"If you tell anyone, we'll make sure everyone sees these paintings," said Michel, buttoning his trousers. He leaned in close to her, and she could feel his spit on her face as he spoke to her. "Don't worry, little whore, I'll still marry you, but this is what you can expect from me." He pulled her head up off the ground by her hair. "Do you understand me?"

With the dress still in her mouth all Juliet could do was nod. He released Juliet and her head hit the ground, hard.

The boys gathered the paintings and headed back down the hill toward the Bussons' house—Juliet could hear Michel's mother calling to him. Juliet heard them whistling and she didn't move until the sound had faded away. She knew that she could not tell her father what had happened here. What could he do? The Bussons owned the land he farmed. They'd never take her word over Michel's. Never. Instead, Juliet pumped out water and scrubbed herself with her torn dress until she was raw. She dumped the water over her head to get the urine and the smell of the boys off her. Then, she wrapped her dress around her and limped home.

Once back at the house, Juliet crawled into bed with Delphine and sobbed. Even a week after her mother's death, Juliet could not stop the chill that seemed to have penetrated to her bones since that night with her mother. No number of blankets or the warmth of her sister's small body could lessen the dull pain of cold.

The next morning, Juliet's face did not look as bad as she'd feared. She told Delphine she had fallen and the little girl accepted the story. Juliet's father was already out in the fields, and he would not notice his daughter's red marks when he came back in at nightfall.

Today Juliet decided that she would teach Delphine to fetch water. With her bruised body, Juliet wasn't sure she could manage getting to the well. She also couldn't bear to see it again after last night. Delphine would have to fetch a half bucket. The little girl could manage that much water.

Juliet opened the kitchen door to find an envelope on the ground that had been stuffed under the gap in the floor. She looked around but saw no one. The envelope was heavy and luxurious like a fine fabric and was addressed to MADEMOISELLE JULIET LACOMPTE in a flowery signature that looked more like art. She could see a watermark under the cream paper. Juliet broke the seal and hoped to find a note from Marchant. This was the letter her mother had told her to expect. She held her breath as she slid out the paper and unfolded it, praying that Marchant was sending for her after all. What she read instead puzzled her:

Dear Mademoiselle LaCompte:

In response to your inquiry of employment, Monsieur Lucian Varnier of XX Boulevard Saint-Germain, Paris, offers you a position as a maid in his home. The pay includes lodging plus 850 francs per month. He will expect you no later than 14 Septembre 1895.

Regards,

Paul de Passe, Secretary

Monsieur Lucian Varnier

11

Juliet LaCompte
Paris, France, 1895

Juliet had only one small bag when she ascended the steps to the Boulevard Saint-Germain. The large black rounded doors were so imposing that Juliet stopped before she knocked. The cab that had dropped her off was turning the block, and she could still hear the hollow clap of the horses' hooves. She breathed in and pounded her hand a little too urgently against the door.

Juliet's father had taken her to the train station in Challans to see her off. He'd needed her help on the farm raising her brother and sister, but the letter had promised money and the offer had been too good for him to let her stay. With the salary Juliet would send back each month, her father could hire two people to help him on the farm. Her only other option was Michel Busson, and the idea of that sickened Juliet. A few days later, a parcel was personally delivered for her father. Inside the package was a heavy bag containing gold francs. With the arrival of the second package with the money, all protests from Juliet's father about her going to Paris or ending her engagement to Michel Busson had ceased.

As they stood on the empty Challans train platform, Juliet's father had a formality that she wasn't used to seeing. He'd worn his Sunday church suit with work boots, something her mother never would have let him leave the house wearing. This little detail caused Juliet's eyes to well up with tears.

He shifted his weight and looked at his mud-covered boots. "Your mother told me that this man is to be trusted."

"Monsieur Varnier?"

He nodded. "She made me promise that you would do as the letter said. She insisted that you wouldn't want to do it, but that I had to make you." His eyes followed the length of the platform. "I met her here, you know." He set Juliet's bag down in front of her as though he were transferring responsibility of it—and her.

"No," said Juliet. "I didn't know." Juliet now realized that her mother had been a complete mystery to her. "I didn't know anything about her."

He pointed to a bench near the center of the platform. "She'd just come off the train from Paris. I'd never seen anything so beautiful in my life, my Thérèse. She was trying to get to the coast to get a boat, but she was too sick to make it any farther. I was so mesmerized by the look of her that I missed my train to Paris, but I never regretted it." He smiled sadly. "I hope she didn't, either."

The death of her mother never had weighed heavier on her than now. Juliet looked away down the tracks toward Paris. "She never spoke of Paris."

"There was nothing she wanted to talk about." He took two steps away from her and put his hands in his pockets. "You be safe with this man, Juliet. This is a better option than the Busson boy. Trust me, that boy is cruel. I never wanted to see you married to him, but, well... the Bussons were keen on it, which was surprising given our financial state."

Juliet felt tears well up in her eyes. She had always suspected he knew the truth about Michel Busson. "Will you promise me something, Father?"

The man did not agree to anything, but he considered her like an adult, a girl heading off to a new life. "Go on."

"Promise me that if Auguste Marchant sends me a letter or comes for me that you'll tell him where I am?"

"I will." He looked behind her at something, and she could see him tense. His face pale, he looked as though he'd seen a ghost. Juliet turned to see a woman in a faded yellow dress, unfashionable even for the country, staring at them. The dress was garish, like a costume. The woman was older—about the age of her father—and the dress was from another time and for a younger girl. Piled up in a nest on her head, the woman's hair was a golden blond, like her dress. The woman looked pale and thin and had deep, dark circles carved under her eyes. It seemed like she hadn't eaten for days.

"Who is that?"

"I don't know."

Juliet didn't believe him. He moved around her like a cat, positioning himself between the woman and Juliet.

"When the train comes, I need you to wait until I tell you to board. Will you do that for me?"

"Why?"

"Just do as I say, okay? Don't be frightened."

She nodded.

The train platform was empty but for the three of them. Arriving on time, the train came to a stop, and one conductor came out and looked around to see if anyone was boarding. The three of them—Juliet, her father, and the woman in yellow—stayed frozen in place on the platform. The woman was looking at Juliet feverishly, like she'd have eaten her if she could get close. Waiting to hear from her father, Juliet heard the "All Aboard" call.

Her father grabbed her and held her tightly. "Go now. Do you hear me?" She clung to him for a moment, nodding. "You have a marvelous life in Paris. Your mother would have wanted that for you."

Small heaves erupted from Juliet's body as they both knew that of all the things her mother had wanted for her, a life in Paris was not one of them. It had been the life she had wanted so badly, but at what cost?

Finally he pulled away, walked over to the woman in yellow, and began to talk to her. The woman seemed distracted, looking only at Juliet, trying to shake him off. The train whistle blew, but Juliet stayed planted on the platform. What Juliet saw next puzzled her. Her gentle father grabbed the woman in yellow by the shoulders and held her firmly, almost like he was in a passionate embrace. "Go," he shouted. "Go."

The woman in yellow struggled to get free of his grasp, but she was no match for her father's strength and there was no one else on the platform to notice the scuffle playing out between her father and the woman. Juliet jumped onto the train as it slowly began to pull away. From a distance, she could see that the woman had finally broken free and had run the length of the platform trying in vain to catch the last car. Her father seemed pleased and turned away, walking toward the steps. The train began to pick up speed, and Juliet saw the Challans countryside pass her. She had never felt more alone.

As a single young woman traveling unchaperoned on the train, Juliet saw the looks she was given by some of the other passengers, but she took her seat and stared out the window as the farmland gave way to the outskirts of Paris with its narrow streets untouched by Baron Haussmann.

Paris was a city bathed in color and noise. As the sun was rising and warming, Juliet had never seen so many beautiful silk day dresses and elaborate hats as during the morning hustle on the boulevard. From the violets and blues of the overflowing flower carts positioned at each corner to the dough balls in vibrant pinks, blues, and greens in the windows of the macaron shops, there were colors Juliet had never seen before. Paris's wide streets and gray buildings were imposing and overwhelming to the young girl. While Marchant's paintings had captured a sliver of Paris, Juliet had never imagined that the world could be so big. How would Marchant find her in a city so big?

She knocked again at the door and pulled out the invitation, matching the address with the number on the door. Finally the giant door opened and a tall man with wire glasses and a full mustache stood there and looked out onto the busy street until he realized the source of the knocking was below him and his eyes peered down over his glasses. Juliet couldn't guess the man's age. She'd never seen a person so strangely dressed.

"Aah!" The man clasped his hands and bowed. "You must be Mademoiselle LaCompte?"

Juliet nodded, unable to speak.

He bowed a moment longer, expecting a retort. When one didn't come, he gazed up at her and a broad smile spread over his face. "I am Paul de Passe, Monsieur Varnier's secretary. I wrote you. Welcome." He pulled the heavy door back, and Juliet entered an enormous hallway with a black-and-white-patterned marble floor and winding staircase. "May I?" Paul de Passe took Juliet's bag and motioned for her to take the stairs. "Sadly, Monsieur Varnier was called away on business today, but he will join you for dinner."

"Join me for dinner?" Juliet shook her head. "Monsieur de Passe, I'm afraid you are mistaken. I am here to work as a maid."

"Yes, yes," said Paul. "Monsieur Varnier has a very different way of approaching things, as you'll learn. He wouldn't dream of having you begin your work without a proper dinner after such a long day of travel. That's all…"

"Do you know what I will be doing for Monsieur Varnier exactly?" Juliet removed her coat. "I haven't many skills."

Paul de Passe took the dirty, worn garment without hesitation.

"Ah! Yes. Well you have what Mr. Varnier calls…*potential*, Mademoiselle LaCompte. Monsieur Varnier *loves* potential. Adores it really. In fact, Monsieur Varnier has a keen *eye* for potential, one might say."

Juliet felt uneasy. The idea that this was some "arrangement" that had been contracted between her mother and Monsieur Varnier was very much on her mind. Her father's change of heart and the money he'd received as though she'd been somehow *sold* to Varnier made her anxious with worry about her mysterious employer. And now she learned it was for her "potential." Her mother had told her to do as the man asked. She assumed "the man" her mother had meant was this Monsieur Varnier. But could she be sure?

Juliet followed Paul de Passe up a steep and winding staircase. When she got to the top, a magnificent grand white hallway unfolded in front of her. Four identical ornate chandeliers hung along the hallway.

"Monsieur Varnier has ten rooms in this apartment—the top two floors. It's actually rather small as far as apartments go, but he likes the Latin Quarter best," explained Paul as he opened the double doors leading into a room with a sofa, piano, and wall of books. Juliet touched the gold spines of the books as Paul opened the doors facing the Boulevard Saint-Germain; the warm late-morning air scrubbed at the sheer curtains, swaying them gently. Paul opened another set of doors that revealed an elaborate table with another chandelier hanging over the table. Juliet counted ten chairs. She followed Paul as he went back into the hallway and opened still another set of doors, these leading into a study with an enormous desk and fireplace. "This is Mr. Varnier's study, but he doesn't mind if other people use it." Juliet had no sense of manners, but Paul made it seem as if it was a gracious move by the mysterious Varnier.

Juliet cleared her throat. A massive painting of a man hung over the fireplace. "Is that him?"

Paul turned and adjusted his glasses to peer at the painting as though it were the first time he'd been in the room. "*Oui,*" he declared with certainty. "*C'est Monsieur Varnier.*"

Juliet walked closer to the painting and looked up at it. The man was seated, and his dark-blond hair was back from his head. His eyes were a shade brighter blue than his navy suit. As with Paul, it was difficult to place Monsieur Varnier's age, but Juliet thought it was similar to her father's.

"He wears a beard now," said Paul. "It is all the fashion in Paris, and Monsieur Varnier is, well… quite *fashionable*, as you will soon see for yourself."

"What does he do?" Juliet looked closely at the artist's signature, her breath catching a moment until she saw an unfamiliar signature scribble in the corner of the painting. The painting was not one of Marchant's. She had known it wasn't the moment she saw it, but the hope that somehow Varnier was connected to Marchant and that the artist had brought her here was never far from Juliet's mind. She peered under the frame, looking up at the painting, studying the artist's brushstrokes. It was something she'd learned from Marchant. A painting was merely a collection of strokes of color. The way the artist blended and subtracted his paints was one of the most important things about a painting. She knew Marchant's brushstrokes like she knew his body—it was as an intimate knowledge.

"Monsieur Varnier doesn't do anything." Paul hesitated. "You could say he has family money." Paul turned to leave the room. "Allow me to show you to your quarters, Mademoiselle LaCompte." Juliet followed him out the door and up another staircase. This hallway featured darker, masculine inlaid wood panels. At the end of the hallway, Paul opened a set of double doors with wood inlays—the tallest doors Juliet had ever seen. With two steps, Juliet walked into a decidedly feminine room with cream walls and wood trim a shade darker. The ceiling was an elaborate design in ecru with leaf patterns along with egg-and-dart and beaded molding designs. The room looked like a dessert. The rug beneath her feet was pale blue, green, and cream with a hint of soft corals. She walked over to the window and found that it overlooked the Boulevard Saint-Germain. The heavy pale-blue taffeta curtains were tied back with a gold tassel. She pulled back the tall cream sheers and opened the windows. Over the bed was a crown cornice with pale-green draperies. The dresser was curved with cream-on-cream stripes and ornate gold handles. A matching gold chair and side table that featured a horsehead design sat next to it. Juliet swallowed back bile from her throat. This room was far too elaborate for a house-keeper. She turned to Paul, who was now opening up the armoire.

"There are some dresses here for you as well, Mademoiselle."

"Tell me please. How did Monsieur Varnier find me?"

Paul didn't meet her eyes. Instead he removed a soft-blue dress with cream lace and placed it on the bed. Inside the armoire, Juliet could see nearly a dozen dresses hanging. "Monsieur Varnier thought these might fit. This one would be a good selection for dinner this evening. Dinner will be at eight. I will now excuse myself." He bowed and walked to the door before turning. "It was your mother, Mademoiselle."

"My mother?" Juliet felt her throat catch.

"*Oui*. Your mother *recommended* you to Monsieur Varnier for this position."

"But my mother is dead, sir."

"*Oui*. Monsieur Varnier was very sad to hear the news."

"Did she know him from when she lived in Paris?" Ever since the night with the circle and the purple robes, Juliet knew that her mother had lived another life—a dramatically different one than at Challans—and she wondered if Monsieur Varnier was connected.

Paul smiled. "Monsieur Varnier will provide you with the answers to your many questions this evening, I am sure of it." He paused. "Your hair, Mademoiselle LaCompte. Should I send Marie to help you with it?"

Juliet touched her long hair. It was pulled back into a loose chignon like she had worn doing chores. She'd never worn her hair in any other style. Suddenly she felt self-conscious. She had not known she'd be expected at a dinner. She was a farm girl who had lived in a simple stone home with four rooms. She had no training for this type of life. She would look foolish. This felt like some shameful trick that Michel had set her up for. Juliet opened up her bag. Inside were two work dresses. Juliet hadn't known if she'd get a maid's uniform. She was wearing her best dress, a long cotton dress that had once been her mother's but one that she had grown into within the last year; she'd started wearing it to Sunday services. Comparing it with the pale-blue creation laid out for her on her bed, hers looked old and dirty.

"Mademoiselle?" Paul de Passe pressed. "Your hair?"

"*Oui*," she said. "*S'il vous plaît.*"

"*Merci*." The secretary nodded and shut the door behind him.

Once Paul left, Juliet began to sob. She was alone and had no idea who this Lucian Varnier was and what he'd want from her. The physical bruises had finally healed after the terrible night with Michel and the other boy, but she was dreading the idea that her mother might have made some similar arrangement with Monsieur Varnier. What she might be expected to do in exchange for this room and these dresses made her sick. She'd heard stories of women who'd fallen and been sold by their families into a life of prostitution.

The only solace she felt was that she was now in the same city as Marchant. As the cab had driven through the streets, she'd strained to look out at the street signs on the buildings, hoping for any name that Marchant had mentioned. She would find him in this vast city, and he would get her out of this horrible arrangement with Monsieur Varnier.

From the open window, Juliet heard commotion and looked down to see the café across the street and three animated men laughing and arguing, their cups hitting saucers. This street was lively, and it was exactly the type of place that Marchant had described, even painted for her. Juliet felt the tug of despair when she realized that the beautiful painting of Paris he had painted for her birthday was now destroyed. Marchant, her baby, her mother, her home—all gone. She had a feeling of permanent emptiness, blackness having enveloped her. But she realized that the cold that had gripped her in Challans was also gone. She was warm in this house. She ran her hands over her forearms and no longer felt the clamminess that had set upon her limbs for weeks. She sat up straight and patted her face to dry her tears. There was little use in crying anymore.

Juliet walked over to the armoire and studied each of the dresses. The first was a long light wool coat and matching skirt with several ornate lapels and a lace blouse with a high neck. There was also a deep-green dress with sapphire-blue jacket, a simple seafoam-green cotton dress with matching stitching and a bow that tied at the waist, a brown velvet coat and skirt, a silver-and-lavender silk dress with cream-on-cream lace décolletage, a pale-pink cotton dress with ornate gathering at the bodice and again at the train with dark-pink sleeves, and finally a black dress with a satin-and-tulle skirt. There was a black velvet coat and a matching wide-brimmed hat. Juliet had never seen such beautiful dresses, each one a confection of color and texture. She heard a knock at the door and a sturdy, older woman entered wearing a maid's plain black work frock.

"My name is Marie," said the woman. Juliet was embarrassed to be holding the pink dress up to view herself in the full-length mirror. "That's a lovely dress, Mademoiselle LaCompte. We didn't know your exact size, so I hope it suits you. Monsieur Varnier has excellent taste, *n'est-ce pas?*"

Juliet nodded. "I've never seen such beautiful things." She looked down at her own dress that hung on her like a box.

"No matter," said Marie. "I'm to help you with your bath and your hair for dinner with Monsieur Varnier this evening. He's just returned."

The fact that the mysterious Monsieur Varnier was now in the house made everything—this house, the dresses, this new life—seem real. This knowledge made her skin tingle. Juliet's heart fluttered with nerves.

Marie opened a door, revealing the expansive bath attached to her room. When Juliet entered the bath, she was shocked. The room was as large as her family's kitchen. She had never had a luxurious bath like this one, content to sponge off most days at the small sink she shared with Delphine.

After her bath, she took a nap while her hair dried. Exhausted from travel and nerves, she fell into a deep sleep until Marie woke her with some coffee and a biscuit. Seated in front of the vanity, Juliet watched as Marie sectioned off her chestnut hair with deep copper and gold pieces around her face and knotted it on top of her head, pulling tendrils down and curling them with pins.

"You have magnificent hair, mademoiselle," said Marie. "It is like the mane of a lion."

It was odd that Juliet had never considered herself beautiful. She'd thought only that Marchant had chosen her from all the other girls in the village because she lived in the next house, never because she was beautiful.

"*Merci*," said Juliet. "May I ask you something?"

"Of course." Marie looked into the mirror at her.

"What is Monsieur Varnier like?" Juliet studied Marie's face for a reaction, but she showed nothing.

"I have only worked for him for a short while," admitted the woman. "He has been quite generous to me. He doesn't seem to care much for details about the house, which is odd."

"Is there a Madame Varnier?"

Marie shook her head. "*Non.* It's a shame, really. He's a most handsome man. The women notice him on the street, and a few have sent notes inviting him to parties, but he doesn't go out much during the day." Marie buttoned her into the blue dress and helped her with shoes that were horribly too large. "Oh dear. We'll have to fix this tomorrow, but for tonight this will have to do," Marie said, stuffing a cotton in the toes. Marie pulled a cameo pin from the jewelry box on the vanity and secured it to the center of the lace blouse, then pulled the pins from Juliet's hair, positioning the tendrils around her face. As Marie studied her work in the mirror, she seemed pleased. Juliet could not believe the figure that stared back at her. The dress was too large in the bust, but the rest of it fit beautifully. Still, Juliet couldn't shake the feeling that she was dressing up in her mother's clothes and shoes—all too big.

Marie excused herself, taking Juliet's old clothes with her.

At eight, a clock from the downstairs hallway chimed and Juliet heard a door creak slowly open from the first floor. She gathered her skirt to avoid tripping on it and tiptoed to the top of the stairs, listening for something, but the house was deadly still. She peered over the railing and finally saw a man pass under her. He stopped.

"Are you going to stand up there, Mademoiselle LaCompte, or are you coming down?" The man tilted his head and looked up at her.

His very presence and confidence made Juliet feel faint. She had never seen a man—or *anyone* for that matter—who filled a room like Monsieur Lucian Varnier. Not even Marchant, who was the most sophisticated man she'd ever met—up until this point—commanded a room with the energy of Varnier. He walked over to the steps and leaned on the banister, waiting for her to descend. Juliet started and then stopped, her heels falling out of her shoes until she pulled them off, holding them in her hand.

She compared every man with Marchant now. Varnier was shorter and slighter, but only a little so. His features were not soft like Marchant's big green doe eyes and sculpted nose. Varnier's features were not delicate. Instead he was all lines and angles. In fact, he looked like a handsome farmhand who'd come into money, where Marchant looked like he'd been accustomed to money and soft things all of his life.

Juliet couldn't tell if she was a disappointment to Monsieur Varnier. She stepped onto the floor, her stockings slippery. She looked down at her shoes and then held them up. "They're too big."

He smiled. "Then leave them there. I'll have Monsieur de Passe buy you new ones in your size tomorrow. Sadly, you won't be able to enjoy a stroll of Paris after dinner, but perhaps we can do that tomorrow."

Juliet bowed slightly. His friendliness had disarmed her.

"You look enchanting," he added and pointed the way to the dining room.

The long table that Juliet had seen earlier was now set up for two with Monsieur Varnier at the head of the table and a place for Juliet to his left. The place settings were elaborate, and a spray of red, pink, and green flowers sat in the center of the table in a colored vase.

A server presented the first course, a soup—creamy vegetable bisque. Juliet ate in silence, only touching a few spoonfuls of the soup, her nerves making it impossible to eat. She watched his moves at the table, mimicking them as she maneuvered through her first formal dinner.

Finally, Varnier spoke. "I trust your travels were fine?"

"Yes . . . quite fine."

"So how do you like Paris?"

"It is overwhelming, sir."

He laughed. "Well, that's an honest answer."

Juliet put down her spoon. "Monsieur Varnier?" She wasn't sure if it was stupidity or bravery that finally made her speak, for both emotions seemed to descend upon her simultaneously. "May I ask you something?"

He pushed the bowl away, folding his hands. "Of course."

"I wished to inquire about my position here with you. I wanted to thank you, of course, first."

He smiled, yet it was a hollow smile, not sincere at all. "You are most welcome, mademoiselle."

"What *exactly* will I be doing for you?"

A door opened, interrupting Varnier as he was about to speak. The server, a man, removed the soup. In another moment the table was cleared and Marie entered the dining room carrying a plate of fish. "It is turbot with lemon and capers," said the woman.

Varnier waited until the servants shut the door behind them. Then he cleared his throat. He leaned in toward Juliet. "You are my guest here, mademoiselle. There are no requirements of you."

"But," Juliet stuttered. "I don't understand. Surely, I have a job. Cleaning or—"

"Or?" Varnier sat back in his chair. "Not to be crass, Mademoiselle LaCompte, but do you *have* any skills?"

Juliet looked down at the dish in front of her and shook her head, finally bursting into tears. "I have none, sir, other than farm chores, which honestly I did quite poorly." Her body heaved in the chair, almost beginning to spasm. "I don't know why I'm here, monsieur. I'm confused."

Varnier took a deep breath and pulled out a handkerchief, holding it out to her. "My apologies, mademoiselle. I thought you knew."

"*Knew what?*" Juliet's voice rose. She awaited the details of some vile arrangement her mother had made with this man.

They were interrupted again by another server, who removed Juliet's untouched turbot plate and returned in a moment with two plates of pressed duck with cherry sauce and stewed vegetables.

He waited until the server left and the door closed. "I *knew*..." He paused again, seeming unsure, and then continued. "Well, I am *connected* to your late mother. In her death, well, your care fell to me. I am an administrator, so to speak."

"You?" Juliet searched the man's face for answers, but he was cool. "I have a father, Monsieur Varnier. I've never heard of you."

He took his knife and fork and began to file away at the duck. His hands were thin but well shaped, his fingers long and slender. "You should eat." He pointed to her plate. Sinking back in his chair, he studied her. "For appearances, we will say you are my niece."

Juliet wiped her face with the kerchief. She stared at the food on her plate, the cherry sauce resembling blood. She was sure she looked blotchy and swollen. "Am I?"

"Are you what?"

"Your niece?"

"No . . . no, of course not. We are not *related*." Varnier spat the word out like it was distasteful and resumed eating, ignoring the fact that Juliet had not touched her duck.

"But I don't understand. Why would my care fall to you, then? I have a family. Did you know my mother from when she lived in Paris? Is that it?"

Varnier stopped chewing. "Yes. You could say that."

"But that isn't the case, is it? I don't understand your connection to my mother." Juliet picked up her fork and knife and put them down.

He leaned back in his chair and picked at his fingernail. "No. I did not know your mother, though she sounds like a lovely woman. The care of you simply fell to me upon her death. No harm will come to you again. It is a simple matter. You don't need to know anything else." He rubbed his hands together, like the matter was finished.

A chill crept across her body. How did Lucian Varnier know that harm *had* come to her? It was impossible for him to know about Marchant and Michel Busson. Juliet suddenly felt faint.

Varnier eyed her. "There is a fine piano teacher. Monsieur de Passe says he is highly recommended. I thought that we could begin your studies immediately. You do like music?"

Juliet nodded, but thought that the only music she'd ever heard had been at church or the crazy old Monsieur Morel who played his half-broken fiddle in the town square on market days when he wasn't shouting at the women to give him a bit of bread and cheese from their baskets.

"Do you know how to read?" Varnier didn't make the question sound insulting. "If not, we'll begin lessons immediately." He didn't seem to notice that Juliet had nodded. Her mother had taught her to read, mostly the Bible, but there were a few other books that her mother had brought from Paris including Alexandre Dumas fils and Gustave Flaubert, who was a particular favorite of her mother. Juliet remembered the woman's weathered hands, raw from scrubbing and butchering, turning the delicate pages of her books; she often had to lick her dry fingers to get a grip on the soft paper.

Reluctantly, she took a bite of the duck, placing it on her tongue and defying her body to take it in. The bird was gamy and wasn't as fresh as those they'd butchered on the farm, but the sweet cherry sauce was a luxurious addition that Juliet's taste buds had never experienced before. The meals on the farm were mostly basic stews and breads, nothing as inventive as this. Everything about this new life was textured and complex. She looked around the dining room at the carved wood panels and heavy chandelier. Her senses were already overloaded from the sights of the streets and the dresses and the sounds of the city outside the window; now her sense of taste was overwhelmed by this intricate blend of simple foods. She missed the simple wood-and-stone structure of the four rooms of her old house, but then she remembered Michel Busson and knew that she could never go back even if she'd wanted to. It occurred to Juliet that she might never see the farm or her siblings again. Her chest tightened.

"I was to marry a boy," she blurted.

"Yes. I know," he replied calmly, not looking up from his plate. "I've taken care of that as well."

"What do you mean?"

He stopped eating. "It means you are free from your obligation, as is your family. Does that make you happy?"

Juliet nodded.

"Good." He began cutting into the duck again. "Now please finish your duck."

"But what about my sister and brother?"

"What about them?" Varnier took a sip of wine. He studied the glass before taking another sip.

"Are they not in your care as well?"

"They are not my concern." He placed the glass down heavily like an exclamation point. "Only *you*."

"*Why* just me?" It was a sharper statement than she'd meant it to be.

He sighed and raked his hands through his soft sandy-blond curls. "Someday, when you are ready, I'll explain everything to you."

"But I'm ready now. Why am I in your care, but my brother and sister are not?"

"No. My dear, you are most certainly *not* ready. But one day, you will be, and then we shall talk." Lucian Varnier laughed heartily. His teeth were those of a man who'd had money and care. "Your brother and sister are in their father's care. You are my charge. Are we agreed?"

Juliet bristled at the suggestion that she was a child and not ready to know things about her situation. She wasn't a naive girl anymore, and she resented the implication that she couldn't handle the truth.

She was about to demand to know more when he abruptly excused himself from the table. "It's been an exhausting day." He smiled. "Surely you understand." He left, not waiting for her reply.

As the door closed behind him, Marie entered the dining room as if on command. "Would you like some bread and cheese, my dear? We also have pie."

Juliet smiled at the kind woman, declining the food and retiring to her room. She fell into a deep sleep even as the sun came blaring through the curtains she'd forgotten to close. The sound of nearby church bells chiming seven times finally woke her.

12

Helen Lambert
Washington, DC, May 26, 2012

A marvelous smell was coming from my kitchen. I checked the clock with one eye. It was nearly three in the afternoon. I sat up in bed, realizing I'd slept most of the day. The pillow beside me looked ruffled and used. Then it hit me. Luke. I remembered breakfast and the nosebleed. And the man in my kitchen—Lucian, then Luke— was now present in both my life and my dreams.

I padded down the hall to the kitchen and rounded the corner. Luke seemed to know I was there without me saying anything. Leaning against the stove, he was searching for something on his iPhone.

"Would you like to go to the opera on Tuesday?" He fumbled with his pockets, finally finding what he was looking for, which turned out to be the key to his Range Rover.

"This coming Tuesday?"

"That would be the Tuesday in question."

"Sure." I sat down at the counter. My body felt heavy. "Well, you finally made an appearance in my dream."

"Did I?" He put the iPhone down and expertly shook a pan. I could see a salmon fillet flipping obediently and an arugula salad sitting in a bowl. "It's about time."

"I don't understand any of this." I put my head in my hands.

"It's complicated."

"I'm sure it is."

"If you saw me, then you saw your mother, Juliet's mother."

"And that bizarre ritual."

"That! Well, that wasn't just any ritual."

It was nice—him making himself at home in my kitchen. I remembered the touch of Juliet's hands on her dresses and the smell of the cherry sauce. He was right, of course. But I knew that already. I'd had a sense of dread about what I thought Juliet's mother had done that night. Before I could ask him more, he plated a gorgeous pink salmon and slid it in front of me with an equally colorful arugula salad. "You need to eat."

He scrubbed the pan and placed bowls into the dishwasher with the casual efficiency of a chef. I met his eyes.

"You could save me the trouble and just tell me everything."

"I know I *could*," he said with a laugh. "But it doesn't work that way. Just keep dreaming, Helen."

I turned as he passed by me on the way to the hall. "You don't strike me as a rule follower, Luke Varner."

He returned to the kitchen, adjusting the strap of the soft leather briefcase over his shoulder. "Well, let's say I've been in trouble enough as it relates to you. I try hard to follow the rules now. Plus, it's better for you to see your own lives for yourself, don't you think?"

He sounded exactly like the Lucian Varnier from my dream, offering little information. I'd have to find my own answers.

"So what opera are we seeing?"

He leaned forward on the counter like he was going to let me in on a secret. "*That* is a surprise." Grabbing his keys from the counter, he ran his hand over my head like I was a six-year-old. "I have to get going. I have a painting to sell."

Before he passed into the hallway, he turned. "The opera...treat it like an opening night."

"So you're saying a gown is in order?"

"I am," he said. I heard the front door click behind him.

After he left, I reached into my bag and pulled out the book of Auguste Marchant's paintings that I'd bought yesterday on my way home. It was sad, really, and I felt a little bad for Marchant—his books had been relegated to the sale bin in the Barnes & Noble in George- town. The store seemed to have an abundance of these tossed-off cof- fee table books, like last year's cat calendars. I thumbed through the book and felt a pang of familiarity seeing the paintings of the children in the countryside. It wasn't so much the faces as the locations.

One plate showed a stone well and a small girl sitting in front of it. Near the back, I reached a painting and my hand drew back like it had been burned on a hot pan. The nude girl—me—looked back in ecstasy, her dark-red curls pooling around her head, which was at the bottom of the painting. The painting was *intimate*. The girl was staring up at the viewer—or was it the painter? This painting was familiar. Not the painting, but rather the scene, the atmosphere it was painted in. Closing my eyes, I could *feel* the folds of fabric surrounding the girl's cold naked body. I knew how the room smelled and that a breeze would come over her head through the window to the right, blowing her hair forward and sending a chill through her, yet she didn't dare cover herself. This was the scene from the dream I'd just had. I read the plate. The painting was titled *Juliet*—the very painting Luke had mentioned to me, now owned by a private collector.

Thinking about the opera and trying to take my mind off every- thing, I rummaged through my closet but found nothing worthy of a surprise opera. I called Mickey for an emergency shopping trip. We stopped at Rizik's on Connecticut—which was a bit of a rush since the store closed at six on Saturday. After looking at several options, I found a gorgeous Reem Acra steel-blue silk gown with tulle overlay and elaborate gold beading—it looked like a dress from another time, inspired by the interiors of Versailles. Perhaps the memory of Juliet lingered, because the dress reminded me of the gowns she had found hanging in her armoire on Boulevard Saint-Germain.

While I was changing, Mickey checked the Kennedy Center website and found that a production of Jules Massenet's *Werther* had just left, but there were no signs of another opera coming on Tuesday. "This is so romantic," he said as he ran his fingers through my hair. "You who knows everything going on in Washington are being *surprised*."

"Go." I pointed to Connecticut Avenue. Gentleman that he was, Mickey carried my gown in a heavy bag. I stopped mid-block. "Do I seem like an old soul to you?"

"Nah, just an old broad." He smiled.

I shot him a cross look. "Do you believe in past lives?"

"Oh shit. Are you getting all spiritual on me since Roger? Just don't turn into one of those cult people…or worse…a Baptist. Don't go there, for God's sake. You'll never have good sex again." He stopped. "You know, there is this psychic that everyone's recommending in Georgetown. We should go and check her out. I had an aunt in Georgia who went all the time to psychics. She told her my mother was dying."

"But your mother is *alive*, Mickey."

"But my aunt died." He raised an eyebrow. "So the psychic was close."

"I beg to differ on that theory, Mick. They're two different people."

"They were *twins*, Helen! Twins. Trust me, it was close."

The nice thing about Mickey is that once he sets his mind to something, you're off on an adventure together. We were in a cab headed to Georgetown for an appointment with Madame Rincky at six thirty.

At six twenty-five, we pulled up in front of the True Religion store on M Street.

"Um, Mickey? This is a jeans shop." I pointed at the window.

"She's upstairs, you nut. Plus, we can get you some Becky jeans when we're done. Those don't make your ass look fat. Not that it is! In fact, I was saying the other day to someone that divorce looks good on you."

"Not sure I agree. And who do you talk about me with?"

He shrugged, opened the door to Suite 202, and pointed for me to go ahead of him. As I walked up the wooden steps hearing the echo of my shoes on the wood, I realized that Mickey was checking out my ass and not in a good way.

Madame Rincky, a large Jamaican woman, greeted us warmly and offered us a cup of tea. Her waiting room was littered with *National Enquirer*s, a 1992 Washington, DC, yellow pages, and a display selling various crystals for $13.25. Behind a beaded doorway, she led us into another room that faced M Street. I knew because we could hear the cars honking with the weekend traffic.

Mickey went first, and Madame Rincky gave him a tarot reading mixed with a bit of palmistry. "I see a child in your future," she told him. "The large man with the dark eyes. You love him, eh? But it will not be without problems."

Mickey had wanted children, so this was in the zip code of accuracy. I don't think it was hard to deduce Mickey was gay, but the large man with the dark eyes was a pretty spot-on description of his current celebrity look-alike boyfriend. So far, this woman was better than I'd expected.

When it was my turn, she motioned for me to sit in the chair, still warm from Mickey who had moved over to a bench, furiously checking his iPhone. I watched the psychic lay the cards out in a cross shape, turning them over one by one. "Let me see your hands?"

I volunteered them, flopping my elbows on the table and looking about the room, bored.

She stared at the cards then back at my hands and looked up at me. "What are you?"

"I'm an editor." I cleared my throat nervously.

She shook her head. "I mean, *what* are you? This is not normal. Have you looked at your hand?"

I turned one over and gasped. The multiple lines that now covered my left hand weren't there a week ago. "I don't understand. My hand didn't look like this before."

"Look here." Madame Rincky touched each line. "You have four life lines, but only one love line."

"You'd been wondering about past lives," chirped Mickey like a helpful assistant and pointed to my palm. "See?"

But I didn't look shocked and Madame Rincky picked up on this. She raised her eyebrow. "But you already know this, don't you? You've lived before."

I nodded. "Three times before."

She shook her head gravely. "This is the devil's work." Folding her hands in front of her in prayer, she mumbled something while her gold bangles clanged against each other. She pointed to my palm. "Bad stuff this is. I need you to leave here. I don't want any part of this."

"Leave?" I asked.

"I don't want you here." She stood up from the table and pointed to the door. "Go."

"Let me see." Mickey grabbed my hand and checked the lines.

"Madame Rincky?" I asked. Beads of sweat had appeared on her upper lip. "I don't know why this is happening to me. Please . . . you've got to help me. I don't know what I am."

"It is simple. A devil has cursed you." Madame Rincky pointed to a line on my hand.

But Madame Rincky didn't tell me anything I hadn't already suspected. This whole thing stemmed from the night in Juliet's kitchen. Her mother had called a demon into the house. Things were now snapping in place for me. I looked down at my hand. Two lines were longer than the others—the second and the fourth. As much as I wanted to deny it, this was real. "Can you help me?"

She shook her head. "No."

"But I need help."

She looked down at the floor.

"Please," I pushed.

"I might know someone."

For the next few days, I waited for Madame Rincky to call me with help. I didn't dream at all those days, which felt like I was wasting time—time I didn't have. Luke called to check in on me—which meant he was wondering if I'd been having dreams and seemed quite disappointed to hear I was sleeping soundly.

On Tuesday, the car left me off in front of the Kennedy Center— the impressive building on the Potomac River that housed five working theaters. Roger and I had been regular opera patrons, so I knew several of the elderly ushers dressed in red jackets. I entered through the Hall of States and walked down the wash of red carpet, admiring the clean marble lines and high ceilings with the names of prominent Washingtonians etched above me. I stopped and read ROGER AND HELEN LAMBERT before continuing on toward the end of the hall where the impressionistic bronze statue of John F. Kennedy sat on the river side of the building.

I couldn't get Madame Rincky's words out of my mind. *A devil has cursed you.*

As if on cue, I heard the familiar tone of Luke's voice. "You look stunning."

I turned to see him walking toward me and wondered if he was, in fact, the devil in a tuxedo. Looking down at my dress, I registered what he was saying. The Reem Acra dress looked like it had been made for me. I'd drawn my hair into a loose, low chignon, leaving the front messy, not unlike Juliet LaCompte. I faux-curtsied. "Thank you. Anything for a pop-up opera—a popera, so to speak."

He smiled but gave nothing away. "Shall we?" He took my hand, more like a parent than a date, and turned right toward the Eisenhower Theater, my favorite theater house and the one that hosts most of the smaller operas. Displayed in cases at the front of the house were two stunning gowns from famous operas. Oddly, I noticed there were no other patrons. "What are you up to?"

Luke opened the door to a dimly lit theater.

"Do we have tickets? With actual seat numbers?"

He laughed and took the stairs. "We have seats, don't worry."

I followed him up the stairs and down the hall, where an usher was waiting to open the presidential box for us. The walls and ceiling of the Eisenhower were wrapped in a red fabric that appeared to be velvet; the cluster of chandeliers above them reminded me of my grandmother's brooches.

Once we were seated, Luke nodded to the usher and I noticed movement in the orchestra box below. As the opening bars started and the curtains parted, dancers flitted around the stage and a muse appeared. I felt a warm rush of nostalgia, although I couldn't figure out why. I'd never seen this opera before. And yet I had. The set was different, it was a more avant-garde production, but I closed my eyes and the prelude of music that washed over me reminded me of a feeling of wonder I'd once had. But where? I thought back to Madame Rincky and my life lines. I also understood the French they were speaking, which was impossible—in this life. I closed my eyes. "*Offenbach.*" I had not known Offenbach. Correction: *Helen Lambert* did not know Offenbach, nor did she speak French. But some part of me knew this music. I knew this time.

"*The Tales of Hoffmann,*" Luke whispered. "It was Juliet's favorite. This company just finished a run in Toronto so I hired them for the night." His words sounded like tin and he was speaking in slow motion. Then the room went fuzzy.

13

T he coloratura's voice died down before the singer slumped over dramatically. Another character cranked the mechanism on the coloratura's spine, bringing her back to life, her voice rising like a bird's. The music and spectacle as well as the theater were all so ornate that between her eyes and ears, Juliet could hardly take in anything else. She sat wide-eyed on the seat, not noticing that Lucian Varnier was studying her.

Once again, the singer's voice slowed and the woman—dressed as a doll—dropped forward, her skirt swinging dramatically as the ensemble gathered around her, disguising that she was not, in fact, a woman at all, but a doll—an automaton—who was deceiving the lovelorn protagonist, Hoffmann.

The entire performance, from the dramatic gaslights to the lavishly painted theaterscapes, had been a feast to Juliet's eyes. The harmonies and haunting melodies gave voice to something Juliet had not been able to grasp until she sat as a spectator in the red velvet chair. This was the sound of loss—her loss—somehow being dramatized in front of her. Hoffmann's love eluded him through the magical and the mundane. The performance was like a knife to Juliet's heart. Every emotion she was feeling had been somehow put to music. It was as though the river of notes flowing from the coloratura had always been hidden somewhere deep inside her.

That night, Juliet wore a gown that featured a navy-and-gold beaded bodice with an ocean-blue-and-gold chiffon skirt. Over the ensemble, she'd selected a dramatic velvet-and-lace navy coat. In the months since she'd arrived in Paris, Juliet had taken pride in being a quick study in everything from literature and music to fashion.

As always, she scanned the seats for Marchant's profile. This production of *Tales of Hoffmann* was not at the grand Paris Opera House but a small theater, where the ragtag performance had been assembled cheaply. Marchant wasn't likely to be here; his tastes were more refined and expensive. Varnier's friends tended to be more in the avant-garde mold, but he'd promised her that one day they would go to the Paris Opera—the real opera.

After the performance, Varnier took Juliet on an omnibus through the streets of Haussmann's Paris—the newer, wide streets pushing aside the smaller, poorer neighborhoods. They got out at the Jardin du Luxembourg, and Juliet walked arm in arm with Varnier. Only in snippets could Juliet see the uglier side of Paris: dirty children, men with threadbare coats, and prostitutes with thin or no coats yet hideously overdrawn mouths and faces like dolls. Always, she searched the dimly lit streets, looking for Marchant's familiar smile, but she never saw him. From a distance, she noticed the small carousel that Marchant had described for her in detail. It had been one of his favorites.

"Did you like the performance?" Varnier lit a cigarette.

Juliet nodded, straining to see the carousel before it was out of sight. No matter how beautiful the performance or gorgeous the street, everything always returned to Marchant. She'd loved him, but at what cost? Her mother? His wife and child? He had warned her that there was no turning back and he had been correct. But had he known how badly they would all pay? She had been pregnant with his child. Often she'd wondered what she would have done had her mother not removed the child from her with dark magic—and she was sure it had been dark magic at work.

"You are far away tonight," said Varnier.

"Not really," Juliet lied.

"Do you know about that opera's history?"

"No," said Juliet, turning her attention fully back to Varnier.

"*The Tales of Hoffmann* is a cursed opera." As the lights of the Panthéon illuminated him, he touched his silk hat and took a deep drag on his cigarette. "Offenbach died before he finished it. Then a fire broke out during a performance at the Opéra-Comique eight years ago. They've only just begun showing it again. It wasn't the first fire to plague the opera, either. There was a gas explosion after the second performance at the Ringtheater as well. So you see, it is a special opera."

Paris was buzzing tonight. The laughing and rhythmic sound of horses' hooves on pavement beyond the gardens mixed with the tapping of Varnier's cane as they walked.

"Do you believe that an opera can be cursed?"

"Yes, Juliet. I do, indeed, believe in cursed things. I think they are all around us." Varnier laughed bitterly, turning his attention back to his cigarette in the chilly Paris night.

In the weeks following the opera, Juliet's new life took on a routine. Over a light breakfast of pastries and tea, she read *Le Temps*, *Le Figaro*, and *Le Petit Journal*, searching for anything on Marchant. During the day, she had a tutor for Italian and English who gave her stacks of books to read as well as piano lessons each week. Varnier was planning a trip to Italy for them in the summer so that she could see the fantastic art and opera of Florence.

Marchant had studied in Florence, Juliet recalled. She clung to every connection, however distant, to the artist. Each night, Monsieur Varnier met her for dinner and they dined on *boeuf*, oysters, rabbit, trout, and salads with white truffles. Varnier taught her about wine and champagne, and introduced her to cherry brandy, which became her favorite. She savored each of these lessons from him, hoping they would make her more desirable to Marchant when she finally reconnected with him.

But it was at the piano that she excelled.

While she struggled at first with the keys, Juliet found that within the year, she began to read music fluently; her pieces increased in difficulty and the delicate fingerwork became more and more intricate, graduating to easier Chopin pieces and then to the études within her second year. Then the notes finally settled in her brain and she could visualize the music, see it before she could hear it. The technicality of the instrument appealed to Juliet. The piano was difficult. Unlike poetry or art, which could be interpreted subjectively, either a note was correct or it was not. The challenge of building her skills each day pushed her. She wasn't sure it was talent, but rather pure determination that made her instructor marvel at her progress. By the second year, the old man thought she could begin composing her own short pieces.

One evening, her head bowed low into the keys, her fingers cramping, Juliet was working out the notes in a song and was so engrossed that she hadn't noticed the smell of light flowers sweet and raw floating into the room. At the end of the piece, she turned her head feeling uneasy, straining to see where the smell was coming from. She found Varnier leaned against the wall watching her.

"Beautiful." He clapped lightly.

"Thank you," she said, dipping her head in a bow. The air stirred with something. She was beginning to understand the musicality of conversation between them and knew this was a longer pause—a fermata—than was normal for them. And for no reason, her throat felt dry.

Juliet knew nothing of where Varnier went during the day or the evening after dinner. Often she waited to hear him coming up the stairs in the early hours of the morning, passing her door on the way to his chambers. Such a presence was he that when he entered the room, he immediately began asking her about the books she was reading or made her play a new song for him, never stopping once for pleasantries. When he finally departed, she found she was exhausted—and exhilarated.

As the months passed, Juliet continued posting letters to her family. Many times, she'd written her father asking if Marchant had ever contacted him about her. She'd broached the idea of seeing her family several times with Varnier, but he'd smiled and told her it was "no longer possible." While news of home came slowly at first, her father never wrote of Marchant, or of seeing her again. She knew that twice a year he visited Paris to sell at the markets, yet there was no suggestion of them seeing each other, and she felt that her father should be the one to initiate it. Surely, he should wonder what had happened to his eldest child? In her letters, Juliet kept up the ruse that she was working as a housekeeper, feeling guilty that she was sitting at the piano for hours or luxuriating in fine linens while her father, brother, and sister were laboring in the fields.

In the summer of 1896, when Juliet had been in Paris barely a year, her father wrote that he was remarrying. To Juliet, it seemed like the life she'd known in Challans was dying. She'd hated the idea of her father struggling to maintain the farm, so she mentioned to Varnier that she hoped her family's life would not be so hard since she wasn't there to help.

The next morning, she found another bag of gold francs on the breakfast table. It was so similar to the bag that had been delivered to her father shortly before she left Challans that she had little doubt Varnier had sent the first one. But why? She was still no closer to knowing the truth about Varnier's connection to her mother than she had been a year ago, and he'd refused to discuss it further. She counted it and found that the bag held more money than Juliet's father made in a year.

"A wedding present to send to him," Varnier said with a smile, yet she had not told him of her father's remarriage. She wondered if somehow her letters were intercepted by Marie and read before they were sent. "Tell him you got a raise. That you're a governess now."

"He'll know that's a lie."

"Oh, Juliet." Varnier shook his head. "You are wrong. He'll want to believe it and so he will. Our illusions are powerful things we cling to."

While she was adorned in the finest dresses and busied herself with lessons and was free to walk about the streets of Paris with Paul or Varnier, Juliet could not shake the feeling that she was a prisoner within the walls of the Boulevard Saint-Germain house. Was her freedom another one of these illusions that Varnier spoke of? She held on to one hope, one longing, and that was that somehow Marchant would find her and take her with him.

Used to running in the countryside unencumbered, Juliet never got used to walking outside with a parasol—and always with an escort, either Varnier or Paul. On her walks, she tried to remember the streets that Marchant had drawn for her. Paris had many angles, and Juliet thought she'd found the setting for his Paris drawing. She searched for him among the bearded painters that gathered along the Seine with their white shirts. Occasionally, Juliet would see a woman in a yellow dress and wonder back to the strange woman on the platform in Challans who had stared at her so hungrily. She never saw the woman again although she was surely headed to Paris before Juliet's father had stopped her. Perhaps she had just been a poor crazy woman.

One of their regular haunts on their walks was Edmond Bailly's Librairie de l'Art independent bookshop on the Rue de la Chaussée-d'Antin. Varnier regularly conversed with men in the small shop, usually an artist—a dwarfed gentlemen with glasses and a bowler hat—and his friend, a composer for the piano with a thick waist and long beard.

As they talked, Juliet spied a small section of piano music. She opened the one for Claude Debussy and another for Erik Satie. While the Debussy piece looked challenging, it was the Satie that fascinated her. Called *Three Gnossiennes,* the piece was complex, composed in free time, with odd note pairings and timings. She went to purchase it from an original printing in *Le Figaro Music* dated September 1893 and noticed a small pile of newspapers. One, *Supplément Illustré,* sat on the counter, nearly forgotten. It was at least a month old but featured an article on painter Auguste Marchant's luxurious life complete with illustrations. Juliet scanned the article quickly, her heart pulsing. It claimed Marchant lived in one of the most fashionable addresses in Paris. Purchasing it quickly, Juliet tucked it in her shawl.

Back in her room at the apartment, Juliet devoured the article again and again to the point where she had nearly memorized it. Marchant's painting had won the Medal of Honor at the Salon this year, and he'd begun decorating several drawing rooms at prestigious Parisian hotels. As the writer noted, his art was thriving and he was looking forward to the yearly Salon at the Palais de l'Industrie, where his nudes would be on display once again. The year apart had made the edges of him less clear to her, and she'd wondered if it had all been a dream. Seeing his likeness on the paper, however, the memories she'd held came flooding back to her—the length of his hair, the upward tilt of his eyes, the way his trousers hung on his hips, the soft belly underneath his crisp cotton shirts, the smell of him. In a final glaring paragraph, the piece mentioned that Marchant, a widower now for over a year with two children, was very much in demand socially.

That evening, Juliet broached the subject of the opera again with Varnier. "I would like to see the opera—the real opera—not these smaller performances."

"But those smaller performances are some of the newest things being created. True artists, Juliet, not some bourgeois version of an artist who paints beauty while all around him is decay."

Varnier wasn't talking about opera anymore. This was about Marchant. Had Marie shown him the copy of *Supplément Illustré* in her room? Gently, Juliet attempted to steer him back. "We were talking about opera, weren't we?" She continued eating her chicken. "You promised we could go to *the* Grand Opera, not *an* opera."

Varnier appeared flustered. "When you are eighteen."

"But that's nearly a year away!" Juliet was furious.

"You can protest all you want, I won't change my mind," he said. "You're too young."

"You keep saying that," snapped Juliet, her knife scraping her plate a little too loud in protest.

"And your childish reaction tells me that I'm correct in my assessment." His voice was a whisper. Juliet stopped cutting her chicken so she could hear him. "I'll only say this once. You thought you were old enough for a lot of things when you were merely a child. You won't be making the same mistake under my watch. Do you understand?"

Juliet fumed.

"Do you *understand* me?"

"*Oui.*"

The following June, Juliet turned eighteen and Varnier took her to Italy instead of the Paris opera. She spent most of the fall being shepherded by a guide through the churches in Rome, Florence, and Milan. At the end of her lectures, Juliet could distinguish a Titian from a Raphael, but her longing for Marchant only increased as she saw his influences in the canvases and church ceilings. She saw Marchant in every line, shade of blue, drape of fabric, blend of oil to paint a nude breast or a thigh. If Varnier had hoped that filling her day with lectures would make her forget about Marchant, he'd been wrong.

As if he'd had a sense of her longing and wanted to snuff it out, he found another piano teacher and they settled in Rome until after the Christmas holiday. This teacher inquired if Juliet had been playing the piano since she was a child. When she told him that she had only studied for two years, the man was dumbfounded. "This must be the work of the devil," the man exclaimed. "You are too good, like Paganini."

"Paganini?"

The little man leaned close on the piano bench. Juliet could smell something foul on his breath. "Niccolò Paganini, the virtuoso. They say he murdered a woman and imprisoned her soul in his violin. His gift to the devil in exchange for his talent. Her cries could be heard in the beauty of the notes."

"That's horrible."

He shrugged. "You might not say that if you'd heard him play," he offered.

The little man implored Varnier to send Juliet to Vienna to study under the greatest piano teacher in Europe. Juliet could travel to London and New York to perform. "She could be famous," said the man. Upon the man pressing him for a decision, Varnier packed them up and left Rome.

They returned to Paris in February, and Juliet felt changed. Gone for good was the simple girl from the country. Now she knew fabrics, food, and wine. She could read books in Italian—slowly, but she could read them. She could close her eyes and smell the olive groves, the cooking garlic, the fresh basil. When she looked in the mirror, the girl that Marchant had painted was fading, replaced by a woman who knew how to roll her hair into ornate waves and high buns secured with jeweled combs and tiaras. Tendrils framed a face that had lost its baby fat. When she walked down the street clutching Varnier's arm, wearing her black velvet walking jacket and silk hat cocked to the side and her hair loosely tied at the base of her neck, Juliet knew that people turned to get a glimpse of her. It did not go unnoticed to her that Varnier liked the attention people paid to her, too.

It was Parisian tradition that in the six weeks before Ash Wednesday, the Paris Opera House hosted its annual masked ball. Varnier secured a box for them for the performance of Saint-Saëns's *Samson et Dalila*.

For the opera, Juliet chose an elaborate soft-pink chiffon dress with beaded sleeves, a gathered train, and a cream-beaded bodice that she'd purchased in Milan. The pinks and creams of the dress were subtle, more texture than color. The dress was exotic and more mature than anything she'd seen in the Paris store windows. She chose a black mask, and her hat was a matching soft-pink-and-cream feather number woven in her hair. When she came down the stairs, Varnier, who was dressed in his waistcoat, was reading a letter that had come in the day's mail. She stood at the stairs until he looked up and was delighted to see that he seemed to teeter at the first glimpse of her. She thought she saw him blink before he spoke. "You're wearing *that*?"

"*Oui.*" So sure was she that she had affected him, she smiled in amusement. "You don't like it?" This had become a thing with them. Varnier seemed to be growing increasingly uncomfortable as she began filling out her dresses. The décolletage on the dress was revealing for a young girl, but not for a woman. And at eighteen, Juliet was blooming. She'd caught him glancing at her as she stood at the piano with the opera teacher. He'd even begun to avoid close proximity to her in the dining room, adjusting his chair away from her.

"It's lovely." His voice cracked and he clutched at his white tie and placed his hat on his head. "Shall we go?" She took his hand and they descended the stairs and onto the Boulevard Saint-Germain to catch a coach.

As they entered the Palais Garnier, she spotted him immediately in the magnificent Grand Foyer. Despite the pure beauty of the room with its ornate carved ceilings and hanging chandeliers, Juliet scanned the faces of the crowds briefly, and it was as though her eyes pulled her toward the marble steps of the Grand Staircase where he stood with his back to her. Even after two years, from the curve of his spine to the color of his hair and his laugh, Juliet knew it was Auguste Marchant. As if on instinct, Varnier clutched her arm tightly, insisting they check their coats. Varnier never looked in Marchant's direction, but he seemed to be aware of the other man's presence.

After leaving her coat, she and Varnier ascended the stairs and she could feel him trying to lead her away, taking her gloved hand and pulling her behind him. It was the break in conversation that Juliet heard first. Marchant stopped speaking in mid-sentence as she passed him on the steps. Varnier's hand continued pulling her up the stairs with a fervor that she hadn't seen in him, as though he were her dance partner. She turned her masked face to the right to see that Marchant had, indeed, gone silent as he stared in her direction. There was a moment of coughing as the men he had been speaking with cleared their throats, and she heard one of them remark, "You were saying?" But Marchant didn't answer, and so Juliet turned again and met his eyes through her mask. From the ashen look on his face, he knew it was her. When she reached the top of the stairs, Varnier led her to their box and shut her in as if she were a treasure.

Marchant entered his own box two away from Varnier's. Marchant's eyes met hers and he hastily took his seat next to a young woman. Juliet felt her heart sink as she saw the woman—a blonde in a sensible black dress—talking closely to him. The woman placed her hand on Marchant's arm, and Juliet could tell they were familiar with each other. Of course, she thought. He would not have waited long to find another companion. His wife had been dead almost two years. She'd been kept away from him for too long. Juliet studied Varnier's profile, his firm jaw and masculine nose, and she despised him then. She barely noticed the opera, positioning herself to get a better look at Marchant.

At intermission, Varnier was forced to excuse himself, leaving Juliet alone in the lounge. She circled the green velvet sofas, watching masked courtesans working their charms on patrons. Juliet knew this was where they conducted business. She was in awe of their style and their command of men. It wasn't just their bodies, Juliet observed. They were wonderful conversationalists. The men laughed and she could hear clips of discussion about art and music.

Buoyed by their confidence, Juliet spied Marchant in the Grand Foyer, standing on the stairs in the same spot she'd seen him earlier.

There was no sign of his blond companion, so she swept past him on the stairs, her head held high. Marchant quickly excused himself from the group of men he was with. Taking her by the arm, he led her carefully down the stairs. When they reached the bottom, he spun her toward him.

"It is you, isn't it?"

"*Oui.*" Juliet could hear the soft sounds of their heels on the marble steps. She stared ahead, enjoying the fact that her face was obscured by her black velvet mask. It gave her a sense of control over the situation, an essence of mystery.

When they got to the bottom of the stairs, he led her around a corner under the chandeliers. Holding her shoulders, he stared at her. Juliet remembered the artist's eye and the way he would examine the changes to her face after each year. He carefully peeled off her mask, and the touch of his fingers on her face took her back to Challans, to his studio and his bed. "How different you look now." Juliet closed her eyes, and when she opened them, she saw his face was pained and bewildered. "But how?"

"I left Challans. I live here now, with my uncle, on the Boulevard Saint-Germain." She touched his arm.

"You live in the Latin Quarter?" He looked surprised.

"Yes. I have for more than two years now. Since that summer." She followed his eyes, which seemed unfocused, hoping to catch them and pull them back to her gaze. "Paris is so different from the one you painted for me." She tilted her head, an angle she'd practiced in the mirror and that she knew was becoming. How had he not known? "You never looked for me?"

He closed his eyes, swallowed, and shook his head.

She'd seen this look before. It was the same look she had seen in his house in Challans with her mother. It was the look of guilt. She reached out to touch him again with her gloved hand, but he pulled back from her.

"No."

"I don't understand." Juliet felt her heart pounding against the bones of her corset. For a moment, it seemed he was afraid of her. She'd rehearsed this conversation so many times in her head and yet it wasn't going as she'd expected.

"It isn't your fault." He smiled sadly. "You were my muse, my inspiration. You held such power over me and I believed—*truly I did*—that I loved you. I suffered greatly for what happened between us." His voice was a whisper. "I was foolish and my wife and child died as punishment for my sin. God took them. I nearly burned my studio down to the ground in despair."

"I'm sorry," said Juliet. She thought it was curious that he'd never stopped to consider that she had suffered as well. While she had scoured every street and newspaper for him, was it really possible he had never looked for her?

Again, he shook his head. Juliet thought his hair looked grayer and thinner, his face both more sunken and sagging than it had been before. He looked like a man who had not fully recovered from a lengthy and progressive illness. "You were just a child. It was not your fault. The fault was entirely mine."

"But I'm not a child now. I'm nearly nineteen." Juliet hesitated before she spoke again. It was the question she'd longed to ask him for more than two years. "Have you thought of me since we parted?"

Marchant seemed to struggle with what to say next. He looked into the crowd. "I tried to *forget* you, but it was not easy."

Juliet smiled. This was the answer she'd been hoping for. She could see the future now. Him painting her in the studio, then making love to her. She was someone more interesting now, worthy of him. She knew French and Italian writers, she could talk to him about the Botticellis she'd seen, the Sistine Chapel, the Raphaels, the Titians, and the Caravaggios. She was caught up in this dream life for a moment, until she saw his eyes catch something behind her and his demeanor changed. Juliet turned to see the blond woman approaching them with a smile. The woman was certain enough of Marchant's affections not to be concerned to find him in conversation with another young woman.

"There you are," the woman called.

He lowered his voice and spoke quickly. It was not unkind, but the tone was low and sharp. "You were my greatest mistake. I saved a sketch of you that I keep in my studio. It reminds me of man's folly— *my folly*. I don't say this to be cruel, Juliet. I say it to be honest. We must never see each other again."

"Surely you don't mean that." She looked up at him panicked, searching for some sign of the man she had known. "Surely not. We've just found each other again. What has happened to you?"

He leaned down. It was a whisper that only she could hear. "You were my ruin, child." He bowed his head and straightened. "You must excuse me, but I hope not to see you again." With that, he passed her, almost knocking her to the side as he slid his arm around the beaming blonde and they were gone.

Holding her mask in her gloved hand, Juliet stood frozen in the Grand Foyer as the opera patrons returned to their boxes for the second act. Needing air, she paced the foyer and finally looked up to find Varnier standing outside their box. He walked to the balcony and looked down at her, finding her clutching her stomach. She saw his eyes scan the crowd and land on Marchant climbing the stairs at a quick pace with the blond woman in tow. Juliet had only to glance at

Varnier for him to know what had transpired between them. Turning, he rushed down to her, passing Marchant on the stairs.

Varnier slid his arm in hers, holding her up as she grew shaky. "Shall we go?"

Juliet nodded. Varnier steadied her against the wall while he gathered their coats. She couldn't speak, and she wobbled down the front stairs of the Palais Garnier. The night chill hit them.

When she was safely seated in a coach, she felt Varnier's hand on hers. "You can't be with him. It's not possible."

"Why?" Out of the public eye, tears streamed down her face. The streets of Paris passed her as horses' hooves pounded the cobblestones. She found comfort in the bustle of people crossing streets, shopping, clutching each other against the cold, laughing. There *was* happiness in Paris. It was all around her.

When Varnier didn't respond, she pressed. "Will you answer one thing for me?"

"If I can." He stared out at the Paris night, looking more melancholy than Juliet had seen him.

"That's not good enough," she said sharply. "I need an answer from you."

"All right." He nodded.

"How did you know about him? No one knew about him. I never told you." Juliet's face felt hot. She pictured Marchant in his studio in Challans. It was impossible to reconcile him with the man who had so coldly rebuffed her inside the Opera House. The gentle man who'd sketched Paris for her was gone.

Varnier was quiet for several minutes in the coach. She waited silently for an answer.

"Your mother."

"My mother? You said you didn't know her."

"You asked how I knew about him—about Marchant. It was through your mother."

"What was this thing between you and my mother?"

Varnier would not look at her. His voice was monotone and he simply stared out at the streets of Paris passing by. "She left me word about you and Marchant."

"Liar. You were her lover?"

"You're wrong." He shook his head. "I was never her lover."

"Then what were you? Because you weren't her brother and you *aren't* my uncle."

"I am in your mother's employ. I told you." He sank a little in his seat, still refusing to look at her, his voice growing smaller.

Juliet had never noticed his profile before, the line of his nose, which looked softer from the side. He was so different from Marchant. Why, she thought, was every man judged against Marchant in her eyes? "That's a lie. My mother couldn't employ anyone. And she's dead so surely any bind that connected you to her is gone."

"I need to protect you. That's all you need to know." He turned to her and took her face in his hands, pulling her so close that she could feel the heat of his breath and smell a faint tobacco smell. "You must listen to me. There is nothing but heartbreak for you with that man. He can never love you."

"I know," said Juliet, tears falling down her face. "He made that very clear."

Varnier still held her face. He met her gaze. As they passed the gaslights on Saint-Germain, she could see the concern in his eyes. "I'm sorry he disappointed you. I'd give anything not to see you this way. I tried to keep you from him all this time for your own good."

"You knew he'd behave that way, didn't you?"

Varnier nodded. "I feared he would." He leaned over and kissed her on the forehead, holding her head to his lips for a moment.

After the ball, Juliet began to see the world cut in two. The world before the masked ball and the one after. Before the ball, her life had purpose—and that purpose was to be reunited with Marchant. Like a little fool, she had believed he'd loved her, even looked for her. Now the fantasy was gone and the days were empty.

She plunked notes out on the piano, read the books placed in front of her by her instructors, but there was only a short-term purpose: finish the sonatina, start another novel, endure another meal. *Endure* was a good description. Juliet found herself simply enduring. Each morning, she woke with an empty feeling in her stomach as if some part of her were missing. In those few moments she struggled to think of what had been lost, so primal was the depth of her pain. And then she'd remember Marchant—the way he'd looked at her with something like contempt—and she could hardly manage to dress herself. Her appearance suffered. She lost weight until her clothes hung on her and her hair became dull. Varnier became so worried that he suggested another trip to Italy, but Juliet begged him not to take her there. All the paintings there—it would be too much. Even the sight of the paintings in the house revolted her, so Varnier had them all removed.

While it had never bothered her that Varnier had always gone out in the evenings, Juliet had begun to wonder where he went. From her balcony, she'd watch him walk down the street, catching an omnibus at the end of the block. Soon she learned he caught the same omnibus each night, and it took him to Montmartre. She'd heard about Montmartre—with its bustling squares and decadent dance clubs.

One morning, over breakfast, Juliet broached the subject. "I hear

Montmartre is nice. I haven't been there." She eyed him, waiting for his response.

"It isn't a place for you." Varnier never looked up from his paper.

"I'm not a doll."

"No, but you are a lady. The place is filthy."

"And yet you go?"

Varnier continued to ignore her.

As they stopped at Edmond Bailly's bookshop on their regular Saturday walk, Varnier found his two friends, the composer and the painter, deep in conversation. Juliet could make out from their conversations that the shorter man was an artist in Montmartre. Montmartre again? The place Varnier kept from her. As she ran her fingers over the leather-bound books on tarot and mesmerism, she heard the men discussing a scandal involving a well-known stage occultist, Philippe Angier, who had been challenged to a duel. Juliet recognized Angier's name from several articles appearing in Le Figaro over the past few weeks.

As the story went, Philippe Angier, when prodded for a private performance at dinner, had reluctantly predicted the fortunes—or misfortunes as they turned out to be—of his dinner companions, all well-known Parisians. The fates were grim—one of the guests was told he would be imprisoned, another poisoned, and the final two would take their own lives. While the predictions did little more than cause a swift end to the dinner, later accounts, if they were to be believed, indicated that each prediction had *actually* come true, to the letter, except for one. Now Philippe Angier, who had once been thought to be nothing but a successful stage magician, was being challenged to a duel by the remaining living dinner guest, Gerard Caron, who had declared him not a stage occultist but—a far more serious charge—a Satanist. Caron had so far escaped his predicted fate of suicide, but given that the writer was known to be a terrible shot, the inevitable outcome of the duel might prove to be another one of Angier's accurate predictions.

Juliet scanned the music section looking for more Erik Satie compositions, her obsession. There were no new compositions and she felt disappointed. The men's voices raised in discussion. So this was what went on in Montmartre? Gossip?

The dwarfed painter was animated. "I heard Angier ate his children."

"*Non, non*," the composer whispered, taking the tone back down as he stroked his beard. "Those are just rumors. True, he killed them in front of the mothers, but he did not eat them. He got his power that way, they say." The composer shrugged as though it were a perfectly normal thing to do. It made Juliet think of Paganini with the dead lover imprisoned in his violin. All of it gossip.

"*C'est barbare.*" The painter shook his head.

"Okay, okay," said Varnier, but he was clearly engaged in the discussion. "There is a lady present." He spied Juliet. She gave him an impatient scowl indicating she wanted to leave.

"Our apologies, dear lady," said the composer. "Are you looking at any of my pieces?"

Juliet held up one of his latest piano works. "I liked the last one."

"She plays it better than you," teased Varnier.

"And she looks better doing it," added the artist.

"Maybe we should be looking for Angier's missing grimoire here, while we're at it," joked the composer.

Varnier waved as the two men began another heated argument about Angier.

"I see what I'm missing in Montmartre."

"You aren't missing anything," said Varnier. "They just love to gossip."

But Juliet did think she was missing something, so over the next few weeks she plotted carefully. She'd lost so much weight since seeing Marchant that her outfit was easy. She purchased elements of her costume one at a time, hoping Marie wouldn't notice the packages containing a cap, trousers, and a waistcoat that she'd hidden under the armoire. One night when the entire costume was complete, Juliet tucked her hair under the cap and waited for Varnier to leave. She was down the stairs and out the door as soon as he got to the corner. The omnibus to Montmartre was on time. Pulling her hat down around her face so she wouldn't be caught, she watched Varnier and noticed how spent and broken he looked when he was out in public. Guiltily, she realized it had to do with her. He had so been vibrant—so alive when they were touring in Italy, showing her around Florence. But now, he seemed as sad as she had been these months, as though their emotions were tied. When she suffered, so did he.

The omnibus stopped and Varnier walked up the steep hill toward the Sacré-Coeur. It was night, and Juliet found it hard to keep up with him as he turned down streets and maneuvered his way at a quick pace through the crowd. Down from the Sacré-Coeur, the street emptied into a square with paintings, thousands of paintings and artists selling them. The sight of the paintings made Juliet sick. She was glad that Varnier was traveling at a quick clip down past the Moulin de la Galette to the Rue Norvins, where she saw him stop to light a cigarette.

Soon he wasn't alone. From the distance, Juliet saw a woman join him with red rouge on her cheeks and lips, color applied so heavily that her face resembled an artist's smock after a day of painting.

Varnier and the woman spoke, and then she saw them turn a left corner farther down on the Rue Norvins. Hurrying to catch them, Juliet could see them ahead on a narrow street that bent around the back of an apartment building. The woman was laughing loudly and fumbling to open a door. Varnier stood behind her silently, holding the door open for her. Juliet thought the woman sounded drunk, and as she got to the door, she noticed that the woman had left it open. Juliet assumed this was for her safety. She knew what type of transaction was about to happen here and the dangers that could be associated with what this woman did each night. She wondered if she'd have been dealt a similar fate had she been forced to marry Michel Busson. Juliet could hear Varnier's voice now, and from the window she could see the faint outlines of them, the woman illuminating the bare room that included a small bed and dresser by lighting a few cheap candles. Perhaps Juliet should have left, but she was frozen in the narrow street as the woman took several coins from him and placed them in a drawer. The woman positioned Varnier on the bed then lifted her skirt and in a swift motion climbed on top of him, reaching for his pants. Juliet did not turn away from the sight nor the intimate sounds that came next. Varnier had been so reserved with her in all their years; there was a joy she took in hearing him reduced to animal sounds. As the noises became more intense, Juliet closed her eyes to recall the sounds of her own lovemaking to Marchant, which were often hushed to prevent his staff from hearing. And then there had been the grunting like pigs from the Busson boy and his friend in the field. She looked back into the room to the final sounds emitting from Varnier, him drawing the prostitute closer for one vital moment before collapsing on the dirty bed that would no doubt be used by another man within the hour. Juliet lingered for a moment, something about Varnier shifting in her mind. So he was a man after all?

Turning, Juliet walked back to the Rue Norvins and down the hill until she saw the windmill above the Moulin Rouge. And in the dark night, she heard the familiar sounds of discordant notes coming from a piano in the open window above her. She knew the pattern that would come next, because she had played it many times with her own fingers. It was Satie's *Gnossienne No. 1.* She stood under the window and closed her eyes, taking in the music until the song ended and Juliet thought she heard a heavy bench sliding away from the piano.

She turned to move past the cabarets of the Boulevard de Clichy. As she passed the Moulin Rouge, she was surprised by the sharp smell of urine. She spotted a woman in a red lace dress standing near the cabaret's entrance. It was the style of dress that seemed familiar to Juliet. She searched her memory for where she'd seen this particular dress before. Then it occurred to her and she began to back away. The version that she'd seen was not red at all—it had been yellow—the woman on the platform at Challans in the yellow dress. This was the same dress in a different color, as though the costumes had been in a variety of hues. Was there a blue one out there somewhere on the streets of Paris? A green version as well? As with the woman in yellow, this dress was also old and faded with a cheap theatrical quality to it, something that looked better from afar. This woman was striking—her red-orange hair clashing with the deep garnet red of the dress. Juliet thought she must be a prostitute who'd bought the dress secondhand, but she was not as heavily rouged as the woman who had been with Varnier. There was an unfortunate feeling about this woman; she did not appear to be earning money on the streets.

As Juliet passed, the woman stared at her with something like familiarity—which was impossible because she was in disguise. It was the same hungry stare as the woman on the train platform, and Juliet felt a chill and an innate sense that she needed to run. From the corner of her eye, Juliet saw the woman begin to walk quickly toward her. Juliet walked quickly, pushing through the thick crowd and turning back to see that she had not lost her. The woman trailed closely behind. Instead of heading toward the omnibus stop, Juliet ran back up the hill toward the Rue Norvins in the hope of turning down one of the winding side streets. At the empty square, Juliet turned to see that the woman was close enough to reach out and touch her.

"What do you want?" Juliet spun on her heels to face the woman. She pushed her with her hands.

"You," said the woman. "It *is* you. I cannot believe it."

"I don't know what you mean."

Juliet was watching the woman's face when he came out of nowhere. The woman was sent backward with such force that her skirt dragged along the road as if by a team of invisible horses.

She got up and began to walk toward Juliet. Again, it was as though she were picked up by invisible hands and dragged backward away from Juliet with such force that the woman's skirt briefly lifted before she was released to the ground in a thunderous, dramatic display.

Juliet's heart was pounding. The woman was now lying on the ground, her head at an awkward angle.

"Leave her." The voice was familiar. Juliet turned to see Varnier calmly lighting a cigarette.

Juliet was speechless. "What did you do?"

"It's not important."

"But you didn't even touch her?"

"We need to leave." He looked at her sharply. "I don't think that my actions tonight are what we should be worrying about." He waited for her to join him as they began to walk down the hill to catch one of the last omnibuses back to the Latin Quarter.

Once back on the Saint-Germain, Juliet spoke. "She knew me."

"She most certainly did not."

"She said, 'It is you.'"

"That was a madwoman, Juliet. They're all over Paris. She probably was suffering from syphilis."

They reached the door to the apartment. He opened it, but Juliet did not walk in. "You killed her, Lucian."

He waited until she entered. "I was protecting you, Juliet. I told you that I always would."

The next morning, Juliet studied the breakfast china with intense interest, as she found she couldn't look directly at Varnier. It was a curious combination of repulsion and something else that she couldn't quite describe. She looked at his hands, remembering them on the prostitute, but also the same hands that seemed to send the woman in the red dress flying in the air on the Rue Norvins. The odd angle of the woman's broken neck. She had seen many different sides to Varnier last night, things she was sure she wasn't expected to see. And it had changed her feelings on him in many ways.

As he lifted his coffee cup, Juliet could see the blond hairs from his arm peeking through his sleeve—the intimate details and spaces of him. Now she wondered about them all. He was both father figure and protector to her, but he was no relation. And after last night, the fact that he was a man was very much on her mind.

Varnier didn't speak to her but opened the morning paper that Juliet had already read and put back to the left of his place setting. *Le Figaro*'s lead story was the news of Philippe Angier: When his pistol had failed to fire on the flats of Bois de Boulogne, he had been mortally wounded in the absurd duel with the writer Gerard Caron. Angier's death had not been easy—the occultist had lingered for two days in and out of consciousness, finally succumbing to his injuries late in the night. It was claimed from his deathbed he had cursed the young writer, who, racked with guilt for shooting when his opponent's pistol wouldn't fire, took his own life—shooting himself with Angier's faulty pistol, which this time fired brilliantly. With this act, he had fulfilled Angier's prediction. Varnier was so engrossed with the article that he did not seem to notice Juliet squirming in her chair.

"You don't make a very convincing boy, Juliet." He folded the paper and took off his reading glasses, something he seemed to need more frequently. "I instructed Marie to find the costume and burn it."

Juliet nearly choked on her coffee. Clearing her throat, she looked at him for the first time. "If you do, I'll just buy another one."

He leaned back in his seat. "I trust you enjoyed your little excursion last night."

"Seems you did as well. At least the first part." Juliet took her knife and began to spread jam on her bread—anything to keep her hands from shaking. "It sounded like you did anyway . . ." Finally she met his eyes.

"That's why I didn't want you near Montmartre," he said, but there was no shame in his face. "You shouldn't see or hear such things. It wasn't safe for you. Instead, I come out to find some madwoman grabbing what I thought was a boy—but then I find it was you."

"What did you do to her?"

"I protected you, Juliet. That is what I do. You know that."

"Why? You didn't even have to touch her. You have powers, like my mother did. That's the connection between you both."

"You're safe now," he said. "And you won't be going back to Montmartre dressed in some ridiculous costume, skulking around the streets getting into mischief and seeing things that are not appropriate for a young girl."

Juliet lowered her voice to a whisper. "You know about Marchant.

What happened between us. You know that I'm not a child, Lucian. I am a young woman. You cannot keep me locked up here like some princess in a fairy tale."

"Oh, Juliet, how wrong you are." He was calm, but there was an edge to his voice that she had not heard before. He took her hand in his, patting it. It was dry and warm. "That's *exactly* what I aim to do."

"And what about what I want?"

"I have a duty to you. I intend to honor that duty."

"What if I don't want you to honor it anymore? What about what I want?"

"Would you like to be tossed on the street?" He cocked his head. "Would you? We can arrange that. How long before you were in Montmartre for *real*? It's one thing to be a spectator and to be able to leave Montmartre, but what if you had no other options? Oh, you wouldn't start on the street. No, not right away. You can read and you look good so you'd work at a restaurant or delivering flowers, maybe a laundry, but that wouldn't pay the bills, so you'd have some encounter with a man who'd give you the money you'd need to meet your expenses for the month. Just once, you'd tell yourself. Until the next time and then the next. Is that what you want?"

"I might get *your* attention that way." She didn't know what made the words spill out, but she knew it was the truth. Once she'd worried that he would have expectations of her, but now she found herself trying to be in a room with him, to see if he would notice her. The truth was, it had bothered her that Varnier had never once indicated desire *for her.*

"You want my attention?" He laughed. "I do nothing but give you attention. This house, this life, the opera, Italy, the piano lessons, the tutors..."

Juliet wasn't aware of what registered on her face, but she felt her cheeks flush. She met his eyes and noticed a change flash across them. "That isn't what I mean."

Varnier put his hands to his face as they stared at each other in silence. Juliet felt her jaw tighten and she was determined she wouldn't cry. Instead she focused on her chest lifting up and down as she began to breathe harder. Varnier looked at his hand for a long moment and then at the floor. She thought she could see the color draining from his face.

"Oh Juliet," Varnier said in nearly a whisper as he stood and walked out of the room, his hand touching the skin on her neck as he passed her.

14

Helen Lambert
Washington, DC, June 5, 2012

The carousel at Glen Echo Park was freaking me out. In all the years I'd lived in Washington, I'd never been to Glen Echo Park and had no idea where to even find it on a map. Not that it wasn't lovely with its art deco architecture, art center, and Spanish Ballroom, but it was all the effort to re-create the turn-of-the-century flavor of the park that so unsettled me after a night of reliving the *real* Belle Époque Paris in my dreams. I'd fainted at the Kennedy Center, blood spilling all over my Reem Acra dress from another nosebleed. Poor Luke had managed to clean me up after I'd come to. After the last dream, the colors of Paris were swimming around me today, from the flower stands to the gold-leaf architecture. Montmartre had the same carousel spinning in my dreams, and the exaggerated organ music was like a hellish soundtrack to me now.

Juliet's story had left me shaken. Marchant's rejection at the masked ball was as raw to me this morning as it had been to Juliet back in 1898. I sat numbly on a bench at Glen Echo with Mickey beside me, both of us holding our morning coffee in our hands. Juliet's images of Marchant—the line of hair that ran from his navel to the top of his trousers, the arch of his back, his stained fingers from the paint he used—were mixing with my own well-worn images of

Roger, the small things I'd missed from our marriage: from the way he chewed on a pen while he was taking an important phone call to the way he wrapped himself around me after we had sex. This was the painter, Auguste Marchant. Maybe a carousel was the right symbol, because as I watched the painted tiger spin by it seemed the images both past and present were circling in my head. My nose had bled again this morning, but I didn't confide this to Luke. I also suffered a throbbing headache that two Advil had not fixed.

My thoughts shifted again to Roger with his big green eyes and the dimple on his left cheek when he smiled, so eerily similar to Marchant in both look and mannerisms. My ex-husband's ten-year effort to bring Auguste Marchant's work to the Hanover Collection haunted me. His relentless passion for those paintings only reinforced my suspicions that I wasn't the only person who was reliving a life. I suspected that Marchant and Roger were, indeed, the same person. This was madness.

We waited for Madame Rincky's cousin, Malique, outside the old bumper car pavilion.

I don't know what I had expected, but an old, thin man with wire-rimmed glasses approached us and introduced himself in a thick Jamaican accent as Malique. He motioned for us to follow him to the picnic tables, which were, unfortunately, directly in front of the carousel.

Malique sat at the picnic table with his back straight—no easy feat, given how uncomfortable the seats were. A man sold barbecue chicken at a stand next to us, and the smell was normally something I'd have found pleasant on this summer day. Malique, who looked like a retired high school math teacher, cut right to the chase.

"Raquel tells me that you have the mark of the devil on you."

"I wouldn't say it's the mark of *the devil*." I closed my hands protectively. Mickey eyed me suspiciously as he stuffed a wad of cotton candy in his mouth and looked back and forth from Malique to me. This was high theater for Mickey.

"She definitely said it was the mark," Malique countered with no emotion, like he was a plumber who'd just discovered I had a clogged toilet.

And the fucking Glen Echo Park carousel kept going around and around with that out-of-tune organ as images swirled of Auguste Marchant making love to me; walking away from me at the Palais Garnier; Roger breaking up with me at Pho 79; and Lucian Varnier's fingers on my neck as he walked out the door in 1898, leaving me alone at the breakfast table—all these images spiraled around in my head like a trippy View-Master. My nose began to bleed again, and Mickey scrambled to get a wad of napkins. Having no shame at this point, I wadded one up and stuck it up the offending nostril, turning back to Malique, not caring how I looked.

Malique took my hand and turned it over. Mickey, sensing his cue, began to point out the lines, helpfully. His touch was sticky from the cotton candy. I swallowed audibly.

"Do you want a Diet Coke?" he asked, edging out of the picnic table.

"Sure," I said to get rid of him. He dutifully headed down the hill.

I turned to Malique. "I need your help."

He kept his eyes on my palm. "You are not looking well, if I may say."

"You may say."

Malique studied the lines on my hand and then held it with both of his, closing his eyes. He seemed to tremor. He released my hands and took my face in his, looking into my eyes—except he wasn't exactly gazing back into mine. His pupils were gone and I saw only the whites of his eyes. Freaked, I tried to pull away, but he held my head firmly with a strength that had me praying for Mickey to return. The carousel went around one time before Malique let me go.

He looked exhausted and out of breath, but he spoke quickly. "As I suspected, it is a binding curse. But not a normal one. It was poorly constructed...rushed...angry. No witch should bind so angrily." He pursed his lips and shook his head, with a distasteful look. "Darkness comes with it—it takes things along with it. Curses should be built with care and precision. It is an art, making a curse. Not this..."

"If you say so." I shrugged, remembering the elaborate ritual that Juliet's mother had prepared. "You said it takes things?"

"It takes *people*," he corrected. "There are multiple people in this curse, sloppy work." He shook his head again. "It loops." He drew with his finger in the air. "That is the mistake. A curse is not unlike a computer program. I see a jumbled mess when I look at...for lack of a better word...the code that created it. It leaves a trace. You"—he pointed to my nose—"are in danger. But there is a third person. He is what I like to call an administrator of the curse."

"So there aren't normally three people in a curse?"

"No. Usually, just one. The cursed."

"So, me?" That seemed obvious.

"No." He shook his head. "In this spell, you are not the cursed."

"Huh?" I almost laughed. "Trapped in someone else's curse. Just my luck."

Malique shrugged. "I don't know the specifics; I just see the outlines of the curse. Its intent was to plague the subject for eternity, hence the looping." He paused before continuing. There was a slowing at the carousel as a new set of riders boarded. "I feel I must tell you something, but I am not sure that I should. Raquel and I often disagree about this."

"Shoot." I stuffed a fresh wad of napkin up my nose a little higher.

"Are you sure?" He looked down at the table and let a spider run over his arm.

I nodded, fixated on the spider.

"You will not live another month."

"Why?" As the question came out of my mouth, I wondered: Did I just say *Why?* Not, *What the fuck?* Why was I being calm about this man—a medium—telling me I'd be dead by July? What was happening to me?

"It is in the outline I see. Whoever designed this curse gave you a guardian from the dark—the administrator to protect you and the curse—but that comes with…" He stopped. "Well, there are concessions that are made when those elements are added. Probably whoever made the curse worried about a minor, so they put an administrator in the mix for protection. The need for an administrator is an odd addition, though. The problem is that the object of the curse who needed protection—presumably you—cannot live beyond the age of the cursing witch herself. It is the cost of the administrator. Kind of like a service fee, so to speak."

"Did my mother know this?"

Malique shrugged. "I wouldn't be surprised that the fine print wasn't exactly spelled out for her. We are talking about demons here."

I groaned.

"This protection also came at a great cost to the spell caster."

"What do you mean?"

"I mean the spell killed the one who cast it. This is a nasty piece of business."

"Oh, of course." I laughed. Malique didn't do sarcasm. "Of course, *my* curse would include a service fee. So, this is bad."

"I've seen worse." Malique sighed. "But not many. Whoever cast this used a bad demon for this one—I won't say his name even for fear he finds me. He's one of the old ones. Really, he's too much demon for this curse. The spell caster didn't have to use one of the ancient ones."

I remembered the night in Challans; I'd seen the name of the demon. I also recalled the age of Juliet's mother from my dreams. Life had been hard and although she looked much older than me, I estimated that her age was in the early thirties at the time of the curse. From the sounds of it, she was thirty-four—the same age that I would be soon. And then, I'd be dead. "Can I stop it?"

"Yes," said Malique. "As the object, you have much power. Your blood is powerful." He hesitated. "Except this is not a modern curse, so that poses unique complications."

"What complications?"

"Typically, it can be reversed with blood and a reverse spell, but in this case *your* blood won't work. You aren't the physical bloodline of the original object. You are a duplicate in another body. You transfer from body to body because the original spell caster wanted the cursed to be punished for eternity. Unfortunately for you, you were caught up in his curse and you travel for eternity with the cursed, but your blood is now different from the original. You have a different body now. Do you see?"

"So I need the bloodline of the original object?" I knew this to be Juliet. I think I said "shit" aloud.

"Yes. I can give you a reverse curse to speak once you have the blood. It is quite simple and fairly straightforward and it just stops the cycle. It is actually the simple part of this."

"And the hard part?"

"That is for later," he said. "Let's take it one step at a time. Just get some blood—even a paper cut amount is fine. One other thing. This is very important. This administrator's purpose is the curse."

"I don't understand."

"The administrator is a soldier of this particular demon. They are lesser demons. Often they're damned souls who work off penance. Usually the curse they work has something to do with their punishment. In your case, your curse is the administrator's purpose. It has been my experience that these soldiers are quite good at executing their orders. In some ways, they don't have a choice and are punished severely for any failure. Do you understand?"

I stared at Malique in his wire-rimmed glasses as he spoke of Luke, my administrator. "So I shouldn't tell him I'm looking for blood?"

"I wouldn't."

15

Juliet LaCompte
Paris, France, 1898

After that morning at the breakfast table, Varnier found reasons to avoid the apartment on Boulevard Saint-Germain, and Juliet continued to follow him. Two days after their encounter at the breakfast table, she followed him two blocks toward the Panthéon, where he stood on the street waiting. Juliet expected to see another prostitute, but instead Varnier checked his pocket watch until he spied a funeral procession. Two black chargers with full plumed headpieces pulled a glass hearse adorned with two wreaths in each back window. Varnier turned into the street and walked behind the procession as though he was a mourner. It was then that Juliet noticed his long black suit jacket and wondered if it had been someone he had known, but it was curious he didn't mention it. People on the street turned to look at the hearse, which was always a curious sight in the normally lively Paris, but this hearse was drawing more attention with people gathering to witness it go by. As two women pointed to the carriage, Juliet stopped and pointed to the elaborate hearse. "Is that someone famous?"

"You could say that," whispered the woman. "It's that devil, Philippe Angier." She motioned Juliet closer. "The magician who was killed in the duel at Bois de Boulogne."

"The one who killed his children," said the other woman. "I once saw him onstage—my husband took us. He called on the dead . . . could tell your fortune . . . that sort of thing." The woman sighed. "He was a tall, handsome man, waves of dark hair . . . nothing like my Pierre."

"Until the devil got him." The first woman poked the other woman.

"Oh, don't be sounding like some half-wit."

The first woman leaned close to Juliet, whispering again as if the dead man could hear them gossiping. "Don't listen to her. That lovely dark hair . . . turned red like the color of hellfire, it did."

"She's right," agreed the other woman reluctantly. "Made a deal with the devil he did. His hair turned as red as the pope's robe."

"Now look at him." They both shook their heads.

Down the Boulevard Saint-Michel, past the Luxembourg Gardens, Juliet caught up with Varnier, who seemed preoccupied, never taking his eye off the hearse. The clopping of hooves stopped and the horses idled before turning into a cemetery with open black gates—Cimetière du Montparnasse. They were far from home now, having walked nearly an hour. Now the hearse turned and Juliet followed Varnier, staying far back, which wasn't hard because the hearse was tall. Only one black carriage followed behind, and it carried several women dressed in black with heavy veils.

Her feet were hurting; she hadn't expected to walk this far in the midday sun. Not wanting to get caught again, she turned and headed back to the apartment.

The next day, Varnier said he had urgent business in Rome and abruptly left Paris. First, he said the trip would last a few weeks, then he sent word that his business would require months.

In his absence, he wrote letters to Juliet inquiring about her piano lessons and updates on books she was reading. Juliet penned thoughtful letters back to him, telling him about the changes on the boulevard.

As the summer passed into fall, Juliet wrote to him frequently telling him she missed him. Needing a chaperone, she was now accompanied by Paul to the theater or on walks. She found the older man patient and kind, but she missed Varnier, the energy he brought to a room. Paul smiled and agreed with Juliet on everything from Zola to the color of flowers to the temperature of the soup. Varnier challenged her on everything. He made her think and defend her reasoning. She had come to trust Varnier as she had not trusted anyone but her parents.

With Marchant's betrayal, her feelings for Varnier had become complicated and feverish. As a young woman of nineteen, she knew most women her age were seeking good matches. Varnier had expressed no such plan for her—he'd said as much. She would remain in the apartment for safekeeping. Did Varnier want her for himself? Once, the idea of that had frightened her, but now the idea of being his wife had great appeal. As she penned letters to him, she told him she longed for their conversations. She longed for Varnier.

A letter came in late November that he would be returning. Juliet was excited. She had Marie and the maids scrub the apartment; she bought a Christmas tree and had it decorated. She was like the real lady of the house. Once again, she had purpose, but this time it no longer involved Auguste Marchant.

On the day Varnier was due to arrive, dinner was prepared in his honor—everything she knew he liked: rabbit, trout, fresh baguettes. Juliet was watching from the window as he stepped out of the carriage, but he stopped and turned, holding his hand out to retrieve another person from the cab. He wasn't alone—a dainty woman with hair the color of the coal in the stoves climbed out of the cab and looked up at the street in wonder. Juliet groaned. What would it be this time? Needlework? Latin? Ballet? Juliet lingered at the top of the stairs as the woman and Varnier arranged themselves in the foyer with Paul taking their coats and organizing their luggage. Varnier glanced up at Juliet with an unfamiliar look—guilt—and she sensed something was terribly wrong in the composition of the scene. He came to the bottom of the stairs. "Ah, Juliet, please come down and meet Lisette."

The woman joined him at the bottom of the stairs. She was pretty, but not beautiful. Her brown eyes were warm and when she smiled, Juliet noticed a small gap in her teeth. Far from making her unattractive, this flaw gave her character. The sum of the woman's features was striking.

"Lisette, this is my *niece*, Juliet." Varnier watched Juliet warily as she descended a few stairs.

"I'm so pleased to meet you, Juliet." The woman had a thick Italian accent, but her greeting seemed genuine. "Luc has told me so much about you." Lisette looked at Varnier for reassurance that they had, indeed, discussed his niece. But Varnier's eyes were only on Juliet. She was wearing a pink-and-gold dress for dinner; her hair had been left down in long auburn waves at Marie's suggestion.

At the name "Luc," Juliet changed her focus from Lisette to Varnier and before he even uttered the word, Juliet knew what was coming next.

"Juliet." His voice was thin. "This is my *wife*, Lisette."

Perhaps it had been the disappointment with Marchant that had steeled Juliet for a moment such as this, but the shock she had shown Auguste Marchant would not be replicated for Varnier and this moment. Juliet clutched the banister and her hand shook, but she stood upright. She looked down at Paul standing below her in the foyer and she was sure he could see her dress move as her legs wobbled from his vantage point under the stairs. "While I'm obviously thrilled, you did not mention that you had taken a wife, Uncle. It was a strange omission given our regular correspondence, don't you think?"

Varnier looked surprised at her composure. "I wanted it to be a surprise."

Juliet gave Varnier a hard glance and then a smile. "Then you achieved your goal." Juliet turned toward Lisette. "Welcome to your new home, Tante Lisette. Please let me know if there is anything I may help you with. I look forward to spending time with you." Juliet bowed her head. "If you'll excuse me, I have some correspondence to attend to. There is a lovely dinner prepared for the two of you, all of *Uncle Luc's* favorite things."

"Thank you, Juliet," said Lisette. "I look forward to learning what he likes." She slid her hand under Varnier's arm.

Juliet walked back up the stairs with her head high. She closed the door and sat on the chair facing the Boulevard Saint-Germain watching the carriages go by. Only when she was seated did she realize how badly she was shaking. In some ways, Varnier's betrayal had cut deeper because he'd known the pain she'd already suffered and he'd known how she felt about him. And yet he'd chosen to deliver another blow.

There was a knock on her door. Juliet expected Marie, but instead Varnier stepped in. He'd never been in her room before, so this in itself was unusual. She was glad that she'd held her composure and that he had not found her crying at her dressing table.

"I wanted to see if you were all right." His gaze was surprisingly soft, almost fearful, when she met it.

"Why wouldn't I be all right?" Still seated in the chair, Juliet turned her face from him.

"I should have told you." He stepped into the room and Juliet heard the door click shut behind him.

"Yes." Juliet stood. "That you planned to take a wife was a key detail that should have been in one of your many letters." She walked closer to him and she saw him take a step back, but the closed door stopped him. Placing her hands on his jacket as if to straighten his collar, Juliet looked into his eyes. He was afraid of her. She could see that now. "I trusted you, but you betrayed that trust." She smiled sadly. "As of today, you and I are done. Whatever this arrangement, we will have to honor it. I will honor it for my mother." Her hands were still resting on his lapels, and she thought she felt him lean in as if he wanted to kiss her. Juliet's words were soft, almost a whisper, and she leaned in close to him, making him believe that she was, indeed, about to kiss him. He made no move to stop her. "You had both my love and my devotion and you *knew* that. You knew it in your soul. Now you have lost both. You have lost me." She looked into his eyes so he could see she was serious. "Do you understand?"

"I'm so sorry, Juliet," Varnier nearly sobbed. "I've made a terrible mistake. You may not understand, I cannot love you. It is for—"

"Yes," she said calmly, cutting him off. "You made a *grave* mistake. Please leave now." Juliet backed away from him and walked to her window. "Would you tell Marie that I need a dress for this evening? Paul and I will be going to the symphony after all."

"Juliet." He held on to the doorknob but made no move to open it. It took him a long time to say the next words and when he did, it was as though the air went out of him. "I am in love with you."

She walked to the window and kept her back to him. "I'm sorry to hear that, Lucian." Juliet's voice was cruel. "Surely your *wife* is waiting for you."

The next few months, Juliet busied herself. She was kind to Lisette, for the woman had not known what she had stepped between and Juliet could not punish her for it. It was a good week for Juliet, though, if she only ran into Varnier once. Paul and Marie both seemed puzzled at the coolness Juliet directed to her "uncle," but they went silently about their duties. Soon Juliet noticed a subtle shift in their loyalty, from Juliet to Lisette, who was now the real lady of the house. Small slights like this only fueled Juliet's feeling of betrayal. It occurred to her that she should request that Varnier marry her to someone—anyone—to get her out of the house.

The thought of returning home to Challans was a possibility, although it had been years since she'd heard from her father or her siblings. The fear of seeing the Busson boy always kept Juliet from seriously contemplating a return home. So that left working at a laundry or a restaurant in Paris, but Varnier had accurately described the descent to prostitution as all but certain for Juliet, and he was not wrong. Each day as she walked to Le Bon Marché or the market, Juliet saw examples of women quietly working day jobs and then paying the bills by doing other "services" to earn money. With a recommendation from Varnier, she might be able to secure a place as a governess with her knowledge of literature and music, but the idea of asking him for anything was appalling to her, so she stewed in her room through spring. The house turned quiet, even with a new resident.

In June, the latest copy of *Le Figaro* appeared on the dining room table. Flipping through the pages, she opened it to the third page to find the marriage announcement of Auguste Marchant to one of his students, Elle Triste. Juliet read the article twice. It referred to the "dark time" Marchant had experienced after the death of his wife and child but that he'd found renewed love with Elle.

That morning, Juliet had come down the stairs to find the place buzzing with workers. Lisette was making sweeping changes to the apartment and had ordered that all fabrics be replaced with softer Italian damasks. Chairs were going out the door with instructions to be reupholstered; new curtains were being hung in the parlor.

Juliet walked to the piano, brushing off the dust that had formed on the black keys since she'd last played. She positioned her fingers over them, not sure what she would play—these piano keys were the only thing that had ever given her solace. She brought her fingers down on a Satie piece. When she finished, she heard clapping and turned to see that two painters had arrived and were looking at her admiringly. Red-faced, she stood and made her way out the door and down the steps.

Juliet walked the entire way to Montmartre, carrying the newspaper in her hand. She found a seat at the Bar Norvins and ordered a glass of absinthe. She'd heard about the dangers of "the Green Hour," but the liquid made her body feel like it was weighed down with stones. Sadly, it was weighed down already. Juliet leaned her head against the wood-paneled wall and closed her eyes. A rough hand shook her awake and she saw a man standing over her.

"You're a beauty." The man was drunk. He looked like a construction worker, and Juliet wondered if he was building the Sacré-Coeur. Juliet looked around the room and noticed several men in his condition. It must have been payday. He confirmed her suspicions. "How much?"

A lady should have been insulted by this remark, but Juliet felt she was no longer a lady—certainly not the lady of the house at Saint-Germain. It had all been an illusion, hadn't it? She was a guest in Varnier's house now, not even a relative, really. Her other fate was this one: pleasing a drunkard with money in his wallet. She considered her original fate, before Varnier had intervened. She'd have married the Busson boy and would have endured horrible things under his control. Varnier had bought her several good years. For that, she was grateful to him. He owed her nothing more. "Another drink." Juliet pointed to the empty glass. "And twenty-five."

The man eyed her. He was repulsive, but Juliet wanted to feel repulsion. She felt nothing. Repulsion was at least something. "Twenty-five? You'd better be worth that."

"I am." She pointed to her empty glass, the last traces of absinthe remaining until she tossed back the glass, draining the contents entirely.

He sat another drink in front of her and Juliet downed the absinthe quickly. This would help. As she headed out the door, Juliet felt oddly free of all of them—Marchant, Busson, and Varnier. At least this was her choosing. With the man following her, she turned the corner and found a space not visible from the street. She held out her hand. "Twenty-five."

He smiled and his two front teeth were missing. Blessedly, the absinthe was hitting her in waves and the taste of the anise was still on her breath. He reached into his pocket, pulled out a coin, and handed it to her. She studied it, more because she thought that is what she should do in this situation, although the weight of the coin felt correct. She unzipped his pants and lifted her skirt. It was a fine dress, the finest in the bar, at least at that hour, and somehow the idea of soiling this dress against the dirty alleyway that stank of urine felt like a proper revenge on Varnier. Expecting to feel disgust as the man pushed into her, Juliet found she felt nothing. The man wasn't quick, but he was not cruel and Juliet was relieved for that at least. The texture of the brick wall cut against her back as the man continued. She could endure this, too. In fact, she'd endured this indignity so easily. As the man zipped up his pants and headed back into the bar, it was this revelation that reaffirmed her decision as to what to do next.

She could feel the man's wet stickiness beginning to run down her leg as she walked around Paris in a daze until she found herself at the Pont Neuf. It was a Thursday night and the Pont Neuf wasn't busy as Juliet climbed on the stone bridge and looked down into the cold black water. This bridge would take her back to the apartment on Saint-Germain and to Lucian, both things she could not bear. With her heavy dress, she knew that once she leapt, there would be no return. Juliet thought she heard fireworks in the distance and she took it as a sign.

"Love, get down from there." It was a man's voice behind her. "Let me help you down."

"*Non*," said Juliet. And it was a curious thing that happened next. Perhaps it was the absinthe, but there was a tingle at the tip of her tongue and Juliet rubbed it against her teeth. And then, from her mouth came certain, exact words, very specific phrasing. "You are going to want to turn around and leave. You'll want to forget you saw me here tonight."

The man laughed, so preposterous was her suggestion as she stood atop the cold stone of the Pont Neuf, but the laughter stopped abruptly and Juliet knew that it meant he'd done just as she'd asked. So sure was she that he'd done as she'd commanded that she didn't even bother to turn, instead focusing her gaze on the dirty, stinking water beneath her.

Perhaps it was the effects of the Green Fairy, but from her vantage point, she swore she could see a hand come out from the Seine to pull her into its blackness. And she was relieved. She would not be alone. And the thought of this comforted her as she leaned out to touch it.

16

Helen Lambert
Washington, DC, June 10, 2012

I was drenched when I woke up. My lungs were wheezing as though I were drowning. Juliet had jumped into the Seine. Wasn't there a statistic about all the people who drowned themselves off the Pont Neuf? I grabbed my iPhone and called my curse "administrator"—which made him sound like the demonic bureaucrat he was. The fact that it was nearly five A.M. thrilled me.

"You are a fucking bastard, you know that, don't you?"

"Good morning, Helen." He sounded groggy and disoriented, which made me happy. "Yes, it is five so I guess that qualifies as morning. As for my being a bastard, you have no idea."

I could hear him shuffling around. "I was up."

"No you weren't."

"No, I wasn't."

"You *married* another woman?"

"Oh," he said. "That's why you're calling. Do you want me to come over?"

"No. I do not want you to come over. I fucking hate you right now. Stay away from me." I considered something that I'd forgotten. "Fuck."

"What?"

"Bastard though you are, I do need a date for this evening."

"I could be busy."

"But we both know you're not."

"I'm not."

"I know. Pick me up around six o'clock. It's a party for an Italian artist, Giulio Russo, at the Italian ambassador's house. Oh, I should mention... Roger will be there."

"Oh, that changes things entirely. I'll definitely be there."

"*She'll* be with him."

"Try not to kill her."

"Very funny. Wear a suit."

"I'm at your service."

"So you keep saying." I hung up the phone.

It was one of those perfect June nights in Washington before the stifling humidity bears down on the city. Up in the hills of Rock Creek Park, the Italian ambassador's house, named Villa Firenze, sat on twenty-two lush, wooded acres. Inside the stone mansion was a blend of Mediterranean meets Tudor with elaborate wood-paneled rooms and stone and tile floors. The house had magnificent views of Washington, so the cocktail reception was held on the blue-green lawn overlooking the woods. After agonizing over the choices in my closet, I decided to wear an Alexander McQueen dress with a white blouse top with bell sleeves and an attached black skirt with a front slit. The entire number was accented with a wide patent-leather belt that pulled it together. It was a striking dress that wasn't going to appear until the 2013 collection. I had gotten close with the Alexander McQueen team in the last year. Topping off the outfit was a McQueen skull clutch. This was the first time I was seeing Roger and Sara in public. I was taking no chances.

In my head, seeing Roger with Sara was distressing, yet equally disturbing were the intense feelings I had for Luke Varner—a man I'd met a little over two weeks ago. It literally felt like yesterday that Juliet had jumped from the Seine; the betrayal from Luke was still raw.

For his part, Luke looked as comfortable in a suit today as he had in 1898 Paris. We swirled around packs of people. Given that Luke was an art dealer, he was very much in his element.

The guest of honor, Giulio Russo, was an Italian painter whose works were large, dark, romantic, and moody. Each painting was a sad scape depicting loss of some sort—love, innocence, life. To stand in front of a life-size Russo painting was to feel pure sadness almost as though he'd dragged you into the scene.

Russo had been making a name for himself in Europe for years, but he was just entering the global art scene in a big way this year with a show in both London and New York. This dinner had been in the works for more than a year, with Roger and I helping to lure him down to Washington. Originally, we had wanted to have him at one of our dinner parties, but those ended when I moved out of the house. Since then, the Hanover had acquired one of his works, and the dinner at the ambassador's was part of the unveiling of a painting featuring a girl about to walk into a lake—the question being whether it was purely for a swim or a more melancholy, final plunge. Knowing it was a Russo, the likely outcome was the latter, but the darkness of the painting drew you into the narrative.

I hadn't seen the painting before the party. Given my dream of Juliet drowning, I found the portrait moving. It had modern-day echoes of Marchant's work except for the fact that behind Russo's beautiful subjects was a darkness. Many of Russo's other works featured elaborate, beautiful settings, but the subject's faces appeared "off" as though they were enduring the beauty around them while aware of something sinister lurking just outside the frames.

Russo himself looked the part with messy black ringlets that just brushed his shoulders and wide brown eyes. Tonight he wore a garnet-red suit with black Gucci loafers, with a black shirt open far enough that you could see the large silver crucifix that lay against his bronzed skin. I was deep in conversation with him when I saw Roger and Sara walk onto the lawn. If I was honest, I felt them before I saw them. Luke's arm came around me and rested lightly on my back even before they came into view, so I know that he had the same sensation. I was grateful for the gesture. For nearly thirty minutes, Roger and I circled each other until we faced each other in conversation.

After the incident in her house when the window had fallen on them, Roger and Sara had broken up for a month, but they were now back together. This was the first time I'd ever seen them together. I'm not quite sure if it was seeing me in public that had him flustered, but we embraced each other stiffly and he gave me a kiss on the cheek. Although I did not like Sara, I still felt tremendous guilt about my role in the death of her mother, Johanna, and I was nicer to her as a result. Curiously, Luke introduced himself by his first name only, and I could tell that Roger was puzzled about my date's identity.

Sara was so tiny that in heels, she barely peeked over Roger's shoulders. Her blond bob was gathered into a "barely there" ponytail, and she wore a snug black sleeveless shift that fell below the knee. The entire look was tidy and polished. Roger wore a look of frustration.

Our entire performance was high theater for the guests around us. There was a sense of everyone holding their breath to see if Roger and I could continue to navigate each other well enough to make everyone comfortable. So we made small talk.

"I bet your phone has been ringing off the hook about the Heathcote interview," said Roger. It was strange. The man who stood in front of me was wooden and sweating even though a cool breeze was coming down through the trees.

As this man stammered to try to find something to say to me, I felt a sense of the larger issues at hand: I was cursed, he was cursed, and my date may or may not be the devil. I did look good, at least, even though the heels of my Louboutins were sinking in the soft grass. I asked him where he was going to hang the Russo painting at the Hanover. To my surprise, Sara answered for them.

As I observed Roger's movements, it seemed that this was a small reenactment of the Paris Opera scene. Had a bearded Roger been wearing a tuxedo, I would have sworn I'd just seen him in 1898 dressed as Auguste Marchant. The two men had never met in this lifetime and yet here was Luke ready to flee with me at a moment's notice if I gave him the smallest signal. I'd witnessed all of Roger's puzzled looks through the years and I knew enough to know that Sara was having trouble reading him tonight. I could tell from her demeanor that it bothered her.

Daylight was fading over the mansion, and the outdoor lights and candles had turned on and begun working overtime. Fortunately, I could hear the distant sounds of dinner chimes. Luke and I excused ourselves.

"Nothing?"

Luke gave me a puzzled look.

"I'm just waiting for the dig on how dull he was."

"I was thinking how dull she was."

And with that wonderful remark, I smiled.

"Seriously, I'm surprised she doesn't have a cardigan on," he said, taking my wineglass.

Luke had a definite way of calming me, whether it was a hand on the small of my back or a perfectly timed sarcastic comment to bring levity to what was an awkward situation. I moved through the sea of party guests with him at my side, shaking hands with a few congressmen's wives, news anchors, restaurateurs, and art gallery owners.

We were seated at a long table with the director of the Washington Opera and his wife. Roger and Sara were on the other side of the room. Dinner began with a rocket lettuce and summer vegetable panzanella followed by porcini-crusted lamb chops and risotto, ending with a chocolate tiramisu for dessert. Wine began to flow.

Luke's understanding of opera was deep, which shocked me. In fact, Luke's knowledge of Mozart operas, Bach concertos, Renaissance painters, Madeira wine, Louis Armstrong, and the city of Oslo, Norway (where the opera director's wife had grown up), was practically bottomless.

"Oslo?" I deadpanned.

"Fabulous city. Efficient airport."

"Oslo?" I cocked my head again.

He shot me a look. But he was exactly the date I needed. By the end of the evening, he practically had three new dinner invitations and a few potential board positions. I found myself staring at him, as engaged as everyone else was. In fact, I nearly forgot Roger until I saw that he and Sara were excusing themselves and leaving early. Reading Roger, I could see that leaving was not his choice, either.

After dinner, Luke and I made our way around the house with its endless hallways and windows dressed in ornate cornices with silk draperies. The rugs and Italian tiles beneath us were all works of art in themselves. Luke led me down a dark hallway into what appeared to be a library, complete with some of Italy's best writers. The room featured two long bisque-colored sofas and a mahogany grand piano.

He pulled out the piano seat. "Sit."

I slid in next to him. "You play?"

"No," he said. "You do."

I laughed. "Don't you get tired of this?"

He coughed and paused before answering. "Never."

"Play me something."

He glanced at me and turned to the keys. I heard the discordant sound of "Chopsticks" forming.

"Nice," I said.

He stopped. "You try."

"I don't think we're supposed to be in here."

"Quit changing the subject. Try."

"I don't play the piano."

"Your mother couldn't afford a piano, even though you wanted lessons like your best friend. She bought you a flute when you were eleven."

I remembered her, struggling to keep us afloat as a single mother. She'd been given an old Armstrong flute by someone at work and had it cleaned and refurbished. She apologized for the battered case. Always keenly aware of our financial struggles, I played the flute and never asked for a piano again. "Then you know I don't play."

"Helen Lambert doesn't play."

"Your point?"

"Juliet LaCompte does play." He took my hand and placed it over the keys. It was a tender gesture and it only infuriated me more because of the feelings it unleashed in me. He aligned my right thumb over middle C. "I think you can handle the left hand."

I shot him a nasty look. "Juliet loved you." I was quick to clarify, "*In Paris.*"

"So that's what this is about." He sighed. "I loved you, too...*in Paris.* But I was afraid of what was brewing between us, I guess. I thought you were too young, too vulnerable."

"You married someone else." As I looked at the keys in front of me, they opened up to me, as if a secret had just been shared. I placed my fingertip on an ivory key and knew exactly how it would sound. With my forefinger, I hit the D, knowing what to expect in tone, but wondering about the action on this instrument. With a sideways glance, I could see Luke watching me intently. I rolled up my sleeves and slammed down on the first chords of Grieg like a girl who hadn't played the piano in a hundred years. Juliet's mind knew the keys intimately, but Helen's muscles weren't used to the delicate finger-work required for the Clementi and Satie pieces that flowed. It was as though Juliet's mind wanted to quickly work through her entire repertoire. I stopped suddenly. "You married someone else."

"I know." He reached out and touched my hand. "I thought Lisette would be a buffer between us. It was my first time as your administrator. As you saw, I fucked the whole thing up."

"You let me down—I trusted you the most." Last night, the pain that Juliet had felt was transferred to me. I swore I could taste the absinthe on my lips; it was that real. I can only describe it as something that resided in my memory alongside my own teenage years. It was as private and as intense as my own dumping at the Bethesda High School senior prom. Now I had Juliet's teenage pain.

"I know what I did. And I can't tell you how delightful it has been watching you marry someone else through our lifetimes together. Cut me some fucking slack, will you? We're not normal."

"Why doesn't Roger remember his life as Auguste Marchant?"

"Well, neither of you are supposed to remember your lives," he said. "You're just supposed to play your parts in the curse, again and again. You're the anomaly."

"Why is that?"

"You're special. I've told you that." He seemed to change the subject. "You don't know what the time is like without you...until you resurface, until you call me. And you always will call me. It's the way the curse works. Until I know you are in this world again, I watch, waiting to see who you will become this time."

"What do you mean, *this time*?"

"You change a little each time depending upon the environment you grew up in—and the times you live in. That's a big part of it, but you're still you."

I thought of Juliet's mother compared with my mother, Margie Connor. Different times, different mothers. He was right. I was different from Juliet and yet we shared the same memories. "What do you do? While you're waiting for me."

"I don't do anything," he said.

"Where are you in the world while you wait for me?"

"You wouldn't understand." He laughed. "I'm not in the *world* as you know it. My purpose is to wait for you. And when I know that you are reborn again, I know that it will be about twenty years or so before you call me into service for you. I set up my next life... finances, homes. I will everything to my son...Lucian Varnier. I'm Lucian Varnier the Fourth. And then I wait until I see you again."

But it had been much longer than twenty years this time. I was nearly thirty-four. "Luke." I closed my eyes absorbing the reality of his life, the cruelty of it. Malique had described Luke as a damned creature—a soldier in the employ of a demon. He was being punished for something and his punishment was—*me*. His employer had been that demon—that thing—that I had seen crawl into Juliet's mother that evening on the kitchen floor. The entire thing was madness.

"You told Juliet you were in the employ of her mother, but that isn't true. Is it?"

"Depends on how you look at it."

From Malique, I had a sense of the basic structure of the curse. "Juliet's mother called on a demon to help her get revenge on Marchant. That is your real employer, isn't it?"

"It is." He purposely changed the subject. "Let's just go away somewhere for a few days while you're working through all of this."

I'd been warned against confiding in him and telling him about traveling to Challans, so I hoped he wouldn't sense the lie I was about to tell him. "I have a business trip in London tomorrow. Three days."

"We only have twelve days until your birthday. Do you have to go?"

"I do."

I looked down at my hands and what they'd just managed to do. This was true, all of it. Luke Varner's crazy story. "I'm going to die on my birthday, aren't I?" My voice cracked a little. "That's why you keep saying we're running out of time, isn't it?"

"Yes," he said softly.

"Do you know what will happen to me?" If I failed in France, I needed to know what would happen.

"It isn't always the same."

"And what will happen to you?"

"I disappear again...and wait."

"Is that what happened to you in Paris? After Juliet...after I jumped off the bridge?"

"Yes. You are my purpose. I have no other reason to be here than looking after you."

"Can I ask you something personal?"

"Of course."

"Is part of your *purpose*, as you call it, loving me?"

"No," said Luke. "I went to extraordinary lengths to distance myself from you in Paris. I told you it wasn't possible for me to love you. I was new and I didn't know how to handle you. As I told you, I failed her."

"What changed?"

"I did." He took my face in his hands and kissed me, slow and deep. The part inside me that belonged to Juliet was brought to tears. My forehead touched his.

"We have so little time now, Red. All I ever want is time with you."

17

Nora Wheeler
New York City, 1932

Clint was taking his time tonight. Norma wished he'd finish so she could send him off. Of course, that wasn't happening until she got him off, so she refocused her energies, hoping this wouldn't be one of the nights he needed his hands around her neck to come.

Norma and Clint had an arrangement. She didn't think about how his short stature and pale stocky body repulsed her at times. He made sure her rent was paid. Before Clint brought her to New York City, Norma Westerman had been on her own—and being on her own at nineteen had been scary. Theater—at least the kind she was doing—didn't pay, and the numbers never added up until Clint. Now they did. Lately, though, this arrangement was messing with her head, blurring the lines between what she was becoming and who she wished she was. It was hard to imagine another year, let alone a lifetime of wearing her legs out dancing all day and Clint wearing out the rest of her at night.

Clint was a theater fixer who took care of "problems" including scandals, abortions, and drunk husbands. He'd found Norma in Akron—where her mother had run a boardinghouse on Dixon Street that catered to musicians.

Norma's mama had an old out-of-tune upright piano in the dining room. Occasionally a boarder with tuning skills would cycle through the house, giving the instrument a new life. After dinner, the boarders would gather around it and Norma would sit in wonder at the singing and tap dancing that would break out, each boarder trying to out-shine the last for the paltry audience. Norma got cheap tap lessons out of it. Something about the instrument haunted her. She showed no interest in playing the piano, even despite her mother's prodding that she could get extra money playing at the Methodist church in town. Norma needed to move—tap and ballet lessons were all she could think about. In New York, those skills were nothing special. Clint found her at a regional theater show.

With her look, he found her a permanent job at the Winter Garden Theatre where he'd placed her as a chorus line girl and set her up in a small apartment. He'd made the terms clear from the beginning, and Norma had wanted out of Akron enough to accept them. In all honesty, she'd had worse terms offered to her by her mother's boy-friends over the years.

But now, Norma wanted more. Clint had contacts at the Holly-wood studios and he'd promised her that he'd set her up for a screen test at MGM, but each time she asked him, he said the time wasn't right. Now, nearly two years into their "arrangement," she knew that Clint was happy with things the way they were. There would be no introductions, and the timing would never be right.

Two years had been the longest Clint had ever stayed with a woman. Norma kept hoping he'd move on to a younger girl, but he remained steadfast that Norma was *his*. At his drunkest, he would unfurl the things that would happen to her if she left him—she could fall in front of a cab, he could cut her insides out and blame it on a crazed lunatic, the accounting went on and on as he got drunker and Norma had no doubt he was creative. Even after his cruelest moments, Clint never apologized. From what Norma had gathered, he'd had a rough childhood—his father abandoned him and his mother when he was a baby. He took care of his mother in an apartment he paid for—for all Norma knew, he could fill up an entire apartment building with the women he paid for in one way or another.

Clint rolled onto his back, pleased with himself. "Get me a drink."

She didn't move fast enough.

"I don't ask you twice."

Norma sighed. Clint was already half drunk, so sex had taken forever with him tonight—a trait he seemed to prize. She was exhausted.

Norma sat up in bed and reached for the black silk robe, but Clint grabbed it from her. "I want to watch your ass while you walk." She knew where this would lead, but she slid out of the bed and walked to the door.

"Stop," he said. Norma turned around.

"Come back and do it again. I don't like the way you did that. It wasn't graceful."

"No," she laughed. "I'm cold." Norma hugged her body.

"I said 'again.'" He twirled his finger and took out a cigarette to light it. "Men look at your ass for a living, sweetheart. I just deserve to see a little more of it since I pay for it."

Norma turned and walked slowly to the door, pausing when she heard him inhale his cigarette. He was satisfied for now. Norma exhaled a little.

In the beginning, she'd pretended she enjoyed herself—it was hard to admit to herself what she was doing, so she convinced herself that she liked—even loved—Clint, but now, she saved the performances for the stage. Her distaste for sleeping with him seemed to excite him all the more and—mixed with the dulling effects of the three whiskeys he'd drunk—made for a very long night and several "attempts" at sex that seemed endless.

She handed him another drink and was ready to get into bed when he shook his head. "Stand there," he commanded. "I never get a good look at you."

Norma stood in front of him and gazed out the window. "You aren't so bad." He maneuvered his cigarette and his drink. "Your tits are too small and you've got a small bump on your nose that I see you try to cover, but your ass and legs are good, at least *for now*." Norma was humiliated that he was assessing her like a Pimlico horse. "You'd have never made it big in Hollywood. I know you think you would have, but you wouldn't have. You think you're better than me, but I saved you from a worse fate, you know. An average-looking girl like you. If not for me, you might be one of those girls in the clubs."

"You mean a whore?" Norma raised her voice. This was a dangerous move.

"It's what you really are, though, anyway," he said, laughing. "You know that, don't you? I could do better than you, you know."

"I know you could." And Norma thought that in this town filled with poor and desperate women, he probably could.

"Then convince me that I shouldn't toss you out of here."

Clint put the drink on the nightstand and Norma crawled under the sheets. She knew that she needed to be smart right now. He'd just opened himself up, in a way. He was bothered by her aloofness and needed to even the score. This was where things could escalate. Clint crawled on top of her and in one movement, the cigarette came down on her cheek and he held it there, the weight of him on top of her. He held her mouth to muffle any sounds. Norma knew the burn would cause a scar; that had been the point. And then Norma felt the hardness of Clint.

It was going to be a very long night.

Norma was the ideal type of dancer, not a smaller girl; nor was she so tall as to be intimidating or gangly. Her auburn hair made her eyes pop from the stage. From years of dancing, she also was able to pick up the more technical, complicated steps that eluded a good percentage of the girls. Plus, everyone was afraid of Clint and it was known that she was his girl, so she rose quickly. But unlike the other girls who leveraged their beauty by entertaining promising businessmen backstage following the show, Norma was off limits. On more than one occasion, Clint had knocked her around and she'd had to use pancake makeup to go out in the daytime. This time it was a burn. She parted her hair on the side until it healed, but the damage wasn't lost on Marvin Walden, the theater director, and although he said nothing about it, he slipped a card in her jacket.

She pulled it out and studied it. It was a card for a Monumental Films talent scout.

"You've got a screen test on Wednesday at two P.M." Walden pulled back her hair. "See if Bettie can get that covered for you. Don't let Clint know about your test. I don't need the trouble."

"Thank you," she said to Marv.

"If that bastard finds out, you won't be thanking me." Marv walked down the hall, his hands in his pockets.

And Norma knew he was correct. If Clint found out, he'd kill her.

The stage was one thing, but Norma hadn't been used to the camera with its harsh lights at her screen test. The test was quick, no more than twenty minutes, and it amounted to her saying her name and turning on the chair so the camera could pick up different angles. The camera guy seemed to spend more time with her than the girl before her, though, and the scout had asked her a lot of questions about Akron. Did she know how to sing? *Yes.* Could she dance? *Yes.* Who was her favorite actress? *Norma Shearer.*

Within a week, Norma received a letter from Monumental with an offer for eight weeks of work for $1,250. Norma had eight weeks to impress the producers at Monumental. If she didn't, she'd be sent home. She'd saved up enough money that she would be able to take care of herself for another two months, but if she couldn't get something in that time period, she'd come back here or go back to Akron—somewhere on her own terms and not subject to someone like Clint. Norma vowed she would never find herself with someone like Clint again.

She was wary of him finding out, though. She had to hide the offer from him until she'd left New York. Her hope was that he'd move on from her quickly. Already, he was out "scouting" regional dancers again, so she might be replaced. Clint enjoyed shocking someone new with his proclivities. Naive women under the age of nineteen were his favorite targets, but there was something about her that he continued to crave. Just to be safe, Norma decided she'd change her name—she would be going to Hollywood not as Norma Westerman, but as Nora Wheeler. She liked the name. People often called her Nora by mistake, and it always thrilled her. The name was more confident than Norma—she was shedding Norma and walking into Nora. The name Wheeler had been her mother's maiden name. Two days before her departure, she bought a train ticket. The trip by train would take four days, first to Chicago and then through Kansas City and then El Paso, Tucson, Phoenix, and on to Los Angeles. Nora needed to be there in five days. She was cutting it close.

It was February and the entire East Coast had been gripped by a harsh winter, so Nora packed two suitcases, wearing a long overcoat that she would really only need through Kansas City. She looked through her wardrobe and picked out several spring dresses and jackets that she would be able to wear. Nora heard the lock on the door and her heart stopped. She shoved the open suitcase under the bed. Clint was supposed to be in Atlantic City tonight, and her train ticket was lying on the table. What was he doing here? Nora scurried to the table to grab the ticket and hide it in her winter coat pocket by the door. Clint emerged through the door, shaking melted snow from his coat.

"I thought you were in Atlantic City?"

"I changed my mind." He shrugged and then coughed. "What? You not happy to see me?"

"Of course I am." Nora wrapped herself around him and gave him a kiss on the cheek. "I'm just surprised, that's all."

"What? You got a fella in here?" He laughed, placing his hat on the coatrack. Nora could see the ticket peeking from her coat pocket so she steered him away, getting him a whiskey. "If you do, he's a dead fella."

Clint's unexpected arrival could mean problems for Nora's plan. She had to be on the seven forty-three A.M. train, but if Clint slept over—and he often did—he wouldn't leave for the theater until late morning. Clint took his drink and pulled her by the arm into the bedroom, and despite the fact that no one was in the apartment, he kicked the bedroom door shut behind them.

As the bed rocked, Nora considered the empty suitcase under them. He would hurt her badly if he found it.

After he'd finished, Nora got up and wrapped her robe around her. She took his empty whiskey glass and poured him another drink. This time, however, she dug a bottle of sleeping pills out of her purse, opened one capsule into the drink, and shook it until it dissolved. And then on impulse, she added a second pill. What with the sex, liquor, and sleeping pills, he should sleep soundly. She tasted the drink and couldn't pick up a hint of the pills.

An hour later, Nora lay awake as Clint snored softly. The longer he slept, the deeper he'd fall. He wasn't a light sleeper. When his snoring was steady, Nora slid the open suitcase out on her side of the bed and pulled a few items that she knew she'd need, feeling her way for them in the dark and hoping she was getting the right things. Clint turned over and she slid the suitcase back under the bed until she heard his rhythmic breathing resume. She dressed quickly in the dark and secured one latch on the suitcase, watching Clint's lack of movement, and then she tiptoed into the living room and shut the second latch. She gathered her purse and her coat, feeling for the ticket in her pocket and only turning the doorknob when she felt the paper in her hand. Sliding the suitcase out the door, she figured she'd buy anything else that she needed on the road. She put her shoes on only when she was out in the hallway, softly shutting the door, but not bothering with the lock. With any luck, Clint would just think she had an appointment in the morning and hadn't bothered to wake him. It would buy her time. Only if he decided to go to the theater would he learn that she'd quit with no forwarding address. There was a chance he wouldn't even realize she was gone for more than a day. Then, even if he tried to find her, it would take him several weeks. She'd been careful to not tell anyone, except Marv Walden, where she was going. By the time Clint finally pieced it together, it wouldn't matter. She'd have a career in Hollywood. Before she shut the door, she made sure she had the envelope with cash in her purse. It was thick with what she'd cleared from her savings.

Nora hurried out of the door, and the cold hit her. She'd be glad to leave this all behind. Only when she was in the warm taxi headed to Pennsylvania Station did she finally relax. As she boarded the train, she looked over her shoulder one last time, holding her suitcase tight against her and then looking out the window until the car pulled away from the station. Once the train was in motion on the way to Chicago, she slept soundly. In Chicago she boarded the Golden State line at ten fifteen P.M., which had her in Kansas City the following morning. She looked through everything she'd packed and realized that she hadn't been able to pack her curlers, face creams, and stockings. She'd have to buy those things once she got to Los Angeles. By the following evening, the landscape was changing to desert as the train entered New Mexico. The desert air was cold, which was a surprise to Nora, but by the time the train stopped at Chandler, she had opened the window to let the dry, warm breeze in. She hadn't had another person in her sleeping car since Kansas.

Arriving at the Los Angeles Union Terminal just after dinner, Nora got a taxi to the Grove Hotel, which was walking distance to Monumental Studios. As she rode in the cab through the neighborhoods, she was struck by the colorful bungalows with perfectly clipped yards, palm trees, and that smell.

"What is that smell?" she asked the cabdriver. It was a sharp scent like an herb with a sweet finish.

"Eucalyptus trees."

The next morning, when Nora cracked open the balcony door, she was greeted by a soft, sultry sun and carefully trimmed hedges mixed with fat palm trees and the smell of warm leaves. The air reminded her of an inviting bath.

Nora was scheduled to meet with Harold Halstead, the number two man at Monumental Studios, who had plucked Nora's screen test out of the pile. His assistant, Penny Bentley, had instructed Nora to be early for their nine thirty A.M. meeting.

At nine thirty-one, Harold Halstead sat behind a desk that was as big as a concert hall piano and pushed thick glasses up the bridge of his nose. Reed-thin, he had an anxious look like a cat ready to pounce. "You've got something…magical. I can't quite put my finger on it, but Marv Walden and I go way back and he says he's never seen anyone like you." The little man slid down in his brown leather chair, and Nora had to straighten her back to see him across his desk.

"Marv Walden talked to you?"

"He called me. Insisted I hire you."

Nora was touched. She had been a reliable girl for Marv, but he gave not a single hint that he felt she was anything special.

Halstead stood up, walked around, and leaned in close to look at Nora's face. The burn had scabbed over and left a smaller blemish. "Billy Rapp has a picture he's working on right now, *Train to Boston*."

"I just got off the train from New York if that helps," quipped Nora.

"You've got a great voice, too." Harold Halstead studied her up and down. "But I need a blonde. Keep talking to me. Tell me about Marv."

Nora reached up and touched her dark-red hair. Her shoulder-length red locks and long legs had been her signature in New York. "Marv was swell. He hired me from a regional theater company where I was performing in Akron."

"Are you a Midwest girl?"

"I'm from Akron. My mom ran a boardinghouse."

"Guess the troupe didn't take you very far if you started and ended up in Akron?"

"Maybe I wasn't trying to get away."

Halstead smiled at her quick delivery. He folded his arms and leaned them on the desk. "I need a blonde."

"How blond do you need me to be?"

"Have Penny set you up with Max." Then Harold Halstead changed his mind about something and picked up the black phone himself. "Get Eve on the phone." He waited, looking out open balcony doors that faced Melrose. "Eve," he said when a voice barked on the other end. "I have a young lady here for Billy Rapp's next picture. I need a blonde. Do you have time this afternoon?" He paused and then studied Nora, pulling down his glasses. "Not exactly. No. Not exactly."

Norma could hear someone—a woman—speaking quickly on the other end of the line. Halstead kept nodding. "Well...just do your best." Then Harold Halstead laughed. "Of course. I *owe* you." Norma could hear the voice on the other end of the phone laughing.

Once he hung up the phone, Halstead scribbled furiously on a piece of paper and handed it to her like a doctor would a prescription. The note read *1660 Highland Avenue. 1 P.M.*

"What is this?"

"That, my dear, is the address for Max Factor."

"The makeup?"

"*The man.* Have Penny take you down to see Eve Long right now. She's Monumental's chief hairstylist. She'll get you blond—butter blond! Then go and see Max Factor, who'll blend the rest. Come back tomorrow morning, same time, and we'll see what we've got to work with." He tapped the note with long fingers. "No promises, though, mind you."

Nora placed the paper in her purse. "I understand."

Twenty-four hours later, a butter-blond Nora Wheeler returned to see Harold Halstead. That Penny didn't even recognize her thrilled Nora. She'd spent the entire morning fumbling with the white screw-off case for Pan Stik that was designed to complement her new coloring. The transformation had been shocking. All of Nora's new makeup cases were blue—the Max Factor color for blondes. Her hair had also been cut to a modern, chin-length bob with soft curls. Nora had slept on a satin-covered pillow that Eve had given her to keep the curls fresh. Eve had liked her and let her borrow a blue suit from the costume department. Nora capped off her new look with tortoiseshell cat's-eye sunglasses she'd picked up and new faux-crocodile pumps. As Nora studied herself in the mirror, there was no resemblance to Norma Westerman—and there never would be again.

"My God," exclaimed Halstead, looking up from his papers. He began furiously dialing. "Is Billy Rapp on set today? See if he is available. He needs to see *this*."

Harold Halstead made small talk, asking where Nora was living. Nodding, he began pulling out slips of paper from his center desk drawer and writing down names of landlords, tailors, restaurants. She was so engrossed in all of his suggestions that she didn't see that the door had opened and a tall man with wavy brown hair and an aristocratic air had come to stand beside her. Halstead shot up from his chair, arm extended.

"Billy." Harold Halstead smiled broadly and patted the man on the arm with his free hand. "Here is your Vivian for *Train to Boston*. Billy Rapp, meet *Nora Wheeler*. What do you think?"

Nora looked up and then rose, straightening her skirt. She knew this was her moment. She smiled slowly, not giving everything away, and extended her hand almost shyly. "Pleased to meet you, Mr. Rapp."

"Call me Billy." The man smiled and the biggest green eyes Nora had ever seen stared back at her, amused. "And where might Harold have found you?" When he smiled, he had a dimple on one cheek—the left.

"New York."

"Broadway?"

"Keep going."

Billy Rapp laughed but didn't shake Nora's hand. Suddenly Nora was concerned that she'd not measured up. Maybe she had been average, just as Clint had always insisted.

"Screen test is amazing, too...not just the look," added Halstead. "We worked on the look." Halstead winked at Nora.

Billy studied Nora for a moment, not even being kind about looking her up and down like a coat he was buying. Nora was getting used to the fact that her body and her face were her product and people in Hollywood made no apologies about studying it. "You're her." Billy Rapp smiled and nodded. "Halstead, you're a genius. You have no idea."

Nora felt uneasy, like there was something unspoken between Halstead and Billy Rapp and that this wasn't going to be as simple as a part in a movie.

18

Helen Lambert
Washington, DC, June 11, 2012

My pillow was a bloody mess when I woke up. The nosebleeds were getting worse and my head was pounding. I was upset that the alarm clock had stopped Nora in Halstead's office.

The plane would take off for London at five P.M. from Dulles Airport. Just in case Luke was suspicious, Mickey had suggested we fly to London to cover our tracks and then take the Eurostar to Paris. Once in Paris, he'd found a train to Challans. I'd been researching the LaCompte family and found that Juliet's brother, Marcel, had died in the Great War. Her father had remarried and had three more children with his second wife. Her sister, Delphine, seemed more elusive. After searching the records, I discovered a marriage certificate in the church between Juliet's sister and Michel Busson. I stared at the screen for several minutes trying to register that I had left my younger sister to suffer my fate. She'd had three children with Michel Busson. I printed out a bunch of records on the grandchildren.

Before I began packing, I did a search on Nora Wheeler. There were 5,654 hits. I pulled up a vintage Hollywood website and clicked on the Nora Wheeler biography. I inhaled audibly as I saw a variation on my face as well as that of the girl who contemplated the step in Marchant's painting, now hanging in the Hanover Collection. It wasn't my face exactly, nor was it the girl from Marchant's painting, but that was mostly because each was the product of its time. Style played tricks on the eyes, making two identical women look similar—like cousins. Nora Wheeler had a platinum-blond bob that fell at her chin. The light eyes peered out from heavy mascara. In the picture, she was dressed in a silk negligee on a sofa, her arm twisted in the same way as *Girl on Step*. The parallel between the two images was shocking.

A few other photos on websites featured stills from *The Hidden Steps* and *A Million Kisses*, which were widely considered to be Nora Wheeler's best roles. In the final photo I found, she was attending a party at the Cocoanut Grove at the Ambassador Hotel with Billy Rapp. I leaned in close to the screen to look at Rapp. He was tan with golden-brown hair, but the man was definitely a version of the Auguste Marchant from my dreams as well as Roger from my present life. Nora was dressed in what appeared to be a silk dress that clung to her along with a white mink coat. I looked over at a photo of Roger and me from Kauai. The two women could certainly be related, and it struck me for the first time how much Roger seemed to resemble both Billy Rapp and a young Auguste Marchant.

I printed out a few biographies and other research material on Nora Wheeler and stuffed them into my bag.

Mickey was waiting for me at Dulles. Our entire trip was less than seventy-two hours, so I wasn't sure how much sleep we'd get once we landed.

I pulled out the biography of Nora Wheeler and began to read it.

Nora Wheeler
Born: June 22, 1910, in Akron, Ohio;
Disappeared and presumed dead July 24, 1935,
near Long Beach, California

Nora Wheeler, born Norma Evelyn Westerman, was an American actress who had minor roles in such films as *Train to Boston* (1932), *The Hidden Steps* (1933), *Max and Me* (1933), and *A Million Kisses* (1934). She was discovered in an Akron G. C. Murphy store by a New York producer and worked as a chorus girl for two years before landing a contract for Monumental Films in Hollywood, eventually landing small parts in films. While she received good reviews for her work in *A Million Kisses* and *The Hidden Steps*, produced by her husband William "Billy" Rapp, she never became a leading actress. In 1935, her husband was found dead in their home from a gunshot wound to the head. The death was ruled a suicide, but there were suspicions that Rapp may have been murdered. The scandal proved too much for Wheeler's Hollywood career and she was never offered another role. While the case of Billy Rapp was never solved, Steve Mason, in his book *Hollywood Murders of the 30s*, concludes that Rapp did not commit suicide but was murdered by his male lover, actor Ford Tremaine, who according to several accounts confessed to the murder on his deathbed. Rapp's biographer, Beth Powell, however, suspects that the director may have been killed by a former associate of his wife's. Further adding to the mystery, Wheeler disappeared off the coast of Long Beach when a boat she was traveling on capsized. Wheeler's body was never recovered and she was presumed dead, although unconfirmed sightings of her continued until 1944. On her deathbed, famed stage actress Lillibet Denton claimed to have spoken to the actress in a Paris bookstore but could recall no real details of the encounter, so the story was largely dismissed.

We were off the Labrador coast at a cruising altitude of thirty-six thousand feet when a wave of sleep hit me.

19

It was a Mediterranean breeze coming in from the Santa Monica Beach Club that made Nora wish she'd brought a sweater. She still couldn't get used to the intensity of the Southern California sun throwing off harsh shadows like they captured in the silent films. And yet in an instant there could be a breeze off the ocean that could freeze her to the bone.

Shielding her eyes, she got a good look at Billy.

The hallway was long. Billy Rapp walked toward Nora slowly, taking his time and smoking his cigarette a little too deeply. Billy knew she was there—waiting—but he didn't acknowledge her. It wasn't his way. She could see the light fabric of his trousers and cotton shirt billowing against the ocean breeze. With wavy golden-brown hair and those piercing eyes, Billy could have been a star in his own right, but that wasn't his style, either. Billy ran hot and didn't like to feel *owned* and make no mistake, the studio owned everyone—including its directors. He wanted his films to be realistic, not some glossed-over studio version or vaudeville comedy. Somehow he had convinced himself that he had some measure of control over his work. Today Billy's soft eyes and full lashes were hidden behind a pair of tortoiseshell sunglasses. Nora closed her eyes. Something about this moment—the way Billy approached her, with his feet softly hitting the Spanish tiles, raking his hair with his left hand and finishing off the cigarette with his other, not to mention the open door that led to the blue ocean framed around him—she knew she should keep this image locked away in her mind, because both it and Billy would be fleeting. Billy took the breath out of her. Even while she was with him there was a strange nostalgia for him, as though she knew that she'd never keep him. Losing Billy felt familiar to her, like a gunshot wound that had scarred over but never fully healed. He was a haunting figure—a loner who seemed to barely tolerate anyone around him, her included. With her, he just pretended better.

He gathered her in his arms when he reached her. Theirs wasn't an equal relationship. He was the director and she his muse. They'd done two films together—*Train to Boston* and *The Hidden Steps*—but she would not appear in his new film, *Starlight Circus*. He'd passed on her for the lead, giving the part to Jayne McKenna. Halstead had let the news slip, but Billy didn't know she'd already been told. Nora wondered how he'd choose to tell her. Would he just be straight about it? Come clean and tell her that he'd passed on her for Jayne McKenna? Would he tell her why? Or would he blame Halstead?

Nora wore a sleeveless tangerine dress with a twist at the neck. She looked up. It was only two o'clock in the afternoon, but it seemed like the sun was already setting. Unlike everyone else, she always thought the California evening sun was a sad spectacle—one of the last places in the world to see the sun of the day. A final bow.

They walked arm in arm to the club and a few couples nodded at them as they passed. Nora was used to getting recognized, although she wasn't a big star. She'd spent less than five minutes onscreen as the victim in Billy's film *Train to Boston* and then fifteen minutes onscreen in the second film, *The Hidden Steps*, playing the shrill and

manipulative first wife. Both roles had been small, yet memorable.
She'd earned a raise six months ago, enough to purchase a Spanish-
style house on a curvy street near the newly constructed Hollywood
Bowl. From a distance, Nora had a view of Mount Lee with the HOLLY
part of the Hollywoodland sign visible. New houses were popping
up everywhere around town, and when the windows were open, the
sound of hammers started early in the morning. Nora's house was a
new Spanish bungalow with rounded doors, cathedral ceilings, and
wood beams. Outside, a fat palm tree stood at odds with a skinny
pine resembling Hal Roach's Laurel and Hardy. On the beige stucco
wall, two lanterns burned at the entrance with a round-topped door
and two stucco planters with overflowing and untended plants. Peeking out above the brown garage doors with brown beam posts was a
double Juliet balcony. It was a romantic house with a three-car garage,
although Nora only had one—a black 1931 Chrysler Roadster with a
white top that she'd purchased from a dealership on Sunset. Inside, the
house overflowed with clothes and books. Nora had everything. And
yet the one thing it seemed that she couldn't have was Billy Rapp.

On her first shoot working with Billy during the filming of *Train to
Boston*, she'd watched him in silence until he called for her. Her part
in the film took only two days to shoot. But she'd been a surprise hit.
She'd done another small part as a gangster's girlfriend in another film
with another director. It wasn't a comedic part like the molls that Jean
Harlow played, but the tragic, ruined girlfriend. She'd been a surprise
hit in that film, too. Billy had requested her again for *The Hidden Steps*,
this time as the first wife. The second shoot with him took one week.
Billy never spoke to her off the set, not even when passing her as she
walked from the dressing rooms to the studio. He was an intimidating
figure, quick to anger and prone to storming off the set, but what he
created was ahead of its time and everyone at Monumental knew it.

As a director, Billy was a true visionary, but that often made dealing with everyday studio employees difficult. The sight of Halstead walking from the set to Rapp's office to cool him down was almost a daily occurrence.

Nora's voice had been an asset to her as she tested for parts. After the release of *The Jazz Singer* in 1927, several actresses who'd had lucrative careers in silent films had failed to make the transition, so Nora's timing couldn't have been more perfect. Her voice was deep and sultry from all the years of voice lessons in Akron. It was too sultry for an ingenue role, so she'd play the femme fatale or the bad girl. With her looks, Nora was a chameleon who could straddle dramatic and comedy pieces. In the past eighteen months, she'd watched fame surround her and she'd been close to it, but had never been given a starring role. When she was passed over for WAMPAS Baby Star of 1933, she'd decided that she'd had enough waiting. She went to Halstead to plead for a better part—a shot. He gave her a card with an address written on it and told her to be there by six P.M. and to look her best.

Four hours later, Nora arrived at a party in Beverly Hills that was in full swing. As she walked through the door, Nora understood what type of party she had been invited to. The men were all executives at Monumental as well as a select group of the "Top Theater Executives of 1933" from around the country. And the women—all young— were clearly there for one purpose: to entertain. There wasn't a wife in sight, but Nora noticed that the serving staff was in heavy rotation for drinks. Nora's face flushed. So this is how it was going to be? She'd hoped that Halstead had been different, but her good reviews were nothing to him. She decided to grab some hors d'oeuvres and a glass of champagne since she had no food in her house. With a plate of deviled eggs, Nora found a quiet corner and sank into a chair.

"Aren't you supposed to be out there shining?"

"That's what the sun is for." Nora took a bite of a delicious deviled egg. She'd be going back for seconds. Nora looked up ready to dismiss whoever was standing there. She found a tall man standing above her, blocking the sun. There was something familiar and precise about his voice. "I think there was a mistake with my invitation."

As the man lowered himself onto the chair next to her, she could make out the sunglassed Billy Rapp, his wavy hair tamed with a pomade. She could see the hint of a sunburn on his forehead. He leaned toward her. "I doubt there was a mix-up."

Nora looked down, stung.

He read her expression precisely. "I didn't mean to offend you." He looked over at the partygoers. "I just meant Halstead knows *exactly* who he's inviting here...that's all."

Nora watched two young girls being pawed by sweating executives. "That offends me." Nora stood up. "Halstead offends me."

"Well, you can't leave." He reached out and tugged at her arm. "If you leave, you'll be branded."

"But I'll have my dignity, won't I?"

"I didn't know you could cash dignity at the bank these days. No studio will touch you. Didn't you just buy a house?" He stood up and took her hand. "Come on. We'll make an appearance and give them what they want. You're an actress, right? We all have to act." Billy Rapp led Nora to the pool where they were visible to everyone. As the sun began to fade and the drinks circulated more frequently, he monopolized Nora's time with small talk. They found out they'd grown up near each other, him in Youngstown, Ohio. "My father worked in the steel mill," said Billy. "He hates what I do. Tells me that I won't be able to get on a shift soon if I don't come to my senses."

As he stood and looked down at her, his trousers billowing in the soft breeze, Nora had a strange déjà vu. "Did you ever paint?" It came out bluntly, and she figured it must be the champagne.

"I tried once," said Billy. "But I saw images that were moving rather than stagnant. That's my passion. Blending sound and image. Using the silences, the spaces."

He smoothly took a cigarette out of the case and pointed it at her. "You know you've got something. It isn't just beauty." Billy scanned the room pointing his cigarette. "There is plenty of that around here. But you...you *command* a scene. You're effervescent, but not like every twenty-year-old that comes off the bus because she's been told she's beautiful. It wasn't Halstead's makeover, either. I pulled your original test tape."

"You did?" He'd never shown interest in her on set, so the fact that he'd done research on her was flattering.

"Your voice and your presence. You stole my last picture and you did it just by walking on the set. Halstead sees it, too. I'm not sure why he sent you here."

"Why are you here?"

Billy held his glass in front of him. "These are the men who finance and distribute my films. Shall we?"

"Then why me?"

"Did you ask him for anything recently?" Billy shrugged. "Everything comes with a price in this town, remember that." And Nora had, indeed, asked Halstead to be considered for better films.

She took his arm and they made the rounds, talking to the clusters of executives, each with a nubile ingenue dripping from his arm. Billy kept his arm around her waist as they circled, and Nora could sense the envy from some of the girls who assumed she would be going home with him.

They passed a piano—a shiny, black lacquer Steinway—and Nora touched it. The wood gave off an electricity, a shock that made her jump. She turned and studied the instrument. She'd hated the piano in her mother's living room, but this one was different—it called to her. A slight tingle began on the little finger of her right hand. She studied it to see if she'd pricked it on a splinter, but the skin was smooth. Soon the tingling had spread to her forefinger.

"Is something wrong?" Billy turned to see she'd paused at the piano. "You play?"

She shook her head. "Do you?"

"A little bit." He slid the bench out and sat down. He played a ragtime song, a simple composition. "My mother taught me," he said. "I also know a fair amount of hymns but I'll save those for some other setting." Billy wasn't a very good piano player; his phrasing was choppy as he struggled to plunk out the keys by memory.

Nora sat down next to him and pondered the confusing set of keys in front of her. Fanning her slim fingers out, she moved them into position. It was the right hand that began first. She plucked out a melody, her brain having no idea what her fingers were doing. The tingle had spread to her left thumb, and the fingers on her left hand pushed on the combination of keys. A beautiful opening melody poured out of them.

"You said you didn't play."

Soon people migrated around them. Nora had no idea how it was happening, but everything but these keys fell away from her and she concentrated on something that she knew to be Satie's *Gnossienne No. 3*. After she'd finished the Satie, she played two songs in succession—more upbeat allegros—and found Billy looking at her.

He began the clapping when she was finished. "That was brilliant. Yeah, you don't play." He laughed. "You're way to modest for this town, Nora Wheeler."

She faced him and smiled, knowing that—just for a moment—she owned the room. "Can we get out of here?"

Billy didn't argue with her this time.

The valet pulled Rapp's Pierce-Arrow Phaeton convertible into the drive. Nora had never seen such a magnificent car. Cream with two-tone brown accents and a side-mounted spare tire. Billy delighted in telling her the car had an eight-cylinder engine.

"Where to?" Billy turned to her.

"I don't know," Nora stammered, studying the cream upholstery in the car. "This is stunning."

He smiled. "We're not dressed well enough for the Trocadero tonight. How about we go to the Derby?"

Nora nodded, not knowing what that meant.

Billy pulled up to a Spanish-style restaurant on North Vine, and Nora understood from the neon signs that they were going to the Brown Derby. Walking into a place like the Brown Derby on Billy Rapp's arm would mean something. Nora grabbed her purse and began searching for a mirror. Billy looked over at her. "I look a mess," she said.

"You look great. You've been burned from the sun today...that and the cocktails you downed at the party have given you a glow."

"Oh no. I'm glowing?" Nora pawed through her purse, not finding her gold mirror.

Billy took the lipstick from Nora's fingers and opened the tube. "Here." He screwed up the tube. "Look at me."

Nora gave him an exaggerated pout, and he dabbed the lipstick on her lips like a painter then wiped the stain off with his fingertip several times until he was pleased. "What else do you have in there?"

Nora handed him pancake stick and some blush. Given it was night, Billy was relying on the neon lights from the Derby to illuminate her face. He opened the tubes and studied her features, dabbing and wiping in smooth, expert movements.

He smoothed her hair and held her chin in position, looking at his handiwork. Nora met his eyes for a moment, but Billy was looking at her as he would if she were on film, not in front of him. Finally, pleased with what he saw, he tossed the compacts and tubes back in her purse. "They need to bleach your hair more."

His comment caught her off guard. "Excuse me?"

"You'd pop on the screen more if your hair was a whiter tone."

"Like Harlow."

"No, that's too harsh, too babydoll, more like early Joan Crawford—almost platinum. Your hair should be longer and your makeup smokier. We want to make you look dangerous. It matches your voice." Billy was studying her. "I'll have Halstead arrange it tomorrow."

After they stepped out of the Phaeton, Nora caught her reflection in the mirror. Her cheeks were flushed, but Billy had downplayed her lips and had put some color on her eyelids. Contrary to what Nora had expected he'd done—adding the harsh shading typical of film makeup—to her surprise the effect he'd achieved in a car with poor lighting was one of an overall healthy glow, like she'd been at the beach all day. He had a great eye.

"Let's make sure Louella sees us," he said over his shoulder. "That'll get her off my back for a while." Nora wasn't quite sure what Billy meant by the comment, but that Hedda Hopper and Louella Parsons, the Hollywood gossip columnists who were regular fixtures, would be seeing her with Billy tonight could propel her out of obscurity.

Inside, the restaurant was buzzing. The dark paneling framed dozens of haphazardly drawn caricatures of famous actors and actresses. Nora strained her neck to see them and to keep up with Billy, who was following the maître d' at a good clip. He suddenly stopped to shake the hand of a man and his wife seated snugly together sharing a plate in a booth for four. After quick conversation, they walked on. Nora caught the profile of the woman and only then did she realize who it was.

"That was Norma Shearer." She tugged Billy's arm, pulling him closer to her conspiratorially.

"*And* Irving Thalberg."

"Of course you'd only pay attention to the director."

Billy's hands were in his pockets and he turned and shrugged. He looked like he belonged here. As they were seated in the booth, Nora leaned in. "Do you come here a lot?"

"Sometimes." Billy expanded his body in the booth, draped his arms over the back, and scanned the room. He leaned in and whispered, "I know you're going to get really excited about this, so try to stay calm."

"What is it?"

"Not a what." He took out a cigarette and lit it. "A who. Carole Lombard."

"Lombard?" Nora's voice blurted out a little louder than she wanted. "Where?"

Billy nodded behind Nora and she spun around to see the blond actress seated two booths behind them. If Nora had an idol, it was Carole Lombard. She was animated, telling a story to an attentive man with a thin mustache. Her golden hair was darker than it appeared onscreen. Nora could see the actress's blue eyes and coral lipstick as she turned her head toward Nora. Nora looked away. "Who is she with?"

"William Powell," said Billy. "They just got divorced, but the talk around town is that they're getting back together."

Nora ordered another cocktail and didn't realize how hungry she was until the scalloped chicken à la king arrived. Billy carved away at the mountain of roast prime rib and pointed out other studio executives around the room. Upon seeing someone standing up to leave his booth, he frowned.

"What's wrong?"

"Howard Hawks." Billy sniffed. "He's Lombard's cousin and was loaned out to Columbia to do comedy." He said the word *comedy* like Hawks had been diagnosed with something terminal.

Nora turned to see a thin man talking to Powell and Lombard before waving and heading toward the door. "You don't like comedy?"

"I don't want my career to be defined by anything that isn't serious or realistic. I'm looking at doing a war picture next."

"But people like to escape for a little bit," offered Nora, thinking about films like Marie Dressler's *Emma* and *Prosperity*. "There's nothing wrong with that, is there?"

"It just isn't true art the way that I see it." Billy brushed some crumbs from the table and ordered the cherries flambé and two coffees when the waiter came to remove the plates. "Hawks is overrated if you ask me. Say, have you been to the Cocoanut Grove yet?"

Nora shook her head.

"You'd like it. Phil Harris is the band leader and he has a nice show. We should go tomorrow night."

Nora wasn't sure if it was the earlier sun, the four cocktails she'd drunk, or Billy, but she found she couldn't speak.

He sat back and nodded. "People haven't been very nice to you in the past, have they?"

Nora looked down. "I'm not sure what you mean."

"I think you know exactly what I mean." Billy was about to say more when the waiter arrived with the flambé and lit the dessert at their table. Nora smiled at Billy, amazed at the cherries on fire in front of them and the perfect day she'd had with him.

Nora was still watching the flaming cherries when she spotted his stocky figure walking toward her. Her face flushed and her heart began to beat. Instinctively, she touched her face where the scar from the cigarette burn had finally faded. The breath left her and she felt something she hadn't felt for nearly a year: fear.

"If it isn't Norma Westerman. Don't you look different? I hardly recognized you. All blond now." Clint looked between her and Billy, sizing up the situation. Clint hadn't changed much. Maybe he was a little wider in the middle with a touch of gray at the temples, but his dark-brown eyes still gave little away. "I'd heard you'd moved here to become a big star."

Billy seemed to read something in Nora's body language because he interrupted the monologue that Nora was sure was about to pour out of Clint's mouth.

"That's great that you're an old friend of my girl, here."

Nora could see Clint bristle at Billy calling Nora "my girl." It was brilliant and she could have kissed him for it.

"It's good to see you, Clint." But Nora didn't extend her cheek for a customary kiss. "I'm glad you're well. How's New York?"

"I wouldn't know." He smiled. "I'm here in Los Angeles now. Working for Palladium Studios. I'll be sure to look you up. We need to catch up." It was a threat and Nora knew it. Clint nodded and walked on past her table.

"Who was that?" Billy took a spoonful of cherry dessert and shoved it in his mouth. "You look like you've seen a ghost."

"He's a very bad man," said Nora, pushing her coffee away. She let Billy finish the dessert—she'd lost her appetite.

"Wonder what he's doing for Palladium Studios?" Billy was asking if Clint was a director.

"He keeps things out of the newspaper," said Nora.

"Oh," said Billy, understanding what kind of man Clint was. "A fixer."

Nora sniffed. "Not sure I've ever seen him actually *fix* anything."

The next night, Billy accompanied Nora to the Cocoanut Grove at the Ambassador Hotel and the Trocadero supper club the following Friday. While Nora liked the statuesque palm trees and music at the Grove, the Café Trocadero on Sunset with its crêpes Suzette and Grand Marnier soufflé became her favorite. Monumental's costume designer, Inez London, began to loan Nora dresses for her dinners. Nora and Billy were getting noticed in the gossip columns, and that delighted Halstead.

But Nora was cautious. Clint was in town, and Billy Rapp was the only thing that would keep him away from her. Clint was like a dog. If he thought she "belonged" to someone else, he might stay away. She needed to keep Billy between them.

It was helpful that the gossip columns covered them nonstop. And Billy, for all his reluctance to go along with the studios, seemed thrilled at the constant publicity their romance stirred in the papers. If the columns were right, Billy Rapp would soon propose to her. Yet each night Billy pulled the Phaeton up to her driveway, opened the door, and kissed her on the cheek before driving off. Nothing more.

The studio was thrilled with the attention that the relationship was getting from the press, so they encouraged her to develop a close alliance with Inez London. At their first fitting, Inez hesitated, indicating that clothes would look better on Nora if she were ten pounds thinner. Sipping bouillon for a week until she felt faint, Nora went back to Inez noticeably thinner. The costumer was impressed with Nora's determination, picking out five outfits for her each week then, as Nora's stature rose, loaning out some of her best costumes. While she took most of Inez's suggestions, Nora also had a great sense for pattern cuts and fabrics, often recommending a longer length for a trumpet skirt or a bias cut on a gown, and she'd return to find that Inez had incorporated her suggestions.

Billy insisted that Nora lighten her hair. The studio was reluctant at first, but Billy met her at the salon, himself, and made his case. The look was a shade up from platinum. Now, when she walked into a room, she was stunning.

Four months went by without any contact from Clint. Halstead had loaned her out for another film, but her best shot at a leading role was Billy's new film, *Starlight Circus*, starring opposite Ford Tremaine. When she mentioned it to Halstead, he became quiet.

"Take it up with your boyfriend," said Halstead.

"He's not my boyfriend and I did take it up with him," said Nora. "He won't answer me. Now I'm taking it up with you."

"I don't think there is a role available." Halstead didn't meet Nora's eyes, and the slight stung. Not only was there no starring role for her in *Starlight Circus*, but it seemed there was no role at all.

Now, at the Santa Monica Beach Club, Nora and Billy sat at the bar. She ordered a tomato juice and vodka. Billy wasn't drinking these days, which was probably advisable since he tended to brawl when he'd had too many. He drank a cup of steaming black coffee quickly.

"About *Starlight Circus*—"

"Halstead said you knew."

Nora was surprised that he'd cut to the chase so quickly and also angry that Halstead hadn't given her the upper hand in his betrayal, if only for a few minutes. "I'm just disappointed, I guess."

"You aren't right for the role."

This remark stung her more than she expected. Not being "right" for a role was personal. "And *Jayne McKenna* is?"

"She'll get along better with Ford."

"How would you know how Ford and I would get along? You've never tested us together. Have I not been your best friend...your drinking buddy? Have I not heard your drunken wailings at all hours...on the phone...in my front lawn...against Hawks...Welles. You have more enemies than friends. Maybe you should take better care of your friends!"

"I didn't know you *required* anything in return for your friendship?"

"I expected not to be slighted by my friend when he decided to cast something big, something important. I guess I expected loyalty from you!"

"You aren't right for the role." He stared into his cup.

"You keep saying that. Look at me, Billy!"

He met her eyes and was witness to her swollen nose and running makeup; she'd begun to cry.

"I know what roles are right for you, Nora. This one isn't, okay? You and Ford. It wouldn't work." He shook his head. "The chemistry would be no good."

"Why?" For a moment Nora wondered if he was jealous of Ford Tremaine.

"I just know." He muttered the reply and she strained to hear while he took a long sip of coffee. "That's all."

Nora was silent.

"Halstead got you something big, as a favor to me."

"I don't want your charity. Yours or Halstead's."

"You just said you didn't want to be passed over."

"By you! I thought I'd *earned* something with you. It matters to me what you think of me. I'm not interested in anything that is given to me out of pity because I lost a role to Jayne McKenna. I thought I had earned your respect, I guess."

"The part. It's a movie called *Max and Me*. You'd be the 'Max'—the lead. It's big, Nora. It could be your break."

Nora let him stammer.

"I passed on directing the movie, but it's got a perfect part for you. I also have another matter to discuss with you." Billy looked pathetic slumped over the bar, his hands cradling a now empty cup.

"Why would I want a part in a movie that you declined to direct?"

"Because the movie isn't right for me, but it is for you." He looked at her defiantly. "Can you just let this go?"

"No." Nora stood up. She tossed the napkin on the counter.

"*Starlight Circus* is Ford's movie. It's *his* picture." Billy turned on his bar stool. "Jayne will let him be the star. Don't you understand? The focal point of every picture that you star in is *you*. Ford can't handle that." Billy had dark circles under his eyes, like he hadn't slept for days. He put on his sunglasses and motioned for the check. With these two moves, he transformed back to the mysterious creature she orbited. "Come with me."

Nora paused and then followed him out the doors and onto the wooden steps that led down to the beach. He was down the steep stairs in what seemed like one movement, not waiting for her or even looking back to see if she'd made it. He was like this sometimes, usually when he was deep in creative thought. Billy was known for dark films with male lead characters who were tortured by inner demons—gambling, war, cowardice, betrayal—but only realistic films. The new screwball comedy trend, led by Howard Hawks, was rattling Billy, who hated comedy and felt it was trite. There was something about him that refused to be the company man.

Nora wasn't running after him. She never ran after him and he seemed to respond to it, so she kept up the charade of distance, hoping he'd notice.

Billy turned and saw she wasn't behind him. He walked back to the step where she stood and what came out next was more of a rehearsed monologue than anything else. "I think we're good together. You understand me more than most people. We could do big things together."

Nora shook her head. The wind was whipping and she grabbed at bits of her hair to keep the strands off her face. "You have a part for me?"

Billy paced in the sand, granules kicking up around his heavy steps. He spun around and laughed. What he said next was so unromantic she nearly fainted. "I...I need a wife, Nora."

"You need a what?" She gulped. Oh, how Nora wished he'd said that he needed *her.*

"A wife, Nora. I need a wife. I'd like for you to be my wife." He was getting used to the words. "Will you be my wife?"

"Oh." She fingered her necklace. She wasn't naive. As much as she wished this was a romantic gesture, the offer seemed to be one of convenience or guilt or something else she didn't understand. Back in New York, Nora had let Clint sleep with her to pay the bills, so she wasn't above a relationship of convenience, but this was the last thing she'd ever wanted from Billy Rapp. Not Billy. Over drives and dinners, she'd listened to him, marveling in his sullenness and genius, and yet his acts of kindness had seemed carved out only for her. Like she was special. Nora had fallen in love with him. This was exactly what she'd wanted to hear, but she'd wanted Billy to love her—to be *in love* with her. She'd orbited him, hoping for that. This proposal felt like a charade. "Billy, do you love me?"

"Of course I love you, Nora. Don't be ridiculous."

"Lord knows, I wouldn't want to be *ridiculous* at a time like this."

She turned her body away from him to give herself a minute to think. She faced him again. "What would Halstead think?"

Billy looked out at the ocean stirring beyond him. "It was his idea."

And there was something so disappointing to Nora about the fact that Billy hadn't even thought of it on his own.

"Well?" Billy stood there with his hands in his pockets, the wind, surf, and sun clamoring around them.

20

Nora Wheeler
Hollywood, 1934

With a budget of one million dollars, *Max and Me* was a hit, earning the studio a seven-hundred-thousand-dollar profit. Of the big studios, Monumental was known for its directors wielding great power—even more than Irving Thalberg at MGM. While Monumental was a smaller studio than MGM, it had a reputation for quality dramas. *Max and Me* was the rare attempt at screwball comedy, with Nora playing a version of Carole Lombard. In the comedy, a husband and wife get switched—the husband waking up in the wife's body and the wife in the husband's. This role reversal gives each spouse an appreciation for the other, and the pure physical comedy required of Nora challenged her for the first time. She'd been rewarded well by Halstead for being overlooked.

But *Max and Me* wasn't the only hit that year. *Starlight Circus* made a star of Monumental's Jayne McKenna, who had dyed her hair from her original Max Factor–coined "brownette" to a darker brown, making the girl look exotic opposite the blond Ford Tremaine. While her role was largely a prop for Ford, she'd become a household name. Billy had been right. *Starlight Circus* was Ford's movie. The camera loved him. The performance he delivered was unlike anything he'd done in his career before. Nora thought it had to be Billy's creative influence.

Three weeks after Billy's proposal and one week before the wedding, Monumental announced that Billy Rapp would direct *Beyond the Shore*, an epic picture about a general who is shot by his wife's lover after returning from the Great War. Ford Tremaine would once again have the lead. Again, Nora would not have a part in her new husband's film.

But one good thing was that she hadn't seen Clint since the night at the restaurant. She was sure it was because of the news of her engagement to Billy. Part of the reason she was going along with the marriage was out of fear of Clint. Billy Rapp would keep Clint away from her.

The Beverly Hills mansion of Harold Halstead, located next door to the expansive Harold Lloyd estate, was lush and green that June as it served as the location of Nora Wheeler's wedding to Billy Rapp. The wedding itself was a low-key affair that had an air of functionality to it that Nora found distasteful. It was her wedding, even if it amounted to another part she was playing.

Nora felt the ivory silk dress against her skin. It was hot that day, and she was worried that the long sleeves would be too confining and the crepe and jeweled bodice too tight, but they were perfect in the end. The dress designed by Inez London was both intricately textured and elegantly simple, complemented by a four-foot silk train. But there was another dress in her head—it was pink and Nora wore a black mask. Each time Nora closed her eyes at the reception, she was haunted by this version of herself and Billy, at least a version of him, telling her that he never wanted to see her again. It was as though the images were slipping through a thin veil, like she was getting a glimpse of something that felt like the past, but was perhaps an omen of things to come?

Photographers got the shots Halstead had wanted: the couple cutting the cake, the couple posed in front of the courtyard fountain. Billy looked happy. From somewhere far away, perhaps an upstairs room, Nora heard a piano playing a rich, sad melody—too sad for a wedding really, but no one else seemed to hear it, or was bothered by its beauty as well as its pain. Nora looked past Halstead's carefully manicured hedges, so precise it was as though they'd been clipped with the aid of a ruler, to see Billy standing with his hands in his pockets, deep in thought. Nora had fallen hopelessly in love with Billy, and although she knew something was wrong, she hoped everything would be better now. He looked up, caught her eye, and smiled at her. For a brief second, she thought that this was a sign they could be happy.

As the ceremony and reception unfolded, there was a topsy-turvy motion to it all, as if the day were moving both fast and slow in tandem, something tugging her backward as events of the day propelled her forward. In moments like this, she was haunted by the details—the lace on her wedding veil, the ornateness of Halstead's fireplace, the smell of the furniture polish—as though she were a visitor in this time and place. As she'd gotten ready for her wedding that morning, Nora felt faint and held on to the vanity until it stopped moving. Instinctively, she knew she needed to absorb what happiness she could from the day.

The wedding was over by two in the afternoon and Nora and Billy drove the Phaeton down to the Agua Caliente Resort and Casino in Tijuana for a small honeymoon. He was due back on the set in less than a week.

Just eighteen miles south of the Mexican border, Agua Caliente was buzzing with Americans for the weekend. Located on more than six hundred acres, the resort had been built by Biltmore owner Baron Long to cater to tourists from San Diego and Los Angeles who'd take advantage of the spa, golf course, casino, or the main draw: the racetrack, home to the richest racing purse in the country. This had been an attempt at a second racetrack—the first built four miles north, closer to the border. The new track drew crowds of hard gamblers who didn't seem to mind mixing with a few locals as well as celebrities, sports figures, and gangsters. No one thing embodied that decadence like the Gold Bar and Casino. Windowless with an elaborate coffered ceiling, the casino even featured real gold chips.

Billy drove the Phaeton past the swimming pool and airstrip before pulling up to the entrance. Guests strained to see who got out of the car as two bellmen rushed to greet them. Since Billy hadn't so much as held Nora's hand since they'd met, she wasn't sure what to expect on their honeymoon—or if she should expect anything at all. When they got to their room, Billy was nervous and twitchy, like a jackrabbit, insisting they immediately head to the racetrack. Dressed in a black-and-white dress with a black bolero hat that Inez had loaned her, Nora followed silently behind Billy as he ignored her for most of the afternoon. After the race, Billy and Nora watched the sunset from their lawn chairs sipping champagne. Then they dressed for dinner, where Billy drank more glasses of gin than Nora could count. Several of the waitstaff dressed in their white uniforms carried Billy back to the room in the early morning. Nora covered him with the bedspread on the couch and spent her first night as Mrs. William Rapp sleeping alone.

Nora was up early, walking the grounds of the Spanish-style resort. She navigated through the palm-lined walkways and the fountains tiled with ornate mosaics and the overflowing terra-cotta planters with yellow and pink flowers dripping over the sides. Groundskeepers had started their days clipping hedges and cleaning chairs. Nora heard the pounding of hooves from the racetrack's morning practice, mixing with some of the workhorses carrying flowers on their carts. When enough time had passed, the sun began to burn brighter and guests began to spill out of their rooms.

When she got back to her room, Billy was on the terrace drinking coffee and smoking a cigarette. His mood was pensive, and he seemed annoyed with her. "Where have you been?"

"Out walking. You were sleeping. I didn't want to bother you."

He tapped his cigarette in the ashtray. "Some of the guys are coming down tonight to gamble."

Nora snorted.

"What?"

"It's our *honeymoon*, Billy."

Snuffing out his cigarette, Billy sank lower in his seat. As his bathrobe gaped open, Nora for the first time saw the outlines of his body, which had been hidden from her until now. There was a familiarity to his body that shouldn't have been possible—a strange déjà vu of sorts of a different man, outtakes of a different life that she couldn't quite understand. Sitting there, she had the feeling that while their marriage was only beginning, she was losing him. Nora was never good at silences, always looking to fill them, but this time she was at a loss for words. She let the uncomfortableness sit between them.

"I can't, you know."

"Can't what?"

"Can't sleep with you the way you want. I had measles as a kid and things don't work like they're supposed to work for me."

"What?" Nora thought she'd misheard him.

"I'm sorry. I should have told you. I can't sleep with you."

Nora exhaled. So that was it? All of the crisp kisses on the cheek as he deposited her home each night. She thought about what she should say next, stopping and starting her response a few times. "Yes. You should have told me." Nora sat down in the chair opposite him. "It isn't like you can help it." As she said the words, Nora contemplated a life of never being with Billy in that way. Suddenly she felt sick. This entire thing—the wedding, the honeymoon—was a sham.

"I'm ashamed," said Billy. "You're perfect and yet I can't do anything. You should have known before we were married. It would have changed things."

It was the nonchalant way he presented this to her that infuriated her. She could tell he wasn't sorry. Nora considered this. "I would have liked to have been married knowing everything."

He held his coffee cup in his hand and studied it. "Halstead thought it was best—"

"I bet he did," she interrupted him. What a fool she had been. An overwhelming sense of betrayal washed over her. She remembered the first day she met Billy in Halstead's office. She'd felt then that there was a strange undercurrent between them; some part she was auditioning for. So this had been it?

In the afternoon, Nora took a golf lesson to try to keep her mind off what to do next. She wasn't sure she could stay in a loveless—let alone sexless—marriage, but she needed to be smart. Personally, marrying Billy had been a stupid move; she'd always known he would break her heart. But professionally, she was now the wife of Monumental Studio's most powerful director, so she decided she wasn't going to be stupid with her career. Right now, it was all she had. Never would she go back to living in a dingy one-room apartment with a man like Clint, nor would she be shuttled around town to parties to serve as entertainment again. She was now Monumental's version of Norma Shearer.

When she got back to the room, Billy had left her a note to join "them" in the casino. Nora took her time getting dressed, wearing a copper silk gown with copper beading at the shoulders. Taking a cue from Jean Harlow, Nora decided to forgo a bra and made her eye makeup smokier—a look less innocent, more vamp. As she gazed in the mirror, she thought it was fitting. She felt less innocent. Ironically, she had never looked more beautiful, and yet her beauty was lost on this man and this moment.

As Nora walked down the hall to the casino, she caught the smell of a flower sitting on the table. She shook her head. Something about the smell pulled her back to another room with another hall table and another man and another copper dress. Something was swirling around her, like events already set in motion. She gripped the hall table to steady herself. It had to be the stress. She straightened her dress and as she kept walking down the hall, the scent of the flowers became fainter and released its grip on her.

With their elaborate dark-wood-beamed ceilings, each room at Agua Caliente seemed to outdo the other. Nora heard them before she spied them at the bar, drinking martinis. The sight of them confirmed what she could hear. They were drunk. Billy was leaning off his chair like he did when he was about three or four martinis in. Next to him stood the lanky frame of Ford Tremaine. Ford faced out to the casino and leaned in close, talking to another man, whom Nora recognized as the cameraman from *Train to Boston*, Zane King. Nora could hear Ford repeating everything to Zane; although he was standing close, he was shouting so loudly that his voice could be heard as far away as the center chandelier. As Nora crossed the Gold Bar, Ford's gray eyes lit up when he spied her. Zane turned and Billy tottered around to face her.

"Billy, your bride has arrived." Ford leaned back against the bar. When he wasn't on set, Ford had the deep Southern accent of a boy born in Oxford, Mississippi. At least he could still stand. "Billy here thought you'd abandoned him for the night."

"Did he?" Nora looked down at Billy, whose glassy eyes showed he'd been drinking since she'd left him earlier. "Glad you boys could join us for our honeymoon."

"Yes, indeed. She's pissed, William." Ford smiled. "William here thought you were pissed. I told him you couldn't possibly be pissed at *him*." Ford's smile had dipped. He was used to turning on the charm for the cameras and the press, and it left him as soon as he had no use for it. His comments were a warning. There was something to Ford's cool tone and barbs. Ford didn't like her. Billy had seemed to have known that would be the case.

"Surely Billy knows I'm not angry at him about anything." Nora tried to catch the bartender's eye. She needed a drink.

Billy looked up at her, but he couldn't focus on her face.

"I think he needs some coffee, boys." Nora could feel Ford's eyes watching her as she ordered coffee for Billy and finished his martini in one swift motion before sliding the empty glass back across the bar. "Another, please."

"Did you know about Phar Lap?" Billy appeared to be talking to his reflection in the mirror behind the bar.

Zane interrupted him. "He's been going on about Phar Lap all night."

"What is a Phar Lap?"

"A horse—known as the Red Terror." Ford came and put his arms on Billy's shoulders. "Isn't that right, Billy?"

Billy nodded and uttered something unintelligible about a ghost.

"That's right." Ford turned to Nora. "Phar Lap was the world champion Australian horse who came here to the States to race, but died under mysterious circumstances."

Nora looked at Zane, who shrugged and shook his head. "He's been going on about the fucking ghost of Phar Lap all night, even when he was half sober." Nora smiled at Zane. A handsome blond linebacker type from Indiana, his face lacked the angles Ford had with his slight, thin build.

"Billy and I saw Phar Lap race—what was that, in '32 or '33?"

"It was 1932," Billy said loudly with the certainty of a drunk.

"No one had seen the horse train." Ford tucked himself into a nook between Billy and Zane. He lit a cigarette. "They wouldn't run him, so everyone thought he was lame or that he couldn't handle the dirt track. Shit, when that big fucking horse—he was *huge*—when he burst through the gate, it was over. About a year ago, Billy and I came back and saw him after he'd died—you know they said the horse's heart was three times the size of a normal horse's heart." Ford pointed his cigarette at us for emphasis. "They stuffed him and stood him out on the lawn at Belmont Park behind some rope. It was a disgrace, wasn't it, Billy?"

Billy nodded dramatically. "Damned disgrace."

"Okay, I'll play along," said Nora. "How'd the horse die?"

"Poison," said Ford, his eyebrow raised.

"Poison?" Nora folded her arms. "Hm."

"Arsenic," added Billy, although the mumbled word didn't sound like *arsenic*.

"Preachers hated Phar Lap...the whole sin and Prohibition thing. You know my daddy was a preacher." Ford reached behind him and grabbed his drink.

"I didn't know that."

"Well, it was big news when Phar Lap came to America. They said that he was the devil. Kind of like Robert Johnson. Made a deal with the devil." Ford seemed to be drawing an audience, but then Nora remembered that he was an actor.

"Or Paganini."

"I don't know no Paganini." Ford shrugged.

Neither did Nora, so why was she suddenly talking about an Italian violinist? She rubbed her head. What was wrong with her? Ford's smug smile brought her back to reality. So, this was it. They were in competition for Billy.

Nora's mouth began before her brain could process what she was saying. It was as though another person entirely had taken hold of her body. "It's an old story, Ford. Did the phenomenon get the talent naturally or did they make a deal with the devil? Before Robert Johnson? There was Niccolò Paganini, the virtuoso." Nora could picture a small man sitting on a piano bench so close she could smell his breath, telling her a fantastic story: *They say he murdered a woman and imprisoned her soul in his violin. His gift to the devil in exchange for his talent. Her cries could be heard in the beauty of the notes.* Nora looked down at her martini and placed it on the bar. Maybe this was a sign that she needed to stop.

"Deal with the devil," repeated Billy, and then he looked up at her almost pleading. "You know what I mean, *don't you*, Nora?"

She thought of Halstead and this wedding she'd hoped for. "Yes, Billy. I know all about a deal with the devil."

"No, you don't." Billy shook his head. "You just think you do."

"Okay. I'm hungry," said Nora. "And he needs something to eat."

"They have a beef tenderloin with mushrooms that puts my French mother's to shame," added Zane. "They put it in this cassolette."

"What the fuck is a cassolette, Zane?" Ford turned to look at Zane with disgust.

"It's a little covered pot."

"Then say *a little covered pot*." Ford rolled his eyes.

No one had noticed that Billy had gone quiet. Perhaps it was the thought of beef tenderloin with mushrooms or Phar Lap stuffed on the Belmont Park front lawn or the addition of coffee to the martini brew in his·stomach, but Billy abruptly turned a funny color of yellow before attempting to stand and throwing up all over the front of Nora's copper dress.

Ford seemed to grab Billy in slow motion like a dance partner and sweep him out of the Gold Bar before the staff had seen what happened. It was always about protecting each other, thought Nora. She could feel the hot vomit seeping through her silk gown and onto her thighs and breasts.

She followed them out through the doors and down the steps to the lawn. Billy was on his knees vomiting. Nora dabbed at her dress with a black cloth napkin, but the dress Inez London had created especially for her honeymoon was ruined. Billy continued heaving for several minutes until Ford and Zane felt it was safe. It took the three of them to steady Billy on his feet.

"Let's get him back to the room," said Ford.

Each time they tried to move, Billy vomited.

Finally, they sat him on a bench.

"We may have to carry him," Ford announced.

"And how will that help?" Nora folded her arms.

"Some honeymoon, huh?" It was Zane, who had started wiping Nora's arm with a rag. She looked up at him gratefully. He held her arm and gave her a sympathetic smile. She could hear Ford talking to Billy, but couldn't make out what they were saying.

"Was he this drunk when you guys got here?" She wiped at her eyes with her arm, the napkin drenched.

"He's always this drunk, Nora." Zane stopped wiping when he got to the front of her dress. "Here," he said, handing her the towel. "Here."

"Thank you." Nora looked down to see that without a bra, her wet dress had left little to anyone's imagination. Disgusted, she threw the towel on the ground. They could look at her tits for all she cared. "Thank you for the effort, Zane, but I think the dress, and the evening, are both quite ruined."

Ford slid Billy up and called for Zane. "We'll walk him back to the bungalow," shouted Ford. When Nora saw they weren't taking him back to her bungalow, she stopped.

Zane removed his jacket and placed it over her shoulders. Nora smiled at him gratefully.

"We got him," said Ford. "No sense in you not getting sleep." Billy, Zane, and Ford staggered down the manicured walkway.

From a distance, Nora heard a band playing, probably in the ballroom. It was the sound of happiness and it made her cry. Walking alone back to her room, she passed several staff members who asked if she was okay. She imagined how she looked, her makeup rolling down her face in a ruined dress. So exclusive was Agua Caliente, it was a wonder they didn't toss her out.

Once in the room, Nora ripped her dress off. Rolling it into a tight ball, she threw it in the garbage. She'd pay Inez back. In her robe, she walked out to the balcony and lit a cigarette. The smell of eucalyptus and the coolness of the air helped clear her thoughts.

Nora was dressed and her bags packed when Billy finally showed at their room around noon. She had been sitting on the edge of the bed all morning, waiting for him.

For as drunk—and sick—as he'd been the night before, Nora was surprised that he looked so good. His hair was rumpled and his shirt was untucked and Nora noticed he wasn't wearing shoes, but he looked bronzed and healthy given the condition she'd last seen him in.

"You're here."

"Where else would I be, Billy?"

He shrugged and tossed his jacket on the chair, then walked to the open door and lit a cigarette.

Nora cleared her voice. "I'm leaving."

He seemed amused and turned to her. "Leaving me or leaving here?"

"Leaving here for now." She sighed. "I'll figure the rest out later."

"Take the car," he offered. "Ford will bring me back tomorrow."

"You're staying?" Nora felt sick. This wasn't happening—this couldn't be happening. He wasn't taking this marriage—or her—seriously at all.

"I can't leave them." He sat on the bed—the opposite corner from her. It was the first time he'd pretended like there was a bed in the room.

"No," agreed Nora. "You certainly can't leave *them*."

He picked at something on his pants until he gave up. He focused on her, his green eyes vacant, his tone cool. "I understand completely, you know. If you need to take a lover."

"What?"

"Zane, for instance." He shrugged and crossed his legs, inhaling his cigarette deeply before going in search of an ashtray, which he found on the nightstand.

"Zane?"

"He thinks you're beautiful."

"Jesus, Billy." Nora stood up. Tears welled up in her eyes. She wasn't sure what she had been expecting, but that he was suggesting she take a lover on their honeymoon was cruel. *Billy* should think she was beautiful. The fact that he was pimping her to Zane on their honeymoon was unbearable. It was something Clint would do. "I can't talk about this. Not today."

"Suit yourself." He extinguished the cigarette and stretched out on the bed. Within minutes, he was snoring softly.

Nora drove Billy's Phaeton up the highway and into the Monumental Studios lot at a breakneck speed. The car was powerful as well as beautiful, she'd give it that. She'd taken her anger out on it as she'd flown back up the highway to Los Angeles. When she pushed through the front doors of Monumental's offices, Halstead saw her immediately.

"He told me," began Nora, peeling off her gloves.

"Who told you what?"

"Billy told me that he can't have sex."

The old man blanched. "He did what?"

"You should have told me," snapped Nora.

"On the contrary, Nora," said Halstead. "Your *husband* should have told you." The man shook his head. "It had nothing to do with me."

"He said you thought it was better that I not know about the measles until after the wedding."

"Did he now?"

"I should have been told."

Halstead leaned back in his chair and folded his hands in front of him, considering his next words carefully. "Oh, Nora. Our Billy is a dear boy and very valuable to this studio. This new picture, *Beyond the Shore*, it's the most expensive film we've ever backed here at Monumental. That's largely because of Billy and Ford. They are a powerful duo, you know?" Halstead cleared his throat. "I fear this is all Louella Parsons's fault. She knew and Billy was afraid she'd leak it. I perhaps encouraged him to court you so she'd think the rumor wasn't true. But I'm afraid dear Billy has treated you poorly. For that, and my role in it, I'm terribly sorry."

"Thank you." Nora sat on the chair in front of Halstead and put her head in her hands.

"My dear," said Halstead gently. "You love him?"

"Of course I love him. He's my husband."

Halstead considered her gravely, like she'd been given a few months to live. "Tell you what I'll do. You haven't done much comedy, and *Max and Me* was a real hit. I think you could be our queen of screwball. There's a play on Broadway that the company is investing in called *A Million Kisses*. If the initial run is good, we're going to make it into a film. I think the change of scenery would do you some good. It's a story about a man who moves his mother in to live with him and his new wife. We've got Lillibet Denton as the mother and a new find from New York, Jack Watt, playing the son."

"This feels like you're paying me off."

"No, my dear. I'm getting you out of town for a while." Halstead reached for his cigarette case in his breast pocket. "You're like a daughter to me."

"You have a daughter, don't you, Halstead? A real one?"

"I do," he said, nodding.

"Tell me. Would you have married *her* off to Billy Rapp?"

Halstead sat in his chair, silently looking down at his cigar a beat before he lit it.

She shook her head. "I didn't think so. How long is the run in New York?"

"Ten weeks. Four weeks of rehearsal and a six-week run. Enough time to clear your head."

Nora nodded. Maybe a break from Billy would do her some good—give her some perspective on their marriage.

Billy didn't have much of a reaction when Nora told him that Halstead was sending her to New York. *Beyond the Shore* was about to start filming and he was wrapped up in sets and production notes. She was also on the opposite coast from Clint again, and that felt good.

While Nora's house was on the market, she'd moved into Billy's newly constructed chalet nestled in the lush hills of Benedict Canyon. They'd continued to sleep in separate rooms there—separate wings of the house—but before she left for New York, Nora and Billy posed for a *Photoplay* photo shoot on the balcony of the canyon in the morning sun, the couple drawn together in a blanket. That they looked happy, Nora thought, was chalked up to her chops as an actress. Only in the evenings did the couple see each other when they made an appearance at the Trocadero or the Hollywood Bowl. There, nestled against Billy, Nora gushed to Hedda Hopper that she loved coming home to him each night.

The studio flew Nora to New York. Her co-star, Lillibet Denton, was a tiny, birdlike woman with cornflower eyes and red hair tint that was rapidly fading to match the color of her flesh. Normally, Lillibet performed in London, but she let everyone know she was making an exception by appearing in *New* York. Seeing the actress from the London stage performing the role of the scheming mother-in-law was like cramming for a test each night. When Lillibet walked on stage, each gesture, word, and pause was given such weight that the woman was sweating after every scene.

Upon the completion of Nora's first scene, Lillibet stood with her arms folded. "Do they teach you to *sashay* on set like that in Holly Wood?" (Lillibet always inserted a rather dramatic pause between the two words.) "I wasn't aware this was *Vaude Ville*."

Lillibet challenged Nora's preparation and taught her timing and proper movement and voice projection. After rehearsals or performances ended, Lillibet invited Nora to join her for a late dinner and drinks. Lillibet suggested that Nora read Gertrude Stein, Hemingway,

Gide, Proust, and—only if she had to—Colette. Nora took to carrying a pad and pencil in her handbag to take notes of all Lillibet's many suggestions. Lillibet tended to dismiss the American writers except for Hemingway and Fitzgerald, but Edith Wharton was a favorite and the woman gave Nora her own dog-eared copy of *The Age of Innocence*.

"Your mind must be constantly challenged, Nora, especially because you are a woman. Don't have them turn you into some mannequin who speaks on command."

If Lillibet exercised Nora's mind, then co-star Jack Watt had a raw sexual quality that was hard to miss and—no surprise even to herself—Nora bedded him by the second week of rehearsals. It was exhilarating to be wanted again. But Jack Watt had his place and Nora knew that she'd be returning to Hollywood. Even though Jack was moving there after the show wrapped, she wouldn't be looking him up. She was still Billy Rapp's wife. While she may have a lover in New York, the relationship wouldn't continue in the same city with Billy.

Once the play's run was over, Lillibet announced, she would take the time between Broadway and filming to get away to Paris.

The word. Paris. The sound of it electrified Nora. As Lillibet described finding the Panthéon while out on a walk around the Latin Quarter or the streets of Montmartre, Nora almost caught herself correcting the woman about the location of a street. There were memories of a young girl and a man, like a flicker, a snapshot on a photo carousel, spinning wildly, each image fading to black. The images seemed like this lifetime, maybe something she'd seen as a child, but where? Ohio? Some things about the colors and the fashions weren't exactly correct, making Nora doubt herself entirely. Hollywood had taught her that reality could be distorted into whatever you wanted it to be, so she didn't trust anything. Even her memories. The idea of "real" to Nora had been irreparably altered. She now entirely distrusted

Billy and Halstead. They'd set up a theatrical performance with her as the unwitting star. And yet there was a larger sense that she'd played another part before on a different stage. Strange images were slipping through—a house in the countryside, an apartment along a wide boulevard, and a girl in a pink dress and mask, feeling exactly as she did: that every illusion she'd held had been shattered. It was this other girl who'd made Nora begin to distrust her very existence. She shared these thoughts with Lillibet, who snorted.

"It's an existential crisis, my dear girl," insisted Lillibet, dismissing her. "Read Kierkegaard. You're seeing another possibility unfold for you because this life has disappointed you. Remember, you are in control of your destiny. No one else."

Nora had an uneasy sense that on this point, Lillibet was dead wrong.

Lillibet had no explanation for Nora's sudden piano talent. Overnight, Nora had become a virtuoso, and she took to playing the piano at the theater during breaks. It wasn't normal to have developed a skill out of nowhere, but Nora played the instrument as though she'd studied it for years, a phenomenon that both scared her and thrilled her, but she liked the skill—it was powerful and mysterious, the physical embodiment of the internal crisis she was feeling and proof that something surreal was happening to her. As she pushed herself further— playing more difficult pieces from muscle memory—she woke up frightened each morning that somehow the talent would disappear just as quickly as it had come.

After the show had ended, Lillibet implored Nora to go with her to Paris, but Nora declined, finally deciding that she had to get home to Billy. Time had only softened her resolve toward their situation. If Billy couldn't sleep with her, it didn't matter. Jack had done that and it had felt hollow. What she had with Billy was true admiration and love. She could work with that.

Lillibet wrote down an address and put it in the girl's hands. "You're an old soul, Nora, and it's a pity that you're stuck in a new city like Los Angeles. Last time I spent any time there, I couldn't hear from all the dreadful hammering. It's quite simply the wrong place for you, but you'll learn that in time so I'm not going to jump up and down about it." She stopped and thought for a moment. "I've been married twice and I can tell you this. Your marriage to Billy is over. You just don't know it yet."

Had Nora let it, this candid assessment of her marriage by Lillibet would have caused a strain between them in those last few moments together. In her heart, Nora hoped the older woman was wrong. Rather than fly, Nora took the same train out of New York that she had taken three years before, quietly taking stock of the changes in her life since she'd left Norma Westerman behind. Armed with André Gide's *Immoralist*, Gertrude Stein's *Autobiography of Alice B. Toklas*, and an Agatha Christie novel, Nora boarded the first-class car this time. When she arrived at the station three days later, the train was early. Excited to see Billy, who had just wrapped *Beyond the Shore*, she arrived home and opened the door to the house to find all of her questions about Billy Rapp finally answered, Lillibet's words ominous. Tangled in the sheets of Billy's bed was a naked Ford Tremaine.

When she thought back upon it, Nora wished she'd said more than "Oh."

It was humiliating, seeing them there wrapped around each other. In hindsight, Nora couldn't believe she'd been so gullible and that she hadn't seen it before. The truth had been in front of her the entire time. Hell, the truth had been invited along on her honeymoon. Even more humiliating, Nora saw Ford smirking at her as he dressed, straightening out his shirt collar. He brushed past her and she heard him mutter to Billy, "You said she knew." Defiantly, Nora stood there calculating who knew and who had lied to her by omission. In the accounting, Nora's fury grew. Who else knew? Zane? Halstead? Hedda Hopper? Louella Parsons?

When Billy emerged from the bedroom and finally faced her, she didn't let him speak.

"The fucking measles?"

He deflated on the chair in front of the fireplace. "I didn't know how to tell you." Nora looked at his open shirt and tan chest. "I'm so sorry."

"You let me believe you were *impotent*." She poured herself a drink and swirled it. "You used me. You humiliated me."

"I'm sorry."

"You used me."

"They were threatening to leak the story about Ford and me."

"There was no love between us...no respect. You don't respect someone you lie to...someone you set up to humiliate the way you did me."

"I never meant to humiliate you, Nora."

"No? What did you mean to do? Did you even think this through? I'm in love with you. Did that ever factor into your plans?"

Billy put his head in his hands. "I can't help it, Nora. Can you see? I might as well have had measles. At least I didn't try with you. I've done that back home in Youngstown with a few girls and if you think this was humiliating, you should try that. I do love you. I thought it could help you...being married to me. I thought you'd understand."

"I might have understood. If you'd thought enough of me to tell me." There was an odd compounded loss to this moment, like she'd felt it before, run through these lines with him before. A door was opening—just a crack—and she was seeing another version of him breaking her heart. Both the present and the past Billy were here in unison—like some grotesque chorus. Nora looked up at the ceiling. She hated this fucking house with a mural painted on the goddamned ceiling like they lived in the Sistine Chapel. Everything about Hollywood disgusted her at this moment. The ceiling trying to replicate something else. Everything a replication like a cheap costume shop. And she and Billy, imposters themselves. Nora gathered up her keys and her luggage.

"Where are you going?"

"To the Roosevelt Hotel, where I will sleep off three days of a train trip that I did at a furious pace so I could see you. Fortunately, my own house hasn't sold yet—too many newer mansions being built, I'm afraid—so I will be going back there once I get furniture back in it. I'll send for my things."

"You can't do that."

With Lillibet's words in her head—*Remember, you are in control of your destiny. No one else*—she turned to look at him before she headed out the door. "Oh yes, I can and I will. You and Halstead had better start thinking of ways to keep me happy." Those marvelous green eyes looked up at her. His sunbaked smooth skin. She could see the blond hairs on his arms, and she took in every last image. "I will not be made a fool of by you or by the studio. If you needed my help, you could have asked me directly. I might have gone along or I might not have, but you knew I was in love with you and you preyed on my emotions. I wasn't a willing participant in this and you knew that. You *took* something from me, Billy Rapp. Don't you see that? I guess it was hope. That is gone now. And I hate you for that."

"If it's any consolation," said Billy, "I wish I were dead."

"I wish you were dead, too," said Nora. "I think it would be easier for me."

She drove her roadster wildly down the canyon turns that night, almost willing something to happen to her but knowing it wouldn't. Even as storm clouds rumbled above her, she knew there would be no reprieve to her suffering. She was a creature who endured suffering and she would endure this, too.

In her suite in the Roosevelt, Nora was woken at seven A.M. to a furious pounding at the door. After several minutes, she realized it wasn't going to let up. Nora located her robe and opened the door to find Halstead standing there with another man. The man's head was turned looking down the hallway, but when he finally faced her, Nora saw, to her horror, that it was Clint.

"We've got a big problem, honey," said Halstead, pushing past her, his voice hushed.

Nora looked at Clint, trying to read him. By comparison with Halstead's rattled exterior, Clint looked calm and in control. His calm demeanor frightened her even more. From her experience, this was the windup before Clint unleashed his fury.

"What's wrong?" Nora directed her question to Halstead.

But it was Clint who answered. "It's your husband."

"Oh shit." Nora struggled to wrap the robe around her clingy satin nightgown, and both Clint and Halstead watched with mouths agape. "I meant to call about that." She poured a glass of water and began to search for something to wear among the pile of clothes flowing from her overnight bag.

"What do you mean you meant to *call* about that?" Halstead's voice had a level of concern that made Nora look up.

She saw him exchange glances with Clint. She wanted to say that she knew about Billy and Ford, but Clint was standing in her room, leering down at her bra draped across her suitcase, so she stopped. Halstead's concern had been about hiding the relationship between his biggest male star and his rising director and keeping it out of the papers. His concern had never been for her. She pulled a cigarette out of her purse and lit it, ignoring Clint's attempt to do it for her. This was her town, not his. She was going to stand her ground with him. "I know about him."

"You do?" Halstead took off his hat and scratched at his thinning hair. He looked pale, purple almost.

"Yeah, Ford was at Billy's house last night when I got there. It was a little crowded if you know what I mean."

Halstead knew where she was going with this and frowned. "I don't think you understand, my dear, but Billy is—"

"Your husband's dead," interrupted Clint. A crooked smile formed on his lips. He took great joy telling her this.

Nora felt her face drain. She looked at Halstead, who seemed to have shrunk six inches. "Is it true?"

Halstead nodded and deferred to Clint. "The studio has hired Clint here to handle this *situation* for us. He comes highly recommended from Palladium Studios."

Clint interrupted. "Norma knows I fix things. Don't you, honey?"

She looked at him with contempt and inhaled her cigarette. "I know you *break* things." She leaned back on the dresser and clutched it to steady herself. This couldn't be real. Her last image of Billy sitting on the chair in front of her and the horrible thing that she had said to him as she left. *I wish you were dead, too. It would be easier for me.* She'd wanted to hurt him and she had. "What happened to him?"

Clint sat down on the chair and pulled out a cigarette. "Ate a bullet."

Halstead looked like he'd tasted something unpleasant. "Do we have to be so crass about it?"

Clint laughed. "Oh, Norma can handle crass, can't you, honey?"

Nora turned away from him to Halstead. "He shot himself?"

Halstead nodded grimly and steadied her, steering her back on the bed. "When did you see him last?"

She gathered her robe tightly around her. "Last night."

Halstead shot Clint a look.

"Did you argue?" Clint was measured, which was so unlike him that Nora wondered what he was playing at. Clint was a hothead; there was nothing cool about him. He'd once bragged that he'd beaten a man to death for picking up the wrong suitcase at the bus station.

"I don't want *him* in the room." Nora pointed to Clint. "I won't talk with him here."

Clint interrupted her. "Ford Tremaine says you and Billy were arguing when he left the house."

"I don't want you here, Clint." She turned to Halstead. "I don't want him here."

Halstead made no move to remove Clint from the room.

"He knows everything, Norma. You see, this one here was a little mousy thing back in New York, Harold." Clint stood up. "I found her in Akron. You wouldn't believe the things they said about her back in New York. I heard she paid her rent—"

"Get out!" Nora pointed to the door. "Now!"

"—by sleeping with every man who would pay her."

"That's a lie," said Nora. "I left you after you gave me enough bruises that I couldn't work steady. I still have a scar from the cigarette burn you gave me." She pulled her hair back from her cheek, knowing that the red mark was where it always was in the morning before makeup. She looked at Halstead. "I need to talk to you. *Alone.* You owe me that."

Halstead looked at Clint and nodded. Clint folded his hands like an obedient schoolboy and walked out.

Nora waited for the door to close behind him, then turned to Halstead. "He's a very bad man."

"I know what he is," Halstead said. "And we have a very bad situation that requires him, don't we?" He sat on the bed, wearily. Harold Halstead wasn't a young man, and the events of the morning seemed to have aged him ten years. "Back to Billy. You found out?" Halstead's tone wasn't accusing.

"I did," snapped Nora. "And not the way I should have. My train arrived early yesterday. I walked in on them."

Halstead sighed. His body seemed heavy. "He should have told you, Nora. I'm sorry."

"*Someone* should have told me, Harold."

Halstead sighed again. "It was going to hit the papers. They had photos. It would have ruined everyone—Billy, Ford, the studio. You were simply effervescent, my dear. From the first minute I met you. I thought that you could help. And you did, but I didn't feel it was my place to tell you everything." Halstead looked down at his hands. "I have something to ask you, dear. It's delicate."

"Yeah?" Nora took one last deep drag from her cigarette. She noticed her nails were chipped and there was dirt under her fingernails.

"Did you kill him?"

Nora spun on her heels. "What are you talking about? You said he shot himself."

"Well, that isn't clear. True, it was a gunshot, but whether he did it or someone else did it and made it look that way . . . well, that has yet to be determined. The gun was placed in his hand, but it looked staged."

"He was a director and maniacal about details. He'd stage his own suicide." Nora paced the room. "What do the police say?"

The man shook his head. "We haven't called them yet."

She raised her eyebrow. "You haven't what?"

"Clint has taken care of the scene. We're calling the police after we leave you."

"Well, Billy was very much alive when I saw him last." The fact that Clint had already been on the scene made Nora even more suspicious. "How did you find out about Billy in the first place?"

"I got an anonymous phone call that he was dead."

"And you don't think that's odd?"

"I think everything about this situation is odd, Nora, but I've got a dead director and an unfinished picture. Monumental cannot afford a scandal like William Desmond Taylor or Fatty Arbuckle. We won't survive it."

Nora walked over to the window and pushed back the sheer curtain. The sun was already shining down Hollywood Boulevard. "Are you sure"—she nodded toward the door—"that he didn't create the situation?"

"What are you getting at?"

"I'm saying Clint breaks things so he can fix them—to create situations for himself. Clearly you see he's obsessed with me."

"I hired him last week, Nora. Every studio has a fixer, you know that. The very thing you hate about him makes him good at his job, sadly. And he's good."

She turned to Halstead. "You'll regret hiring him."

"Not today I won't, Nora."

She turned back to the window. "Thank you, Harold, for letting me know. Now I have to make arrangements to bury my husband."

21

Helen Lambert
Paris, June 12, 2012

Mickey shook me awake. "Dear God, you've been asleep the entire flight, and there was drooling."

"Sorry," I said. "I've been sleeping more than usual."

Mickey shook his head. "You say sleeping, but it was more like you just went unconscious. I thought you were dead at one point."

He wasn't wrong. It was sleep, but then it wasn't. It seemed that the energy needed to make me whole again—gathering Juliet, Nora, and me together into one—required me being unconscious. Upon waking from this latest dream, I felt a strange affection for Nora Wheeler. She didn't have Juliet's vulnerability. Nora was a survivor, and I needed her strength over the next few days. While Billy was most certainly Marchant, Luke had not yet made an appearance in her life yet. I had to admit I was waiting to see him again, if only in my dreams.

Our kiss the other night had left me rattled. I'd felt guilty lying to him about a work trip. I made up some crazy interview that I was going to conduct with a famous British actor for *In Frame*. Was all of this crazy? This secret trip to Paris to get blood? Witches and curses didn't happen in real life. Part of me thought I should just go back to Washington and live my life, ignoring Luke Varner, and everything would be fine. But how to explain these vivid lives that were downloaded into my brain each night? I had a heightened sense of color…reds and soft blues with Nora…greens and cornflower blues and gilded golds with Juliet. I knew the smell of eucalyptus even though I'd never been near it; I could see the brown flowered wallpaper pattern that had hung in Nora's mother's boardinghouse in Akron that didn't exist anymore; I knew the way the icebox sounded when she shut it. *And I had always hated the smell of cloves.* As I remembered the stinking paste that Juliet's mother had applied all over her body, it finally made sense to me.

No, the reality was that my mother had cast a spell more than a hundred years ago in Challans and now I had less than two weeks to stop this madness or I'd resurface again and keep repeating these mistakes like some fucked-up version of *Groundhog Day*. Was Roger Lambert someone I should have been with or was he just an actor—a slug—that had been placed into my life thanks to some mistake made by an angry woman? From the way Luke described it, these parts we played were like roles on a stage. And of course, part of the reason I couldn't admit to myself that this thing was real was Sara's mother, Johanna. If all of this was true, then I had unwittingly been the cause of her death. This curse was dangerous and I needed to stop it.

Mickey and I cleared customs and caught the train from Heathrow into London, then catching the Eurostar at the St. Pancras Station. Although I'd slept through the flight, I didn't feel rested.

"You're awfully quiet." Mickey ordered a glass of wine even though it was barely noon.

"I'm trying to process all of this."

"You don't really believe this curse stuff?"

"Well, don't you?" I raised my eyebrow skeptically. "If not, why are you here?"

"I'm here because *you* believe it." He looked over at me gravely. "Promise me something. If this whole thing in Challans is a fluke, will you go to a doctor back in Washington and get an MRI like a normal person? I'm worried you have one of those brain tumors like that John Travolta film where he gets superpowers."

"*Phenomenon?*"

"A great film." He swirled his wine.

"I don't have a brain tumor, Mickey."

"That's right. You have a curse. How could I forget."

"I think I'd rather have a brain tumor."

We arrived at the Gare du Nord and decided to stay the night in Paris. We'd take the first morning train down to Challans, where I'd look for Michel and Delphine Busson's granddaughter, Marielle Fournier, who was now seventy-eight years old and living in an apartment in downtown Challans. I was still haunted by the fact that Delphine had married Michel Busson. Had the young girl been forced to marry him after Juliet had left for Paris? Closing my eyes, I could see the innocent little girl who couldn't even carry a full bucket of water. Imagining her married to that monster made me sick. Why hadn't the money Juliet sent home been enough to keep her safe?

The next morning, we arrived at Challans by ten. Marielle Fournier's apartment was in one of the huge buildings with big open foyers and walk-up steps. When Mickey and I knocked on her door, there was no answer.

A neighbor was bringing her groceries in for the day and saw us standing in front of the door. She eyed us suspiciously. "Are you looking for Madame Fournier?"

"We are." Hearing the woman speak French, I, in turn, answered in perfect French.

"She doesn't live there anymore." The small woman struggled with the lock on her apartment door. She slid her cat's-eye glasses up the bridge of her nose with her finger. "She moved to a care home on the other side of town."

"Oh...do you have the address?" I began rummaging through my bag for a pen.

"Are you her family?" The woman's guard was up.

The question struck me as odd. I straightened myself. "Yes. I am her great-niece."

"Oh," said the woman. "She never mentioned you."

I met her eyes and smiled. "I have come all the way from the States to see her."

The woman looked impressed by this last bit of information, and her face softened. "I had assumed you were Parisian. Your French has no American accent to it. I will give you the address."

Up until last week, I didn't speak French at all. Now I spoke it like a Parisian.

The woman, Eve, did more than just give us the address. She called the care home and told them to be expecting Madame Fournier's great-niece. Then she made us a wonderful pot of coffee.

As we left the building and walked up the street, Mickey unfurled the map that Eve had drawn for us. "Who said French people aren't nice."

"She *was* friendly, wasn't she?" I studied my iPhone, which was on a crazy roaming data plan so I could get Luke's messages, but he hadn't left any.

"Hey, I didn't know you spoke French," said Mickey. "And with no American accent."

"My tumor must be Parisian."

I swear I heard him snort.

"So, are we going to stick Madame Fournier with a pin?" Mickey was still reading the map as we walked up the hill toward a newer complex that Eve had described to us. "You *do* have a plan for getting blood from this poor woman, don't you?"

"I'm thinking," I snapped.

"Don't be pissy with me," said Mickey. "You have about five minutes to figure it out."

The Challans Center for Aging could have been located in Topeka. All of the French charm was lost the minute we stepped through the doors. It seemed as though all assisted living communities in the world look the same: dusty-pink Chippendale sofas with floral pillows and cherry end tables covered with a thick glass protector. A French version of the Carpenters' "Close to You" played softly while file drawers banged open and closed. There was a sign-in sheet. I'd noticed the French were sticklers for procedures of any kind, and the distantly pleasant concierge made it clear we weren't going anywhere until we had properly signed in and checked to make sure all the fields were properly completed. In protest of rules, Mickey signed his name "Lorenzo Lamas" and handed me the pen in a challenge to be equally creative. I signed my name as "Dorothy Hamill." Mickey and I did this sometimes with our name badges at conferences to fuck with people. The concierge checked to see that there was, indeed, something in the form field for "nom" and "visite." The bored woman pointed us toward a hallway and said, "*Quatre gauche.*"

"What does that mean?"

"Fourth room on the left."

The hallway smelled of pee, face cream, and some kind of unappetizing cooked food that I could remotely identify as carrots. It was a disgusting combination. The place my grandmother had died in smelled like this. The cleaner they used to cover up the pee smell only ended up magnifying the odors.

In the fourth room, a nurse stood over an old woman in a chair, *drawing blood* from her left arm. Mickey turned to me with wild pony eyes. "Get that vial," he whispered under his breath.

I walked into the room while Mickey stood back near the nurse's cart. If the cart was left out while the nurse went to the next room, then Mickey could just swipe the vial. All of this was said without words—I had looked at the nurse's cart and Mickey nodded. "Don't fuck it up," I whispered. "Get the right vial."

"Get your brain-tumored ass in there, Dorothy Hamill."

I smiled at the nurse as she approached, stripping off her latex gloves. "You must be the relative?"

"Yes," I said. "I came all the way from the United States. Doing a bit of genealogy." I looked down at the blood vial. "Is Great-Aunt Marielle all right? You're drawing blood?"

"Diabetes," she said, "with some kidney issues. I hope you aren't planning on talking to her. Her dementia has gotten worse. That's why she moved from her apartment. Some days are better than others, but..." She looked over at Marielle Fournier. "Sadly, today is not one of those days."

I considered that French health privacy laws must be more relaxed than those in the US because I couldn't believe the information this nurse was providing me without much provocation. Something was odd here. Then I remembered that Eve had been so kind to us as well. The nurse looked puzzled, and I realized I'd seen this look before—on Senator Heathcote's face when I'd suggested that he tell us about his nomination for VP. I had a hunch.

"There is something on your shirt." I pointed, starting with something simple. "Here, I'll hold the vial while you get it."

Mickey stood in the doorway, eyes widening.

The nurse handed me the vial without hesitation and began

brushing her shirt at nothing. "Oh dear," she said. "What have I gotten on this shirt."

"Dunno. It looks like dirt," I suggested, pointing to her perfectly clean white button-down. "Perhaps you should go and wash it off *right now.*"

"I'll do that," said the woman, hurrying down the hall. "*Merci.*"

I gave her a little salute and a smile.

"Let's get the fuck out of here," said Mickey. "That was brilliant."

"Wait," I said. I walked into Marielle Fournier's room and saw the woman looking out the window. She did not look like Delphine in any way; nor did she resemble Michel Busson. I wasn't sure what I was looking for, but the woman noticed me and smiled.

"Madame Fournier." I leaned down. "I am a blood relative of yours."

The woman's face was kind but bland, and I felt a pang of guilt for what I was doing.

"The soup was good," said Marielle, hopefully.

"Yes," I said. "The soup *was* good today! May I ask you something?"

The woman blinked and nothing more.

"It's important if you can remember, okay?"

"Hurry up," hissed Mickey, who was on lookout.

I held my hand out to shush him, and he folded his arms indignantly. I turned back to Marielle and crouched down beside her.

She looked at my face and touched it. "I've seen you before."

I shook my head. "No, I don't think so."

Marielle Fournier shook her head back at me. "Yes. You're the girl from the painting in the attic. It was covered by an old cloth and I was told not to look at it, but I did. It was burned on the edges. It was you." She thought for a moment. "But that's not possible, is it?"

I remembered Michel Busson taking that painting with him, the earlier version of *Juliet* that the maid had tried to burn in the fire. It had not been the final version of the painting. That one had been taken by Juliet's mother. "*Oui*," I said. "*C'est possible, Marielle.* Tell me, did your mother talk about her childhood at all? Was she happy as a child?"

"Oh no," said Marielle. "Mother had a terrible childhood. Grandfather Michel was a bastard." The woman motioned for me to come closer. "The soup was wonderful. Mother liked soup."

"Was Grandfather Michel terrible to your grandmother?"

Marielle looked out in the distance like she was trying to retrieve an image. "I believe he was." She looked at me. "But I can't be sure anymore."

I smiled. "You get some rest, Marielle." My heart sank again at the thought of Delphine miserable. She had been a delightful child. The spell Juliet's mother had cast had ruined everyone's life. I touched her on the shoulder and I could feel heat emanating from my right hand. I lifted my hand and studied it, even touching it with my other hand, but it was cold to the touch. I shook my head. Now I was feeling things. But once again, I placed my fingers and then flat palm on Marielle and she gazed up at me. Her focus become more intense, like a lover's.

"Who are you?" It was a clear statement.

"That's the million-dollar question," I said with a laugh.

"An angel?"

I smiled. An angel was the furthest thing from truth, it seemed. "Yes." My hand was hot, like I had placed it on an open flame, but I didn't remove it. The longer I held it, the clearer I could see the old woman's gaze become. When I couldn't hold on any longer, I pulled my hand away. "Goodbye, Marielle."

As I left her room, I could see her looking around the unfamiliar furnishings, wondering where her apartment had gone.

"About time," said Mickey as I brushed past him into the hall. "I thought we were having a family reunion."

"Oh shut up."

I had the vial hidden in my hand as we left through the front door, walking slowly past the concierge desk like people who hadn't just stolen a vial of blood from an old woman.

Once we were outside, Mickey sped up. "We're like outlaws."

"You're enjoying this way too much. I think you can slow down," I said. "No one is coming after us."

He slowed. "What happened back there?"

"I don't know."

"Don't be cute, Helen."

"My brain tumor now seems to be able to bend the wills of others... oh, and heal, too."

"Really?" Mickey touched his forehead. "I've had a slight headache since we landed. Can you heal that?"

I glared at him.

Then he spied a café. "Let's see if you're right."

He took me by the hand like a child in trouble with its mother and marched me into the café. "Order me a coffee with cream and that delicious-looking pastry." He pointed to an almond croissant.

I frowned, tapped on the glass at the pastry, and ordered two café au laits. As the woman prepared them, Mickey whispered behind me, "Now tell her you have no money to pay for them, but that you're hoping she won't mind if we just take them."

"*Pardon, mademoiselle. Je n'ai pas d'argent... mais... je voudrais un café au lait et croissant, s'il vous plaît.*"

The woman looked relieved, like she'd longed to have an unpaying customer standing before her. "*Mais oui,*" she exclaimed, pushing the pastry to me, almost insisting I take it, like it was her idea.

"I love this," sighed Mickey.

"Well, you only get about two more weeks of it before I'm dead, so enjoy it." I handed him the bag with the pasty. "What was it you were saying about an MRI?"

"Don't be using this mind-bending shit on me!" He pointed a finger and began digging in the bag. "Do you think we need to refrigerate the vial?"

"No," I said. "It's being used for a curse, Mickey, not a transfusion."

I tucked the vial safely in my bag wrapped in a piece of bubble wrap that I'd had the foresight to bring.

"Mickey," I began, "could we do something? I mean...since we're here." I walked over to the cab stand near the train. I asked the driver if he was local, and he said that he had lived in Challans all his life. I asked if he knew how to get to La Garnache. He nodded and we were soon out of the commune of Challans and into the countryside. In one hundred years, the immediate outskirts of the city had changed, but as we moved farther into the country, the white stone houses that had stood for generations began to resemble what I had seen through Juliet's eyes. The roads were different, having been carved out of what had been farmland. I asked the driver if he knew the Fonteclose manor, and he nodded. "I am from La Garnache," he responded.

"Maybe you can suggest we not pay," whispered Mickey.

I ignored him and focused on the driver. "Did you know the Busson family?"

"*Oui*," said the driver with little interest. "They are an unpleasant bunch. Madness runs in that family." I suspected that he was offering up more than he normally would in a casual ride, and the poor man had no idea why he was doing so.

"They lived near the Fonteclose estate, didn't they?"

"*Oui*," he said. "I know it well. They sold the house when I was around twenty." He paused. "I am sixty now."

"Can we go to the Busson house? I just want a glimpse of it."

We drove swiftly through the valleys, the ripe greens and wheat-colored hills. When he turned right on the road, I had an overwhelming sense of déjà vu. I had, literally, been here in my dreams last week, but it was no dream. It was like a bottled memory, a little like *Through the Looking-Glass*. I'd walked these roads when they were dusty. My feet had been dirty and I had been brown from being in the sun and the sweet sweaty scent of a child in the summer was something I could still smell remnant traces of, like yesterday's perfume lingering on your pulse points.

He drove up the road about half a mile and pointed down the hill. The Busson house was still standing, but it had a different paint color now. The porch where Michel Busson had grabbed and pinched my arm. I looked up the hill and I could spy it: my old stone house. To my surprise, it remained unchanged.

"Would you wait here for us?"

"But of course," the driver said, nodding.

As if I were in a spell myself, I stepped out of the cab and walked up the hill toward my old house. There were signs of life in it: wash hanging on the line, and a terribly odd sight: power lines connecting to the road. There were toys scattered throughout the yard in the primary colors of children. As we walked closer, I could hear the familiar sounds of chickens. I smiled.

Mickey was close behind me. "We'll probably have some angry Frenchman with a shotgun after us."

"Not if I can talk to him first," I said. Truth be told, I liked my new suggestive power and I was so comfortable with it, like an old shirt, that I knew it wasn't the first time I'd been given a gift such as this.

I saw an overgrown patch of grass. Clearing away some of it, I uncovered the stone well where I went daily to draw water. Instinctively, I looked around for a bucket. The house was not well kept; farm equipment and junk littered the grass in haphazard piles. Five yards from the well, I knew the exact spot where Michel Busson and his friend had held Juliet down and raped her in the night. And that left only one more hill to climb. Trekking up, I could see Marchant's roof peeking out. Seeing that house again stole my breath away. I came to the beginning of the stone wall and touched it. It was not as tall as I remembered. Memories and images came flooding back like old home movies in my mind. Not the key memories that I'd been shown, but the entire flood of them: my feet on the cool stones, the sound of my mother's voice, the soft drape of the fabric in Marchant's studio, and of course Marchant himself. The door to the gate was held open with a plant in a badly broken pot. I walked through the courtyard to the outdoor studio. It was empty. Somehow this detail made the space bearable. It needed to be empty. My Auguste Marchant was long gone.

I understood in a flash how tricky time can be. It's unnatural to witness so much sweeping change brought on by time. People were meant to live in their small pockets of time with events proceeding in digestible intervals. To see so many lifetimes of progress unfurled before us is far too jarring—almost incomprehensible. It makes us doubt our significance in the world. And a feeling of significance is so important to our survival.

What I was feeling was unnatural. I wasn't supposed to be here in this time and this place. Juliet shouldn't see the plastic toys and power lines. But here she was and here they were.

The smell of the musty stones, the feel of the soft breeze, the sound of his brush scraping canvas...the flood of feelings for Auguste

Marchant came rushing back. I was reminded of the way that Juliet loved him so completely, so foolishly.

"Your nose is bleeding." Mickey pulled off the button-down shirt he'd been wearing over his T-shirt and handed it to me. "Sit down."

"No," I said. "We need to go." I wiped my nose with the back of my hand. I had an odd sense that I was gaining strength. Getting a glimpse into my past had been exactly what I'd needed.

The driver was waiting for us as I had expected. Mickey was again delighted that I'd "cast a spell" on the man like I was a modern-day Samantha Stephens.

We boarded a train at Challans. As we headed toward Paris, I realized that the last time I'd had this view with rolling hills and green hues of fertile farmland was more than a hundred years ago. It had been the last time I'd seen my father, my sister and brother.

Mickey was quiet the entire ride back, as though he could tell what the trip had taken out of me. We made the most of our night in Paris. I found myself gravitating toward the Latin Quarter, toward the Boulevard Saint-Germain. Mickey was agreeable. We dined at a café two blocks from the old apartment. When I had lived here the café had been something else entirely. Over dinner, I told Mickey the story of Juliet.

"What was it like living in Paris a hundred years ago?"

"Dirty yet colorful." I smiled. "It stank and yet had some of the greatest opulence I've ever seen."

"And you lived here with *him*."

I shook my head. "Not in the way you think."

"But you loved him."

I drank my wine and considered my answer. "Not at first, but yes, I grew to love him. I was convinced I was in love with him when I died."

"And what about now?" He smiled. "I think you *like* him."

As we walked the two blocks to the old apartment, I thought about this. Standing under my window, I looked up at my old balcony. It was like returning to your hometown and finding that the streets aren't as big as you remember. Things looked smaller, dingier than I remembered them. But as I looked up at the building, I remembered the fear and loss of control I'd felt as that girl coming here from a farm in Challans with no knowledge of the agreement my mother had made with Lucian Varnier. I was in awe of Juliet's ability to so blindly trust her mother's word given what had happened in the kitchen and after the trauma of being raped by Michel Busson.

"Yes," I said. "I do like him." But as I spoke the words, I realized that all of these lifetimes later, I still didn't fully understand the agreement my mother had made with Varnier.

Mickey had his hands in his pockets and was watching me carefully. "Do you want to go to the Pont Neuf?"

I shook my head. The Pont Neuf was one destination that I feared I could not see again.

"Can I say something to you?" Mickey's hair was shining in the moonlight.

"Of course."

"You're different now. You're you, but not exactly the same anymore. You aren't the old Helen anymore."

I smiled, knowing exactly what he meant—I was now Juliet, Nora, *and* Helen.

22

Nora arranged to have Billy buried at the Forest Lawn cemetery, buying a space in a private mausoleum for him. His parents arrived by the end of the week, and Nora made sure that everything was taken care of for them. There had been only one request they'd made of her and it had come by way of a letter to her delivered to her room at the Roosevelt. They'd asked to see his house, wanting to know where their son had lived. Nora met them in the ornate lobby to give them the key and the use of one of Monumental's drivers. Billy's mother looked up at the opulent ceiling and clutched her handbag tightly.

"Why did you want to see us?" Billy's father was a tiny, wiry man. She couldn't imagine him working a full shift at the Youngstown steel mill.

"Billy spoke of you both very fondly."

"He never mentioned you to us," his father said. It wasn't meant as an insult, more of a fact.

"I loved your son very much," said Nora, smoothing her skirt, wanting something to do with her hands now that she'd given the key away.

Billy's parents looked at each other, but neither spoke at first. Nora realized Billy's dad did most of the talking. He took his hat off. "Miss Wheeler. We know what our son was, so I'm not sure what you're getting at."

The color drained from Nora's face. "I don't understand..."

"It was a source of pain for Billy's mother and me, but yes, we knew all about it."

"I didn't know," Nora blurted out. "When I married him. He didn't tell me."

"I'm very sorry to hear that." Billy's mother finally spoke. "You seem like a nice girl."

"Thank you," said Nora. "If I can do anything for you, please let me know."

They nodded but made no further requests and declined the offer of a driver.

While her house near the Hollywood Bowl was still vacant, Nora couldn't bear to be alone, so she had decided to stay on at the Roosevelt. The hotel noises, voices, doors shutting, and sounds of carts being wheeled down the hallway were a comfort to her. Halstead had jumped into action with the suicide story and the police were quietly looking for other theories, but Clint, to his credit, had done a decent job setting the crime scene. Then a suicide note was found in a copy of Billy's director script.

"Thinking this has to end. Forgive me."

She considered that it was perhaps a note to her about their marriage. Billy often kept notes in his scripts, like a list of reminders he needed. It was likely notes for a rehearsed speech he was going to give her.

The day of Billy's funeral, Halstead had ordered a large black car for her, and she was dismayed to see Clint had inserted himself as her driver. He was now coming and going at all hours at the Roosevelt.

So far, he hadn't touched her or even hinted at it. Nora had asked for assurances from Halstead that she'd be left alone, stopping short of saying that he owed her that much. The man had agreed, but Nora knew that it would only be a matter of time before Clint crossed the line. Clint crossed lines. Did he still somehow believe that Nora was his property? Now that she was a star, he felt like an early "investor" in her and he would certainly demand his share. And without Billy's presence to protect her, Clint beating her up again was all but guaranteed.

Had Clint killed Billy out of some obsession with her? After all, Billy's death had made him indispensable to Harold Halstead and had made Nora vulnerable. These two things were far too coincidental.

Clint let Nora in the backseat and jumped into the driver's seat.

"Do you know where you're going?" Nora looked out the window and adjusted her black dress.

"Yeah, I fuckin' know where I'm going." He drove a few blocks down Sunset. Clint was a talker, he couldn't help himself. "So did you do it, doll?"

"Do what?"

"Kill your husband. Because that scene that I walked into . . . well, it was a murder scene. Took me a fucking hour to straighten it out."

"Of course not." Nora adjusted her black glasses. "I loved Billy. I didn't kill him."

"How about his boyfriend? Did he kill him?"

"How would I know."

He laughed. "Clearly you didn't."

"Fuck you, Clint. Can you have some respect at least?" Nora could see sweat forming above Clint's lip. Soon he'd be sweating through his shirt in this heat.

At the stop sign, he spun in his seat and grabbed her arm. "You think you're better than me, don't you?"

Nora didn't miss a beat. "I do," she spat.

"I could fix it so *you* do time for this, honey. You'd better start being *really* nice to me again." Her arm was twisted toward him and it was killing her.

"Watch it. You gonna leave a mark like you used to? I'm sure Halstead would love that, especially today. Use your head, Clint."

He smiled and let go, driving on down Sunset Boulevard after the car behind him honked.

The funeral service was held at the Spanish-style Church of the Epiphany on Altura Street, his parents insisting on some religious ceremony. Nora had chosen the church because of its name—she'd certainly had an epiphany through this whole mess. She and Billy had not been real, she knew that now. They were merely another illusion created by Monumental Pictures. Directed by Billy, produced by Halstead, and with Nora in the starring role.

Still, Nora was racked with guilt over Billy and what she'd said to him that night. He'd paid the ultimate price for a secret that he was forced to hide. Couldn't she have just gone on with it for him? Nora's grief was so visible that Louella Parsons would later write in detail about Inez London and Harold Halstead having to hold Nora upright for the funeral procession. Conspicuously missing from the funeral was Ford Tremaine. The official word was he was on location in Mexico, but Nora knew it wasn't true. He was on a four-day bender, she'd heard, so drunk he'd nearly drowned himself in his own swimming pool.

In the weeks after Billy's death, there were sentiments of sympathy for the widowed Nora, but there was also an undercurrent of rumor running around Hollywood that she had driven Billy to suicide. Ford

Tremaine's disdain for her—and his frequent drunken articulation of this disdain—began a wave of bad press for her. There was even the suggestion that Tremaine had been *her* lover. Nora thought that had a hint of being planted by Halstead. The whispers did their damage. The movie version of Nora's Broadway show had been delayed, then permanently shelved, due to Billy's death, leaving Nora without any future work—a first since she'd arrived in Hollywood. Billy's funeral had cost her nearly four thousand dollars. While she was still under contract and she doubted Halstead would fire her, she knew that he would not likely renew her contract next year. Knowing that she'd need to reduce her expenses, Nora put Billy's house up for sale, but given the house's recent history, there were no buyers and she was told to wait and relist it in a year. Reluctantly, Nora accepted an offer on her own house. Next, she sold her car, but refused to sell Billy's Phaeton. It was the one thing she had to remember him by, and driving it made her feel like he was still with her.

A month after Billy's funeral, an invitation was left for her at the front desk of the Roosevelt:

Mr. Luke Varner invites you to be his guest

At a Weekend Cruise Honoring Lillibet Denton

July 24, 1935

2:00 pm

On Board "The Aurora"

Pier 12

Long Beach, California

The birthday party is a surprise

This was just the diversion she needed. Her old friend Lillibet. Nora packed her bag for the weekend and was standing in the Italianate lobby of the Roosevelt waiting for her car when Clint walked through the doors.

"Going somewhere?"

"Indeed I am. A party for the weekend." She was cool. Taking a cigarette out of her purse, she put it to her red lips and lit it. She turned away from him.

"You've run out before." He studied her. "You look different now, but you're not as pretty as you think you are."

"Oh Lord, are we going to do this again?" Nora blew smoke in his direction. "I'm fucking Nora Wheeler, Clint." She was afraid of this man, but she needed to stand her ground with what power she still had.

"I'll drive you."

"No need. I've got my car coming."

"I sent it back to the garage." He picked up her luggage. "I said, I'll take you."

Nora was alarmed. She didn't want a lengthy drive in the car with Clint, but he pushed her out the door and onto Hollywood Boulevard, taking her suitcase with him.

He opened the passenger's-side door for her, but she opened the back door instead and got inside as though he were a hired car. "Get the fuck in."

At a stop sign, he took time to take out a cigarette and light it. "I looked for you for several months, you know. I even went to Akron thinking you'd gone back there to your mother." The idea of him showing up at her mother's boardinghouse alarmed her, yet her mother had never mentioned a visit from Clint.

"You knew I wanted to come here. I never made that a secret."

"But leaving in the middle of the night. You sure kept that a secret, didn't you?"

"I'd asked you to help me. You said you knew people."

"You just went around behind my back?" Clint shook his head. "You made me look like a fool. Then I hear you're in a movie—and you're not Norma Westerman anymore, now you're *Nora Wheeler*." His voice was mocking. The car was going at a faster pace now. He was getting angry, working himself up. "Well, I had to see this for myself. And what do I see? You have a fancy boyfriend." He laughed. "So I figure this is the way it's going to be." They were driving too fast. Nora gripped the door handle. "You're going to go on this little trip and when you come back, you're marrying me."

"That can't happen, Clint. I'm a widow," said Nora. "It would look bad to marry you so soon."

"You think I fucking care how it looks to you? Do you?"

Nora needed to think fast. "It should matter to *you*. Halstead needs to renew my contract. You work for Halstead and I make a lot of money. The public needs to like me. Marrying you would make people not like me, and therefore I won't make money."

"You really don't get it, do you?" He tossed the cigarette out the window and with his free hand reached around to the backseat and grabbed her hair, pulling her across the divide into the front seat with one firm yank. "You are—always have been—and always will be *mine*. Do you understand me? Do you?" Still holding her head, he nodded it for her. "Say 'yes.'"

Nora nodded.

"Say it."

"Yes. I'm yours."

He let her go with a shove and she moved herself over to the passenger's side of the front seat, gathering herself into a heap.

"We don't even have to make the marriage public—at first—but I'm done with chasing you around the goddamned country. Look at you." He studied her. "You look like a tramp—a fucking whore. I heard he made you look like this. Billy Rapp…"

Nora closed her eyes.

"You aren't even pretty." He shook his head. "I don't know why I even care about you like I do. I'm just a nice guy. You're gonna get back and wipe that shit off your face."

Nora sighed loudly like she was bored. It was dangerous, but she couldn't help herself. She was tired of running from this man.

This move infuriated Clint. The veins on his neck began to swell and his face began to turn red. "Still think you're better than me?" He hit her on the head. "I can make it so you go down for his death. You know that, don't you? You stupid, stupid bitch." He grabbed her head and began hitting it on the steering wheel again and again. "Don't you know I *made* it look like a suicide. I did that! You cross me…or you don't marry me? You're going down for his murder. You get me?" He held her up by the hair.

Quietly she mumbled, "You killed him, didn't you?"

"Of course I fucking killed him, Norma. You are mine. Why don't you see that? Are you stupid?" He laughed. "Funny thing is, I didn't need to kill the bastard. He was never sleeping with you. The whole thing was a farce." He looked over at her, went a few miles, and put his hand between her legs. Fortunately, she was wearing trousers. She shuddered and Clint mistook it for desire. "You wanna pull off the road? Does the fact I killed him turn you on?"

"No," Nora snapped. "I have to get there before the boat goes out."

"I figure I'll manage your career," said Clint, gaining his composure.

Nora closed her eyes. After a few more miles, they pulled into the harbor and Nora quickly got out of the car. Clint came around and pulled out her suitcase. Backing her against the car, he kissed her hard and his hand found its familiar place around her neck. "You little bitch. You go on this fucking little trip and then you get your ass back here and you're going to do it my way or I'll fucking kill you, too. Do you understand me?"

Nora couldn't breathe, but she tried to nod.

"Is there a problem here?" It was a voice behind Clint. On instinct, he released her. She saw him smile before he turned.

Nora saw a man with caramel-colored hair lighting a cigarette beside the boat.

"No problem," said Clint. "The missus is just being difficult."

At "the missus," Nora thought she'd be sick. She would have to run again. Clint would eventually kill her. She knew that she had to leave Los Angeles and never return.

"Are you Nora Wheeler?" The man took two steps to retrieve her suitcase.

"Yes." She stepped away from Clint toward the man.

"We've been waiting for you," said the man. He turned to Clint, dismissing him. "Thank you."

Nora could tell that Clint didn't care for the man and cared less for the dismissal. He was handsome, in the way that the camera picked up—the cheekbones, the thin face. The man had tanned skin and deep, soft-blue eyes. He looked like he'd been in a few bar fights in his life. There was something about him that put Nora at ease.

"You remember what I said, Nora." Clint turned and got into the car.

The man helped Nora onto the boat. There was another man in a white server's uniform holding a silver tray of food.

"I'm Luke Varner." The man put Nora's suitcase down and put

out his hand. "This is my boat, the *Aurora*." He pointed to her head. "You're bleeding."

"Oh." She touched her hair and could feel a sizable lump where Clint had hit her head against the steering wheel. "Am I the only one here?"

"You are the first," said Varner. He motioned to the man in white. "Can you take Miss Wheeler's bag down to her cabin?" Varner walked around to the bar, poured a full glass of champagne, and handed it to Nora. "Let's have a drink. I'll get you some ice and a towel, too."

It sounded like a good idea to Nora. Luke left the room and returned with a white towel twisted around several ice cubes. She put it to her head.

"To new journeys." Nora downed the champagne quickly, and Luke refilled it. "That man," he said. "Is he as bad as he looks?"

"Worse."

Varner came around the bar and looked at her neck. "He left marks here, too."

Nora looked into a mirror that was hanging near the door. Red handprints were painted across her neck. She closed her eyes, embarrassed.

"You're safe here," he said. "I promise you."

She laughed bitterly. "Oh, Mr. Varner. I'm afraid I'm not safe anywhere." Nora took another big gulp of her champagne.

"Do you want to rest for a bit in your cabin?"

Nora nodded.

"Come on." He helped her down a set of stairs. "I'll be upstairs if you need me."

"Can you call me when Lillibet arrives?"

"Of course."

The room was modest but comfortable. It had a window and she could see out to the expanse of the Pacific Ocean. A sudden wave of drowsiness overtook her. Nora sat down on the bed. She would just rest for a minute. Her eyes were heavy, and she rolled up in a ball onto the bed.

Church bells. Seven of them. Nora woke slowly, getting adjusted to the light that was pouring into the room. Something seemed off with the scene around her. She sat up and looked around the room—and it was a room—on land, she was sure of it. Confused, she tried to remember the last memory she had. She'd been in her stateroom on the *Aurora*, where she'd had several glasses of champagne. She felt her head. The bump was still there—at least that was still normal. Looking around now, she was in a bed—a big bed with drapes and an elaborate rug. Light was streaming in through the French doors—two sets of them. This was not a stateroom. She looked down—she was dressed in a silk nightgown, not the sweater and trousers she'd worn on the boat. Sliding out of bed, she walked over to the window and pulled back the sheer drape. It was a strange sight. She was on the third floor. Cracking open the door, she stepped out onto the balcony and looked down at the busy street beneath her. This was definitely not Hollywood—this wasn't even America. She could hear people laughing and calling to each other. "*Allez*," said a man calling to a young boy. Where on earth was she?

Nora looked around the room for her suitcase. Opening up the armoire, she found six dresses hanging. She pulled the first one out—a knee-length powder-blue dress that she knew would fit her perfectly, as well as a silk-and-velvet gown that clung tightly through the hips and hung just below the knee. Nora checked the labels. They were all from the top French designers and perfectly sized for her. At the foot of the bed, a matching silk robe was draped. Nora pulled it around her and opened the door to the hallway. Everything was quiet, but she could hear the ticking of a clock. At the bottom of a grand staircase was a foyer with a round table and fresh flowers. Nora padded down the stairs, wondering if she should be wearing shoes. Off the foyer, she opened the double set of doors and peered in. It was a sitting room with a grand piano and bookcase and marble fireplace. Nora did a double take on the piano. Something about that particular instrument felt familiar. The painting above the fireplace caught her eye. It was a curious thing. Standing under it, she contemplated the mournful look on the girl's face.

"It's called *Girl on Step (Barefoot)*."

Nora turned to find Luke Varner, the man from the boat, standing behind her.

"Where am I?"

"Paris." He walked into the room calmly, as if he'd just said, *Pasadena*.

"Paris?" Nora thought she needed to sit down. "How did I get here?"

"I brought you."

"How?"

"That isn't important."

"I think it *might* be important."

"Trust me." He laughed. "That is the *least* important thing."

"I have to get back to Los Angeles."

"That isn't wise." He leaned on the chair. He wore a gray V-neck sweater with a white shirt and loose-fitting black pants. "But you know that already. You were planning to leave Los Angeles after the cruise."

"How did you know that?" She frowned. "Let me guess? It's not important."

He shrugged.

"Well, I can't stay here."

"Why not? This is your home."

"I'm confused, Mr. Varner. This is a lovely apartment, but it is not my home."

He smiled. It was a kind smile. "You are my guest here for as long as you need to stay. That man, Clint, he can't find you here."

At the mention of his name, Nora blanched.

Mistaking her look for hunger, Luke reached out for her. "Do you need something to eat? I can have the staff get you something."

"I don't know yet."

"Why don't you sit down." Luke Varner walked over and positioned her over the Chesterfield sofa.

She eyed him suspiciously. "I don't understand any of this."

He sat down beside her and touched her hand. "There is nothing to understand. You're safe now."

"This place." She looked around the room with its dark walls and elaborate wood moldings. "It feels familiar, but that isn't possible. I've never been to Paris."

Luke began to speak, but stopped. "Why don't we get you a little something to eat. I'll have Marie bring it up to your room."

Nora nodded.

Luke behaved as though she had been hospitalized. He helped her up. "You will be okay. I promise."

She smiled. As they crossed the foyer, Nora was so struck by the flowers. They were clusters of hyacinths, and the greens and blues and spray of leaves seemed to be glowing. Nora nearly teetered over from dizziness at the intensity of the color.

"What is it?" Luke looked alarmed.

"Just the flowers."

He looked down at them. "I'll have them taken away."

"No." She held out her hand. "They're beautiful. It's the colors. They're just too much for me right now. They make me a little sick."

Nora climbed the stairs to her room, clutching the banister. Upstairs in her room, she had a little bread and cheese that was brought to her by an older woman named Marie.

Marie stayed to be sure Nora was eating enough. After she'd left, Nora sat at the dressing table and instinctively reached for the middle drawer to pull out a hairbrush. That her fingers, indeed, touched a brush in the middle drawer was not a surprise to her. She'd known the silver hairbrush would be right where it was, like a muscle memory. Studying the hairbrush, she found several long reddish-brown strands in it. She pulled them out and studied them. They were not familiar and they certainly weren't her own chin-length, almost platinum-blond hair.

After eating, Nora fell into a deep sleep. The next morning, she woke in a sweat. The dream had been so vivid. The girl, Juliet, had felt like her. She had been wronged by her lover Auguste Marchant and raped by Michel Busson. At the end of the dream, a letter had come for her to work for a man named Lucian Varnier at an apartment in Paris.

She looked around the room. *This* was an apartment in Paris.

What struck Nora the most was Juliet. The painting that hung downstairs, Nora had dreamed about it. In the dream, she'd *posed* for it. But this idea was mad! There is no way she could be this girl. The hairbrush sat next to her bed, and Nora stared at it before picking it up and looking closely at the remaining strands of brown hair. This had been Juliet's hairbrush.

She opened the doors to the street and let the air hit her. This street. Juliet had known it well.

Nora drew a hot bath and crawled into the water, letting the warmth relax her until the water was tepid and she began to shiver. She dressed quickly into a silk shirt and a pair of wide-legged wool trousers and went down the stairs, finding Luke reading the paper at the dining table. He looked up, careful. "How are you?"

"I'm okay."

"Coffee?" He lifted the pot to pour some into a coral-and-aqua-striped porcelain cup.

She nodded, waiting for him to finish and set the pot down before she added cream and began to stir. Nora fingered the delicate jewels on the cup. "May I ask you something?"

"Of course." He leaned back in his seat, folding up the paper.

"I don't know how to ask this without sounding crazy."

"Try me."

"I'm having dreams. There is a girl in this dream."

He raised an eyebrow, which emboldened Nora.

"Am I her?" She blurted it out more forcefully than she'd been rehearsing it. "I know this makes no sense, but...these dreams are so real...and it's the girl in the painting...the one hanging on your wall."

Luke looked at the floor. "Well...uh..." he stammered. It seemed liked he'd also been rehearsing what to say next. He hesitated.

His struggle to speak piqued her interest even more, so she pressed. "Am I?"

"Yes," he said quietly, as if he was defeated.

"But that isn't possible."

He seemed shocked and flustered. He folded his napkin in front of him gravely and met her eyes. "How much do you know?"

"That Juliet was Auguste Marchant's model. That picture hanging over your mantel"—Nora pointed to the next room—"is her. Is me."

Luke nodded, but Nora wasn't sure if it was a nod of acknowledgment or agreement.

"These dreams?" He sat back in his chair. "How real are they?"

"Very real. Like we're the same person." She raised an eyebrow. "You seem surprised at this?"

"It's just odd, that's all. That you're seeing Juliet in your dreams."

"No," Nora corrected him. "I am Juliet in these dreams. They're from her vantage point. I see everything that she does. I feel everything she feels."

"And they're progressing chronologically?"

"It appears so."

"Hmmm." Luke tapped his fingers on the table.

"What is it?"

"This is just odd, that's all."

"Odd how?"

"Odd as in, you shouldn't have any memories of Juliet LaCompte."

"Should I be concerned that you seem as confused as I do?"

"No." Luke waved her off, but this only worried Nora more. He was keeping something from her.

Nora pressed. "My mother, did she do this?"

He seemed resigned to something. "She was what you call *une sorcière mineure*."

"A *minor* witch?"

"An amateur."

"As opposed to?"

"A *real* witch."

"There are such things?"

"You'd be surprised." He raised an eyebrow.

"And what are you?"

"I'm the administrator."

"The administrator of what?"

"Your mother's binding curse. You live in a binding curse."

She stared. "That doesn't sound very good."

"It's not so bad."

Finally, Nora sat down. "Can you just start from the beginning? What is a binding curse?"

He added some cream to his coffee, the spoon hitting the fine china cup like a bell. "You saw the...eh...*performance* Juliet's mother put on."

"The one in the kitchen?"

"*Oui*. Your mother chose an odd curse. Either she didn't know what she was doing or she meant to bind you to Auguste Marchant. Knowing that she was angry at Marchant, I doubt she wanted you bound to him for eternity, so I'm left with the conclusion that she made the mistake of a minor witch. She did, however, want him to suffer for eternity, so you get the problem that you both suffer and you're both bound. And now, we're all stuck—you, me, and Auguste Marchant..."

"For eternity."

"Correct."

"This curse she cast. It killed her?"

"Follow me." He stood up and walked down the hall to his office, turning the lock on the center drawer. From there, he took a piece of parchment paper and a sharp knife. In one swift move, he sliced his forearm, sending blood pooling on the paper. Nora yelped as he cut his arm, but Luke didn't flinch. Within minutes, the paper seemed to absorb or drink the blood, causing words to appear.

"Is that a contract?"

"Of course. We're not barbarians," said Luke. "It just was created by a blood sacrifice, so it requires blood to read it. You see, when a minor witch levels a large curse—one really out of her area of expertise—well, there are payments required, especially when she invokes the curse from a major demon and especially when she requests the help of an administrator."

Nora looked over to see that the gash on Luke's arm was now perfectly healed. "Death?"

"In this case, yes." He put on his glasses and read. "You see here that THE INVOKED has the right to request a sacrifice up to, and not excluding, the immaterial essence of the sentient being who has invoked the malediction..." He stopped. "It goes on, but it means the soul of your mother could be used as payment."

"So she knew that?"

"Well, Nora, it's not like she was doing business with the pope." He sat on the edge of the desk, like a professor. "This is an agreement with Althacazur—one of the original demons, a bad one at that. The consequences must have been so dire that she felt she had to enter into it—either that or she failed to read it, but I do think the fact that she added an administrator is proof that she knew she wouldn't be around to protect you."

Nora remembered the fury of Juliet's mother when she realized the girl was pregnant. She looked over his shoulder at the contract, but it was in some bizarre language. At the bottom was what appeared to be a seal in old blood that had turned black in stark contrast with the writing on the paper, which was still a crimson from Luke's fresh blood. "Is that what I think it is?"

"Your blood."

Nora remembered the vision of Juliet's mother cutting the girl.

"What about Billy?"

"Ah yes," he said. "Billy Rapp and Auguste Marchant are the same essence. Your constant concern for Marchant is charming in both of your lives. The problem is that you weren't *supposed* to be with Auguste Marchant in your first life. Your life was supposed to send you on a different pathway, but your mother had other plans for you, whether accidental or not, and now you are bound to him. Thanks to this curse you will *always* be bound to him, but you will never be happy with him, because it was not the natural course of things. Minor witches tend to fuck these things up."

"That is my mother you're talking about."

"My apologies."

"Can't we just rip up that contract?"

He frowned. "Sure, because that will make it null and void. You have no idea who you're dealing with, do you?" He handed it to her. "Just try to rip it up. Go ahead."

Nora remembered the demon's name that Juliet's mother had chosen in the book, and she remembered what he looked like coming through the kitchen door. Yes, she knew who she was dealing with. Nora took the paper in her hand and pulled at it, trying to halve it, but it was like steel. When she tried to again, it cut her and she began to bleed. "Ouch."

"You can try all day." Luke folded his arms. "It only gets angrier."

"And what happened to Billy?" She handed the contract back to him.

He sighed and handed her a hankie. "Do you really want to know? Of *course* you want to know. It's Marchant...you want to know every detail, don't you?"

"Yes, I want to know."

"Okay." He shrugged. "Have you met me yet in your dreams?"

She shook her head. "Paul de Passe sent an invitation from a Lucian Varnier to Juliet. I'm assuming Lucian Varnier is you?"

Luke sighed. "It works like this. You and Auguste Marchant were not supposed to be together, but now you are bound. You will always think you love him, but you never do. Frankly, it's boring, but the curse is written that way so you both play your parts. Fitting you're an actress this time. Your relationship with Marchant—or Billy, as you called him this time—always goes bad. When it does, you call me and the curse gets invoked. Voilà, my duties as your protector begin."

"Because you're the administrator?"

"Correct."

"How did I call you this time?"

Luke cleared his throat. "Are you sure you want to know?"

"I want to know everything."

"Everything?"

"Are you always this insufferable, Mr. Varner? Don't you work for me?"

"No. Technically, I'm in the employ of your mother."

"How awful for you." Nora poured some more coffee. "To be at the service of a *minor* witch."

He smiled. "You have no idea." He cocked his head. "It started when you wished Billy Rapp dead."

"You *killed* him?" Nora put the coffeepot down with more force than she meant.

"No," said Luke. "Technically, *you* did. I mean I had a hand in it, of course, but it was you. The request for help has to come from you."

Nora looked stricken, but somewhere in her mind she had always known this. The words she'd said to him. "I wished him dead."

Luke cleared his throat. "Actually, Clint shot him, but Clint only did that because you set the chain of events in motion. You will *always* set the chain of events in motion. It's the way the curse is constructed. You can't blame yourself. You have no control over it, because you're connected to Marchant."

"This is crazy." Nora pushed back her chair.

"And yet you know I'm telling you the truth. We can go round and round about this. You can storm off to your room . . . you can jump . . ." He stopped. "You will always be what you are—on some level you know this."

Nora studied the rug beneath her, anything to avoid looking at Luke. "I loved Billy Rapp."

"An annoying habit," said Luke rather bitterly. "Like I said, it's how the curse works."

"And I have no control over it? I have no free will. I don't fall in love with a random stranger."

Luke shook his head. "You can't."

"What if Billy's family had moved to Africa? What if he'd never moved to Hollywood?"

"If Billy Rapp had decided to tag along with Sir Edmund Hillary to Mount Everest itself, you'd have been hiking right behind him. You're bound. You two find each other. The earth opens up to facilitate this little exercise in futility again and again. It plays its part, too."

"But it makes no sense."

"Precisely," sighed Varnier. "Thank the minor witch for this—and Althacazur, the demon she invoked. He actually does most of the work."

"I don't think I'll thank either of them, Mr. Varner, if that's okay with you."

Luke put the contract back in the drawer and walked back to the dining room. As if on cue, a door opened and Marie came out carrying a plate of eggs. After they were seated, Nora slid the plate closer to herself and looked at the eggs. Instead, she took a piece of toast and began to spread butter on it followed by jam. Something about the dining room, the toast, Luke, Marie, everything felt so familiar.

Luke was studying her face.

"What?" Nora stared back at him as she took a bite. Far from hungry, she choked it down.

"Nothing," said Luke, his voice softening. He handed her a napkin. Blood was pouring down her face from both nostrils. "Let's get you upstairs."

Luke picked Nora up and carried her up the stairs just like a scene from a Hollywood movie. Once upstairs, Nora's nose bled heavily for a day and she was in and out of consciousness. When she finally woke, she found that Marie had stuffed tightly packed cotton up her nostrils. Luke sat by her bed, a worried look on his face.

"You look worse than I do," she said.

"I'm not so sure about that." He left the chair and sat next to her on the big bed. "I'm sorry. I told you too much." He looked pained, but something else was wrong. "This is all new to you, and you need time to adjust." Luke shifted his weight, and for a moment Nora thought he was going to get up from the bed. She had a surprising feeling of disappointment at the thought of him leaving the room. With no basis for it, she felt safe with this man. He smiled sadly and Nora knew, from the anguished look on his face, without even knowing Juliet's thoughts, that there had been more between them.

It took more than a week for Nora to recover from the violent nosebleeds, and Luke didn't visit her room again. On her way to breakfast, she found him heading out the door.

"If you have to go, will you take me with you?" She seemed to surprise him.

"I'm not sure you're up to it." He was putting on a raincoat.

"It's exactly the thing that I need," she insisted. "Please."

"It's raining," he said adjusting his coat. "You'll need an umbrella."

Nora smiled and grabbed one from the ceramic stand in the hallway. "I'm assuming they work the same in Paris as they do in Hollywood?"

Paris, with its wet morning streets, cafés, and bookstores, was exactly as Lillibet Denton had described it. Black cars and bicycles passed her and Luke as they walked down the busy Boulevard Saint-Germain. The Latin Quarter was a part of Paris and yet possessed its own unique character. As they passed the Sorbonne to the left, Nora was struck by its imposing architecture. She'd heard wealthy patrons in the theater in New York talk about sending their children to the Sorbonne to study, but it hadn't seemed like a real place until now. As she turned, she saw the top of the Eiffel Tower peeking above a building. Luke took her hand, and they crossed a street and headed toward what Nora assumed was Notre Dame. She had not had any dreams in a week and had no recollection of these streets although Juliet must have passed them hundreds of times. "Where are we going?"

"We are taking a walk," said Luke. "Here, take my arm."

Still wobbly from losing so much blood, Nora slid her arm into Luke's.

"I haven't been here in quite some time and I still haven't gotten my fill of it, I'm afraid."

"How long? Weeks? Months?"

"Years," he said.

"How many?"

"Too many," he answered.

"Too many as in…"

He stopped on the street and turned, placing his hands on her face in a gentle way. "Longer than I wanted to be away."

His eyes lingered on hers, and she saw pain in them. "I'm sorry. It's just that I have a lot of questions."

"Have you had more dreams?"

She shook her head.

"That's probably for the best. Just give it some time. I'm not pushing you again to remember. You bled terribly."

"Do you think that's why?"

"I don't know for sure, but may I suggest that while you're giving it some time, we just walk the streets of this breathtaking city together? Preferably in silence?"

She smiled and slid her hand under his arm. She thought she saw the tiniest smile cross his lips.

The next morning, Nora woke drenched. This time, it didn't seem like sweat; it was more like a rebirth—Venus emerging from her shell—only if Venus had been choking. Was it water? She jumped from the bed and fell on the floor coughing. Her nightgown was damp. As she sat on the floor, the pieces of her dreams and the missing story of Juliet's life came to her in waves, and she was so overcome with nausea that she threw up all over the blue-and-green silk rug beneath her.

Her lungs ached, which was impossible, but none of this made sense. She drew a hot bath and managed to slide herself back into more water. She sat in the bath for nearly an hour, until she was pruned. Marie had come into her room and placed a few more dresses in her closet. Nora could see her peering into the bath, but she didn't say a word. If someone had been looking at her, Nora was sure she would've looked mad—wet hair and dark circles under her eyes, bitten lips. *So Juliet jumped off the Pont Neuf and drowned.*

Nora finally made it downstairs after several attempts at makeup. She'd heard the door shut earlier, so she knew Luke was not in the apartment. She'd wanted to be alone in the place so she'd waited until he'd left to come down.

She crept downstairs and studied the main rooms as she entered each of them. Everything was as she'd left it back in 1897. The changes that Varner's wife—Lisette—had been in the process of making had all been reversed. The day she'd died, Juliet had seen them bringing in fabrics and taking out the chairs to be reupholstered, but these were the chairs that had been here before Lisette. The only change to the house was the addition of the Auguste Marchant painting of Juliet that was now where Varner's portrait had once hung. Nora walked over to the piano and sat down, positioning her fingers over the keys and pressing them down in an order that she knew would result in the perfect tone she was looking for, just as she'd done at the party in Beverly Hills. But this piano was different. *It was hers.* Her fingers moved in ways she had never known them to bend and spread. It was as though she had been reunited with a friend—a lover even. When she finished, she closed her eyes and placed her hands on the piano. It was at the piano keys that the realization hit her. *She was Juliet and she was alive again.* Instinctively, Nora turned to see Luke standing in the foyer, his face pale. He took several steps toward her. She turned on the piano bench to face him.

"You've had more dreams?"

She nodded gravely.

"Juliet again?"

She looked up at him and could feel the pain that Juliet had felt before she'd jumped into the Seine. He must have seen it on her face, because he took another step toward her and leaned down and kissed her forehead. "Juliet, is it you?"

She found that she was overcome. Tears began to flow down her cheeks and she stood—or Luke pulled her up, she wasn't sure, but Nora wrapped her body around his and kissed him softly on the lips.

"Have you come back to me?"

"I have."

"I'm so sorry, Juliet." He held her face in his hands. "I behaved horribly."

Nora knew what he meant. The memory and the pain were close to her like they'd happened not forty years ago, but hours ago. For all Nora knew, it could have actually happened yesterday. Nora was—and wasn't—a different person. The lifetime of memories as Nora had put flesh on Juliet's skeleton—had expanded Juliet's experiences and both amplified and softened her pain. "I loved you, but you knew that. How could you not?"

"And I loved you, but I was terrified of it. I didn't think we could be together. You will never know how ashamed I was after…" Nora could see the tears in his eyes and the tightness in his jaw. He was trying not to break down in front of her.

"After I died."

Luke closed his eyes.

Nora pulled him toward her and kissed him. Then there were the stairs, his room, his bed. A long day into night and then into morning as if they had a lifetime to catch up on.

23

Nora Wheeler
Paris, March 1940

Paris was eerily quiet as Nora turned onto Rue des Écoles. She'd gotten used to seeing the sandbags, the missing statues, the trucks driving out of the city—always out of the city. The Parisians, so proud, were terrified their buildings would end up in rubble, so they'd begun quietly packing valuables and placing them in trucks that had been running south in a steady stream since the fall of 1938. The children were also gone, parks emptied of them, packed like treasures and sent to Burgundy.

And those who had remained in Paris had their eyes focused sharply on one thing—a line of fortresses and fortifications that ran from the north in La Ferté to the Rhine River. The Maginot Line promised to keep German forces from entering France...Paris. Whether the line would hold was the discussion at all the dinner parties. Paris had to hold, both the city and the way of life. There was something special about Paris to protect, so Parisians removed things and sandbagged, looking up for the sounds of anything coming. Over the past year, the dinner parties had gotten noticeably smaller, people turning down invitations because they were traveling south or to America to see family "only for a short time." But no one ever returned. The quiet emptying of everything in the city was a silent vote of no confidence in the much-heralded Maginot Line.

Nora stopped in at the bookstore on Rue des Écoles. Each week more shops closed, and it was quite common for Nora to reach a store only to find it shuttered. She'd have to begin the quest to find something that was still open, even if in another arrondissement. When her memories of Juliet had come back, she walked the streets looking in at the windows, marveling at the changes. And for a long time, she stood at the Pont Neuf, trying to find the courage to look down. The girl who'd jumped felt so close to her in recent memories, yet Nora had lived another whole lifetime with different sadnesses carving indelible marks.

As she passed the newsstand, she eyed the cover of *Le Figaro*. Mussolini had announced that he was joining Hitler, and the British had not succeeded in an air raid in Sylt. They'd handed out gas masks last week, but she doubted she'd see that news in the paper. In the small English section, Nora spied Lillibet Denton. More accurately, it was Lillibet Denton who spied Nora. And that was a problem.

Standing on a stool, Nora was reaching for a Collected Works of Shakespeare edition that was just out of her grasp.

"It is you?" said a voice from below.

Nora looked down to see her friend smiling up at her. For a moment, Nora was overcome with joy, but then she realized that she couldn't be recognized. The safe world she'd created with Luke was now shattered.

"It is you. They said you'd drowned." Lillibet put her hand to her face and laughed. "Something about a party for me on a boat in Long Beach," she continued. "Did you know that? As if I'd ever be caught *dead* in Long Beach. I thought it was all a bunch of bull shit."

Nora smiled at her friend's habit of cutting words in two. Bull shit. Where Nora, the girl from Akron, would have simply said *bullshit*. She'd missed her friend and realized how absurd it was that she, herself, had believed that Lillibet had invited her on a birthday cruise. Had Nora not been so despondent over Billy's death, she might have been more clearheaded about the invitation.

"Well, I didn't die," said Nora, stepping off the stool to hug her friend.

"So it would seem," said Lillibet, touching her hair. "I almost didn't recognize you."

"It's my natural color," said Nora. "Hair dye is getting harder to come by these days."

"Yes," said Lillibet. "I'm headed back to the States on a boat in two days. I'm hoping we aren't torpedoed." The woman stared at Nora like she was trying to absorb every line and pore on her face. "Nora Wheeler, what happened to you?"

"Oh, Lillibet... it's a long story," began Nora. "I was rescued from a very bad man."

"They said you'd killed Billy. I didn't believe it."

"No," said Nora. "I did not shoot Billy." Nora felt the distinction was correct. She had killed Billy—or the curse had; she just didn't pull the trigger. Clint had done that.

The clerk tapped Nora on the shoulder and told her that the Émile Zola translation she was looking for was not in stock. Nora smiled and asked when it might be in. The clerk put up a finger to check. Upon turning back to Lillibet, Nora found her friend's eyebrow raised.

"Your French is quite proficient," said Lillibet.

"Well, I live here now," admitted Nora. "Paris is as beautiful as you described."

"You have no trace of an American accent," pushed the woman. "How odd."

Nora knew she owed her friend an explanation, but honestly, how could she explain that she was actually a French girl from Challans who'd jumped off the Pont Neuf before the turn of the century? She couldn't say that sometimes she visited the Louvre and sat in front of the paintings by Auguste Marchant just to look at herself as a young woman who'd posed almost forty-five years ago. The truth would not make anything clearer for Lillibet. The truth sounded crazy.

Pulling up the collar of her raincoat, Nora was concerned that Lillibet was drawing attention to her; this fear she felt in being discovered was visceral. And just as she'd felt a tingle in her finger before she'd played piano in Beverly Hills, now a tingle began at the tip of her tongue and began to flow through her. Remembering this feeling from the Pont Neuf the night a man had tried to help Juliet before she'd jumped, Nora knew what would happen next. Her mouth began to speak words that were not hers. "Lillibet. You don't want to tell anyone you've seen me. Do you understand?" It was more of a request, a plea even, but Nora noticed the strange effect her words had.

Lillibet blinked and cocked her head. "What?"

"You want to forget you ever saw me," said Nora. "For your own good." Nora was thinking about Clint. If Lillibet began telling everyone she'd seen Nora alive and Clint got wind of it, neither she nor Lillibet would be safe. "Do you understand?"

Lillibet stared at her, expressionless, blinking rapidly.

"Lillibet?"

The woman seemed to sway, and Nora reached out to catch her. "I'm so sorry," said Lillibet. "I seem to be dizzy." She smiled at Nora, but it was a strange smile, one without past or recognition. "You seem to have rescued me, my dear. Would you be so kind as to find me a chair so that I could sit for a moment? I feel like I've had quite a shock."

"You have," Nora agreed, guiding the woman to the chair that sat unoccupied in the French drama section.

She looked up at Nora and patted her hand. "Thank you, dear," she said. "I'll just sit here a moment. You look like you're leaving." The woman pointed to Nora's coat.

"I was," said Nora. She backed away from Lillibet. "Are you going to be okay?"

"Oh yes." The woman smiled. "What was your name again, dear?"

Without hesitation, Nora answered, "Juliet."

"Such a beautiful name," said Lillibet. "So Shakespearean."

"Yes," said Nora. She turned and looked back. "Goodbye, Lillibet."

"Goodbye, Juliet."

Nora left the bookstore and turned the corner quickly, going out of her way two blocks before cutting through another unmarked street that got her back to the safety of the apartment. Lillibet was in her sixties, so Nora doubted that the woman had followed her, but she wasn't taking any chances. She'd hated deceiving her friend like that, but she couldn't risk being found. Her hands shaking from adrenaline, she struggled to get her key in the lock. She looked down the street but saw only a paperboy.

She found Luke in the library, evaluating a new painting.

"Someone saw me." Throwing her raincoat across the sofa, she shook her hair. It was wet from the fine mist outside.

He didn't look up from an array of books strewn across the mahogany desk. "Many people see you, my love."

Nora shook her head. "I mean recognized me."

At this, Luke looked up over his glasses. "Who?"

"Lillibet Denton."

"That's not good," he said. He leaned back in his chair and folded his hands in front of him. "Did you speak to her?"

"It was strange." Nora came around to the desk and leaned against it. "I was in the bookstore. She saw me and asked me a bunch of questions, mainly about how stupid everyone must have been to believe she'd have a birthday cruise in Long Beach." Nora shot Luke a look.

"You fell for it," he said with a shrug. "So?"

"So, she was pressing me about where I'd been and how my French was too proficient."

"Did you tell her anything?"

"Like that I was born in the 1870s in Challans and jumped off the Pont Neuf to my death?"

"For starters."

Nora gave him a look. "But that wasn't the only strange thing."

Luke pushed the painting aside and stood up. "I'm listening." He walked around and began packing.

"I don't think you need to do that." Nora stopped him from gathering things. "I told her that she needed to forget that she saw me."

"How'd she respond?"

"She forgot me," said Nora. "It was as though she'd never met me before." Nora began to cry. "It was upsetting, actually. Someone knew me. It was nice, and then to just see that blank look of nothing, like I'd removed all memory of me. It was terrible."

He returned to his desk and glanced down at the papers in a neat pile. "I've been meaning to talk to you about something." He picked up *Le Figaro*. "I think we might want to leave Paris soon. With Italy joining, we're surrounded."

"Where would we go?"

"Back to America. Europe is too unstable right now."

Nora dreaded the thought of returning to America. She groaned.

"Nora, listen to me."

"I don't want to go back to Hollywood."

"I'm not suggesting that we do." He sat back down. "It's a big country."

"So where were you thinking? New York?"

"No." He smiled. "Too unwieldy, plus Clint knows New York."

At the sound of that name, she shuddered. While Paris had been a nice diversion, she had not really escaped her past. She sat on the desk and crossed her legs. "San Francisco?"

"Warmer."

"Oh God! Not Las Vegas? That place is horrid."

"No, but you're getting warmer."

"This is sounding more dreadful by the minute. What's left? Oklahoma?"

"Taos."

"Taos? What is a *Taos*?"

"It's a place in New Mexico. There is a fantastic little Spanish house I found. Lots of acres... secluded. You can have horses."

"Tell me, Luke. Have I ever expressed an interest in having horses?"

"Not exactly."

"Never exactly."

"It's a vibrant community of artists. It might be a great place to hide for a while."

"You've given this a lot of thought, I see."

"Are you angry?"

"No." Nora shrugged. "Luke?"

He sat in the chair across from her.

"Luke, why did Lillibet do what I asked her to do? This wasn't the first time this happened, either. Juliet did this same thing to a man who tried to stop her from jumping off the Pont Neuf."

"I don't know."

"You didn't do it?"

"No. Maybe you have some special powers of your own." He was deep in thought about something.

"What's wrong? What aren't you telling me?"

Luke looked uneasy. "It could be." He got up and busied himself at his bookshelves, but it was all theatrics. He was working something out in his head and didn't want her to notice.

Nora knew this meant he wouldn't be giving her a straight answer. Since her terrible nosebleeds when she was having dreams, he'd stopped telling her things. She hated being in the dark. "You're not going to tell me?"

"Anything that I would say would be purely a guess, and I don't want to do that until I know more, okay?"

"I thought you knew everything."

"I know what's in the contract, Nora. You've seen the contract." He shrugged and put his hands in his pockets. "What you did with Lillibet is definitely not in the contract."

Nora sighed. That didn't make her feel any better.

They arrived in New York City in April 1940. Within a month, the Nazis had slipped through the Maginot Line in Belgium and were headed toward Paris. Although they'd locked up the apartment, neither of them knew if they'd ever see it again.

The boat had taken much longer to get them to New York because it had to evade German torpedoes. As they arrived in New York, Nora was strangely happy to be back in her own country. Unlike Paris, which was shuttering, New York was alive and vibrant and seemingly untouched by the fear and war that had defined Europe over the past year.

Luke and Nora took a train to Chicago. This was Nora's third time on this line and she knew it well. While she was happy to be back in the States, she was also uneasy, given what had happened with Billy and Clint, and the idea of this desert house was not ideal, no matter how much Luke promised her it was a thriving artist community.

The house featured a massive wooden door that led into a grand foyer with dark wood. A long bench lined the hall; Nora realized it was a church pew and found names carved into the old wood seat. With its textured white walls and high dark-beamed ceilings, it was a house that yearned for people; Nora worried it would swallow the two of them up.

"Paul and Marie are coming in a few weeks," Luke assured her, as if he'd read her mind.

"They got out?"

"Of course, they're like me," he said, but he didn't elaborate further. She had suspected they were like him since it was the second life she'd seen them both in, but there was definitely some pecking order in that they worked for him.

As if sensing her potential boredom, Luke had purchased a mahogany grand piano—a Steinway Model M. Until Juliet had illuminated the instrument for Nora, she'd never had any opinions about pianos. Every pathetic piano Nora had seen growing up at the boardinghouse or at church had been a broken-down thing with chipped, missing, or stuck keys. But Juliet *did* have opinions about pianos, and those were now Nora's opinions. She'd never tested an individual key to sense whether a new piano had been tuned properly. Instead, she'd liked the heavy feel of Chopin's "Tristesse" to get a sense of the personality of the instrument. As Nora pulled out the bench and sat down, she felt her familiar fear that an instrument of such physical perfection would be lacking in sound quality and disappoint her ear. Some of the best-sounding pianos had not been beauties.

She pounded the first chords with more force than she would normally use. This instrument had a full-bodied sound with deep, lush bass keys and clear treble ones; not a tin sound emitted from any of them. Nora still marveled at what came from her fingertips—a skill that had developed overnight—and the sounds she could create by feel. The action was perfect.

As she finished the piece, a marvelous smell came wafting into the room. She smiled, slid the bench back from the piano, and followed the smell to the kitchen. This house was not home to her yet and she wasn't sure it ever would be, but all that mattered was that she had Luke and she was happy. In the expansive kitchen with hanging copper pots, Luke was cooking chilies and garlic for a pork dish. For a kitchen in the desert, this very much resembled Juliet's own rustic kitchen. "We need a better stove." She folded her arms as she watched him. "I didn't know you cooked."

"You've just never seen me."

"True," she acknowledged. "You could order cooks around a lot, but I've never seen you actually create something."

He laughed. "There are a lot of things you don't know about me."

"I know that," she said. "I have a lifetime to learn about you."

He smiled uneasily but went back to his task

"They're showing a Ford Tremaine film in town. Did you know that?"

Luke looked up from chopping potatoes. "I had no idea."

"I might go." She walked around the stove and stirred at what was in the pan. "Even though he is a bastard."

"Do you miss it?"

"What? Making movies?"

He nodded.

"A bit, I'm afraid." She shrugged.

Luke pushed the potatoes away and came closer, pulling her toward him. "I'm sorry."

She tried to shove him away, but he pulled her closer. "I know you're sorry." She smiled. "There are other things that can make me happy." She walked over to the cupboard and pulled out a small stack of plates and began setting the table.

"Such as." Luke's voice was wary. "You can't perform. It isn't wise. Even a local theater production is risky. You can't be recognized. You're supposed to be dead, and there are still people out there who think you killed Billy Rapp."

"I'm not talking about that." She moved on to the silverware drawer, the sound of the metal knives clanking against each other in her hand. "I'm talking about kids. This house is too big... too empty. The timing is perfect."

Luke's face fell. "That isn't such a good idea, Nora."

"Why not?" She looked into his eyes. A stab of fear hit her. "We love each other. No one is looking for me here. We can be happy here."

"We are happy," he said. "Just the two of us."

"What if I don't want it to be just the two of us?"

Luke exhaled and ran his hands though his hair. He looked defeated, like a man on a sinking boat. "It's not that simple."

"Why isn't it?" She thought she might faint. "What aren't you telling me?"

Settling himself uneasily against the sink, he folded his arms. "I promised you that I would tell you the truth this time. No matter how painful."

"Yes?" She walked around to the table and dumped the silver on it, sending it scattering. Bracing herself, she faced him.

He literally winced. "You'll never be able to have children." He moved around to the table and reached for her hand, but she pulled farther away. "I'm so sorry."

"Oh," she said as she sank in the chair below her. "Oh."

He bent down in front of her. "Oh honey. I'd give anything to give that to you, but—"

She cut him off. "So I'll never be normal then, huh?" Her eyes were cold. She recalled the scene in Challans in the kitchen, Juliet's nightgown dripping with blood and her mother telling her that she had been with Marchant's child, but that it was gone, too. Marchant's pregnant wife had been killed and their baby along with her.

He took her hands in his. "I'm trying, Nora," he said. "I'm trying to give you as normal a life as I can."

She shook her head. "It isn't your fault, Luke. None of this is your fault."

In the fall of 1940, Luke opened an art gallery near the Taos Plaza. The town still consisted of a dirt road with a few storefronts, but he began dealing in local artists' work and selling it. Each week, Nora would come into town and catch a movie, preferring to go alone. The movies were changing from the 1930s, and there were names she didn't recognize. After a few years, she couldn't imagine herself on the screen anymore—the fact that her peers were mostly gone gave her some comfort. Monumental Studios had closed shortly after Harold Halstead died of sudden heart attack in 1939, neither ever recovering from the deaths of their top director and his wife. She didn't know where Clint had gone and she'd stopped looking over her shoulder for him. She'd let her hair go back to its red, and it fell to her shoulders. Nowadays she wound it back in a chignon and had taken to wearing boots with long wool duster blankets. No one would have suspected she'd once been the actress Nora Wheeler.

It was during the viewing of *Rebecca* in the South Side Plaza that she was struck by the film's score. Racing home, she found herself at her piano, and the ideas in the form of notes came flooding out of her. Becoming a composer had never been something she'd ever considered. She'd been content to play the works of others—with increasing difficulty—but her own work, her own voice, had eluded her.

She drove to Albuquerque and found a music store and bought them out of blank music paper. Sitting at her Steinway, she began to piece together her first and then her second composition. In the next four years, Nora would create twenty-eight pieces of music for the piano.

On June 22, 1944, she woke to find that Luke had made her a plate of Spanish eggs—her favorite. While he made her breakfast every morning, to have it delivered was something out of the ordinary. "What have I done to deserve this?"

"It's your birthday."

She groaned. "Thirty-four. I'd hoped you'd forgotten."

"Sadly, no." He slid in the bed beside her and arranged her hair, an intimate act that she loved. "We've done well, haven't we?"

She laughed, snorted almost, arranging the tray in front of her and admiring the flower he'd placed there. "What on earth has gotten into you today?"

"I'm just asking." He sank into the pillow next to her, watching her. "We've been happy, haven't we? Despite the hand we were dealt."

She picked up her knife and fork and began cutting into her poached eggs. "Yes. We've been very happy." She smiled. "I couldn't be happier."

His face looked grim, and there were tears in his eyes.

She reached over and touched his face. "What is it?"

He shook his head, studying her face for a long time. "It's nothing. Nothing at all."

"Well, I can't eat with you doing that." She laughed and held out her hand, placing it over his eyes.

After she ate, she agreed to accompany Luke to his gallery. She'd had other things to do. She'd requested the score from Offenbach's *Tales of Hoffmann* and it had taken months to get it from a store in Montreal, but Nora had gotten a note that it had arrived. She'd planned to get it as soon as the store opened, but Luke had been insistent that they spend the day together.

He was busy hanging a painting when she looked out the window to the square and noticed the marquee for the newest picture, *Going My Way*. It was a musical starring Bing Crosby, and Nora was dying to see it.

"I'm going to go get tickets for tonight," she called to Luke as she fumbled with her purse. After she got the tickets, she'd swing around to the music store to get the score. She'd be back in a minute.

She thought she heard him yelling something to her. Something like "Don't go," but that was ridiculous. Nora was smiling, walking toward the theater, admiring Bing Crosby's name in letters when the truck hit her with such force that it sent her flying ten feet into the park. One minute Bing Crosby's name was there; the next it wasn't.

She heard *his* voice and saw *his* face. "Just stay put. Don't try to stand."

Nora put her hand to her head. "The pain." She could see that a truck had struck a statue. The crushed hood was smoking from the impact. How funny was it that she hadn't heard it? She hadn't even seen that accident and yet she'd been in the square.

He pulled her toward him. "It's okay."

"Funny," she said, deflating like a balloon in his arms. "It doesn't feel okay."

"You're okay." He rocked her back and forth on the ground. "You're okay." He continued rocking her, long after she'd stopped talking. Long after she'd stopped breathing. Long after she'd begun to turn cold.

24

Helen Lambert
Washington, DC, June 14, 2012

I'd landed at Dulles Airport in the afternoon and although I was playing it cool with Mickey, I knew I would be calling Luke as soon as I got back to my apartment. I'd hidden the blood vial in my makeup bag, and it had gone through security without a hitch. Now I rolled it up in a gym sock for safekeeping and locked it in my safe.

I was reeling, both from going back to Paris, which had ripped open many of the raw wounds I had from Juliet, and from learning about Nora's death—reliving my death, rather. While I couldn't admit to Luke that I'd gone to Paris, Nora's story answered a lot of questions I had about my own life, mainly my failure to have a child.

I set my suitcase down in my foyer, remembering to take off the tag declaring it had come from Charles de Gaulle Airport to keep up the ruse that I had been in London. I hit Luke's number on my speed dial. The conversation was short.

"Can you come over?"

"When?"

"Now?"

"Yeah."

I'd had a chance to shower from my flight. My nose hadn't started bleeding, and I didn't think it would anymore. With each story, I felt

I was building strength from each of my lives. This was different from what had happened to Nora when she'd bled so profusely. Pouring a glass of wine, I was halfway through it when I heard a knock at my door.

Nora's story was such a fresh wound to me that when I saw him I started crying—sobbing really. The poor man hadn't even gotten through my doorway and I was already a mess. He held me in the foyer telling me he was sorry. He was different from Juliet's and Nora's Varner, but he'd only changed for the times—from the formal coat and beard of Juliet's Varnier, to the cardigan and wavy hair of Nora's Varner, to the current leather-jacket-and-jeans version with shorter, spikier hair. I hadn't realized how many times he'd had to do this before with me, the dizzied explaining and piecing together of who I was and who he was in relation to me. It occurred to me that this must be maddening to him, but he just held me. It was the silence and the feel of him breathing that was the most romantic thing about it. And then I untangled myself enough to kiss him.

Something in my kiss caused his eyes to search my face. "Nora?"

"I'm so sorry, Luke." I nodded. Now I understood why Nora had been so special to him. They'd had a full life together.

It was as though we were both starved, barely making it out of the foyer. Me, pulling off his jacket in the hallway and peeling off my sweater like an unwanted shell. I knew his body from my dreams—I knew his body through Nora's eyes, which was a little strange because both were me and not me at the same time. I recalled feeling a pang of jealousy toward Nora in my dreams. I wasn't Nora or Juliet exactly, having both their memories but also a lifetime of my own different experiences...lovers...a husband. I was different. And he was different with me, too.

Hours later, we were eating Thai takeout sitting on the floor of my living room, using my coffee table and red plastic disposable plates. I stretched out my legs and scooped up a spicy eggplant bit. "Why did you not tell Nora what would happen on her birthday?"

He leaned against the sofa. "I couldn't do that to her. She just wanted a normal life. You know the disappointments she suffered... Billy...Clint..."

"Children." I shook my head. "Do you know how many fertility treatments I went through?"

"I'm sorry," he said.

"No one could figure out what was wrong with me."

"They wouldn't," he said. "You're just not like a normal person with normal fertility problems, I'm afraid. It's a curse, not an actual medical problem. You were pregnant with Marchant's child. Your mother got rid of the child—but unfortunately she did that for all versions of you. Marchant, Billy, Roger, too."

"Because I live in a binding curse." It wasn't until that moment that I fully absorbed everything that had happened to me in the past few weeks. And then the other truth hit me—really hit me. "I'm really going to die?"

He looked down at my rug and then met my eyes.

"I take that as a yes, then."

He nodded.

"This is just bullshit," I said. "I can't imagine my mother—my current mother, that is—casting some spell because Ryan Garner fucked me in the back of his parents' Buick on prom night."

"But the times were different," he said. "You and your family would have been ruined back in Challans."

"That makes no sense. Wipe out a man's whole family—kill his pregnant wife and child and force some fucked-up demonic miscarriage on my sixteen-year-old daughter, plunging them both into an eternity of hell, for revenge," I said. "It was an extreme reaction, don't you think? Even for 1895."

"I think your mother saw a lot of herself in you. I think it scared her."

"What aren't you telling me?"

"I'm telling you everything that I know about the curse, Helen."

"How much do two people—three people—have to suffer? Not to mention innocent people like Sara's mother, Auguste Marchant's wife. They had nothing to do with this and they're dead." I studied his face and the lines of his bone structure, trying to see if I could render an artist's sketch of him if I had to. He had a slight widow's peak, lines on his forehead, a masculine nose, and stubble that was graying.

"You can't blame yourself. You can't control it."

"But you can."

"No. I can't. I have limits."

"You're prepared to do this for eternity?" I knew he didn't want to answer this; he was always cagey about this.

"I am."

"Forever is a long time, Luke."

He touched my hair. "It is."

"Were you ever mortal?"

"Yes."

"When?"

"Not too long ago."

"Are we talking five years ago or 1595?"

"I think it was the 1700s."

"You *think*?"

"Honestly, Red. I don't know. I've been stripped of all memories, but I earn them back with each tour of duty, so speak."

"With me?"

He nodded.

"That's convenient." I considered that his lack of memories was the opposite of my life, where I was fitting several lifetimes into one body. "How can that be?"

"It's the nature of the punishment. To know you're punished, but not why. They think it's better for my suffering if I have no context at first. I just take orders."

Malique had told me as much. I hadn't fully considered what Luke had done to find himself in the employ of a demon. "Punishment for what?"

"I was rash in my real life, so now I'm forced to wait and watch you love someone else over and over. My hell is the waiting and watching. It's perfect punishment, really, watching you pine for different versions of Auguste Marchant again and again, even after we've had a marvelous life together."

"What did you do in the 1700s? Steal a loaf of bread?"

"I killed a man over a woman who didn't love me. That much I do know."

He leaned on the coffee table and stacked my plate on top of his, then pulled me completely over him on the floor. "I've thought a lot about it and I think this is my punishment. Eventually I'll earn back all my memories until I become truly cognizant of my crime. Then I'm given a choice to return as a mortal or continue as a demon."

"That sounds like an easy choice."

"Is it?" He laughed. "You're very sure of yourself because no one chooses mortality, Helen. The power of being a demon is too heady. By the time I'll have earned back my essence, I'll have been *this* for too long." He looked down at his body. "No one chooses mortality over this power. No one."

"Maybe you'd be different." The idea of him choosing something so dark made me sad for him. I took a loud breath to try to change the direction of the conversation. "What will happen to me when I die?" I could see he was prepared to be esoteric in his answer so I sharpened the blade a bit with my question.

"There is no *one* way that you can die," he said. "It could be peacefully in your bed; it could be...an accident like Nora. There isn't any set pattern to it, but I would be with you."

"Like you were with Nora."

He nodded. "I had thought about just going somewhere...like Tulum...Barbados...and just riding out our time together. Anywhere with water." He smiled sadly.

The idea of being somewhere at the end made it so real and final for me that I began to sob, deep long heaves. He held me for a long time. "I don't need to be on a beach somewhere," I said. "My fucking luck, I'll get eaten by a shark." I thought of that silly game Roger and I used to play. Would you rather die by guillotine or drowning? Eaten by a bear or a shark?

But I wasn't okay with dying in less than two weeks. I was more determined than ever to find a way to break this curse.

Luke and I didn't leave the apartment the entire next day; the take-out bags and boxes piled up in my kitchen. I had about twelve missed calls from Mickey on my phone when Luke went back home for a few hours. Malique had finally called back and told Mickey he would meet us tomorrow at his cousin's shop in Georgetown at noon.

When I placed the blood vial on the table, Malique looked impressed.

"I told her she needed to refrigerate it," said Mickey helpfully.

At that, Malique gave a full belly laugh. He opened the blood vial, poured a drop onto my hand, and rubbed it on my palm. Then he studied it again, falling into a trance where his eyes rolled back into his head. He came to a few minutes later and looked dazed, like he was drunk. "You got the right blood," he said. "But now I require something of his."

"Whose?"

"The other one in the curse. The object—the original object."

"Auguste Marchant? Fuck. I have to get his blood, too?"

"No," he said. "I just need something of his. The curse was bound with something of his and your blood. It can only be unbound with those original elements."

"Fuck, fuck, fuck," I said. "I wish I'd have known that when we were in Paris." And then, I had a thought. "Can it be any object?"

"Anything he owned or touched."

"*That*, I think I can do." I pointed.

Twenty minutes later, my cab pulled up at the Hanover Collection. I pushed through the doors and across the concrete foyer and up the loft stairs to the executive offices where Roger worked. It occurred to me that I might run into Sara and honestly, dead in ten days or not, I still wasn't sure I was ready to face her and her pixie self, always in some shade of beige with her neat blond hair and little makeup.

Roger's assistant recognized me and looked frightened at my sudden appearance, anticipating the calamity that could befall the office.

"Hi, Maggie." I smiled. I literally saw her gulp. "I have some quick paperwork for Roger to sign. He's *going* to want to see me."

She met my smile. God, I loved this gift. "Sure thing, Mrs. Lambert." I'll admit her referring to me as *Mrs. Lambert* gave me a tiny thrill. "I'll get him right away!" She jumped up and scurried to his office. Through the glass divider, I saw him spin around in his Herman Miller chair and watched as a wave of sheer horror crossed his face. It had occurred to me that my new superpower might not work on him. He was the other person in the curse. This was my only shot, though.

I looked at Roger—a younger, more clean-cut version of Marchant—charging toward me. There was no pretense of a smile when we met, and I felt like Juliet at the Paris Opera House that night so many years ago—traces of both of them between us somewhere. I could see him glancing down the hall, worried Sara would see us. This made me angry enough that I could literally feel the power pulsing through me. His voice was low and not welcoming. "What are you doing here?"

I decided to try something light, in case he was immune to my suggestive skills. I needed something that let me save face and get the fuck out of there if it didn't work. "I need your help with something. Would you be able to help me?" It was an innocent enough suggestion. If he maintained his scowl, I could offer something that I needed him to do for my mother. He liked her. (She hated him.)

He gave me a puzzled look and I froze. *Oh shit*, I thought. But then he smiled. "Of course I can help you! What do you need?" His face shifted. He put his hands in his pockets like we were the old college buddies that we were.

I lowered my voice, causing him to lean close. "I need to see the Auguste Marchant personal items you have here at the museum. The paints, the brushes. Would you take me there?" I smiled. This was fun!

"Of course, Helen," he said. "Let's go." He trotted down the stairs like he was giving a tour. Since the museum had only been finished when we were separated, I admit that I hadn't spent any time here, other than my late-night visit with Luke. It was a stunning space that Roger had lovingly created. Other than the circular Hirshhorn, most of Washington's museums were serious places with Greek architecture. It was a city of columns and marble. This was concrete and glass. It was fitting that Roger had chosen to put this museum in the newly

developed Waterfront. Looking around, I couldn't help but feel proud
of my ex-husband. Although I wondered if Roger ever weighed what
he'd given up for this.

Like a war charge, he led me down the steps into a private part of
the basement. He swiped his key and escorted me into a room that
smelled of dust and paint. Something that can only be experienced by
living it, not by reading history books, is that the smells of a time are
unique. Foods, body odors, soaps, flowers, chemicals—they change
through time, and their brewing conjures entirely different olfactory
palettes, but smell is the hardest of the senses to describe, so the floral
scent of a perfume in Belle Époque Paris is not the same as one today,
nor is the smell of garlic cooking since the oils are different. Bodily
odors are different, too—the combination of chemicals used on them
changes with time. I passed through time as I entered the room. I
could smell Marchant's open paints in the courtyard. I spied the old
wooden paint case he always had in the studio. Immediately drawn to
it, I pulled it off the shelf and placed it on the table. Opening it, I felt
my heart stop. It was really *his* case. I closed my eyes: Oh, how I had
loved this man! Loved so many versions of him through time, including the one standing beside me, but this was the original—the genesis
of it all. The pure love that I'd felt for *this* man in *this* time with *this*
case. I pulled out a brush—one I'd seen him use on my own painting.
"I need to borrow this. Is that okay?"

"Of course, Helen." Roger smiled. It was kind of Stepford and
creepy the way everyone wanted to help me with such enthusiasm,
but I needed the brush and Roger needed me to have the brush, even
if he didn't realize it.

I was about to shut the case when I noticed the depth of the tray
didn't match that of the case. Reaching in, I pulled down on the brush

tray to reveal a false bottom. Inside the space was a piece of paper. Before I even unfolded it, I knew what it was. Unfurled on weathered paper was a sketch of my nude. It was the face study from the *Juliet* painting. The outlines of my body were rough—although in true Marchant style they were almost perfect—but the face detail even after all these years was better than my own current DMV photo. He'd told Juliet that he'd kept her portrait to remind him of his folly, but this picture wasn't about folly, nor was it about lust. It was Juliet drawn by a man who'd wanted to keep a detail of every line and curve of her face etched in his mind. I could see it had been held and opened, the stains on it from fingers—his fingers. Auguste Marchant had loved her and kept it in his most secret spot.

This paper reflected the way their romance was to end: Juliet and Marchant going their separate ways to face different fates. I smiled sadly and felt entitled to do what I did next. I folded the sheet and, instead of sliding it back into the space, I put it in my back pocket. Roger seemed in a weird trance of happiness that he was helping me and didn't notice I'd discovered a secret compartment in Marchant's paints. Had Roger been about his wits, he would have knocked me over to investigate the secret compartment. I snapped the lid shut. It would be my little secret with Marchant. "All done," I said.

He proudly escorted me to the front door, even opening it. From the corner of my eye, I saw Sara watching us from the executive suites with a combined look of disgust and shock. "Roger," I said. "Why don't you kiss me lightly on the lips?"

"Of course," he said. His kiss was enthusiastic, like the old Roger. It was even a little longer than our wedding kiss.

I adjusted his collar. Mind you, there was nothing wrong with his collar, but it was an intimate act and the thrill of being watched by

Sara now felt like the universe had righted itself for just a second. "You know, Roger," I said, "I think you are getting tired of Sara."

He thought about it for a moment. "You know, Helen, I think you might be right."

"Take care, Roger." I could see Sara stiffen, and I had to admit that I smiled a little more as I hailed a cab back to Georgetown.

25

Sandra Keane
Los Angeles, May 1970

As Tom Jones crooned over the speaker above her, Sandra Keane snapped open another paper bag. She pushed the button and watched the food inch closer toward her on the belt. Mrs. Gladney was buying an array of meat products in every shade of blood. "You making something special, Mrs. Gladney?"

Mrs. Gladney clutched a coupon in her hand with some tenacity. "Oh yes, Sandra! I'm making Italian roast beef sandwiches and potato salad. Jared is coming home this weekend. It's his favorite."

Jared Gladney's number had been drawn in the first lottery last December and he was coming home from army basic training before being shipped off to Vietnam. Among their regular customers at the store, it was common knowledge who was over in the jungles of Southeast Asia and who was on their way. Now that she was twenty-one, Sandra knew a dozen boys she had gone to school with who had been drafted. Jared Gladney had only been out of high school one month when he had gotten the news.

Sandra's dad was the regional manager at A&P with five stores in the Southern California area. This was only a part-time thing for her, courtesy of her dad who was always sure to point out how lucky she was to have the job. Today he was looming somewhere in the front of the store watching how fast she keyed in the prices on the register. Her mother, who worked as a secretary at the UCLA provost's office, was very pleased with the fact that they'd recently sold their house in Los Feliz to move to a larger house in Hancock Park, surrounded by neighbors who were dentists, entertainment lawyers, or television stars. Although her mother would never admit it, Sandra suspected she missed her friends in the old neighborhood where they drank and smoked cigarettes out of sight of their husbands and discussed the amount of Paregoric they'd been prescribed for their bad stomachs (usually caused by the husbands or wayward, unappreciative children). There were also the ceramics classes and macramé classes, with nearly every house in Los Feliz sporting the same ceramic cat duo. The new neighbor in Hancock Park had a housekeeper who used to work for Lana Turner. Sandra's mother was now determined to get the woman to work for her just so she could say she'd employed Lana Turner's housekeeper.

Sandra snapped another bag open with one hand, a skill she'd developed in the three years she'd worked here, just the right amount of wrist. She'd be a junior at UCLA in the fall. Her parents still thought she was majoring in nursing—a bit of an intentional oversight on her part to not tell them she'd switched to music performance last year. Practical people with jobs managing the order of finite places, her parents saw no certain future for their daughter unless she was going to be a music teacher—a profession that Sandra had no interest in. At their urging, she'd majored in nursing, but by the end of her freshman year, she decided she hated it.

"Mr. Tremaine." Sandra looked up to see her father patting a bony-faced man on the back. While there were throngs of old movie stars who came through the A&P doors, Ford Tremaine, a 1930s film star, was a stranger bird than most, always waiting in Sandra's line even if the other checkout counters were empty. The old stars came in two varieties: those who came decked out waiting to be noticed in the canned goods aisle and those who bundled themselves in hats and scarves trying to avoid being seen, only to draw more attention for their poor attempts at shopping incognito. With his quaking fingers and thick mane of brown hair with white roots, Ford Tremaine was one of the former. He smelled of hair dye and cheap cologne and wore gold rings and a bracelet—a man who was trying hard. Sandra always noticed his rings as he composed a check for three cans of cat food that could total less than seventy-five cents. Her father, a big film buff, knew them all by name and their entire oeuvre. He'd started out a ticket boy at the Pantages Theatre and still recognized all the old contract players, dramatically approving their checks and making them feel like they were still Hollywood royalty, if only within the walls of this grocery store. Her father was good at that.

"Did you find everything you needed, Mr. Tremaine?" Sandra's father pushed Sandra out of the way and began ringing up Tremaine's items. This was all show. Sandra picked the emery board from her pocket and filed at an errant nail.

Ford Tremaine stared at her like he always did: as though she were a ghost. It was unnerving, and she tucked herself behind her father's girth to avoid the man's stare.

"That'll be one dollar and nine cents," said her father, who reached for a bag, bringing the aging movie star once again into view.

Sandra smiled weakly, meeting Ford's eyes, glad she wasn't approving a check for one dollar. Her father took the rubber stamp out and dramatically pressed it against the check, signing it and then placing it under the cash drawer.

Once Tremaine had told her that the devil was playing tricks on him and said "Nora? Is it you?" She assured him she wasn't Nora.

"Have a lovely day, Ms. Keane." After all these years in Hollywood, Tremaine still had the thick Southern accent from Mississippi. At least she thought that was where he'd told her he was from. She pushed the bag toward him.

He turned around at the door to get one last look at her. His staring gave her the creeps.

"That man is weird," said Sandra.

"He was a big star in his day." Her dad was busy counting ones from the register.

Sandra snorted at the thought of it.

"No." Her dad stopped counting. "He was really good...nominated for an Oscar—one of the first ones for that Billy Rapp film... *Beyond the Shore*. It came out after Rapp died." Satisfied with the thick stack of one-dollar bills, her dad snapped the cash register shut and headed toward the office.

After her shift was over, Sandra walked down Larchmont Avenue to her car, tugging her long, strawberry-blond hair out of the required ponytail and shaking it free. Despite being in a city of beautiful women, Sandra was "a looker" and it wasn't uncommon for a motorcycle to pull over or a car to honk as she made her way home. As she headed west on Melrose away from Paramount Studios, she rolled down the window on her light-blue Corvair.

The sun was nearly finished for the day, and it sent a soft, warm glow toward the ocean like a dying campfire. While the warm weather was great here, Sandra always thought that growing up in Hollywood fucked you up. Kids like her who grew up in the shadow of the Hollywood sign saw the glaring disparity between the real and the fake, making its teenagers abnormally cynical. The ideal mom from the favorite 1950s TV show that you watched after school might now be giving blow jobs at the bowling alley parking lot off Sunset.

Seeing aged and hunched '50s movie stars pushing grocery carts, chasing kids off their lawns, or riding their bikes drunk through their suburban neighborhoods fucked with the idea of Hollywood perfection. It was a city that was good at tricking the eye. It had to be hard, Sandra thought, all these old stars seeing ghosts of themselves everywhere with tour buses circling every fifteen minutes like they were installments in a zoo.

It was Saturday night and by the time she got home her mother was busy preparing herself for her regular weekly dinner with her father at Musso & Frank. From the look of it, Sandra would have thought her mother was headed to the opera. Betty Keane teased her hair into a bouffant that Sandra thought was a little dated; it was a bit much for an avocado cocktail or calf's liver with onions. Betty turned and posed in front of the mirror, waiting for Sandra to say something. Her mother was wearing a pink-and-orange polyester shift that went to the knee and was snug across her newly wide hips. Sandra had a sneaking feeling that she had fit into the dress last summer.

"Well?" Her mother shifted her weight from foot to foot, the sound of her nylons swooshing as her inner thighs scraped together. "What do you think?"

"You look good." Sandra could hear her voice rise. It was her lying voice.

Her mother eyed her. "You aren't going out with those kids tonight." It was a statement, a warning, really.

Those "kids" were Hugh Markwell, Lily Leotta, and Ezra Gunn. Together the four of them had formed a band, No Exit. With the exception of Ezra, whose father was a somewhat famous television producer, Sandra's parents hated these friends.

As with most parents, the murder of actress Sharon Tate by Charles Manson's family of teenagers last August had unnerved them to the core. No Hollywood script could have produced something so terrifying as the actual murders and the macabre scenes at the courthouse with Manson's followers carving symbols into their foreheads. It wasn't the actual Tate murder that had unsettled *her* parents as much as the murders of Leno and Rosemary LaBianca the following night. The LaBiancas had been normal people who lived in the same Los Feliz neighborhood as the Keanes. Normal people just didn't get murdered in their bedrooms in Los Feliz, so with pressing from her mother, the family had moved to a two-story Italian Revival house in Hancock Park and her mother bought two Boston terriers—Buster (as in Keaton) and Basil (as in Rathbone)—for protection.

As Sandra looked down at Buster and Basil, snoring on her parents' bed and oblivious to her presence, she wondered what on earth those two could possibly protect.

In particular, her parents had taken one look at Hugh Markwell, with his dirty-blond hair and straggly brown beard, and determined he was exactly the kind of boy to lead their daughter astray. "That Hugh called earlier." Her mother was now plucking her eyebrows.

"When?" Sandra leaned against the doorframe, trying not to act too interested.

"When I got home from work. I told him you weren't here and that I didn't know when you'd be back." Her mother pivoted and faced her. "You know how we feel about that band of yours."

The band was a sensitive subject. Sandra was the keyboard player, but that was being modest. Halfway through her first piano lesson at the age of ten she'd mastered "Row, Row, Row Your Boat" and "Green Gravel" while the instructor was brewing a weak cup of coffee on the stove. By the second lesson, Sandra noticed that she felt an

electricity coming from her fingertips, not unlike the feeling she got
when she ran her socks over the carpet and touched the light switch.
Within the hour, Sandra was playing sonatinas as easily as she could
recite the alphabet. Her teacher, so animated about Sandra's swift
progress through the Hal Leonard instruction book, used words like
"never seen anything like it before," and "we need to take her to
New York." Sandra's parents heard "savant" and wanted no part of
some strange, unexplained talent that had sprouted overnight from
their daughter's fingertips. Despite Sandra's begging and repeated calls
from the teacher, they never took their daughter back for another lesson.
Within a month they'd sold the piano to a family down the street. Sometimes Sandra would walk by and look at it through the window. So
she took to playing alone at school and hiding the fact that she didn't
need lessons at all to master Chopin and Rachmaninoff by the age of
eleven.

To avoid any further conversation with her mother about the band,
Sandra changed quickly into a white gauzy top, grabbed her purse,
and headed out the front door and down the steps to her car with a
quick "Bye."

The heat was stifling and she rolled down the window to let some
air in the car. She was already late meeting Hugh, who was getting off
his shift at Vogue Records in Westwood in an hour. Since they didn't
have a gig tonight, they were planning on practicing at Hugh's place
in Laurel Canyon before hitting the Strip to check out other bands.

As she pushed through the doors of Vogue Records, the bell jin-
gled. Hubert Markwell III stood behind the counter, his dirty jeans
and cowboy boots looking like he'd slept in them. Sandra was always
surprised to see him with his shirt buttoned. Most days, he didn't wear
shoes.

For a Saturday, Vogue Records was dead. This was the place where everyone gathered to listen to new music that came out each week. From teenagers to rock stars who came in from neighboring Beverly Hills to pick up the latest, everyone knew Hugh. He walked over to the record player and, after searching for what seemed to be five minutes for what he wanted, placed a big stack of records on the player and set the arm. Dutifully, the record dropped from the stack and the familiar bars of Crosby, Stills, Nash & Young's "Ohio" echoed through the shop.

When she'd first met him, Hugh grilled her about her own record collection, and she was afraid to admit that most of her stuff was classical piano—Debussy, Satie, and Chopin. The last album she'd purchased was Bobby Goldsboro's *Honey*. So Hugh sat her down in front of his own collection asking her what she liked. He was satisfied enough that she'd liked the Rolling Stones, Eric Burdon and the Animals, and was a big fan of Ray Manzarek of the Doors.

As "Ohio" spun on the turntable, a small voice came from somewhere in the aisles. "That's so groovy." The voice belonged to a tiny thing with long brown hair and a cupid face. Lily Leotta seemed to float rather than walk through the aisles, wrapping herself in a Pendleton blanket over her T-shirt and bell-bottoms. She hugged Sandra tightly—something she did to everyone she met so she could feel their aura. Lily said she was from Florida although which part of Florida remained vague as did everything else about Lily, except that she seemed to know Hugh intimately and she'd lived in Los Angeles's Laurel Canyon with a semi-famous musician before moving less than a mile down the road to live with Hugh instead. Hugh's "place" in the Canyon was a tepee he'd built in his sister's wooded backyard a little too near the fire pit than Sandra thought prudent, but Hugh didn't concern himself with such things.

After Hugh's replacement showed up, stoned and twenty minutes late (they were glad he showed at all), Sandra followed him and Lily up Laurel Canyon Boulevard. Finding Hugh's house was tricky. It was a gingerbread cottage, brown and low, blending in with the trees just before Lookout Mountain Road where musicians like Joni Mitchell and Cass Elliot owned homes. The driveway was never marked, so the first thing Sandra always spied as a marker was the tepee sticking up past the house. With its tree houses and all-night partying, Laurel Canyon in some ways felt like a never-ending summer camp for adults. Never mind the fact that real kids were everywhere with their bikes littering the winding roads. The Canyon was magical.

While everyone called it Hugh's house, the house actually belonged to Kim Markwell Nash, Hugh's older sister. The prodigal children of an oil millionaire from Bakersfield, Kim was four years older than Hugh and a freelance writer. Kim's husband, Rick Nash, was a photographer for the *Los Angeles Times*. Neither of those jobs would pay for a house like the one they rented in the Canyon, so Sandra knew that their dad was likely footing the bill for the place although Hugh was currently estranged from his father for marrying his mother's nurse after her death two years ago. Kim, however, was still tight with her father, so according to Hugh the money still flowed.

Around the living room with wood floors and paneling, scattered sofas covered with garish afghans, and orange shag rugs were black-and-white photos that Rick had taken. Several covers of the *Los Angeles Times*' Sunday magazine, *West*, featuring Rick's photos were framed and hung on the walls.

"Is Rick working tonight, too?" Saying his name sent a wave of electricity through Sandra's body. Hugh had introduced her to his brother-in-law a few months ago, and Sandra found herself trying to get into the same room with him every chance she could.

Kim, wearing purple octagonal sunglasses that made her look a little like Janis Joplin, was lying across the sofa smoking a joint. For the first time, Sandra noticed a photo of Janis Joplin sitting on that very sofa, holding an ashtray, with those very glasses. Sandra spotted nearly eight ashtrays on the coffee table, all of them brimming with old ash.

She passed the joint to Sandra, who debated smoking it for a moment. They were supposed to practice, and it was hard for her to focus stoned. She inhaled twice and sat back on the sofa waiting for that moment the pot hit her and the floor dropped out from under her like the Whirl Pool ride at Pacific Ocean Park.

"Yep," said Kim, a beat behind the conversation. "He should be here any minute." Kim had long red hair, freckles, and wide hips. The combination of Kim was beautiful and, in fact, her nude form currently adorned a giant photo over the mantel, obviously another photo taken by Rick. It was customary for Rick to call from the pay phone on Doheny to see if anyone wanted food before he headed up the Canyon. It was unclear to Sandra whether he'd done this yet tonight.

"Is he bringing food?"

"Indeed, dear brother. Pizza. He's covering Creedence at the Forum tonight. I haven't seen him in a week. I'd really love to do more than just *think* about having sex with my husband so you all might need to leave." Kim turned her attention to a cat who had parked itself on the cushion next to her and began rolling around on its back.

Sandra hadn't seen this cat before at the house. Cats were everywhere on the Canyon's winding roads, sunning themselves and moving from house to house. When she looked up, she saw Rick walk through the doors, bags of food in hand. Sandra felt the breath go out of her. She never got tired of seeing him.

Rick Nash was one of the best-known photographers in Los Angeles—if not the country—known for taking the photos in most of the features sections. He'd been on Sunset Strip at Pandora's Box during the 1966 riots and at the Whiskey when Jimi Hendrix had taken the stage. In the last year he'd photographed the Doors, the Flying Burrito Brothers, Jimi Hendrix, and Stephen Stills as well as covering the construction of the 405 freeway.

Rick was loading film in his Nikon camera. "Hey, asshole, are you practicing tonight?" He directed this comment to his brother-in-law.

Hugh nodded as he dug through bags looking for something to eat.

"I was thinking it might be cool if I took some photos to document what's going on? It might be nice, capturing the start of a band."

"That's cute, honey. How many bands has this been for Hugh now?" Kim was bored with the cat and had sunk herself deeply into the sofa and closed her eyes.

Rick shot Hugh an apologetic smile.

"When will you be home?"

"Midnight," said Rick. "I just need a few shots of Creedence tonight."

"Someday, your husband will say he knew us before we were famous." Hugh had positioned himself on the floor directly in front of Kim's nude photo. Sandra wondered if that was weird for him.

"And I'll sell tickets to your tepee, you little bastard." Kim yawned.

"Got any extra tickets for tonight?" Hugh lit up a cigarette. Rick was always good for some tickets.

"I do, indeed." Rick glanced at Sandra. "I've got four with your name on them, Hubert." He leaned his tall frame against the doorway and reached into his pocket. He was wearing flared, faded jeans with a giant silver belt buckle on his light leather belt. While he talked, he cleaned the Nikon with his shirt.

"Ezra's going to be late tonight," spurted Lily, walking through the door, like she'd been keeping a secret."

"How do you know?" Hugh's voice rose a decibel.

"He called." Lily was looking at her shoe, purposely trying to be vague so Hugh would think there was something possibly brewing between her and Ezra. Sandra was sure there was nothing going on, but Lily liked to yank Hugh's chain when she could.

"When?" Hugh was clearly taking the bait.

Oh shit, thought Sandra. Lily had piqued Hugh's jealousy right before practice. Lily knew exactly what she was doing here. Lily's strategy was twofold. She liked to make Hugh jealous but she also enjoyed reminding everyone that Ezra, with his drug problem, was the weak link in the band because it took the attention off her. Lily played the tambourine. That was the extent of her musical skill, other than being Hugh's muse, which was a position she both jockeyed for and tested from time to time to make sure she was still on solid footing. With Hugh's reaction, it seemed she was and that had been the point.

It was one thing for the band to smoke pot—everyone in Laurel Canyon grew and smoked pot, rolling joints before, during, and after practice. But Ezra seemed to be missing more and more band practices because he was now strung out on heroin. His parents had sent him to a hospital to clean him up in February. Clean, for Ezra, had lasted about a month. He was a remarkable drummer, so they'd waited for him while he had been in the hospital. They'd found someone to cover for Ezra, but Sandra just wasn't sure they could do it again.

Sandra got up from the sofa and decided to move to the garage so she wouldn't hear another row between Lily and Hugh. As she stepped out into the night, the fresh smell of eucalyptus and pine hit her. The night was cool for May, but she took her time, enjoying the fresh air because the house always smelled sweet, like a stale joint. Somewhere off in the distance farther up the Canyon, she heard laughter and then a bottle breaking. The garage where they practiced must have been a pottery studio at one point because there were still kilns and pottery wheels in several states of repair around the place. They'd cleared off one side to put a drum set and Sandra's Gibson G-101 with several amps. Over it, a center beam appeared to be sagging, and Sandra wondered where they'd all be when it finally gave way. Hugh and Kim were like children playing house. They didn't concern themselves with things like plumbing. This was the opposite of how Sandra had grown up.

Rick followed her down the path to the garage. After pulling the strings on all the old lightbulbs to illuminate the space, Rick shot a few rolls of film of the equipment. In any band there was lots of waiting, but tonight the extra time was allowing room for the battle brewing between Lily and Hugh. Under the glow of the only working porch light, Sandra could see them fighting, pushing each other to the brink and then declaring their love for each other.

Rick smirked and took photos of them in the doorframe, their voices rising occasionally.

"Does this happen often?"

Sandra looked up from her notebook. "You mean do I sit here by myself a lot while they fight and Ezra shows up wasted?" She cocked her head. "Yes." While she talked, Rick snapped her picture. She frowned at him.

"You don't like your picture taken?" He ran his hand through his brown hair, which was like a mop. He'd grown a beard over the spring. It balanced his piercing green eyes, which nearly erased the rest of Rick's features. "You look like Peggy Lipton."

Sandra snorted. "I *wish* I looked like Peggy Lipton. And no, I don't like being the focus of attention." She returned to her notebook but smiled. She'd thrown a long light-blue coat with light-brown fake-fur cuffs and collar over her shoulders. The garage had no heat, and if she wasn't playing, she was always chilly.

"Then you're in the wrong profession, my lady."

Was he flirting with her? Sandra twirled her pencil and considered this. Rick moved around the garage, taking photos of the empty drum set, the unplugged Fender. Sandra couldn't help notice everything about this man—his yellow Western shirt, faded jeans, and cowboy boots, the way the Nikon sounded when he advanced the film, and the way he stopped between each shot, rarely taking multiple photos.

Sandra picked up Hugh's unplugged Fender and began to strum chords that she thought would work. Hugh loved this guitar and took it everywhere. He said that it had belonged to Roy Clark but Sandra had her doubts that Roy Clark ever owned a Fender; more than likely she thought someone had told Hugh the story to sell it to him at a steep price. It was a battered guitar and Sandra knew that Hugh could call his dad for money for a better one, but he never did and that raised Hugh in Sandra's estimation.

"So how many bands has he been in now?" Rick kept snapping her photo as he motioned to Hugh.

"Hugh? I think he said he's up to six now." Hugh seemed to have a history of forming bands, but little success in keeping them together beyond jamming. In the spring, he'd been between bands and posted flyers all over the campus to form a new one, first finding Ezra Gunn, a drummer who was majoring in philosophy.

"How did he find you?" She noticed Rick's eyes for the first time over the camera frame—they were a light green with dark lashes, a stark contrast.

"He'd seen Ray Manzarek at London Fog and became convinced that a keyboardist was what he needed this time."

"For band six?"

"Band six has a name. No Exit," Sandra corrected him.

"Oh, they all had names," said Rick. "They were terrible. The name has to be your influence because it's good. Sartre?"

"Ezra said being in a band was like a form of hell. The music was fine; it was the bandmates that he hated. Hugh and I both thought of Sartre's play—only we had four people living in hell together for eternity instead of three."

"How did you get hooked up with Hubert?" He snapped more pictures as she talked, here and there like small pecks on the cheek.

Hugh was a powerful pull, like the tide. If you weren't careful you could get sucked into his surety, the way he thought the world should work. But there had been something about him that Sandra had needed—maybe she needed him to defy his father so she knew she could do it herself. Until Hugh, Sandra had never thought she could be in a band—never imagined she could be a part of something bigger. For his part, Hugh needed Sandra's discipline. While he was blurry, she was focused. Where he started songs, she finished them.

"He started searching UCLA's practice studio rooms, going up and down the halls, peering into windows and listening for the right sound. I was working on something—a bit of a blues composition—when I heard this awful pounding noise. The door even shook." The memory made her smile and she pointed at Lily and Hugh, entwined and silhouetted. Sandra felt a pang of envy. "I found those two peering in the window at me. Hugh kept shouting 'I found her.'"

"I think this one might make it, though." Rick switched the flash. "Kim thinks so, too, but she likes to tease him."

"Why do you think band six will make it?"

"You." He pointed the camera directly at her and snapped.

Ezra came rushing in, bursting through Hugh and Lily, who were still deep in discussion. With his mop of dark hair that he rarely cut, there was a child-like sense to everything Ezra Gunn did. Often Sandra thought that it would have been easy to fall for Ezra, but there was something dangerous and tragic about him that forced her to keep her distance, almost like he was impermanent.

"I got held up," Ezra said, plunking himself down at his drum set.

Hugh and Lily had called a truce and come into the garage. The band starting warming up with a few covers "Sunshine of Your Love" and "All Along the Watchtower"—stuff they knew well. Ezra counted them in.

They moved into their own songs, "You Slept On" and "The Fall," both deeply confessional lyrics written by Hugh about the death of his mother. Sandra had written the music to both songs. "You Slept On" had a more classic piano melody that had been in her head. Sometimes, music came to Sandra in her sleep. When she woke, she'd often race to the practice rooms at UCLA to see if she could capture on the keyboard the fleeting melody in her head.

They'd been experimenting with another section to "The Fall," a transition that was on the verge of working. Hugh stopped. "I don't think that's it."

Sandra had a melody with a different time in her head. She'd been holding it back, hoping that they could use if for another song, never exactly trusting that another melody would be there, but something about this riff felt right for this song. She flicked a few switches to get a different sound and tried it. Hugh's face lit up. "That's it . . . that's fucking it, Sandra."

Sandra could hear Rick's camera advancing. For a moment, she'd been so engrossed in what they were creating that she'd forgotten about Rick. He was sitting on the floor, taking his time capturing the exchange between Sandra and Hugh.

Hugh picked up the Fender and added another flourish to Sandra's riff until it felt more complete. A solid self-taught guitar player, Hugh's true gift was lyrics. He wrote poems and lyrics on little pieces of paper and in his large array of notebooks. Upon hearing what Hugh was playing on the Fender, Sandra layered it with a few additional flourishes on the Gibson. It was this push and pull between them that made the band work. Sandra's tastes were more classic and folk while Hugh was embracing the psychedelic sound that she thought was coming to an end. She could almost feel what was coming next, the stripped-down sounds of acoustic folk paired with simple, almost country-influenced melodies.

"Let's try it from the top." Hugh turned to Ezra to count them in and then he played the first few chords of "The Fall," singing in his nasal baritone, which had become the signature sound of the band. The melodies were haunting and the music had a timeless quality to it, with people sure it was a cover of something older.

Still, the band needed a bass player. Sandra had seen Ray Manzarek perform; inspired by him, she'd learned to mimic the bass line on her Gibson's black bass keys. It would have to do until they could find a fifth member of the band.

Midway through "The Fall," Ezra's timing was off—way off.

Rick shot Sandra a look of alarm as he kept snapping photos.

Hugh kept trying to work around Ezra's timing, but it was becoming slower then faster. Lily, Hugh, and Sandra exchanged looks.

"I'm going to break for a moment," said Ezra, coming to an abrupt stop. "Beer anyone?" All three of them sighed and exchanged glances. Tonight was only going to get worse and they knew it. While Ezra opened doors for them, got them into parties and after-parties, he didn't know how to stop with the drugs. Always flush with cash from his dad, Ezra couldn't resist getting the best weed and heroin he could buy. And there was never any problem finding drugs on the Strip.

"Sure," said Lily, her voice falling as she tried to figure how wasted he was.

After he walked toward the main house, the trio looked at each other.

"I think you should say something to him," said Lily to Hugh.

"Do you think he's shooting up in the bathroom?" Rick was loading film.

"Who knows. He only listens to Sandra." Hugh kept working through some fingerpicking he was thinking about for a new song. "What do you think of this, Sandra?"

But Sandra couldn't focus on Hugh. In the distance, she heard something hit the ground—a beer bottle perhaps, then two. She saw what looked like a figure, which became Ezra as he became illuminated under the porch light staggering out of the back door and collapsing in the yard near Hugh's tepee. On instinct, Sandra bolted from the room and into the yard.

"Ezra." Dropping to her knees, slapping him lightly on the face. Sandra could see he wasn't breathing. She checked Ezra's pulse, which was weak.

Hugh and Lily were at her side.

"Call an ambulance." Her voice was sharp.

"He's turning blue," said Hugh.

"I know," said Sandra. "Call a fucking ambulance. Tell them he OD'd."

Looking up at the trees and the remaining light that was shining down, Sandra wondered if an ambulance would ever find them so deep up in the Canyon with the unmarked roads and hidden driveways.

Sandra touched Ezra's chest and she could feel—not really feel, but see—that his heart was slowing. The drugs were relaxing his lungs to the point he was unable to make himself breathe. As she touched him, she felt a buzzing in her fingertips. She pulled them back as if she'd touched a hot stove and looked at them, wondering if it was the weed she'd had earlier. It had to be a bad trip, some weed laced with some other shit that Kim must have gotten. But there was an overwhelming sense that she felt could pull the heroin out of his bloodstream through the pads of her fingers like she was draining a snakebite. This was some fucking weird trip.

"What the fuck." It was Rick beside her.

Ezra had begun to foam at the mouth and it seemed he was attempting to vomit. Sandra turned him on his side, but he was making noises.

"He's choking." Rick came around and helped her sit him up, but Ezra's body was limp.

Sandra met Rick's eyes.

It was then that a smell began emit from Ezra. From experience, Sandra knew that she was the only one who smelled it. Since she had been a little girl, Sandra could sense death via smell. The first time it happened, there was this kid in school who'd come down with a fever. As she sat next to him on the school bus that Friday, Sandra smelled something sweet yet foul on him. He was admitted to the hospital with bacterial meningitis and was dead by Monday. She'd smelled this same rotting sweet scent again after her grandmother's heart attack. As the woman lay in her hospital bed, Sandra remembered her doctor patting the woman on the shoulder and declaring her "lucky," except that Sandra knew better. When she kissed her goodbye, she almost choked on the sweet and rotten fragrance ebbing from the woman's pores. An hour after they'd left for the afternoon, her grandmother died in her chair in front of a cheap hospital gift shop Chinese checkers board.

And she smelled it now on Ezra. Her hands began to tingle, as if they were coming alive. She placed them on him and a sharp burning sensation shot through her. It was an odd sensation, but she could see that Ezra's chest moved as long as she touched him and stopped when she pulled her hand away.

"What are you doing?" Rick stared down at her.

"I don't know," said Sandra. "When I touch him, he seems to respond."

"So touch him then."

Sandra placed her hands firmly on Ezra's chest, and it began to rise. Sandra's arms began to shake from the pain, but both Rick and Sandra could see him getting more lucid.

"Are you okay?"

She nodded to Rick and held her hands firmly on Ezra until he began to vomit violently. Rick held Ezra upright, slapping him on the back. When she couldn't bear it any longer, she pulled her hands away, expecting them to be blistered, but they were still pale and pink.

It was then that Ezra opened his eyes and inhaled a raspy breath. "What the fuck." He sat up and wiped his mouth.

"Sandra saved your life, asshole." Rick stood up. "What the fuck are you on?"

"Nothing, man." Ezra shook his head. "I'm clean, I swear."

Ezra looked up at Sandra and something unspoken occurred between them. *He knew what she had done.*

Somewhere in the distance, Sandra heard the sirens getting closer— the ambulance on its way up Laurel Canyon Boulevard. They wouldn't find anything in Ezra's body, of that Sandra was sure. And with the same certainty, Sandra knew that she could still smell death lingering on Ezra. She had only saved him for tonight. There would be another night.

After Ezra's collapse, practice was done for the night. The paramedics couldn't find anything wrong with Ezra. He lied and said he often had seizures, and the team packed up their gear and headed back down the Canyon.

The group broke for the night, unsettled by what had happened. Hugh and Lily headed to the Forum. Ezra said he was headed home. Sandra decided to go down to the Shack to see about getting the band a gig for Thursday night. She needed to be alone for a while. As she was heading to her car, she heard a voice behind her. It was Rick.

"Hey, I wanted to see if you were okay?" He was juggling two camera bags, and Sandra could see he was headed to his Jeep. "He was lucky you were here tonight."

"It was nothing." Sandra shifted her weight. Why was she so nervous talking to this man?

"I was there, Sandra." said Rick. "It was *something*." He reached out and touched her arm lightly. It was an innocent, protective gesture, but Sandra felt her stomach flutter.

"Are you headed to the Forum?"

She shook her head. "I'm going to try and get us a Thursday night gig at the Shack."

"Do you want me to call Milo for you?"

Milo—for he had no last name, at least not one that Sandra knew of—was the owner of the Shack, one of the oldest clubs on the Strip.

"Sure," said Sandra. "If you don't mind."

"I don't mind," said Rick.

They stood there at his Jeep for a moment.

"I should go," said Sandra.

"I'll run up to the house and call him," offered Rick.

Rick had always had enough sway in LA to get the owner of the Shack to give them a slot. He had that kind of power. So why was he doing this now? His brother-in-law was a member of the band as well, so he could have offered this favor up at any point. It seemed like it was a grand gesture for her for what he'd seen tonight. While she was downplaying it to Rick, she had to admit, what she'd done had been extraordinary. She had no idea how she'd done it.

Sandra drove down Sunset past the Trocadero and Ciro's, relics from another time in Hollywood. The Strip was at the center of something bigger. Most of the mile-and-a-half stretch of Sunset Boulevard known as Sunset Strip was littered with fading, seedy clubs. Its location outside Los Angeles city limits made it a place where the underbelly of Hollywood's nightlife had thrived. She had a soft spot for the old haunts although she wasn't sure why. Maybe it was that her dad knew everything about this stretch of LA. He'd drive her down through here when he was running errands and give her the history of every establishment. If he thought she wasn't listening, he'd quiz her on the return trip. She knew all the good stories: Betting that Prohibition was going to be repealed, Billy Wilkerson, owner of Ciro's and the Trocadero, spent every penny he'd brought with him on a European cruise to buy French wine. The wine sat in San Francisco Harbor until Prohibition was repealed, but it established Sunset Strip as the place to go for nightlife. Or the untrue legend that Lana Turner was discovered at Schwab's Pharmacy (she was not). To her father, the *real* story was that F. Scott Fitzgerald had suffered a mild heart attack outside the store (he would drop dead after eating a candy bar two months later). It was a warm night so Sandra rolled down the window to let the breeze in, and she turned down her radio. KHJ-AM was playing some B. J. Thomas song that wasn't her favorite. Instead she focused on the sounds outside: horns, the hum of crowds, drunken laughter, and music—sitars and something that was Indian, but also makeshift drums. Saturday nights, the Strip was so crowded that pedestrians often took to walking in the streets, so seeing musicians carrying their gear was not uncommon. It was taking her a long time to get down to the Shack. Traffic was at a standstill, motorcycles idling and lurching. She had time to read the vanity billboards that lined the streets, artists looking for comebacks, little-known celebrities hoping an executive would notice them on the way to the studio. On the billboard in front of her, a cowgirl statue peered down at a sign advertising the Sahara Hotel in Las Vegas. She knew it was a prop for some new Raquel Welch film but was not sure which one.

What had happened tonight? The smell of death was something that had followed her since she was a child, but the ability to heal someone was completely new. Her life had been filled with incidents where she had to cover to appear normal, try to fit in. First she was a piano savant, and now she could apparently heal people. She studied her fingers at each stoplight, looking for something different about them, but they looked like they always did.

With its burned-out bulbs on the sign, the remaining letters reading ACK, the Shack was one of the older clubs on Sunset Strip. It had taken Sandra weeks to work up the courage to ask Milo for a shot at an off night like a Tuesday. Tonight the little man greeted her warmly and said that Rick Nash had just called.

"Nash was right. He told me Julie from *Mod Squad* was coming to see me." Milo winked. Sandra had dressed the part. Knowing Milo was a flirt, she'd changed into a yellow blouse, brown suede mini skirt with fringe, and boots. He showed her to a seat at the bar and asked what she wanted to drink. Sandra asked the bartender for a gin and tonic.

She had expected to have to do a bigger sales job, but the man said Rick vouched for her and she was beautiful—he didn't need to know any more. He wore a white suit with extremely flared pants. The suit was so small that she wasn't sure it hadn't come from a children's shop.

"Can you play?"

She nodded.

"Then come by Thursday night. Setup begins around five. If I like you, you can come back. Agreed?"

"Yes."

"Good!"

To get a job as a house band on the Strip was a dream for any band. While doing a regular paying gig, the band could work through their sets, make some money, and perfect their sound in the hope they'd get a studio interested and a fan following.

On Thursday they took the stage for the first time at the Shack. Hugh was the focal point of the band—a force onstage—something Sandra was grateful for. There seemed to be something that caused her to feel she needed to not be seen.

They ran through a total of twelve songs for a forty-minute set. Hugh had taught Lily some basic guitar chords, and she could handle a few of the electric guitar parts while Hugh layered on the acoustic. Ezra had cleaned himself up, and his drum playing was never better. The crowd responded. The confessional lyrics, the harmonies between Hugh and Sandra, the haunting melodies with such a hint of nostalgia. The band had transformed. The show was good.

Rick showed up at the Shack at their opening show, a Nikon and a Leica each dangling from a shoulder. The fact that Rick Nash was photographing them performing live was huge since he was known for usually covering bands that had already made it. He walked around the room composing the shots. The band setting up, the frustration of waiting, the anxiety on Hugh's face, and then the show itself: the band and the crowd.

The next day, after Sandra's shift at the A&P, Hugh called her to tell her Rick had developed the photos from the Shack. "They're so groovy, Sand," he crooned. "You've got to get up here and see them." She heard something. "Lil says you need to see them, too."

After she'd closed the store with her dad, she drove up to the Canyon. She'd gotten there later than she'd hoped so everyone at the house was gone except for Rick, who was in the darkroom. The darkroom was created by another shed space around the corner from the house and like the pottery studio, it also seemed to have a sagging roof. Sandra had never been in a darkroom before. Rick seemed to be expecting her and was happy to see her. In the soft glow of the room, she worried it would be awkward around him, but as he moved through the studio, putting paper into a solution, dipping and swishing it around, he talked to her about the band.

"You really need an official photo," he said. He watched the photo like it was cooking in a pan, pulling it out and clipping it to a line, where other shots swayed like laundry.

"You think?"

"You guys are getting better. You're going to need some publicity shot for posters. I was hoping I might have something here, but I didn't get one of the four of you."

Sandra studied the photos drying on the line of an actress.

"She's beautiful," Sandra said. "Great shots."

He stopped what he was doing and came around to stand behind her.

"Where was it?"

"The Roosevelt." Sitting by the pool, his subject—an exotic and moody brunette—was dressed in a bathrobe, looking bored and smoking a cigarette.

"Were you lying on the ground to take this shot?" Sandra leaned in closer. The angles of the photo were dramatic and irreverent.

"I was." He laughed. "She was completely strung out. We had to get her in the shower to wake her up. That's why her hair is wet. I did what I could. I thought a more artistic shot might work. It's for the style section. They'll like it."

Around the darkroom were shots of Jimi Hendrix at the Forum, Jim Morrison at the London Fog, Elton John at the Troubadour, the riots on Sunset, another actress Sandra didn't recognize at the Chateau Marmont. Her favorite photo—and from the position it enjoyed in his studio, she suspected it was his favorite as well—was another outtake of Janis Joplin at a party in what appeared to be Rick's living room, wearing a feather coat and octagonal purple sunglasses, deep in conversation on his sofa.

"These are amazing."

"Here." He handed her the stack of photos of the band.

As Sandra went through them, she could see the difference in the photos—there was a progression in their confidence and in their music, and it was evident in the photos. It was as though Rick captured something that they hadn't even seen in themselves; his documentation of them almost breathed life into them as a unit. Sandra wasn't so sure they'd have seen themselves this way if not for Rick.

She looked up at him, the glow of the room highlighting the whites of his eyes. "You really captured us."

"You think?"

"I do. You captured us as even we don't see us. Does that make sense?"

"True reality? It's an illusion. We never see ourselves truthfully, but this camera comes close. Sometimes it shows us things we don't want to see." He pointed to the photo of Ezra and Lily in what appeared to be an intimate moment coming out of the Shack's bathroom, Hugh nowhere in sight. Rick took the photo and tore it up. "Hugh tells Kim that your family doesn't support your music career." He was placing another set of photos to dry. "That's bullshit. You can write music, you know."

Sandra hadn't remembered sharing much about her family with Hugh. That he'd shared it with Kim felt like a small betrayal. She was oddly silent.

He looked up from the trays of solution when she didn't respond. "I didn't mean to make you uncomfortable," said Rick.

"You didn't," Sandra lied. "They want a normal life for me, that's all."

"But you are normal." He folded his arms and leaned against the wall. "You're talented. They should be thrilled."

Sandra nearly snorted. "You should have seen the looks on their faces when my piano teacher called them after my second lesson. They were expecting some fat-fingered version of "Row, Row, Row Your Boat" and what they got was the beginning of a Grieg piece." Sandra was still thumbing through the photo stack Rick had taken at the Shack. What she was beginning to notice was that she was the focal point of all of the photos. She looked through them a second time just to make sure.

"You're a fucking virtuoso. They should have been happy."

"I'm hardly a virtuoso. My parents didn't want a freak for a kid. I never went back for another lesson. I think the teacher called them for a year."

"That's awful."

"After that, playing the piano is all I wanted to do, but they sold it."

"They sold your piano?"

She laughed. "Yes, they encouraged me to try the flute instead."

"How was that?"

"Oh, I was terrible so the flute stayed." She smiled at the recollection. "But every chance I got, I'd stay after school and I'd find the piano in the auditorium and I'd play."

"I never had normal," offered Rick. "When I see Kim and Hugh with their father, I realize that I feel like an outsider to a normal life."

"But Hugh hates his father."

Rick laughed. "Hugh is a spoiled child who doesn't know how good he has it. Hugh's just upset that his father remarried. Kim is, too, but she's working through it. My mother fed us by working a bunch of low-wage factory jobs and the kindness of the boyfriends she brought home. Maybe that's why I view life through a lens. It's a barrier of sorts. Everyone is over there." He held his arm out. "I'm over here. I'm a voyeur, viewing life from a safe distance, trying to capture a moment. That's really what we're doing here right now. We're living in a moment in time like we'll never see again and I just want to capture it all. I swear I was a painter or something in a past life, like I didn't get enough of it—chronicling life. Do I sound crazy?"

Sandra hadn't known any of this about Rick's childhood.

"I can tell if someone will live or die," Sandra blurted. She had no idea why she felt the need to tell him this. "Is that weird?" She looked down at the photos—three of them of her. He shifted, an awareness of her that he didn't seem to have before.

"I would say it was strange except I saw you the other night with Ezra."

She looked down at the photos and fanned them out. The confession had made her bold. "These are all of me."

He hadn't stopped staring at her. "I know."

It was the simplicity of the statement—no denial on his part—that gave the room a strange electricity.

"Why?"

He didn't answer. The silence forced a tension that seemed to draw them together. He reached out to touch her hand, and she didn't pull away.

With Buffalo Springfield's "Mr. Soul" playing on his radio, he pulled her to him, lifted her chin, and kissed her. His lips and hands felt so foreign to her, and yet he was so familiar. And even though it was her first kiss with him—what should have been a beginning between them—there was also a profound sense of loss that she couldn't shake.

The next day Rick suggested that the band head down in the early evening to the bed of the LA River and take some publicity photos for posters. The stark concrete of the covered river was a perfect backdrop. Rick moved them around getting the right shot. With the angles of the covered river, he could put them on different heights. He had them sitting in one set and standing in another. There was a heightened awareness she and Rick had of each other, but they kept their distance.

It wasn't until the weeks dragged on and she saw him sitting next to Kim in the living room or taking photos of the band that her desire for him was cemented. She was now more attuned to his stories. There was a vulnerability in his eyes that Kim, with the confidence of a child raised by a millionaire, didn't sense. They were both damaged creatures—Sandra and Rick. Hugh and Kim were just pretending.

But there was one more photo that would become *the* photo. Kim and Sandra tagged along with a backstage shoot at the Hollywood Bowl on an empty evening. A piano had been set up for a performance and Sandra had sat down to play; the Bowl was empty except for the cleaning crew.

Rick had gone backstage to take a photo of a jazz pianist who'd been practicing, leaving Kim and Sandra alone on the empty stage.

"I don't know where Hugh gets it," said Kim.

"What?"

"The desire to perform." Kim shook her head. "I don't know how you do it."

Sandra sat down in front of this instrument—a Mason & Hamlin—and set her fingers over the keys. "Let's pretend you're on stage."

Kim slid in the seat beside her.

"Are you terrified now?"

Kim laughed looking out at the blackness. "No. The seats are mostly empty."

For Sandra, the grand piano was where she excelled, and when her fingers hit the keys it was as if something played through her. Never had she hit her runs with such marked precision; never had the delicate notes been so carefully plucked. So mesmerizing was the performance that the cleaning crew sat down in the front row to watch. Sandra ran through Chopin, Rachmaninoff and Beethoven, Debussy and Satie with fury, her hands pounding down with surety.

So caught up in the moment was she, she didn't see that Kim had slid off the seat and Rick had snapped a shot of her playing to an empty Bowl with the exception of the three-person cleaning crew who sat mesmerized in the front row. The shot was unique in that the view was Sandra playing to empty seats with the setting sun behind the Bowl. The composition was a great example of negative-space manipulation, which happened through sheer luck. At the end, Sandra made a deep curtsy and wave to the crew, which Rick captured. As she turned away from the empty seats, she saw Rick's face. He was pale. Sandra couldn't tell you if the moment had been five seconds or five minutes in length. It was as though time stopped as they stood there looking at each other. Finally Kim tugged on his jacket sleeve for them to all leave.

Rick used the photo of Sandra on the cover of *West* magazine. It became the defining photo of Rick's career.

The following week Sandra was leaving practice when Rick,

knowing her schedule, pulled up in his Jeep. "Do you want to go somewhere?"

"I do," she said.

He'd found a little motel, Le Bon View on Olympic Boulevard, and she followed him there. As they were lying there between scratchy sheets after a clumsy, haggard first attempt at adultery—a combination of guilt and nerves that resulted in a performance that neither of them considered their best—Rick said, "I think I've been in love with you since I took *that* photo." At that confession, Rick ceased being Kim's and—at least in Sandra's mind—became hers.

Their second attempt at lovemaking was not marred by any of the awkward guilt, and they settled into a rhythm with each other and a sense of completion. It led to hours in bed together and a familiarity that Sandra had never felt with anyone else. And yet she was haunted by Rick—a feeling that everything about them was short-lived. It wasn't the impermanence of the situation between them. It was as though Sandra understood how it felt to lose Rick like a muscle memory.

As summer dragged on they saw each other a few minutes a week. One Tuesday afternoon, they both sneaked away and stopped at the Santa Monica Pier. It wasn't unusual for the group of them to go places together, but Rick and Sandra were careful not to touch each other in public for fear someone they knew might see them. Still, on the beach in Santa Monica, Sandra felt an incredible sense of déjà vu—one of another version of Rick standing on the beach and of her being so cold. Sandra, who spent countless hours at the Pasadena Fair each year playing Skee-Ball, racked up seven feet of tickets to win a stuffed giraffe.

As she got into the front seat of the Jeep, Sandra had begun to feel incredible guilty at what she and Rick were doing. She knew that Kim had started pressuring him to have a baby. This desire for a child seemed to topple him, creating a larger contrast between the two women in his mind. Rick wasn't ready for kids or settling down; he was focused on his art. He'd started talking about how he and Sandra could go to New York together—he was fielding offers from other magazines. It could be a new start for them.

As they drove on the Pacific Coast Highway, she couldn't shake the blurry image of another Rick—this one tanned and smoking, walking down a hallway with the ocean behind him, his pants flowing in the breeze. This Rick was smiling at her. With this Rick loop playing in her head, she remembered clutching the cheap giraffe when the other car crossed the median in front of them. She saw the car, but she wasn't sure that Rick ever did.

Like a fade in a movie, Sandra came to. She was still in the Jeep.

"We have a four-car pileup," said a voice. "Two more behind—"

The paramedic didn't even finish but Sandra could hear him. She climbed out of the Jeep, clutching the giraffe in her hands, rubbing her hands up and down the cheap scratchy fur, sure that she was dead. She found Rick thrown from the Jeep and spied a stretcher with what appeared to be lifeless arm hanging. There was the smell of smoke and burning oil. She heard the scrape of boots.

She heard them talking over Rick, but couldn't figure out what they were saying. The paramedic looked up at her, his face grim. A look exchanged between them. Sandra knew what it meant.

Her legs gave out. She saw a huge gash on her jeans with blood trickling out, but Sandra knew she'd survive. On her hands and knees she crawled over to Rick, the concrete hot. "You should stay put," yelled a voice, but Sandra crawled on.

"Do you know this man?" The voice was urgent, but everything for Sandra was slow and clouded, like she was seeing it through the fuzz in the television.

Did she know him? She'd traced every inch of Rick's body. She'd stared into his eyes, shoved cotton candy between his lips, gripped the back of his hair when she came. "Yes."

"We'll need a name."

"Rick Nash."

The next few minutes were all instinct. Sandra pleaded with God—with anyone—to save Rick. She worked out a negotiation—if Rick lived, she'd let him go. It was the only thing she had to offer—meager though it was. She hoped it was worth enough.

The paramedic was shaking his head. Sandra placed her hands lightly on Rick's arm, and so dire was the scene that they let her do it. And there was the smell. Warmth emanated from Sandra's hand.

"Have you looked at her?" barked a fireman. Sandra brushed off a pair of gloved hands.

As she looked down over Rick, she could see that his eyes were open. He looked up at her, raw and unsure. "You're going to be fine," Sandra assured him. She touched his face and it was burning, but she realized it wasn't Rick, only her. The burning sensation grew hotter until touching Rick's arm was like holding her hand to the stove, but with Rick she never pulled her hands away, holding on to him until she nearly toppled with searing pain. Only when the burning feeling disappeared did she finally pull away.

As with Ezra, she could clearly see what was happening beyond his skin. She saw clearly the tear in his spleen and another in his heart—both from the impact. She wished the wounds closed and to her amazement, like she was looking through a peephole in his skin, she saw the rough edges of the wound melt together. The pain for *her* was unbearable, as if she were absorbing it, but with every second she held him, she could see him stirring. Taking her hands off for just a moment, she steeled herself to hold his hand. Rick's hand gripped her. It was like a fiery mitt, but she held on and she could feel herself pulling him back, the smell of death subsiding. Something—somewhere—was giving way to her will, returning him. He stared at her wide-eyed and unable to speak, seeming to understand that there was something going on and that Sandra was at the center of it. "You *will* live," said Sandra. "You will be fine."

They loaded Rick onto the ambulance and Sandra finally let him go, Rick's fingers reaching for her after she'd released him.

Sandra stared at her hand. It was fine. No burns, even though it had felt like her flesh was searing. To no one, Sandra said aloud, "If he lives, I will let him go."

When Kim showed up in the waiting room, she was red-faced, flustered.

"What happened?"

"A car crossed the median."

"And you were in the car with him?"

Sandra looked up. She was holding a paper cup of tepid coffee in her hand. She'd been looked at by a doctor in the ER and only had scratches, but there was blood—Rick's blood—all over her T-shirt. She nodded. "He's going to be fine."

"How do you know that?"

"I just do."

"What the fuck, Sandra?" Kim's voice was rising. She was looking out at the hallway trying to figure something out. "Are you in love with him?" She stopped. "Is he in love with you?"

Sandra stared at the wall, thinking about Kim's questions. They didn't matter anymore.

In two hours, Rick was out of surgery. They hadn't found bleeding anywhere, but Sandra wasn't surprised. Another victim from Rick's crash died on the operating table, and a third was dead on arrival.

Sandra stayed away from Rick for a day. Finally, when she knew Kim had gone home, she went to his room.

When he saw her, he smiled. "I've been wondering where you've been."

"I couldn't come." She sat on the chair next to him. "She knows."

He touched her hand, ignoring her. This time, there was no burning feeling. His hand was warm, normal. "Come here." He pulled her hand toward the bed.

She kissed him softly and touched her forehead to his.

"What happened the other night?"

"A driver crossed the median and hit you head-on. Another car slammed into you and another into them."

His voice was far away. "That's not what I mean, and you know it," he said. "Don't be coy. I was dying. I knew it. You knew it. Now I'm sitting here. It's like what you did with Ezra, isn't it? What are you?"

"I'm nothing. You just had a brilliant surgeon."

"It wasn't the surgeon, Sandra."

She sat up and looked at him. "It just wasn't your time to die, I guess." She slid off the bed and gathered her things in her hand.

"Don't go." He pulled her closer with his hand.

"I shouldn't be here."

"Yes, you should," he said. "Nearly dying has changed me."

"How?"

"I need to be with you."

"Don't say that. I told you. Kim knows."

"I don't care."

"You should care."

"I love you, Sandra." His fingers ran over her hand. "I know you love me, too."

Sandra sat back down on his bed, heavily. She leaned over him and kissed him lightly on the lips. "When you were lying on the highway, you were dying. I begged God...anyone who would listen...to save you. I bargained for you. And you lived."

He watched her intently.

"I swore that if you lived, I would let you go. Do you understand?"

"I don't accept that, not over some crazy superstition."

"But you know it's true. Something happened. You felt it. I don't know what it was. I really don't." She stood and tried to steel herself for what she was about to say. She could see monitors beeping, reminders of what had been given back to her, of what she'd bargained for. "Don't ever doubt my love for you, Rick, but we can never be together again. I won't tempt fate. Not with you."

He sat up and grabbed her hand, pulling her back.

"You need to accept it."

"I don't have to accept it. I won't live without you." He held on to her hand, not wanting to break the connection.

"You can and you will. Don't make this harder, Rick."

She turned and shook his hand free, turning.

"Sandra?"

She turned back.

"Will you just give me one last minute. Just pretend that we're a normal couple, saying goodbye like we'll see each other again tomorrow. Can you just do that for me?"

Slowly, Sandra walked back over to the bed, savoring the moment and knowing somewhere in the back of her mind that this scene had played out for her before. The knowledge was both a comfort and a heartbreak to her. She leaned over and kissed him. As her lips touched his, she was overcome with the most remarkable sense of something larger. At that moment, Sandra knew for sure that there had been other Ricks—other versions of him with other versions of her. But this idea was impossible. Yet as her skin met his, she knew that this wasn't the first time she'd said goodbye to him. This sorrow was like an imprint on her.

Rick reached out and touched her face. "I love you." His tears mixed with hers and he held on to her head, not letting her go, small heaves lifting his chest.

"I love you, too. I always will." Sandra turned and wiped her eyes and didn't look back. One turn and she wasn't sure she would have had the resolve to leave him. Walking around the corner, she slid down the wall, breaking into full sobs.

The following week, No Exit got a prime gig at Gazzarri's based on their shows at the Shack. Gazzarri's was a bigger venue and a huge opportunity. Sandra wasn't sure how Hugh would be with her following the accident. If he knew about her affair with Rick or if Kim had told him, though, he never let on.

Hugh's nasal baritone blended with Sandra's harmony in a way that they hadn't before and he seemed to feed off the energy of a bigger venue. After the show, a tall man was standing in the corner waiting for her. As she made her way through the crowd, she noticed he was still following her out onto Sunset. It gave her a slight thrill that people wanted to talk to her after the show. She'd even signed a few autographs tonight.

"Mademoiselle." The man's accent caused Sandra to turn around.

"Yeah?"

"You are a hard woman to catch up with." The man's face was pleasant, and there was something familiar about it that put Sandra at ease. "That was a fabulous show."

"Thank you."

"Have you thought about making a record?"

Sandra laughed. "Are you kidding? That's all we think about."

"I can make that happen." The man handed her a card. "We have availability in the studio in two weeks if you're interested." He nodded, put his hands in his pockets, and walked past her down Sunset.

Sandra looked down at the card. It was pale blue with a gold embossed logo—an expensive card:

Pangea Ranch Studios

Kit Carson Road

Taos, New Mexico

Luke Varner, Producer

"Hey," Sandra called after the man. "What's your name?"

"Paul de Passe." The man smiled and turned, walking back down Sunset.

Hugh was at the wheel of his mother's 1965 Chrysler Imperial Crown convertible. It looked like a woman's car—white with a cream interior—but no one dared say a word to him because it was the only memento he had left of her.

The timing of Paul de Passe's invitation to cut an album had been perfect. Sandra had needed out of Los Angeles for a while. She had to honor the deal she'd struck so that Rick would live. Perhaps she was superstitious, but she felt Rick's continued well-being was dependent upon her keeping this promise.

They'd loaded their gear in a small U-Haul—Ezra's drum kit, the Gibson organ, and Hugh's guitars—that the Chrysler now towed behind it. Clutching two blue suitcases that her mother insisted she bring, Sandra wasn't sure what to expect, but she'd never seen a trunk as big as Hugh's. Ezra rode in the backseat with Sandra; by the time they reached the Mojave Desert, he was sound asleep on her shoulder.

"Did you know these were here?" Lily pulled out some eight-tracks from under the front seat.

"No. What are they?"

Lily turned them to read them. "Patsy Cline."

"That's the *Story* album," said Sandra, peeking over her shoulder. It was one of the few albums she owned that Hugh approved of. "I love that one." She began to belt "Strange" at the top of her lungs, her voice powerful enough to send a sleeping Ezra climbing across the seat.

"Fuck." Ezra rolled into a ball on the other side of the car. "I was asleep."

"There are two of them." Lily studied them.

"It was a double album." Hugh sounded far away. "My mother loved it."

The eight-track started midway through "She's Got You." Sandra, a big Patsy Cline fan, picked up the lyrics. To her surprise, Hugh joined her and turned his head, shooting her a smile.

Ezra put his hands over his ears.

They drove through the stark Mojave Desert, peppered with shrubs, the sun cooking them.

"It looks like Palm Springs," said Ezra.

"It looks nothing like Palm Springs," declared Lily.

At these moments with them bickering like siblings on a family trip, Sandra thought the four of them could make it as a band—and as friends. Somehow Ezra could stay clean, and Lily and Hugh could stay focused on the band and not each other. Sandra worried she wanted this band to work too much.

"How much longer, Dad?" Ezra leaned back in the seat and covered his face. "I have to piss."

"You should have gone before you left," said Hugh, mimicking his father's voice—something he often did. "We don't stop for *anything* in this car."

"It's a fucking fourteen-hour drive," laughed Ezra. "Unless you want these precious white seats soaked with my piss, you'll pull over."

"Please pull over," deadpanned Sandra. "We've been on the road since three A.M. I don't want to be sitting in Ezra's piss."

"No one wants that," added Lily.

She'd pictured fine, neat sands like *Lawrence of Arabia*, not dirt, brush, and rock. There were few markers on the roads, and each turn-off looked the same. They drove through Flagstaff and Albuquerque, finally turning north in Santa Fe and heading up into the mountains. By five P.M., they entered a town square, and then Hugh took a turn and steered the car down a narrow lane with a tall cactus patch at the entrance and a sign that read PANGEA that they almost missed. The fence was a haphazard collection of slim tree branches.

The house was like a beige sand castle with a bright-red roof. It blended in with the rest of the terrain, and that seemed to be the point. As she stepped out of the car, a smell hit her. "What is that smell?"

"Fireplaces." She turned to see the tall, thin man from Sunset, who now sported a terrible sunburn that was visible even in the dark, holding out his hand.

"Paul de Passe?" Sandra extended her hand.

"Mademoiselle Keane." He bowed. He looked at the car with the U-Haul. "May I assist you with your bags? And anything else you may have."

"Sure." Sandra reached into the trunk and handed him the bigger bag, keeping the smaller one that held her underwear and toiletries.

"I've never been to New Mexico." Sandra wasn't sure why she was babbling, but Paul simply nodded and kept walking.

"I hadn't been to New Mexico, either, before I started working at Pangea, Miss Keane," he said. "I'm not sure what I think of it. Taos. I'm not sure the weather up here likes me."

His accent was thick, and she didn't understand him at first. "Do you mean *agrees* with you?"

"Yes." He smiled. "I'm not sure this desert weather *agrees* with me. I'm also not sure it likes me. Soon enough, you'll understand." He laughed.

"That smell." Sandra inhaled. "It's wonderful."

"Yes, mademoiselle. People use their fireplaces here all year round. It's the smell of multiple fireplaces burning. It's the smell of Taos. Quite wonderful isn't it?" Paul cleared his voice and pointed a suitcase ahead. "This house is what they call a hacienda-style," he said. "It's quite old."

The house in front of her was vast. Two large brown—almost ebony—double doors opened to a foyer with dark-brown round beams and stark white walls. Hung from the center of the foyer was an imposing crystal chandelier with delicate gold branches. From the foyer, a large courtyard unfolded; beyond that was a tepee.

"Is that—"

"A tepee? Yes." Paul tapped on the window. "Mr. Markwell wrote us that he insists on staying out there—called it 'living amongst nature.'"

"Did he?" Sandra looked over her shoulder back at Hugh and Lily. "I'm sorry. I hope it was no trouble."

"On the contrary, mademoiselle. You're going to be locked away here recording for a month. Mr. Varner wants you to be comfortable."

"Hugh is all back to nature—until he needs a modern shower, that is," said Sandra under her breath. She touched one of the ornate carved double doors.

Something about the Spanish-style architecture gave Sandra a surprising pang of sadness. Weird things had begun stirring in her since she'd brought Rick back from the dead. The green cactuses in the courtyard were almost glowing, like she was tripping on acid. Plus, she was having strange dreams about a farm in France and she swore she could understand what the people were saying. "Where are you from?"

"I am from Paris," said Paul, pronouncing the city *Paree*. The sun-burned man hoisted Sandra's suitcase from the floor and walked over to the staircase. "Mr. Varner will be expecting you all for dinner around seven thirty."

"We'd love to see the studio." Ezra was hoisting his own bags. "And I do not like sleeping in the great outdoors."

"Not to worry, Mr. Gunn. We have a room for you up here." Paul ascended the stairs. "Mr. Varner will be happy to give you a tour of the studio later."

Shaking off a strange déjà vu feeling that Paul had carried her bags before, Sandra passed the courtyard toward the stairs, noticing an antique church pew that spanned the entire length of the wall. She paused for a moment and decided to poke around the downstairs spaces before going to her room. There was a sitting room with a rustic beamed ceiling and a large fireplace that blended with the rest of the stucco walls. Bookshelves lined the walls, and Sandra thought the place looked more like a library than a ranch with a grand piano at the window.

"You must be Sandra." She turned to see a middle-aged woman with long hair and low breasts leaning against the doorway. "I'm Marie. Welcome to Pangea Ranch."

"Thank you."

"You must be exhausted after your long drive. We've helped Mr. Markwell and Miss Leotta into the…tepee." The woman's French accent was not as thick as Paul's. "Did Mr. Paul take your luggage?"

"He did." Sandra followed Marie back into the foyer and up a flight of ornate tile stairs.

"You've come at a great time. All of Taos is in quite an uproar," said Marie. "The actor Dennis Hopper just bought the Mabel Luhan house down the road, so there is much, much excitement. Lots of people from Hollywood in town. They say Michelle Phillips from the Mamas and the Papas is with him. You don't happen to know her?"

Sandra smiled. She'd seen the Mamas and the Papas many times on the Strip. Their music was similar to No Exit. Being as famous as Michelle and John Phillips was something she and Hugh were hoping for. "No, but I've seen her."

"I would just love to see her." Marie kept walking, pointing out things. "Mr. Varner, who you will meet soon, dabbles in both art and music. He is most famous here in town, though, as a healer. I just work for Mr. Varner—I have for a long time."

"A healer?" Sandra stopped. "Really?" The mysterious Mr. Varner was getting more interesting all the time.

"Oh yes," said Marie. "He is well known here. We have people coming and going at all hours of the night. The man is a saint."

"What is he like?" The name Luke Varner had a familiar ring to it.

Marie smiled as she got to the top of the stairs. "He's an amazing man. He has a gallery in town, but this new creation—this recording studio—*c'est magnifique*. He is what you would call…a Renaissance man. He's an old soul. But I'll let him tell you his story." She stopped at a door and opened it, revealing a bedroom with a double bed, simple bedspread, and wool rug.

The room faced the courtyard and had its own private balcony. She heard doors opening and shutting and the sound of Lily laughing somewhere.

Alone in her room, Sandra collapsed on the bed. This whole thing—Taos and cutting a record—seemed unreal. She fell asleep and woke when the sun was low in the sky. Checking her watch, she saw it was nearly seven. Sandra brushed her long strawberry-blond hair until it shone. Not sure what to expect, she picked a gauzy long-sleeved sundress and brown boots and frowned at her reflection, thinking she looked pale. Marie had worn an elaborate concha belt and turquoise jewelry, her bangles clanging as she walked the stairs. This was the best she could do, though. She sighed and headed downstairs to dinner.

Outside, lights were strung all around the back of the house. As it got dark, the desert got cold—Sandra hadn't been expecting this. It was cold in Los Angeles at night, especially up in Laurel Canyon, but this was nearly freezing. There was a shotgun near the door and Sandra wondered about it until she heard the sounds of animals breaking the desert calm with their wailings.

She heard Lily already deep in conversation. "We like to live among the land." She was holding court, seated on the floor in front of the record player talking to a captivated Paul. "We live in the Canyon." Sandra was pretty sure that Paul had no idea what living in "the Canyon" meant.

"Yeah. We're grew most of our food this summer," agreed Hugh, sliding in next to Lily and squeezing her hand. They were both clearly stoned as they leaned on each other. "Green beans, squash, chilies..."

"*C'est magnifique*." Marie came around the corner just in time to perk up at the word *chilies*. "Dinner is ready."

"I'm still dying to see the studio," said Ezra.

"After dinner." Marie shooed him off the chair.

Sandra walked down the hall past the grand piano and was instantly drawn to it. Since no one was around, she had a desire to hear what the instrument sounded like, just a quick stop before dinner to play one song. Sliding quickly into the seat, she positioned her hands and began with the Grieg warm-up she'd done since she was a child. From there, she moved to a Satie piece that had been her favorite. When she'd finished with the first movement, she let her hands pause and took her foot off the damper pedal. The piano's sound was clear and deep. It was the most perfect instrument she'd ever played.

"That was quite lovely."

She turned to find a man seated in what must have once been used as some type of ebony Gothic bishop's chair. While completely engulfed in the chair with its seven-foot spires, ornate back carved with winged figures, and clawed feet, the man sitting in it was certainly not overpowered by its opulence. His tan face, stubble, and dirty boots seemed to mock such indulgence.

"I'm sorry. I didn't know anyone was listening."

"I know you didn't," the man said, smiling. "That made it all the more interesting." His hands were folded and he took his time studying her face, like he hadn't seen it in a long time.

"That's a pretty big chair you're sitting in," said Sandra.

"It is, isn't it?" He stroked the arms. "I love it! I got it at a Catholic mission in Albuquerque. It's a bishop's chair. But pardon my manners." The man stood. "Luke Varner." He was slight, not nearly as tall as Paul de Passe or even the chair he was sitting in, but tanned like he'd been outside all day. Luke's skin was the color of butterscotch from the sun, his brown hair had waves, and the beginnings of a slightly gray beard were forming. His button-down burgundy shirt and worn jeans made him look like a ranch hand from *Gunsmoke*.

"Sandra Keane." She offered her hand. "But you already know that, Mr. Varner."

He said nothing, but motioned for her to head down the hallway and outside. There was an outdoor table set and a blazing fire pit nearby. A turntable sat on the porch, and Hugh had already put on a stack of records. By now, the record had been changed to Donovan's "Hurdy Gurdy Man." Dinner was mole chicken that Marie had slow-roasted. As she'd passed the living room, Sandra had also seen a blazing fire in the fireplace.

Everyone took notice when Luke Varner walked into the space. Marie fussed after him, and Sandra could see Lily shift her attention from Hugh to Luke. Hugh seemed to notice the shift, but accept it.

Sandra was surprised that she'd found Luke Varner so attractive. It felt odd so soon after Rick—it felt like a small betrayal of him—but there was something about this man that felt like a tug from the past. A door opening.

They talked about Lily seeing a roadrunner that morning, her first. The conversation moved quickly to Karl Marx, Hugh's favorite. The conversation always moved to Karl Marx when Hugh was around.

"Man has become alienated from his own work," said Hugh. "Don't you agree?"

"I think Marx is overrated," said Luke.

"What Luke is doing is amazing," added Lily. "Marie says that he's not letting the corrupt capitalists exploit the work of local artists here."

Hugh began talking about art. Sandra wasn't sure Hugh actually knew anything about art, but that never stopped him.

The doorbell rang and Marie excused herself to answer it. There was a noise in the foyer and some murmuring. Marie came to the door and motioned for Luke. Everyone, so deep in conversation, kept talking and drinking. Curious, Sandra waited a moment before getting up and following Luke out into the foyer.

A young man was lying on the floor, blood flowing from an abdominal wound. An older man speaking Spanish was relaying something to Marie, who apparently spoke fluent Spanish. The translation delay was frustrating as the boy struggled. Oddly, Luke took his time listening to the story rather than tending to the boy.

"It's his son. He was accidentally shot," said Marie. "He didn't know what to do. They heard about you."

Luke knelt down beside the young man. A thick pool of near-black blood was forming around his hip. Sandra could smell the death—the sweet rot that always wafted up from the bodies. This boy was dying.

So this was the "healing" that Marie had spoken of. She held her breath.

Luke looked up at Sandra. "Do you want to try?"

Sandra shook her head vigorously. *How did he know what she could do?*

"Try," he said. It wasn't a command, but it wasn't a request, either. He stood back, giving her room, but also sizing up what she was about to do. This felt like some strange test.

Pushing her hair aside, Sandra got on her knees and looked up at Luke for guidance. The fact that he thought she could do this gave her confidence. She'd try. The older man was wailing, Marie holding him back. Just as with Ezra and Rick, she touched the young man's stomach. As she did, Sandra closed her eyes and could see the path the bullet had taken, tearing through tissue and bone. It had gone in on the right side, ripping through the liver. Her wet, bloody hands began to heat up, and she could see the torn edges of this man began to fuse as though she were a surgeon. Not sure what to do with the bullet, she looked over at Luke. He was watching her intently. In her mind, she began to shrink the bullet until she imagined it to be the size of a benign speck of sand.

The blood was still flowing out of the man, so Sandra stopped it and began thinking about new blood forming in this man's arteries. The man's body responded, creating new blood and fusing the wound.

She'd gotten used to her hands feeling like fire, but this was a tougher case. The man began to cough, which was encouraging. Sandra could see she now had Luke's full attention. When she couldn't bear the searing pain anymore, she took her bloody hands off the man's stomach and fell backward, nearly propelling herself across the foyer. She turned her hands over; it felt like they were blistered, but instead she found that they were still pink and smooth. Looking up, she saw everyone in the house—Marie, Paul, Hugh, Lily, Ezra, and the man's father—peering down at her.

In what was a true existential dissonance, the boy, his clothing soaked through with his own blood, got on his knees and stood with help from his father. So bloody were his clothes, it was impossible to imagine him living let alone walking.

The father turned to Sandra, who had made a similar slow ascension back to her feet with help from Paul. "I have heard about magical things on this ranch, but nothing like *you*." He grasped her bloody hands. His were cool and Sandra was grateful to hang on to them for a moment to quench the burning of her skin.

Sandra didn't know what to say. This was all new to her. There was silence in the room, and she couldn't tell if she'd done the wrong thing or not. She looked at Luke, who seemed pleased but not shocked. She tried to read his expression, but he gave little away. She, however, was shocked and confused. She'd been virtually commanded to heal this boy like a parlor trick.

Seeming as stunned as Sandra, the boy pulled up his shirt. There was the appearance of a scar where the bullet had entered. It was as though the bullet had done its damage years ago, not minutes.

The father turned to Luke. "I don't know how to thank you."

"It's what we do here." Luke shepherded the man and his son away from earshot and toward the door. The giant black door shut with a loud thump and Luke leaned against it. "That was *fucking* brilliant, Sandra."

"That's the shit she did to you, Ezra." Hugh grabbed her and kissed her on the mouth. He was drunk.

"Far out." Lily rolled her eyes. "*That* was the most incredible thing I've ever seen. And I've seen some groovy shit."

"She has," concurred Hugh.

Only Ezra stood there, silent. Sandra met his eyes. They'd never talked about what she'd done to him, the night of the overdose. He looked stricken.

"I'm going to go and get changed." Sandra looked down at herself, caked in blood, two handprints remaining where she'd absentmindedly wiped her hands on her dress. She staggered toward the stairs and then found the handrail and pulled herself up.

Fortunately, she had her own bathroom that included a deep clawfoot tub. Drawing herself a bath, Sandra sank down into the water. What was happening to her?

Later, as she sat on the balcony, wrapped in a bathrobe, she heard a knock at her door. Opening it, she found Luke Varner standing there.

"I wanted to check on you." His hands were in his pockets.

She motioned for him to come in. She moved toward the bed and sat, but he leaned against the dresser instead. They were silent. Sandra didn't know what to say anymore. Words seemed not to be as important to her as they'd once been. "What was that?"

"You just saved a man's life."

"How did you know that I could do that? I don't even know how I do that."

"It's complicated."

"Was it a test?"

"It was." He sighed and looked like he wanted to say more. "What you did down there. I've never seen anything like it."

"I hear you're a healer, Mr. Varner. Surely you've seen *something* like it."

"Other than me, I meant," he added with a laugh. "No, I haven't seen anything like that."

"You can do *this*?" Sandra leaned toward him, her hands out.

"Yes." He sighed. "But I've never seen you—" He stopped. "I've never seen anyone else do it. Can I ask? How does it work?"

"I don't know," she said honestly. "I can tell if someone is dying or not. It's a scent they have. I've learned that I have the power to change the outcome. I coax the body into doing what I want it to do."

"Have you always been able to do this?"

"The smell thing, yes. Ever since I was a child." She looked down at her hands. "But the healing, that's new. It comes through my hands, I think." She flipped them over and studied them. "I don't know that for sure, but they burn while I'm doing it." She considered something.

"Anything else?"

"What do you mean?"

"Power of suggestion? Can you get into anyone's mind?"

"Are you kidding?" She looked at her hands. "I think it all comes from my hands. I've never had a piano lesson, either. Well, not after the first one."

"And you played like you did downstairs?"

She nodded.

"Your gift is powerful."

"It's not a gift. It's a curse," she whispered as though afraid to voice what she would say next. "I'm a freak."

"You're not a freak." He smiled, sadly. "I'm sorry you've been made to feel that way. Welcome to Pangea, Sandra. You have a home here." He turned toward the door and tapped his hands on wood. "And you haven't even seen the recording studio yet."

She smiled. "Thank you, Mr. Varner."

"You can call me Luke."

"Thank you, Luke."

The next morning, they started recording. Luke opened the entire back wing, which was divided into two rooms. The first was a control room; through the glass was the studio.

"This shit is awesome," said Hugh, his hand looming over the knobs and levers.

"Don't touch it," said Luke.

Hugh quickly moved his hand away.

This board was the most elaborate thing she'd ever seen, with well over three hundred buttons and levers. This whole thing seemed impossible—that they were here in this studio and someone like Luke Varner believed enough in what they were doing to let them record an album.

"We'll start with the drums," said Luke to Ezra. "Once we get that sound down, we'll lay down that track."

"How does it work?" Ezra stared behind the glass at his drum set, which had been set up with least six microphones placed around it. "How do we cut an album?"

The setup was intimidating. Between Hugh and Sandra they had five original songs. They'd rehearsed them at the Shack for the past two months and smoothed out the rough parts, but they locked eyes over the Neve console and almost read each other's minds. *Holy shit! Are we up for this?* They had a month in here to work on their music together under the direction of someone who could shape their sound—it was a once-in-a-lifetime opportunity, and they all knew it.

"It's never going to be better than this, is it?" Hugh said it so quietly that only Sandra heard him.

"No," she answered. "It isn't."

Luke looked up. "Oh good. The cavalry has arrived." He turned to Ezra. "These guys can explain to you how you're going to cut an album."

Two men stood in the doorway.

"This is Bex Martinez," said Luke, pointing to the taller man. "He's your bass player for the session. Paul says you don't have a bass player. Bex here is a session musician originally from Santa Fe." Bex was tall and lanky. He wore a cowboy hat and a T-shirt with the sleeves ripped out. Rather than speak, he just nodded to everyone. "I think Bex can also play lead guitar and steel guitar if you need him to."

"Banjo too," offered Bex.

"And banjo, too." Clapping his hands together, Luke turned back to the second man at the door, a tiny, bald man with a long beard. He looked like an elf from a Christmas special Sandra had seen. "And this is Lenny Brandt. He's your sound engineer—all the way from England." He turned to Hugh. "*He* can touch the equipment."

"Far out," said Lily.

"I want to hear what you've got," said Lenny, who was not English but Australian. During the next twenty-four hours, Lenny and Luke had the band play the five songs they'd written. Lenny would stop them and make corrections and suggest changes, his fingers moving quickly over the dials with a great ear; his fingernails were bitten to the quick. He made furious scribbles in a small notebook, each song taking up seven or so pages before he moved on to the next.

By the evening, they were exhausted. Marie had brought dinner in for the group in the studio. Other than trips to the bathroom, the group hadn't left the studio all day.

"Anything else?" Lenny looked at Sandra and Hugh.

"That's all we have so far," said Hugh.

"I have two songs." Ezra poked his head up from the drum set.

"Have you guys played them?" Lenny turned to Sandra and Hugh, who shook their heads.

"Okay, you guys practice those two songs at night if you can, to get them ready. We've got five songs to work with for now for the album. Let's try to record a song a day if we can—although that's aggressive because I think they all need a little more work." Lenny turned to Bex. "What do you think?"

Bex nodded. "I think Hugh and I can layer the guitars a bit more."

"My thoughts exactly." He turned to Sandra. "I want a regular electronic keyboard in here. Either that or we haul in that beautiful Steinway, although I get it needs a tuning."

"It does need a tuning," Sandra agreed.

"I think all these songs have too much reverb. You've got great, meaningful lyrics and you are trying to pretend you're Hendrix. Only Hendrix is Hendrix. Got it? Find your own voices." Lenny was leaning against the glass. "Okay, let's all go roll some joints."

"Fuck yeah," said Hugh.

The next morning, they began recording the first song, laying down the drum tracks, the rhythm track next, followed by keyboard and finally vocals. When the first song was finished, Lenny handed them an eight-track tape and a bottle of tequila. "Take it somewhere special, man."

Hugh smiled and the five of them—for Bex Martinez was now fully a member of the group—all sat in the Chrysler with the top down listening to the master track and passing the tequila around the car as the sun beat down on them. They'd never heard themselves before.

Lenny had pulled the drums forward to balance them and blended the guitar, layering on Bex's tracks as well. The finished product was a song that wasn't overcomplicated with reverb, but it was polished.

"Jesus," said Ezra. "That's us."

And Sandra's throat caught and she had to swallow hard so she wouldn't cry. The parts of them had never been as great as the whole. *They were good. They could do this.*

Over the next two days, they'd go their separate ways in the morning and work on individual pieces and then come back together to see what they had. As they laid down two more tracks, Sandra's strange dreams continued. France became something out of *Alice's Adventures in Wonderland*—and Sandra felt like she was inhabiting another person. There was a painter in her dreams. Sex with this painter, whose name was Marchant, was wild, brutal, and intense. She came down the stairs in the morning exhausted, but had more clarity about things around her like colors and sounds.

Oddly, these dreams made her more creative in the studio, and it showed up in her writing. While listening to a song they'd played for six months, Sandra began to see the song differently. She thought it should be dreamier, slowing the tempo down. Bex, seeing where she was going with it, pulled out a steel guitar and had Ezra soften the snare. The result was a lush, haunting sound that felt like her dream.

On the third night, the strangest thing was that a version of Luke Varner appeared in them as well. The girl in her dreams, Juliet, had begun living with him in Paris. She played the piano—she played the Grieg, the Satie—pieces that were very, very familiar to Sandra.

When the girl jumped off the Pont Neuf, Sandra was startled awake choking—spitting actual water out on her pillow. "Jesus."

Sandra stared up at the wooden beams above her. "What the fuck is happening to me?"

At breakfast the next morning, Luke sat down across from her at the table. "Can I show you something?"

She followed him down the hall and into the room with the Steinway. He pulled out several composition books; Sandra could see they were musical compositions, at least four volumes. "You might get some inspiration from these? Lenny says you need four more songs."

Sandra looked down at the writing, and something struck her. She recognized the first few bars and she leaned in, studying them closely. "Who wrote these?"

"That's not important right now," he said. "Just try a few."

Sandra opened them and sat down at the Steinway, spreading open the books that seemed to have been shut away for years. The spines on the pages were yellowed and had spread to the edges of each individual page, but the black ink remained clear. There was something familiar about the twists of the quarter and half notes. She kicked off her high-heeled cork sandals and slid her bare right foot over the damper pedal. Reading the music on the page faithfully, Sandra stumbled over the first few bars until something struck her. She stopped and pulled back from the keyboard, like she'd touched a hot pan.

"I know this song." Sandra scanned through the rest of the book, placing another composition in front of her. After playing the first few bars, she closed her eyes and played the rest from memory. When she'd finished, she took her foot off the damper pedal, and the instrument gave a reverb noise as it held on to the last note. "What is this?"

"Do you really want to know?"

"Of course I want to know. These songs come to me in my dreams.

I've spent years trying to lay them out as compositions, and here they are." She flipped through the book, scanning through the rest of the songs. "There are some songs that I couldn't figure out." She opened up a song and started to play it, stopping midway through the first page. "It's here, too. *How* is that possible?"

"Because you wrote them."

Sandra looked at them and then at Luke. "No."

"You don't believe me?" He sat down next to her on the bench. "But the problem is that you don't *not* believe me."

"No one in their right mind would believe you, Mr. Varner."

"Luke."

"No one in their right mind would believe you, Luke."

He slid the bench out and stood up, holding his hand out. "Let's go for a walk, shall we?"

She followed behind him, hesitant to hear what he was about to tell her. The cold morning air hit her as they opened the door and stepped onto the back porch. Last night's full ashtrays and empty beer bottles littered the ground. Sandra kicked at a stone and folded her arms.

"Are you having dreams?" He began walking down the path to the road.

She looked at him warily. "I am."

"Am I in them?"

Sandra stopped walking.

"I'll take that as a yes." He broke a stray tree branch and began clearing a path to an old campfire site. "I'll bet there is a painter and a girl named Juliet. Do you want me to name your cat while I'm at it?"

She frowned, feeling the blood drain from her face until it became tingly and she touched it just to anchor herself before she spoke. "How do you know that?"

"Didn't I look familiar to you when we met?"

"You did, but I thought it was something subconscious, or I'd done too many drugs." Sandra flicked some tall shrubs with her hand, sending a rabbit hopping out and startling her.

"It is something subconscious, by the way." He retrieved a pair of gloves from his back pocket and began moving small stones while he spoke. "It's best to do this in the morning before the sun really comes down. These dreams are you. Haven't you ever thought you were different?" He looked up at her. "Well, you are."

"That's never been a good thing."

"Actually, it's a fabulous thing. You played the piano, but your parents stopped you."

"How did you . . . ?"

"You were afraid you were weird—or as you said the other night, a freak—but you weren't. You saw the dream with your mother—Juliet's mother. You saw what she did."

Sandra nodded.

"It's a curse—specifically a binding curse. You come back again and again."

"You're saying I'm this girl? That makes no sense."

"Yet part of you knows that I'm telling the truth."

"Is that why you brought me here? Was this recording-an-album thing all a ruse?"

Luke ignored her. "If you've seen Juliet in Paris, you'll soon have another dream, of being Nora Wheeler. It's Hollywood in the 1930s . . . it will be interesting viewing for you at least."

"Will I be visited by the Ghost of Christmas Past while we're at it?"

He laughed, hard. "No, just the ghost of Nora Wheeler, but I shouldn't say more. You need to feel this thing for yourself."

"And the healing?"

"That has been a big surprise." He turned and walked back into the house, making it clear he was done talking.

In the afternoons, while the band was in the studio, Sandra would find Marie watching *The Secret Storm*. "I love television this time," she remarked in her thick French accent. Sandra wasn't exactly sure what she meant by "this time," but she swore she'd seen Marie and Paul in her dreams as well.

Luke had been right. Like something out of a Dickens novel, Sandra was visited again by the ghost of Juliet and then Nora Wheeler. The compounding of Nora's and Juliet's stories gave Sandra more of an appreciation for Luke. Nora had loved him. They had lived together until Nora had died right in the Taos town square where Sandra had stood the day before, buying postcards.

Sandra began poring through Nora's composition books—her composition books. It was as though she'd found some lost piece of herself. The answers to all her questions were all written in these faded pages, one of the few physical connections she had to Nora. Sandra kept the composition books with her at all times, never letting them out of her sight. Nora had sent these to her through time, and they were precious.

Two days later, Luke found her sitting at the bench rewriting some of the compositions into workable music for the record.

"What are you doing?" He took a seat in "the throne" chair again, which made Sandra smile.

"You look ridiculous in that chair."

"Anyone would look ridiculous in this chair. That's the point."

Sandra's focus returned to her composition book. She had a pencil and had drawn several new staffs on a blank piece of paper. "I can use this if I rework it. I didn't know how to find a melody line for one of

Hugh's poems, but this really works." She plunked out the bars on the Steinway. "You see."

Luke stood up and paged through the original composition book, opening up a spread farther back. "But you changed the tempo here." He pointed to a spot three pages later. "This is a better one, don't you think?"

Sandra looked at the music and then played it. He was right. "How did you—?"

"I know all of these songs."

"Of course you do," said Sandra softly.

In the recording studio, though, something magical was happening. A crew moved the Steinway into the studio and Sandra had tuners on hand all day getting the instrument where she wanted it. Lenny then switched Hugh from his Fender to an acoustic guitar. "Take away the theatrics," he said to Hugh and Sandra. "Just trust the music you wrote."

Hugh wanted to try a new song. He'd written down some lyrics and had a basic riff he played. Bex picked up the idea and began to lay down a bass line for it that really made it come alive. Sandra thought Hugh's riff could blend well with one of Nora's compositions. On the piano, she began to improvise the riff. The three of them—Sandra, Hugh, and Bex—worked out the major melody and lyrics. By the afternoon they were ready to add Ezra's drums. Lenny hit the RECORD button with the band playing through the song for several hours. This would become the pattern for the rest of their songs. Each night, they'd listen to the day's work, talking about what could be added.

In the rare day they had off, Sandra and Marie explored Taos. Marie was up early every morning making coffee. Rambling around the big house in the morning was one of Sandra's favorite things. She liked to get up early—Marie was usually the only other person up at that hour—and they'd sit on the back porch sipping coffee. Marie was a wealth of knowledge about the artistic history of Taos—D. H. Lawrence, Georgia O'Keeffe and Alfred Stieglitz, Paul Strand and Rebecca Salsbury James, and Mabel Dodge Luhan.

As they headed into town, Sandra noticed that everything in Taos was worn, from the jeans to the boots, to the Navajo blankets with thin places like bald spots, to the old Chevy truck that Marie drove around the town square to canvass the outdoor market for chilies. Marie was an excellent New Mexican cook, roasting red and green chilies with garlic and adding them to pork and chicken dishes. Sandra had never seen, smelled, or tasted anything like Taos. In contrast with Los Angeles's busyness, Taos was calm.

Hugh taught Lily and Sandra how to shoot a gun. They'd get on dirt bikes and head deep into the desert to shoot beer cans, jackrabbits, and—once—even a rattlesnake. Bex and Ezra routinely went into Santa Fe, everyone keeping a watchful eye on any changes in Ezra's behavior, but he maintained focus during the recording sessions.

As the weeks passed, the four of them recorded a total of eight songs for the album. The time locked away together both as artists and people had made their songs better. They had been so proud of their first recording—the one that Lenny had given them to preview in the Chrysler—but upon listening to it again Hugh had requested they re-record it. They'd developed a sound around the fourth song that they didn't have in the earlier works.

Despite his Marxist lectures, Hugh made an allowance for one big capitalist industry—music—receiving new shipments of records from his friends back in LA: new Janis Joplin, Melanie, and the Doors.

Sandra's favorites were the 13th Floor Elevators' "You're Gonna Miss Me," the Guess Who's "No Sugar Tonight," and Can's "Mother Sky," although Donovan's "Season of the Witch" was the song she played the most, leading Hugh to call it "her song." Upon hearing the news of Janis Joplin's death of an overdose in early October, they all spent a whole day together on the sofa mourning, playing "Try" over and over again, until they had to go into town to buy another record needle.

After dinner one evening, Sandra saw Ezra standing alone looking at the sunset. She closed the door quietly so as not to startle him. "You okay?"

"Don't you wonder how many times you'll see the sunset again?"

"Very Paul Bowles of you," said Sandra.

He laughed.

Sandra knew how many times she'd see the sunset. She'd die at thirty-four, just like Nora, unless it all became too much for her. But Ezra was different. He could choose a different ending for himself if he wanted. "I want you to be happy, Ezra."

He shook his head. "That's not possible, I'm afraid. I want this record to matter, Sand. As proof that I was here."

Her legs almost buckled when he said it, but Sandra understood exactly what he meant. Like Nora leaving her the composition books, this album was her proof that she'd lived and that she'd done something good with this fucked-up situation she was born into.

"I've promised myself that I'll see this record through."

Sandra could read the spaces between Ezra's words—he knew he didn't have long. She reached out and touched his hand. They stood there together for a silent moment and she leaned her head on his shoulder.

The final two songs on the album were ones that Ezra had written.

The first was called "Angel of the Canyon," and the lyrics were poignant. By now, the group could get a suggestion of a riff or basic melody line and begin to layer a song around it. Hugh went back to the Fender and upped the reverb on the chords. The song had a distinctive lushness to it. It was a fuzzy, atmospheric song, and Hugh went off on a guitar solo after the first two verses. Lenny was glad he'd recorded the whole thing because everyone in the room felt it was a departure from the other songs and really pushed their sound.

By now there was a feeling that what happened in the studio was sacred—this thing among them would never be re-created with another group of people—it required them in this moment. As Halloween approached, there was a heaviness in the air as the album was coming to an end and a feeling that every moment from then on for them would somehow be lesser.

"Does every fucking musician feel this way?" Hugh had worked his way around the recording console by now and he knew exactly which combination of buttons and levers made their songs come alive.

"If they know their record is good, they do." Lenny leaned back in his chair. "And this is a fucking good album. There's a superstition to it, that you'll never be able to create it again. Any artist feels that way, I think—that everything they've done, every ritual they've created is sacred."

Right before Halloween, Sandra found a letter for her sitting on the hall table. The writing was familiar. She'd seen it etched on photos in grease pen, offering cropping suggestions or captions on the back. Opening it, she was surprised at how she'd been able to put Rick out of her mind. The sheer foreignness of Taos and the dreams she'd been having had overloaded her senses and given her space from him. But seeing his handwriting again made her ache for him, like he was imprinted on her.

October 20, 1970

Sandra:

I hope you are well. Hugh tells Kim that the recording sessions are great. I always knew that band six would be the one. I think about you all the time, but strangely I can't imagine you in New Mexico. I hope you are happy. You surely deserve to be.

I've written and rewritten this letter so many times. Words just seem to come up short for the emotions that I feel for you. I understand why you left, really I do. Distance and time have given me perspective on what happened between us, but they have not diminished my love for you. Nothing can do that.

I've accepted a photo assignment in Vietnam. There is a story to be told over there and I'm going to capture it—I guess I need to feel a part of something bigger. I learned that from you. There is something about us that transcends this time and place. I know I'm not describing it well, but the whole thing—my feelings for you and what happened to me in the hospital have changed me. You've changed me.

When I'm done, I'm coming to find you. You are my "raison d'etre" as the French say. We should be together—I think you know that, too.

I'll love you always,
Rick

Luke found her, letter in hand, sitting on the old church pew in the foyer.

"Bad news?"

"Rick is going to Vietnam." She gathered her hair up into a rubber band to give her hands something to do. She sniffed and when she did, she felt something trickle down her lip and she touched it—blood again.

He moved to get her a tissue, but she waved him off, wiping it on her shirttail. He tried to help but she put her hand out to stop him.

He sat down beside her, the old boards on the pew creaking.

"The bargain I made with you." She looked over at him and down at the letter. "It was for him. He died——"

"I know," said Luke. "Marchant."

"Of course you know." She laughed. "Or you think you do, but you don't. He was Rick."

"No." He sighed, sounding bored. "He's Marchant *disguised* as Rick, but he's always Marchant. Never forget that. You've seen him in your dreams—first as Marchant, then as Billy Rapp . . . he's like an actor playing a part."

"But he's Rick. He was special this time. And you're wrong—Marchant, Billy, and Rick—he's always different. This one was unique." She folded her arms and turned to look at him.

Something in her stance or features seemed to make him pull back and look at her. "What's wrong?"

"So we're tied together—you, me, and Rick?"

"You and Marchant."

"Rick," she corrected him. "How does this curse work?"

"Well, your life is pretty normal, until you meet Marchant or some version of him, and then it always goes wrong and you . . ." He paused. "Well, you call me to intervene. It's like a loop, always the same. The dreams you have are part of it. All the different versions of you need to reconcile into one person, so the dreams start, but they don't start before you call me. I'm your administrator. I look out for you. Think of me as a guardian angel."

"Or the opposite."

He nodded. "Or the opposite. How you look at it is up to you."

She held up the letter. "Rick is volunteering to go over there...to take pictures. Then he says he's coming here, after."

"I wouldn't recommend that he do that, nor that you encourage it." Luke leaned over and put her face in his hands and pulled her close—so close their lips were almost brushing against each other. "You made a bargain and there are consequences." He shook his head and laughed bitterly. "It has always... *always*... been you. I have a choice, remember that. Marchant *doesn't*, but I do. It's forbidden for me to love you. There have been consequences for *me* to love you and *still* I choose to do it over and over. You are mistaken if you think this version of him is genuine. He isn't. He's not capable of it."

"What consequences are there for you?"

"It doesn't matter."

"But it does. You can't say something like that and not finish it. What are you? What consequences do you have for loving me?"

Luke got up and walked away but seemed to rethink something and came back. He grabbed Sandra and kissed her, deeply. She stood up and pulled him closer, swaying for just a moment. Like an imprint, she remembered every patch of stubble and smooth part of Luke's face as she touched him.

Finally, she pulled away. "No."

He shrugged his shoulders for her to continue. "What?"

"I'm not falling for this again. You controlling the shots of what I know and don't know. What are we, Luke?"

He looked puzzled. "I don't know what you mean." His eyes were the deep blue of the sky in Taos.

"I don't know *what* I am."

He looked down at the floor. "Does it matter?"

"Very much. I'm not mad about you not telling Nora she was going to die, but I've noticed something—you keep things from me. You think it's best that I not know them, but that isn't your right."

He looked down.

"You think you're helping me, but you're not. And since I'm here because of a curse, I assume that you're a demon of some sort? Isn't that what my administrator is? Paul and Marie, too? There's a version of them in each of my lives."

He met her eyes, and there was defeat in them as though he'd been kicked. "They're lesser demons."

"So, by the same token, should I assume that I'm some kind of demon as well?"

"No." He ran his hands through his hair. "You're a witch. Like your mother."

She looked down at the letter. "That's bullshit. This whole thing is bullshit. You saved Rick, *not* me. This power that I have, let's not fool ourselves. You've created it for some entertainment purpose this time around, just like you created this sham of a recording studio. If making this record wasn't Hugh's dream, I wouldn't let the charade that we're making an album continue." She pulled back from him and began to walk toward the steps.

"You're wrong, Sandra." His voice was quiet. "I didn't save Rick, you did. Do you recall Nora being able to make Lillibet forget she'd seen her? That was the first time I noticed that something was going on. Something more. You're getting more powerful in each life."

"What are you talking about?" Sandra cocked her head.

He was silent.

"Oh. You won't tell me? This is madness, you know. That you let it go on again and again is madness."

"You don't think I hate this?" Never had Luke looked at her with such intensity. "I am powerless. Do you know what my sole reason for existing is? *You*."

"Well, if I'm your sole purpose, then you do a lousy job." As she said it, Sandra knew she'd gone too far.

He laughed bitterly and looked up at the chandelier above them. "Maybe I have done a lousy job. It doesn't matter that I watch you fall in love with someone else again and again. I'm always picking up the pieces after Marchant is done with you, like now."

"Well, that's the job, isn't it?"

He nodded. "Yeah. It's pathetic because I know as I stand here that in *another* forty years, I'll do it again with another version of you. My only fucking hope in the next life is that the new version of you isn't as big a bitch as this one seems to be."

He walked off and didn't look back.

The house was quiet for the rest of the day. He didn't come to the studio.

Late that night Marie fried up burgers with chilies and melted cheese and left one on the counter for Luke, but it went untouched. On the radio in the kitchen, President Nixon was giving a speech to the nation about the war. Now, with Rick over there, the war was more personal to Sandra, and she found herself sinking on the sofa next to Marie to hear him. As night fell and the temperature dropped, Sandra excused herself to go to her room. As she walked down the hall, she knocked on Luke's door. His face was weary when he saw it was her.

"I thought it was Marie with dinner."

"Can I come in?"

"Sure." He stood back from the door.

"I don't want to fight with you." The feeling of his lips on hers still burned.

He sat on the bed and folded his hands in defeat. "I'm sorry for what I said earlier. It wasn't true."

"Me too. You don't do a lousy job. I know you try your best." Sandra thought he resembled an inmate in a prison cell, biding his time. "I think you hoped that I'd get my Nora memories back and we'd just resume as things were. Where we left off."

"I did. We were happy." He raked his hands through his hair, looking strained. In the lives she'd been shown, he hadn't looked this strained, old even. "You don't seem happy. I can help you, if you'd let me."

She laughed a little too loudly. "Well you *could*, but you never really do. You keep things from me. Don't you?"

He tensed and Sandra knew he was expecting another fight. As a conciliatory gesture, she sat down on the bed next to him. "I want a real explanation for why I recall my lives, but Rick or Billy do not? Let's start there."

"Because you're a witch and Marchant is not."

"That doesn't make sense. I'm having an existential crisis here, Luke, and I don't know why you aren't. The three of us are pawns. We don't even have free will."

"It's pointless to have a crisis, Sandra. I had one on my first go-round with Juliet. I agonized at my failure when she jumped off the Pont Neuf and I thought..." He paused. "I thought I'd served my sentence. That I was done after she'd died—they'd send me on to real hell or give me back some of my memories—but I ended up with another version of her. I was in agony. I'd loved Juliet and she was back but had no memory of me. That was the way it was supposed to work."

"Except Nora came back with Juliet's memories."

"Not at first. Like I said, it was agony seeing her. And then one day, I came through the door and she was sitting at the piano and I saw the recognition—the love in her face."

"Won't this spell just wear off eventually?"

He shook his head. "No. It binds for eternity, but you're getting stronger each time you come back." He kept rubbing his head and then fell back onto the bed. "Look at it this way. You live in a curse. I control things within the curse. Like I kill Billy Rapp or make Clint do it—it really doesn't matter. I also protect you—I keep our finances flowing for generations, buy us houses, that kind of thing." He stared at the ceiling like he was staring up at the stars, his tan skin against the crisp white sheets. "But this healing, the mind control—that doesn't have anything to do with the curse. It's coming from you. In fact, this power you have actually makes it harder for me. Each time you come back, it's like you want to reassemble yourself, so Juliet starts with her memories and she sends you the piano skills. That's the essence of who you are at heart."

"Why?" The kiss had stirred something in her. She knew what it was like to make love to him and it was tempting to crawl on top of him now, but yet they *were* strangers again. She wanted to reach out and touch him, knowing exactly how he'd feel, but she stopped. He'd always kept things from her, no matter what she'd given him. While she had the stirrings of love for him from the past, she couldn't forgive him for his omissions.

"You're sounding like a six-year-old. You know that, don't you?"

Sandra paced the floor in front of the bed. "Then help me. So my mother was a minor witch, so what. I've seen her. She dabbled in herbs and love potions. So what?"

"Because you're a major one."

"Very funny." She took a sock from on top of the dresser and threw it at him. He reached up and caught it with perfect precision.

"I'm not kidding." He leaned forward on the bed, playing with the sock in his hands. "You're a major dark talent, like your father."

"That's crazy. My father—Juliet's father—was a farmer."

Luke shook his head before he spoke, preparing her for what was to come next. "No. Juliet's father—your father—was Philippe Angier."

The name sounded familiar. She cocked her head. "Philippe Angier?" Sandra searched her memories working backward—first Nora's memories, and finally Juliet's—until she found it. "The magician killed in the duel? The one you were discussing at Edmond Bailly's shop that day?" Sandra remembered the composer and the artist, discussing Angier.

"Your mother was his assistant for many years. She was also his lover. He was notorious for impregnating his assistants and then killing his children as sacrifices. He was a real prince. You have his dark skills—in every one of your lives."

"You went to his funeral. I followed you."

He nodded. "I had to be sure he was dead. And I wanted to make sure that one of his brides wasn't following you again."

"The woman in the red dress? The one you killed on the Rue Norvins?"

"That's the one. But that wasn't the first one you saw, was it?"

"No," said Sandra. "Juliet was followed to the train station the morning she left for Paris—a woman in a yellow lace dress."

"Oh, he had a harem of them for sure." Luke laughed. "Your mother wore the blue dress. When she got pregnant with you, she fled Paris for Challans with Angier's grimoire. That's where she met Jean LaCompte, who raised you as his own."

Sandra absorbed what Luke was telling her. It had such a true ring to it and finally put all the pieces of the puzzle together for her. Juliet's mother had said she'd lived in Paris. She recalled the purple costume and the face paint. It had been so theatrical because that was all the magic the poor woman knew. She hadn't realized she was out of her element—or was so desperate she didn't care. And the grimoire. She remembered the old book with the name of the demon.

"Philippe Angier never stopped looking for you. He was frantically searching for you before the duel—especially before the duel. He could sense you were in the city, so that's why they were out looking for you."

"To kill me?"

"Sacrifice you. Had they gotten to you, he wouldn't have died. That's why I didn't want you dressing like a boy and cavorting about Montmartre, but you had other ideas."

It was a moment of levity, and she poked him. "You'd have none of that." She lowered her voice to mock him. "Lock you away? Why, Juliet...that is exactly what I plan to do." She sat back down on the bed, heavily.

"I wasn't that bad."

"Hell you weren't. It was like Alcatraz on the Saint-Germain."

He put his hand over his face and laughed. "I was protecting you. It was a game of cat and mouse with him."

They both stared up at the ceiling. He touched her lightly with his fingers, held her hand.

"Why would Angier want Juliet dead?"

"He thought his children gave him power. As long as you lived, he was weaker. Your death would give him power." Luke stopped and considered his words. "And it would have given him power, Sandra. Philippe Angier was real. He wasn't doing parlor tricks and theatrics. His powers came from a real demon. When your mother found

out about you and Marchant and she realized that you were pregnant, that's when she got the crazy idea for this spell. She was angry
at Marchant, for your ruin, but also because Angier would know you
were pregnant. He could feel it. You were in real danger; she was
right. Her anger at Marchant was wrong, but she was so angry she
wanted him ruined. She just screwed up the fucking spell."

For the first time, her mother's anger at Marchant made sense. It
also explained why she never wanted Marchant painting her—the risk
that Angier might see some likeness of himself hanging in a Paris salon
and get one step closer to finding her.

"Sadly, your mother wasn't a talented witch, like Angier. She was
just a stagehand. She'd seen him do things, so she mimicked those
things. But summoning demons? More emotion than skill, I'm afraid.
The sad irony of the whole thing is that she never had to do the spell
at all."

"Why would you say that?"

"She'd stolen the grimoire." Luke shrugged like it was a simple
explanation.

"And?"

"Well, a grimoire is a living thing. It was the contract between the
demon—in this case Althacazur—and Angier that was passed down
through the bloodline. It's also why Angier wanted no bloodline. The
demon gave up some of his magic to Angier in that grimoire. The
more heirs you have the weaker you get. You were a legitimate heir—
a blood heir. You had possession of the grimoire and you had power.
Angier really couldn't have touched you. Althacazur would have seen
your claim to the grimoire."

"But my mother didn't know that."

"So she called on him for a protection spell, by accident."

"Why'd he do it?"

Luke laughed. "Do you have any idea how many people, right now, are trapped in binding spells...going about their daily lives as though they are the architects of their own fates?"

Sandra didn't answer.

"Millions."

"Millions?"

"It's the business, Sandra. It's what we demons do. We collect people and tie them to contracts for eternity. It was fun for him—and he collected your mother's soul in the contract..." His voice trailed.

Finally he continued. "Which all pretty much sums it up. That's why it has been so unpredictable with you. It's like trying to cork a genie. When Nora started having recollections of being Juliet, I was stunned. I didn't know what to do. You weren't supposed to have those memories so it made my job more complicated. I hear Althacazur thinks it's terribly funny watching me contain you. You were supposed to just come back a blank slate, grateful for the help. I was just supposed to renew your contract every thirty-four years or so. Simple."

"And you?"

"What about me?"

"What are you?"

"You know what I am. I'm soldier—a lesser demon."

"Sounds awfully close to a major witch."

"Demons—the big ones like Althacazur—don't like to deal with humans. Major witches are humans. Lesser demons, like me, do their dirty work. I'm hoping to get my freedom when the curse is done. I can move up or become human again."

"Luke."

"Yeah?"

"We're trapped until the end of time. Exactly when do you think you're winning your freedom?"

He didn't say anything.

She saw something in his face. "Wait! There's a way out of this curse, isn't there?"

He still didn't say anything.

"But you can't tell me."

"Enough answers for you tonight?"

She kissed him on the forehead, still holding on to his head. "Thank you." She was so tired of having things that didn't belong to her. She ran her hand through his hair. The feel of it—of him—was so familiar to her. They didn't speak. Sandra unbuttoned her blouse halfway and Luke finished, sliding it down her shoulders. In the amber glow from the bathroom light, she studied his face and traced the outline of his lip. He pulled her down toward him and she fumbled at his clothes, pulling his shirt free. In the heat of the desert, she'd learned to slow down and to savor things. As she ran her hands along the smooth skin of his back, she took her time undressing the rest of him, her hands touching every inch of him. When they finally made love, it wasn't the intense interlude of Luke and Nora, but rather the subtle intimacy between two people who know each other's bodies and minds so well.

After, Sandra traced the thin patches of hair on his chest and then kissed him, the saltiness of his skin and his reaction both so familiar.

"You were human once?" He laced her fingers in his, and she knew that he was about to share something with her. "So you remember nothing of your life before?"

He shook his head. "What I know is that I killed someone in my real life. I acted against a man in anger for a woman I loved, but in fact she did not love me."

Sandra studied his face. This was a painful memory for him. "You killed him."

"I did and it was wrong. And now, this forced—inaction—this is my punishment."

"For action."

"For my rash action."

"So I'm a form of hell?" Sandra ran her hand over the cool sheets. From a distance, somewhere downstairs, she thought she could hear music—an accordion. "Is that Lawrence Welk?"

"I think so." He laughed. "Marie loves television."

"Another form of hell."

"Yeah, that really kills the mood, doesn't it." He pulled her to him and kissed her deeply. His voice was quiet, almost a whisper. "You've always had such beautiful hair." He touched the strands. "It's blonder now. You come back and everything is new and you don't remember a thing about me, but I remember every detail of you. And the worst of it. I have no idea *who* you'll be this time. You say Rick is different, well, you're wildly different each time. This *is* hell for me."

"You miss Nora?"

"I do miss her. We were happy. You have her memories, but you aren't her. I thought so, too. Once, I thought all the versions of you were the same, but the three of you are not the same. Nora's dead. *My* Nora is dead. Just like your version of Rick."

What he said stung, even though he didn't mean for it to. "I loved him." She said this because it was true, but also because what he'd said about her not being Nora had hurt her more than she'd thought it would.

He stroked her hair. "All the shit that you're asking me to tell you. It's stuff that doesn't matter. It's simply the mechanics of this thing. *All* that matters is the time you are here with me. Nora understood that."

"But you're wrong," said Sandra, touching his face and pulling his chin down so she could see his eyes in the darkness. "Nora didn't ask questions because she didn't want the answers. She was afraid of the answers. You know that, Luke."

"She was happy."

"You made her happy, that's true," said Sandra. "But she never wanted to dig too deeply."

"I can't blame her. I won't blame her for that. She'd had a tough life as Juliet and then Nora." She could hear something in his voice. Was it jealousy? "Rick made you happy."

"He did. I know you say that it was impossible for me to be happy with him, but I was."

For the first time, Sandra felt that Luke wasn't hiding anything from her anymore, but she also felt something that she hadn't felt before with him—he was disappointed in this version of her. He'd loved Nora, and sadly Sandra hadn't come back exactly as she'd left him. They were like a couple who'd been married a long time—they loved each other deeply, but they knew the limits of each other—having etched those places through regret, sorrow, mistakes, and time.

Over the next few weeks, they finished the album—nine tracks in total. Right before Thanksgiving, Lily, Ezra, and Hugh went back to Los Angeles. Sandra knew she wouldn't be going back for Thanksgiving or any other time. She wasn't a creature of this time. She belonged here with Luke, Paul, and Marie.

26

Helen Lambert
Washington, DC, June 16, 2012

On the way back to Georgetown to see Malique, I'd apparently fainted in the cab. I woke to find the driver standing over me, swearing as I drooled on his pleather seat. After swearing I wasn't drunk and that I could, indeed, pay him, I roused myself from the backseat and walked up the stairs to Madame Rincky's shop. *So, I'm Philippe Angier's daughter. I'm a witch. And I'm a witch who lives in a binding curse.*

From the waiting room, I could hear that Malique was doing a reading. I studied my fingers. I'd felt that same tingling then burning sensation when I'd touched Marielle Fournier in the nursing home. At the time, I thought that I'd seen an improvement in her condition, and I had been right.

I was curious about the band, No Exit, so I did a quick Internet search on my iPhone while I heard Malique wrapping up. I'd coughed a few times so he'd know it was me out here.

Wading through the millions of Jean-Paul Sartre references, I finally found one curious entry, a post on a Los Angeles website that talked about seeing the band in 1970 at Gazzarri's on Sunset. The post said that the band had been a highlight on the Strip that summer, but they'd disappeared from the scene just as suddenly as they'd arrived.

There were several other theories of what had happened to them. A few other posts mentioned rumors of a lost tape, and one post mentioned Hugh Markwell's address in Texas. What the hell, I thought. I was running out of time and wanted to find out Sandra's story as quickly as I could.

Searching for Hugh Markwell, I found a phone number in Austin. He was a professor of environmental studies at the University of Texas, Austin. From the image of him, I could see that it was the same Hugh. Now gray-haired, he really hadn't changed much, still looking like a 1970s hippie only with a fuller face marked with deep lines.

I rang the extension for UT Austin and got his message. I left him a voicemail saying I was Helen Lambert, publisher of *In Frame*, and was interested in hearing the story of the lost tapes of his band, No Exit, for a features piece in our September issue.

Sandra's story was the last one for me, but as with any cliffhanger I was dying to know what had happened to her. So Luke had been producing records back in Taos? I could sense Sandra's confusion at her powers, her desire to be normal. In piecing together my own fractured lives, I realized that I was not yet a whole person, but a group of women.

I looked at my watch.

The door opened and Malique ushered a crying young woman out of the room. She appeared to be crying with joy, however, hugging Malique. It occurred to me that I hadn't hugged Malique and wondered if I had some social flaw for failing to do so. It did occur to me that few people would hug him for saying they were living in a binding curse.

I sat down as Malique took a decorative dagger from his bag and placed it on the table. Then, dipping the paintbrush in the vial of blood, the older man began to paint a thin layer of blood on the dagger, turning the knife every direction to cover the blade entirely. Finally, he set the dagger down on the table.

"What are you doing?"

"I'm letting the blood dry."

"Do we just say some kind of spell?"

He nodded. "As soon as the blood dries."

I could hear a clock ticking loudly from somewhere. I wondered why Madame Rincky would have a clock so distracting in her salon. The smell of stale incense was clinging to the curtains long after it had burned away.

When Malique was satisfied, he placed his palms down on the table on either side of the dagger and began to speak. It was a strange singsongy sound. I'd heard it before. As Juliet, I'd heard my mother sing this same way the night she placed the curse on me. Malique's eyes rolled back into his head, but he kept speaking in the same rhythm and voice, high and unsettling. Finally he reached out and grabbed my hand, startling me. He began to shake and then convulse. My hands began to burn, and there was a strange taste on my tongue; I realized my nose had begun to bleed. Malique fell out of the chair and rolled onto the floor, still shaking.

I wasn't sure if I should call an ambulance. I leaned over Malique, slapping his face. "Malique?"

His eyes opened suddenly, sending me reeling backward from fright. "You scared the shit out of me. Are you okay?"

But it wasn't him looking at me—his voice was altered, not his own. "Oh, my beautiful girl!" Malique sat up and turned mechanically like the doll from *Tales of Hoffmann*. "*Est-ce toi?*"

I pushed myself back against the wall as far as I could get from him, my boots squeaking on the floor as I scrambled.

"You are frightened of me? Don't you recognize me?"

I cocked my head. "*Maman?*"

"Juliet, Juliet." It was Malique, and yet it wasn't.

"*Maman*, is that you?" I looked closely at Malique for signs of Juliet's mother. "Sorry…You just look a bit different than you did before. Well, you look like a rather old Jamaican man."

"You look different as well." Malique smiled. "I don't have much time. I did a terrible thing to you. I need to tell you how sorry I am."

"Which me?"

"What do you mean?"

"There are many mes, *Maman*. I've been living for a hundred years, over and over, plus I die at thirty-four." I was a little bitter at the last thing, and I think she picked it up in my voice.

"Oh *non*," said Malique. "I am so sorry, Juliet."

"Yeah, well…" I leaned in. "Where are you exactly?"

Malique shook his head. "I cannot talk about it." But from his face, I could see pain.

"Are you suffering, *Maman*?"

"Please don't ask me about this place. I just want to look at you. My beautiful girl. Your hair is red." Malique/Maman seemed disturbed by this detail.

"It is." I touched it, knowing that I must look like Philippe Angier.

"*Maman*," I said. "I know about Philippe Angier." It was uncanny how Malique had captured Juliet's mother's speech patterns. At times, I could overlook that it was actually Malique, so perfectly animated was Thérèse LaCompte in his body. Malique's face twisted.

"I never wanted you to know. He and I were on stage every night together. I can still see him as I saw him then. He was tall with jet-black hair and he commanded the stage. He'd start with hypnosis, grabbing someone from the audience, then he'd move to the cards, and finally his big act was levitating me. I never understood that it was supposed to be a trick. He never used wires so I just assumed that was the way all of the magicians did it. It didn't occur to me that there was another side to him. That his magic was real.

"Yes, I was his most prized assistant—and also his lover. But I didn't know that there were many of us. I was with him for a year when I became pregnant with you. Things changed then, but the changes were subtle at first. My door locked at night when it had never been locked before, for my 'safety.' When he was sure that the pregnancy was going to come to full term, he told me that I was to be of service to him. And I *wanted* to be of service to him. I loved him. He was magical—the grandest man I had ever seen. But that's not what he meant. He took me to a house and told me that it was to be ours after your birth. I was given a room and locked in it. By then, he'd hired another assistant to replace me. I passed her once in the hallway. She was young and blond and she had a rouge dress. I never wore rouge. I was the bleu girl, always in bleu. That's how he referred to us, by the color of our dresses. I was soon to meet rose girl, violet girl, and jaune girl, for we were all locked in this house together. Jaune and I were both pregnant."

I could see the dress that *Maman* was describing. I'd seen the jaune and the rose versions.

"Oh yes. It was violet girl who helped me the most. Her real name was Esmé. I refuse to call her by any other name. You see, she warned me of what was to come. That I would give birth to you and you would be 'offered' to service."

This story made me uneasy. I'd just heard Luke telling the bones of it, but something told me this would be an unpleasant tale to hear.

Maman continued. "Well, rose girl had become his deputy. She had recruited us all. She told us that service was an honorable thing, that to give you to him would be the greatest gift I could give. But I didn't want to give you up. Esmé told me that you would be slaughtered at the first full moon after your birth. I still had several months to go before that happened, but I would not let it happen. Esmé told me that I had to make them believe that I would offer you. Esmé and I were caged when another girl—one who had been on stage before me—brought her child, a boy, to the altar. The girl was weak from childbirth, which had only been two days before, so I forgave her. I don't think she fully understood. At least I hope she didn't. Esme and I were chained for the ceremony, but we were required to watch. It was a horrible ceremony. I had to witness it three times. There were candles that burned quicker, robes, and then..." Malique's voice went quiet. "I knew I would never let that happen to you, but I had to go along or they'd kill me upon your birth and take you anyway."

"Why?"

"When I was several weeks from giving birth to you, Esmé told me that I needed to escape. She pretended she was ill. She was an actress and she was good enough to distract the rose girl. She'd cut her arm and drained the blood into a cup. When rose girl looked away, she dumped the cup all over her violet dress. Rose girl was horrified, thinking something terrible was happening, like consumption. While Rose was tending to Esmé, who was rolling around on the floor very dramatically, I escaped while the door was open and ran through the hall. It was my only chance, Juliet. I had to run past the great altar and I saw the grimoire on its pedestal. Esmé had told me to try to take the leather book—your father's grimoire—if I could manage it. She said that without it, the demon would be angry at your father and I might have a chance to get away. I grabbed your father's purple robe and turned it inside out. It was black on the inside and I was able to use it to keep warm. I heard them torturing Esmé as I went out the side door and into the night. She'd told me that she wouldn't endure another pregnancy—and that was certainly what they had planned for her. She said that she'd rather be slaughtered. And that, my child, is exactly what they did to her."

"I'm so sorry, *Maman*." This news was overwhelming. I felt like I'd been kicked. "Where did you go?"

"I broke a window and stole some shoes from a shop. They were too small, but they were better than nothing. I must have looked ridiculous with my long black cape and small shoes. That is how I looked when I met your father—the father who raised you—at the train station at Challans. I was so sick from hunger and so pregnant. I was thrown off the train at Challans because I had not bought a ticket. Well, I had no money. At this point I assumed it was all futile and that we'd be discovered, that I hadn't ran far enough, but no one ever came for you. It was the strangest thing. As you grew up, the fact that you were alive and growing stronger would have been appealing to your real father. You would have been a greater sacrifice. When Marchant began to paint you, I was worried that you'd be found out. You look like your real father." Malique touched the hair. "The hair, especially. His only turned red after. I thought he'd see himself in one of those paintings and discover where you were. I spent those years learning magic in the hope of trying to protect us. I knew the grimoire was powerful, so I called upon it. I was foolish."

"*Maman*," I said. "You weren't wrong. Rose and Jaune *did* come looking for me, but I was protected. You protected me. Philippe Angier died in a duel a hundred years ago."

"The administrator kept you safe." Malique smiled.

I nodded.

"Then it was all worth it."

"Well," I said. "There were complications."

"What complications?"

"Your spell kind of tied me to Marchant for four lifetimes."

Malique looked stricken.

"But I'm going to try to break the curse. Any ideas?"

"You must know it will be dangerous."

"I do know that, *Maman*."

"I'm so sorry, my beautiful girl. Please forgive me," said Malique before collapsing on the floor.

I sat there, looking at Malique, making sure he was breathing.

"I do," I whispered.

He woke up several minutes later, rubbing his head.

"Malique?"

"Yes."

"Is it you?"

"What do you mean?" He grabbed the chair and pulled himself up.

"Well for starters, you were possessed for a few moments."

"That explains the headache." He rubbed his temples.

"Does this happen to you a lot?"

"It is an unfortunate occupational hazard, but that was an unusually long period to be out." He looked over at the clock—twenty minutes had elapsed. He sat down on the chair, picked up the knife, and slid it into a leather case.

"What's wrong?"

"Nothing," he replied, but he seemed distracted.

"Nothing?"

"I think you are becoming very powerful. I can't even summon the world of the demon for two minutes."

"And?" I got up from the floor and sat opposite him.

"You're a very powerful witch, but this curse binds people for eternity—through time and space—you get the idea. They're nasty little things."

"Do you come across a lot of these?"

"Sadly, yes. My spell. It unbinds. Very simple." He rubbed his head. "Who was I...just now?"

"My mother. The original witch."

"That is very good, but also very bad."

"Why very bad?"

"Very good in that it means we got the right spell. Very bad in that we've called attention to ourselves. The demon will know."

"What do we do now?"

Malique reached out and touched my arm. He slid the knife toward me. "Here."

"What do I do with it?"

"I thought you knew."

I felt a sense of dread spreading across my body. "Knew what?"

"You must stab your administrator. You must kill him. Stab him in the heart. It nullifies the contract." He put his hand over his chest, like a child saying the Pledge of Allegiance.

I stared at the knife, resting in its leather holder. I felt the air leave my lungs. My stomach began to churn to the point I feared I would vomit. He was looking at me, horrified, and I realized that blood was dripping from my nose into a pool in front of me. "Malique, I don't think I can."

"Why not?"

"Because I'm in love with him."

He shook his head gravely. "Then we have a serious problem."

And then the room began to spin.

27

Sandra Keane
Taos, New Mexico, December 1970

The group agreed to return the first week in December to finish two more songs, but a week before they were due to arrive Hugh called to say that Ezra was back in the hospital. They'd have to push the recoding to the New Year. Lenny Brandt wasn't available again until February, so they agreed to try again then. Hugh was anxious to finish the rework of the first few tracks, but without Lenny it was impossible.

Taos got eighteen inches of snow in the mountains, a thinner layer blanketing the Pangea Ranch. The town was lovely at Christmas. Sandra and Marie went into town to see the lighting of the Christmas tree, sipping hot chocolate with cinnamon in the spot where Nora had been killed.

On Christmas Eve, Luke suggested they drive to the Taos Pueblo to see the Christmas Eve Procession—a sacred ceremony where the statue of the Virgin Mary was carried down the church stairs. At dark, as she walked among the bonfires that lit the sky red against the pink adobe walls of the Pueblo, it occurred to her that she'd never seen so much fire before she'd moved to Taos—from the fireplaces, to the fire pits and smudge sticks, to the bonfires that surrounded them at the ceremony.

"All the fires?" Sandra asked. "What are they for?"

Luke was quiet. "They are supposed to ward off the darkness."

As the chimes began to ring from the church, she looked at him and he couldn't meet her eye.

They were the darkness.

"We shouldn't be here, Luke," she said, taking his hand as they made their way back out of the pueblo.

After Christmas, Sandra was surprised when Luke got a letter first from Lily, then Hugh, saying they'd gotten married in Las Vegas. Ezra had continued to go in and out of the hospital as though being back in Los Angeles had unmoored him. Although it had been the early energy between Sandra and Hugh that had driven the band, something about Ezra not being able to come back had been the final nail in the coffin. Without him, the strange energy they'd created in the studio was gone—they needed all four of them to continue it. There was a finality to Hugh's letter, as though he knew the band was over. His getting married was also an indication that he felt it was time for them all to grow up. She'd wondered how Luke had managed to stage a recording studio, but considered it probably hadn't been that hard to promise a shot at stardom to four naive kids. But there was no need for the pretense of other people at Pangea Ranch anymore. The world consisted of her and Luke now. She thought it was sad because those months with Hugh, Lily, Ezra, Bex, and Lenny locked in the studio recording that album had been one of the best times of all her lives.

There continued to be knocks on the front door at night, and Sandra healed people when she could and finally began accepting money from grateful patrons. While she now knew that her power came from a dark place, she convinced herself that she was using it for a good purpose. She was helping people with it.

While looking at the composition books one day, Sandra found a curious thing. A blotch of ink had formed a fingerprint—Nora's fingerprint. To Sandra it was a precious thing—proof of her existence. Globbing up ink on a piece of scrap paper, Sandra pressed her own finger in the ink and then onto the composition book. Side by side. Identical fingerprints.

On an early-spring morning, Sandra answered the door and found a man standing on the front porch. His hat was low and she looked down at his black bag, which resembled a full garment bag, the kind that carried a rented prom tuxedo. But it looked too bulky.

Marie came to the door and began translating. The man said his daughter had been hit by a truck while walking on the highway. The man insisted on seeing Sandra—he'd heard about the Pangea Ranch—before taking her to the funeral home.

When the man unzipped the bag on the floor, Sandra realized the girl's head was not attached. Nothing was attached. She gasped loudly and then knelt down by the bag.

"I was hoping," said the man.

Sandra could hear the cadence coming down the steps and knew that Luke was standing behind her. Sandra shook her head and turned, touching Luke and whispering in his ear, "I'm sorry. I can't. She's... she's too far gone." Sandra looked up at Luke, grateful he was there.

The man shrank in front of them and then reached for the bag.

"I can do it," said Luke. "Leave her here. Come back in the morning. Daybreak."

The man took his hat off. "You can?"

"Come back at daybreak." Luke was rolling up his sleeves.

When the father had gone, Sandra spoke. "How can you fix *that*?"

"You don't want to know."

"Luke." She reached for his hand. "Don't. Listen to me. This is unnatural. This is wrong."

"None of this is natural, Sandra. Just give in to it."

"I mean it's dark, Luke. We have a choice."

"We're dark, Sandra." He sat on the church pew and stared at the bag. Sandra reluctantly joined him. He began to laugh. "We really don't have a choice."

"What can I do?" She put her hand on his leg.

"Nothing." He stared at the floor for a moment and then nodded toward the bag, which had begun to stir. Sandra thought she'd throw up; the idea of what was about to come out of the bag terrified her. "It's done. I'm going to go get a drink. I feel like a nice bourbon tonight."

She watched him walk down the hall, as if he'd done something banal like sweeping the front porch.

From the body bag came more stirring. Within minutes, a complete and whole girl unfolded. Her long dark hair emerged first, sitting atop a pair of shoulders, then slim hips and long legs. She was naked and Sandra ran to get her a blanket. When Sandra touched the creature—and the thing was still a creature at this point—it pulled back like a beaten dog.

"Luke!" Sandra yelled.

"She's confused," said Luke calmly from the hall, holding an amber glass of bourbon. "That's why I told her father to come back. She needs time to adjust to the world again." He shook the drink.

"What the fuck have you done?" Sandra wrapped the blanket around the girl. "We will pay for this, Luke."

"She needs to sleep," said Luke, ignoring her. He stood and began to walk back down the hall. "Put her in Ezra's old room."

"Luke," Sandra commanded.

He turned.

"This is wrong."

He turned again and walked away.

In the morning, the man came to collect his daughter, offering Sandra a horse and a bag of cash. She declined both. Oddly, Luke had been missing all morning and had given no instructions about this newly formed girl, so Sandra simply handed her back over to her father. She was still quiet, but the man seemed to anticipate some change was to be expected.

Sandra found Luke sitting on the back porch. It was cold—too cold for him to be sitting out. His lips were tinged with blue, which was contrasted by the occasional orange glow of the cigarette he smoked.

"Why did you do that?"

"I don't know." He shrugged. "Because I could, maybe. Sometimes it's fun being a demon, Sandra."

"Will she be the same?"

"No," he said. "That isn't his daughter, but he won't care. It will be enough for him. You'd be surprised at the illusions we sell ourselves."

Sandra remembered him telling Juliet that once about her own father. There was something bitter in Luke's voice, something she was missing.

She sat down next to him, took the cigarette from his hand, and took a drag. There was something about what they'd done that had excited her and made her feel connected to Luke again in a way that she hadn't felt before in this lifetime. She took another deep drag of the cigarette before putting it out with her boot. She put her hand out and, after a few seconds, he took it. Sighing and seeing her breathe in the air, she stood and pulled him up, the warmth of his body when it touched hers enveloping her. Then she led him upstairs to her room and closed the door.

A week later, Sandra found the mailman putting a letter in the mailbox early in the morning. He nodded to her as he started the Jeep. They never got letters. Seeing the postmark from Los Angeles, Sandra assumed it was something from her mother, but the writing was off. Looking closer, she'd seen the scribble on countless patient charts. It was from Hugh.

March 2, 1971

Dear Sandra:

I can't believe it's been three months since we saw each other. I miss the four of us. Being the one left behind is the hardest—the ghosts of Ezra and you are everywhere here in Los Angeles.

There's no easy way to say this. Rick was killed in Vietnam a week ago. I'm not getting a lot of details on what happened. Kim thought you'd want to know.

She's been waiting for reports from the army division he was traveling with, but I understand they took heavy casualties. The lack of detail gives us all hope that someday he'll walk through the door, but I know, deep in my heart, that my sister won't get a third chance with him. Kim said he wasn't the same man after the car accident, but I think you knew that.

I'm going to graduate school in Berkeley in the fall. I don't have another band in me after what we experienced in the last year. I don't think we'll ever get closer than those tracks and those months together. Lil and I talk about you quite a bit. We miss you.

I hope that New Mexico is treating you well. Tell Luke, Paul, and Marie we think of them often.

I hope to see you again sometime!

Hugh

Sandra closed her eyes and steadied herself against the railing on the front porch. After collecting herself, she found Luke in his study.

"Rick is dead," she said.

He nodded.

"You *knew*?"

"I always know when something happens with the two of you. You're both my responsibility."

"Why didn't you tell me?"

"What would I have said?"

"'Rick is dead' for a start…"

"Hugh should have been the one to tell you. Not me."

Sandra walked over to him and put her hands on the desk. "I loved him."

"I know. It's always that way—"

"No," Sandra cut in. "He was different to me, like Nora was different to you. He was a better version of himself, like Nora was a better version of me."

"I didn't say that…"

"You don't have to, Luke. It's written all over your face every time you look at me."

He sat back on the chair, and it tilted a little. His eyes met hers. "I never got over her."

"I understand completely," said Sandra as she turned to leave. She spent two days in her own bedroom, mostly lying in bed thinking of Rick dying. The loss of him again, unbearable.

On the third day, she finally got up the nerve to take a shower and make her way to the kitchen. Luke was making breakfast. He ignored her, busily moving around whipping things in bowls and putting them in pans. The tension between them was noticeable. Marie had given up trying to help and she and Paul were now reading the newspaper, like the good supporting actors they were in all her lives.

Luke handed Marie an omelet first, followed quickly by one for Paul and then Sandra. Thin and crispy potatoes and toast were placed in the center of the table. All three ate their eggs in silence, waiting for Luke to speak.

He set his own plate down heavily at the head of the table and grabbed the section of the newspaper that Paul had just finished. "That girl...the one in the body bag."

"What about her?" Sandra looked up, relieved he had finally said something. Everyone around the table appeared to breathe.

"You should go and see her. Make sure she's okay. I mean...as okay as she's going to be."

Sandra found herself wanting him to make eye contact, actually lowering her face to try to catch his eye as he read the paper, but he stayed fixed on whatever he was reading. "You don't want to go with me?"

"No." He turned the page on the paper. "I don't."

Luke's behavior around the girl was odd, and it piqued Sandra's interest enough to go looking for the address. The post office told her where she'd find the house and indicated it had a green mailbox. She drove Marie's old GMC pickup truck deep into the desert and had to drive slowly, looking for non-numbered mailboxes that seemed identified by names and colors. Pulling up the truck in front of the house, it seemed silent, like an Old West ghost town. There were no cars in front of the simple adobe ranch. From the looks of it, this family wasn't poor. The house was well maintained. Pulling her hair into a ponytail, Sandra slid her sunglasses onto her head so she could get a better look. A three-legged barn cat hobbled near the porch and crouched down observing her like the locals do before a big shootout in films. She stepped on the porch loudly enough that she'd be announced and rapped firmly on the door. The feeling that something was wrong here was overpowering.

A woman opened the door and gasped. She began speaking Spanish and Sandra shook her head, saying, "*No hablo Español…*" The woman paid no attention and seemed to be telling a lavish story involving something down the hall as she pointed. Finally, Sandra understood that she was to go down the hall. As she moved through the long hall, she could smell the medicinal odor of sage and knew that a smudge stick was burning. Knowing that someone had likely purchased one to ward off evil spirits, she crept hesitantly. These superstitious things didn't work—didn't ward off evil spirits or keep her out. She and Luke were as much the embodiments of evil spirits as anything she'd ever seen. In this case, the family would have been more likely to keep her out if they'd filled the place with cloves. Photos lined the walls, and Sandra recognized the woman, the father with the hat, a young man, and the girl who had been in the body bag. From the living room, the woman nodded when Sandra arrived at the correct door. She knocked, but there was no answer. The woman motioned for her to go in anyway.

Sandra opened the door slowly to find not a decaying body—as she had feared—but the girl sitting on the windowsill, smoking a cigarette. "Oh, I'm sorry…I didn't know…"

The girl's long dark hair cascaded in ringlets down her back. She was a stunning young woman with chiseled arms and thin fingers. "That I was in here?" The girl didn't look Sandra's way. "I don't speak a bit of Spanish, so there is no point in trying to talk to them. They think I've come back damaged in the brain." The girl finally turned to look at Sandra. "Wow, you've really changed, but not as much as I have, huh?"

"I'm not sure I understand..." Sandra took a step back.

"You don't recognize me? I'm hurt, baby." The girl blew smoke.

"I'm sorry...I don't..."

"Let me fill you in." The girl's voice was bitter, causing Sandra to step back into the hall. "One minute I was in a Jeep with three other journalists. We were doing a story in Hanoi and were given assurances that we'd be safe. We were just telling the story without any political ties. I was a fucking photographer." The girl laughed. "As if that's possible."

Sandra's stomach began to twist. In her head, she did the calculation of the date of Hugh's letter and the night that the girl's body was brought to Pangea. "Rick."

Ignoring her, the girl continued. "Next thing I know, I feel something heavy in my back, like I'd been stung and then stung again. Strange thing is that getting shot doesn't hurt like you think it would. It doesn't hurt at first and then it comes in waves." She inhaled. "Anyway, for me it was painless but maybe it's the shock, I don't know. I saw the other guys in the Jeep, their bodies twisting as the shots hit them, and I knew I must be twisting, too, my body was getting hit from all angles. I was reacting like you do when you're a kid playing with toy guns. It was only when I saw the blood that I knew I wouldn't make it out. The final shot must have been to my head because after that what I saw was a white sheet with a light behind it."

The girl rubbed her arms, seemingly surprised they were there.

"I'm sorry," said Sandra. "I don't understand."

"This went on for a while. And I saw the craziest things. I was painting in a little studio with a stone floor and then there was this opera and you were there, but it wasn't you really. I mean you looked a little different than you do now. And I could see that I was making you cry. You were trying hard to hide it from me, but I knew that what I was saying was making you cry. And then there were these flickering images of the sun, like a damaged film reel. Then there was a goddamned racehorse and you different again, but crying in this bronze dress, you looked like a goddess. Then I really felt pain. It was like someone was trying to put me in a heavy raincoat and it hurt so badly getting shoved into it, like I was being pulled out of my raw skin and into this raincoat."

Sandra felt her legs wobble. How was this girl describing her lives? What was wrong here? "I—"

The girl cut her off, her voice husky. "When I woke up, I was on a floor...in a bag." She paused and looked at Sandra as though she were waiting for an explanation, putting her cigarette out in the nearby ashtray and immediately lighting another. Something in the way she lit the cigarette was familiar.

"I thought I was still in Hanoi and then I looked down and I didn't understand. I thought I saw you, handing me a blanket, and I thought to myself, *This is the most absurd vision of heaven I can imagine. Sandra is handing me a fucking blanket.* And then you sent me away the next day, handed me over to this man who didn't speak a word of English, and I realized that it wasn't a dream—it was a horror show."

Sandra closed her eyes, the feeling of bile rising up in her throat. "Oh, Rick."

"Yeah, but I don't look like him anymore, do I? How the fuck am I here, Sandra? You know I saw what you did to Ezra." The girl swung her legs off the sill and onto the floor, planting them with a tiny thud. She took three steps toward Sandra, who towered over her now. "How?"

Sandra spied the edge of the toilet in the room across the hall. She ran, heaving into the bowl, choking on her own vomit. She slumped to her knees and squared herself with the rim of the toilet seat before vomiting again. She could feel the girl—Rick—behind her, looming.

"Is this what you did to me before?"

"I *didn't* do this to you."

"After my car accident. You brought me back."

Sandra nodded. "But not like this. That was different."

"Well, someone brought me back again and put me...in this." The girl tugged at her skin.

Sandra stood, not bothering to flush the toilet, and pushed past the girl, staggering from the house into the truck and driving off. After missing several dirt roads, she spied a patch of cottonwood trees and pulled off the road. This was a nightmare. Finally, a motorcycle passed her and she pulled onto the dirt path, following the motorcycle out onto the main road. When she got back to the Pangea Ranch, she found Luke in the kitchen on the phone.

"Get off the fucking phone." She paced the floor in front of him, grabbing at her hair. Finally, she pushed down on the lever to hang up the phone.

"What is it?" He wasn't angry. After putting the handset back on the wall, he folded his arms in front of him. "This should be good."

"How *could* you?" Sandra spat.

"How *is* Marchant?"

"He's a fucking mess. How do you think he is?"

"Well, he's not dead at least."

"He'd prefer to be."

"Oh, they all say that. None of them mean it." Luke started down the hall. "Marchant was always such a fucking prima donna."

"Don't walk away from me." Sandra took off after him.

He spun around, sending her reeling backward. "Tell me. What is so bad about what I did for you? This version was different, right?"

"You were jealous?"

"That you *loved* him…Lord knows I've heard that enough, so I found a fucking loophole for the two of you to be together. You're welcome. Go and be happy together."

"It isn't natural."

"Oh, I'm sorry." He laughed. "And you and I are both *natural*, are we? We're the *fucking* Addams Family, Sandra, in case you failed to notice."

"You had no right—"

"Don't lecture me on right. Would you rather he was dead? Would you?"

Sandra took her time answering. "Have you stopped the curse by doing this to Rick? Will it end now?"

"Oh honey," laughed Luke. "If only it were that simple. But I assure you, as the *administrator* of this fiasco we live in, I could pull that bastard Marchant out of his body at any time and put it in that cookie jar over there and guess what? He'd still bounce back to meet you in the next life. I'm powerless to alter the spell, but it doesn't mean I can't enjoy fucking with it—and him a little!"

"You're an awful man," said Sandra. "How'd you do it?"

"What do you mean how did I do it? How do I do everything? How do we do everything we do? I'm a fucking demon. You keep saying so, reminding me how *bad* we are."

"Rick is confused." She knew it sounded pathetic.

"Jesus, Sandra." Luke raked at his hair. "*Enlighten* him. Plus, he's back now in a pretty casing. If Rick is such a soul mate to you then

you'll accept him in any package, won't you? Go fuck him…her…
whatever…to your heart's content, until he isn't confused anymore.
Love the one you're with, right? Just get out of my sight with this. I'm
done. Really."

"You did this out of spite."

He sighed, exasperated. "No, Sandra. Really…I did it for you with
pure intentions. Fool that I was, I thought he'd make you *happy*. I'm
sick of you going through the motions. You sure as hell aren't happy
here with *me*."

The last word hung between them.

"I was trying to be happy…with you."

"Well, go *try* with someone else." He pushed through the screen
door and out into the backyard.

Sandra waited a few days and went back to see Rick, now Aurora Garcia. She found Aurora sitting on the porch, drinking a beer like a man.

"You're back." Aurora eyed her warily.

"You're not very ladylike," said Sandra. "You could at least try."

"I've had no practice being ladylike, Sandra." Aurora shrugged and
nodded toward the house. "Can you at least tell them that I have lost
the ability to speak Spanish as some consequence of trauma? I think
they're planning an exorcism. I'm not sure they're happy with you,
either, so you might not be welcome in there." Aurora tipped her beer
toward the kitchen.

"Want to get out of here?"

"Fuck, yes." Aurora dropped the bottle on the floor and stepped off
the porch.

They drove down to Santa Fe for the day, walking around the town
square, Aurora taking everything in. They stopped at a café on Santa
Fe Plaza, with windows facing the square. After sitting in silence for a
few moments, Aurora nodded to the window. "It's not LA, is it?"

"No. This is the opposite of LA."

"I miss it. Maybe I'll go back."

"To Los Angeles?" Sandra's voice rose. She tried to imagine the horror of Aurora trying to fit back into Rick's life. It wasn't possible. He couldn't tell this crazy story to Kim and Hugh.

Sandra slid back in the booth. She was conflicted. She wasn't attracted to Aurora, but this was Rick. There were hints of Rick in Aurora, mannerisms, inflections. It was likely that Aurora's appearance was visibly different to everyone who had known her before. If Sandra closed her eyes, she could almost picture the face that Aurora was *supposed* to have, the one before Rick moved into it. "You can't go back to LA."

"Why not?"

"Because you're dead to them."

"I'd be someone new."

"Aurora Garcia?"

"Aurora Garcia."

"That probably wouldn't work, Rick."

"So, I should stay here and marry some farmhand?"

"I'll take care of you." But as she said this, Sandra felt a strange anger well up inside her. Auguste Marchant had been fine leaving Juliet to marry a farmhand when he'd abandoned her. Now, two iterations later, Rick couldn't abide the same fate for himself. Sandra hid her irritation. "Quit being a pain in the ass. You still know how to take pictures. Think of yourself as the modern-day Georgia O'Keeffe. You can be a photographer again, but just...as Aurora Garcia."

Aurora looked at her with contempt. "I'm glad you've decided things for me. But then again, that's what you do, isn't it?"

"I didn't do this to you. You have another chance at life. Think of it as a gift." She could hear Luke in her own words.

"Let me put it to you this way. If I hadn't known *you*, what would have happened to me?"

Sandra looked down at her hands.

"This is your doing, you see..."

Sandra paid for lunch and they walked back to the truck. Outside of town, Aurora pointed to a motel. "Can we just stay here tonight? I can't go back to that house."

"Sure." Sandra pulled in and got a room. When she got back to the truck, she found Aurora gone. Walking around to the pool in the back of the motel, Sandra discovered her swimming nude while two men—hotel workers—watched her with delight.

Sandra leaned down. "Get the fuck out of the pool, Rick."

"Why don't you come in."

"Get the fuck out of the pool, Rick."

Sandra waited while Aurora lifted herself out of the water. She handed her the wad of clothes that had been discarded around the diving board. Aurora walked behind her, not even attempting to dress. Sandra opened the door to the room and Aurora fell on the bed, leaving a big wet spot on the bedspread.

"You need to dry off," said Sandra, a little too much like her mother for her own liking. Was she turning into Betty Keane? She looked up and saw the painting of praying hands over the bed. She got up and removed the painting.

"You need to come here," said Aurora.

Sandra sighed. She wasn't sure what was about to shake down, but she also wasn't going to go back to Luke without having tried. Sandra sat on the bed next to her. There was a tug on her shirt and Sandra was pulled down next to Aurora on the bed, side by side like planks on a floor.

"It's like Le Bon View." Aurora leaned up on one elbow and kissed Sandra, which was only more confusing than Sandra had imagined. She hadn't kissed a woman before and this wasn't a woman, it was Rick, but it was still a woman. And then Rick as Aurora was peeling Sandra's clothes off.

But the whole thing was off, it was macabre. This wasn't Rick; this creature had had its head severed nearly two weeks ago. Rather than feeling aroused, Sandra thought she might vomit. "Stop."

Aurora seemed pleased about something.

Sandra got dressed and walked over to the Rambling Coyote Bar across the highway. Aurora followed her, but sat on the other side of the bar. The beer felt great and so Sandra had another and another, drinking alone because Aurora was doing shots of whiskey with two men—a mistake that Aurora was making, thinking she could hold her liquor like Rick. By two drinks, Aurora was swaying and bumping into the man next to her.

Sandra ordered another beer and could hear Aurora's voice, loud over the music. Tired of being ignored, Sandra paid the bartender and went to the bathroom before stumbling back across the highway to the motel—only to find Aurora up against the side of a red Ford truck fucking a white man in a cowboy hat.

Sandra opened the door to their motel room and slammed it a little too hard, but not so hard as to miss Aurora's final moans.

"That was fucking awesome," said Aurora as she spun into the room, putting her panties back on. "I like being a woman."

Sandra glared at her.

Aurora sat down on the bed. "Don't be shitty about it. You're telling me if you woke up with a dick you wouldn't do the same thing? It's not like you're putting out."

"Fuck you. Every illusion I thought I had was shattered today." Sandra sat in the cheap, scratchy chair with wood arms. She looked down at the arms and found women's phone numbers carved into it.

"I never realized you were so uptight."

Had Rick always been this much of an asshole? Perhaps Sandra hadn't seen it before?

"I gotta go," said Sandra, grabbing her purse and keys. "The room is paid up. Can you find your way home?"

"Sure, baby."

While Sandra started the truck, Aurora stepped out of the motel room, held her finger up for Sandra to wait, and walked around to the driver's door. Sandra rolled down the window.

Aurora pulled Sandra close to her and kissed her long and tender. Sandra felt something deep and sad coming. "I think this is the end of the road for us." Aurora had tears in her eyes. "Let me go this time, okay?"

Sandra stared at Aurora's brown eyes. She could see Rick in them, but this wasn't *her Rick*. Rick turned.

"Hey," called Sandra. Rick turned back. She decided something and as she did, it came to her: the proper phrasing for something. "It's a good idea that you not remember me anymore or your life as Rick Nash." Aurora stared at her for a moment, blinking.

"You shouldn't remember Rick Nash or me."

"Can I help you?" Aurora looked puzzled.

Sandra didn't say a word—she couldn't. She simply nodded, numb.

Aurora walked into the motel and shut the door behind her.

When she got back to Pangea Ranch, she found Luke stacking firewood.

"You *knew* he would be different."

"I knew no such thing. These things are fluid." He sighed, his voice monotone as he kept stacking. He sat down next to her and pulled her legs over his, peeling off his work gloves. "I didn't know anything, but I figured. It's usually the case."

"That *thing* wasn't Rick."

"Oh, it was him all right, but a different body or different circumstances can alter the version."

"You mean like Nora and me?"

He met her eyes. "I didn't do it to be mean to you, if that's what you think."

"It's exactly what I think. Look around this place. You brought me here, not Paris. You haven't changed one thing about this house since she died. Since I died… You're mad at me because I didn't come back like her."

He leaned back in the seat. "True."

"You were teaching me a lesson."

He shrugged. "Maybe."

"No 'maybe' about it. You wanted me to know what it felt like to be you," Sandra said and pointed to him. "Well, for starters, I can't keep a girlfriend."

"You weren't that bad."

Sandra looked at him, horrified. "How do you know?"

"I know everything you do. Part of my job."

"You're an asshole." She kicked him lightly with her leg. "Doesn't it bother you? What we do? Because it bothers me. After seeing all of this. We interfere with nature. People die. We're *bad* people."

"You're cursed; you have no choice." He paused before continuing. "I'm aware of what we do. It's not that I don't know right from wrong, but if it's *wrong* and it protects you, then, no, it does not bother me. You can hate me for that if you want, but that is my purpose here."

"Your purpose is long over, Luke. We need to end this thing," said Sandra. "You need to help me."

He walked away from her.

At nightfall, there was a frantic knock on the door. Privately, Sandra groaned. They'd had two people show up tonight with illnesses, needing healing. After the last one, she'd gone back to her room to discover that her nose had started to bleed. She'd kept it from Luke, like she did most things these days, but it had taken most of the night for it to stop. She wasn't sure she had it in her to heal anyone else tonight.

Opening the door, she found the porch empty. She stepped out and looked around, but no one was there. Uneasily, Sandra stepped back into the foyer. She turned and found Mr. Garcia standing near the kitchen, having come in from the side porch.

"Mr. Garcia." Sandra laughed. "You scared me."

The man kept his right hand at his side and was turned so she couldn't get a look at what he was carrying. As though he had been practicing English, he formed the following words: "What kind of devil are you?" He raised his hand and aimed a shotgun at her.

"I don't know what you're talking about." Sandra's voice rose.

The commotion on the porch brought Marie, who spoke the most Spanish. She began to plead with the man. "He says his daughter didn't come back to him. Some monster came back instead."

"Tell him no monster came back," said Sandra. "And I didn't know."

Marie began arguing with the man.

"He says you play with people's lives. You are a witch."

Sandra was surprised he'd been so correct in his assumption.

The man shook his head. He was animated, and the gun was moving between Marie and Sandra as he spoke.

"Oh no," said Marie, her face pale. "He says he killed his daughter tonight. So he could send her back."

"No!" Sandra exhaled. Not Rick. Not again.

"You are the devil." Mr. Garcia said in broken English as he walked two steps toward her. Instinctively, Sandra backed away.

"What did he do to Aurora?"

Marie asked him the question in Spanish. She seemed pained to tell Sandra.

"Tell me."

"He drowned her," said Marie. "He said he drowned her like a dog then burned her body like a witch so you can't bring her back again."

"You came to us," said Sandra, trying to reason with the man. "You brought Aurora to *us*."

The man spoke in animated Spanish. Sandra knew what he was saying not by his words but by his expression. Sandra could see that the gun was heavy and unfamiliar to him.

"You..." Sandra didn't even get the words out of her mouth before she saw the man pull the trigger. It was so fast that there was no time to react. Just like Rick had said, at first, she felt no pain, only a sense of faintness and the dripping of blood. Then, searing pain. She looked down. For a man with little experience with guns, Mr. Garcia's shot had been oddly accurate between her ribs. Sandra felt a heaviness over her body and fell to her knees. Next, breath wouldn't come easily. She felt as if she were underwater. Blood was pouring into her lungs, and she was beginning to drown. She started to laugh, wondering if she could heal herself by touching the wound. Then she heard another shot and knew it was Mr. Garcia. He couldn't live with what he'd done, either.

"No, no, no!" Luke was running and she heard his boots slip on the worn wood, sliding on her blood. Grabbing Sandra's head, he lifted her up in an attempt to help her breathe.

While it is said that your life flashes in front of your eyes when you die, what Sandra noticed was the indignity of the moment. With the knowledge she was dying, Sandra took a ten-second accounting of her life, the biggest moments rising—the checkout at the A&P, Ford Tremaine staring at her at the door, holding Ezra's lifeless body in Laurel Canyon, the band on stage at Gazzarri's, kissing Rick and Luke, of course. This was all she got? Like a written obituary, the fact that it ended here and now was such a disappointment.

Luke had a ferocity to his face that she hadn't seen before.

"I doubt I can heal myself," she laughed. "Maybe I should try, though, huh?" When she did try to sit up, she tasted blood and knew it was streaming from her lips.

"I can do it," he said. And he touched her and she felt she could breathe again. "We can have more time." He pulled her tighter. "I'm so sorry, Sandra. I was such a jealous fool."

She met his eyes. It was so tempting to stay with him a little longer and to make things right between them, but she shook her head. "Don't."

The very last sight of him was one of a man crumbling. She recalled the same sight when Nora died, but this one looked even worse. He shifted to his knees and still cradled her head with his hands. "Please, Sandra. Don't leave me. Let me try."

"Don't," she repeated. "Luke," she said so softly, as she struggled to breathe, that he leaned down to hear her. "Maybe next time, huh?"

"Don't say that," said Luke, shaking his head.

"Next one…" Sandra was nodding.

She felt him kiss her forehead. "I'll see you in the next one."

Then there was a sudden heaviness, like someone tugging on her from below the floor. It felt as if she were being sucked through the floorboards, but the hands were so warm and Sandra was so cold.

28

Helen Lambert
Washington, DC, June 17–18, 2012

I was dizzy—Sandra's story had put so many of the pieces together for me. It was, in some ways, the story I'd been waiting to hear. Sandra had also known the curse had to end. She just died before she could figure out how to do it.

Sandra had been shot. I reached down to touch my ribs, almost expecting a scar, but it didn't work that way and I knew it. But it was also the realization that Luke had known everything that Sandra had done with Aurora Garcia—every intimate detail—that sent a shiver down my spine.

He'd said it was part of the job, but that meant he had to know what I was planning—the trip to France, the knife...And yet here he was sleeping beside me pretending that he didn't know. I also remembered Sandra's question to him about whether the curse could be broken and his refusal to answer her. Did he know the curse could be broken? Was he letting me map a path to breaking it?

I took a shower quickly and pulled on a Missoni dress that had always been my favorite. As I held it up, it reminded me of the house in Taos. It was a knit dress with a chevron pattern in pinks, browns, and beiges. I'd worn this dress a dozen times and never noticed it fully and never even wondered why I had been so drawn to it. I looked in my closet to find I had six versions of it.

There were two missed calls from my mother and one from an Austin phone number, which I thought must have been a return call from Hugh Markwell. I felt guilty for ignoring my mother. Five days to go until my birthday and my mother had started asking me for present ideas. I didn't have the heart to tell her that the likelihood that I was going to need a cake this year was slim. And then that made me sad. What else was I going to miss in this world?

Pushing through *In Frame*'s doors, I saw that the July issue was fresh from the printer and sitting in boxes in the lobby. Cracking open a box, I pulled out the shiny issue with the horse cover. It would probably be my last. What would happen to the magazine after I was gone? Everything I owned went to my mother, but I couldn't see her running a magazine.

I thought about my mother a lot. I didn't share Sandra's feelings that my mother was a stand-in. This mother felt like my mother. I sat on the sofa, rather than the desk chair, and curled up, kicking off my heels. Perusing the issue, I was hit by the sweet smell of ink. It was one of my favorite smells, ink on paper. I looked around the office and considered my life. I liked my life here. It wasn't perfect, but if I failed at breaking the curse, this life had not been a bad one. It had its ups and downs, but that was normal. I considered Juliet, Nora, and Sandra—my life had been mundane compared with theirs. Roger and I had not had the drama of Billy and Nora or even Rick and Sandra. We'd been normal people.

My phone buzzed to remind me that I had an unanswered message. I listened to it.

Hi. This is Hugh Markwell returning your call. Wow. I'd love to talk with you about the band. I don't know how you found me, but I haven't spoken about that stuff for years. My number is . . .

Sandra's story had left me feeling strangely whole. So many things about who I was were clear to me now. The fact that it all might be erased again in five days just felt so senseless to me after the gathering of all the memories of my lives. I had such a nostalgia for Hugh and the band. I could almost smell the eucalyptus trees outside Rick and Kim's house. I dialed his number, and he answered on the first ring.

"This is Hugh Markwell."

"Mr. Markwell. It's Helen Lambert from *In Frame* magazine."

"It's so good to hear from you, Ms. Lambert. I did a bunch of research on you before I called you back. You have a really nice publication." He chuckled. It was Hugh's wonderful, pure laugh that I'd missed so much. "Tell me something. How did you hear about No Exit?"

I hadn't anticipated this question. Why hadn't I anticipated this? I tugged at my hair, searching for an answer. "I was out in LA recently. A friend of mine was saying he'd seen this great band play once and he didn't know what became of them."

Hugh sighed. "To think that someone remembered us . . . well that's pretty special." He had a slight lilt to his voice—one he'd likely acquired from living in Texas. "We had no idea what we were doing. It was my sixth band and nothing had stuck. Lily and I were young and in love—Lily was my first wife."

Hearing those names again. I'd just lived this life over the past few days. It was so fresh to me and Hugh was giving life to it. It *was* real.

"Lily Leotta?"

"Yes. She became Lily Markwell, but . . ." His voice fell. "Lily drowned off Stinson Bay in 1978. So many people were lost in those times. We used to practice at my sister's house up in Laurel Canyon. We were up on Lookout Mountain where all the really cool bands were. Hell, Mama Cass was our neighbor. My brother-in-law died over in Vietnam. My sister moved back with my dad. The whole thing just kind of came to a dead stop. We'd been down in Taos. This guy offered us a chance to cut a record so we all piled in the car—Lil, Ezra Gunn, Sandra Keane, and myself."

I could tell from the silences that these memories were something he hadn't wanted to think about for many years.

"Those eight weeks we spent in Taos were some of the best in my life. There was this sound engineer—Australian fellow—I forget his name."

Lenny Brandt, I wanted to say, but didn't.

"We cut about eight songs, and that man really put together a hell of an album. I think it could have gone somewhere. We went back to LA for a quick break and that's when I found out that my brother-in-law had been killed. My sister needed me too much—their marriage had not been good toward the end. And then Ezra Gunn overdosed right after Christmas. At that point, I think the house just started falling down. Lil and I got married. We just wanted something solid. I got accepted to Berkeley and we lived there for a few years."

I hadn't known about Ezra's death. I closed my eyes. It wasn't that it was a surprise, but just to hear that the sweet boy with the mop of curls had met his end was heartbreaking.

"That's the mystery of this whole thing. We left Sandra at Pangea Studios. She'd started something up with the producer—Luke someone, the name escapes me now—but we left her there and drove back to LA with the idea that we'd be back. I never heard from her again. I just assumed we went our own ways—you know, it was the

'70s. But then I'd heard she'd gone missing. I tried to find Pangea Ranch Studios again—anyone who knew what happened to her." He laughed. "It became such a thing that Lil and I drove down to see the place again. Almost—and I think this will sound strange to you—but almost to make sure the whole thing had been real."

"And what happened?"

"The whole thing was gone. The house was empty and the ranch sign gone like it had never existed at all. It's haunted me all my life, Ms. Lambert. The house belonged to a French man, but no one could ever remember really seeing him. The tape we'd made—the album— all gone. I know there were photos of the band that my brother-in-law had taken. I clung to those for many years, proof that it had all been real. You know?"

"I know," I said. And I did.

"I have to go and teach a class, but it's been really wonderful talking to you. As luck would have it, I'm up in Washington in two weeks. I have a conference and I've got something else I've got to do while I'm there. I'd love to have coffee with you. Just talking about it has really been good for me. That album. Ms. Lambert, that album was something special...if it ever existed."

I closed my eyes. Most likely, I'd be gone in two weeks—disappeared like Sandra. I felt a huge sense of guilt about this man. He'd spent his life wondering if Sandra, Pangea, the album, Luke were even real. "I'm actually in Europe for a month beginning next week, but I do get down to Austin and I'd love to get together with you sometime."

"That would be nice."

"Take care, Mr. Markwell."

"You do as well."

I broke down and cried—the lives I'd led, the history I'd seen. As

I'd been talking to Hugh, I'd been flipping through the latest issue, something I always did by habit the minute it came back from the printer. It was in the back arts section that I saw the ad. Where had this come from?

I jumped up and hailed a cab and told the driver to take me to Maine Avenue—the Hanover Collection. The museum had just opened for the morning. I stood in line to buy a ticket, but then decided I could walk right through and no one would stop me.

"I'm just going to walk in." I smiled to the ticket booth attendant, who waved enthusiastically.

I turned the corner and headed down the stairs to the photography floor that looked out onto the Potomac. At the bottom of the stairs, I saw the elaborate installation from the ad: *Richard Nash—A Photo Perspective*. The next panel was a photo of Rick as I'd remembered him. It was a photo of him that I'd taken at the Forum. Me. That was *my* work. Proof that I had lived. Rick was looking down and smiling away from the camera.

"Oh, Rick."

As I walked through the installation, I saw photos of the house in Laurel Canyon, the police lined up along Sunset Boulevard during the riots, Jimi Hendrix playing the guitar, Dodger Stadium, the Watts Towers, the construction of the 405, Janis Joplin sitting on his living room sofa holding an ashtray, and—his most famous picture—Sandra Keane bowing to the cleaning crew at the empty Hollywood Bowl, the sun setting over the top of the nosebleed seats.

The final panels were of Rick's Vietnam assignments. Airfields, jungles, jeeps, the VC, American soldiers, hookers, priests, snakes in baskets at the market. He'd captured everything—it was a body of work that anyone would have been proud of over a lifetime, and he'd achieved it in twenty-eight years. In a glass case, I was drawn to a series of objects that was captioned: ITEMS FOUND ON RICHARD NASH'S BODY. The display featured an old Leica camera, a pack of bloodstained cigarettes with a hole in them where a bullet had passed through, and an old red plastic key holder. It was the door key to Le Bon View. As though it were yesterday, I could visualize Room 41. I tottered on my heels, tears welling in my eyes. He'd taken this key with him to Vietnam.

On a hunch, I took the elevator to the second floor—the film and media center. As the elevator doors opened, there was a direction sign for a special exhibition: HOLLYWOOD'S HIDDEN TALENTS: LOST DIREC-TORS OF THE 1930S. Walking down the hall, I found the familiar posters of *Train to Boston* and *Starlight Circus*. Nora Wheeler was in the *Train to Boston* poster in the corner, flashing an over-the-shoulder look. There were collections of photos of Billy Rapp, behind the scenes. Billy and Ford Tremaine and even a rare photo of Billy Rapp's wedding to Nora Wheeler and Billy's casket being carried to Forest Lawn by celebrity pallbearers. The next showing of Billy Rapp's film *Train to Boston* was in fifteen minutes. I kept wandering through the photo displays. Billy Rapp's letter from Halstead offering him a con-tract at Monumental. The Monumental logo and Halstead's signature brought a wave of nostalgia for me. As Nora, I'd gotten a letter just like this.

Outside the theater, there was a notice that on June 25 at eleven A.M., Elizabeth Tremaine would be giving a talk on her grandfather, Ford Tremaine, and his work with Billy Rapp. I hoped I'd be alive to come to it, but I doubted I would be.

Until Sandra's story, I hadn't factored in that Luke knew everything I did. I was sure he knew where I was at this very moment, sitting in this theater. But why hadn't he confronted me about it? The answer was obvious—I was no threat to him. I would fail at this task and be sent back again for another lifetime. These short lives seemed wasted. I never had a chance to learn enough before the reset button was hit again. Somehow the thought of that was unbearable to me. I liked this life that I'd created. It was far from perfect—the end of my marriage to Roger and the fact that we'd had no children had nearly broken me a few years ago—but I was always hopeful that something better would be around the corner.

Sitting inside the theater, I watched as the old Monumental logo made another appearance in the crackled film roll with a dramatic score. After the main actor credits, INTRODUCING NORA WHEELER appeared. The screen faded to black, followed by the shot of a platform of a train and the sound of a whistle. It was Nora Wheeler's shoes that were captured first. She was walking briskly, moving to a run to catch the train. Dressed in a fur-trimmed long coat, her blond bob peeping out from under a black hat, Nora was the epitome of 1930s style. Watching myself onscreen, I was captivated. The images in my dreams had felt real, but seeing the actual film was haunting. She *had* existed. I had existed then. I remembered that day on the set. The stage was hot and I was bundled up in that coat but had to pretend I was cold. Billy was barking orders at everyone. I would soon learn that it was because he was terribly hungover, but I didn't know him well then. I closed my eyes and remembered the smell of the suitcase prop I carried—its fine leather scent and soft-blue color, not white as it appeared on the film. I could fill in the missing colors—the blue-red of my lipstick, the fact that my coat was brown, not black, that the attendant uniforms were bright red, not gray. The halftone film images did not do justice to the vibrant colors of the 1930s.

"What are you doing here?"

I turned to see Roger in the row behind me.

"I'm watching the film. Why are you here?"

"It's my museum, Helen."

"I'm a big Billy Rapp fan."

"Since when?"

"Oh, shut up, Roger, and let me watch this in peace."

He came around and sat next to me. "I didn't know you were a Billy Rapp fan. Since when?"

"Shhh."

"Helen, there is no one in the theater but you and me. We can talk at a normal volume."

I looked around. We were alone. "He wasn't appreciated like he should have been, and he died too young. This film is one of my favorites. That actress, Nora Wheeler." I pointed to me on the screen. "She is one of my favorites. You know she only appeared in about four films, but she was magnificent. I hear Billy never cast her with Ford Tremaine because he and Ford were lovers. You know Billy was married to Nora."

"Yes," said Roger. "I did know all of that. I brought these films to the Hanover *because* I loved Billy Rapp's work. I never knew you felt that way about him."

"It was a symptom of our marriage," I said, transfixed by the screen. "We never talked enough."

"Helen, are you okay?"

"And Richard Nash," I added. "His exhibit downstairs. Wow! Another lost talent. You know, there are outtakes of that famous photo—the one of the girl bowing to an empty Hollywood Bowl."

"Sandra Keane."

"Yes," I said, touched that he'd done so much research. "There is another great photo series that he took of a band called No Exit. Sandra Keane from the *West* photo was in that band. Do you have any of those?"

"No." He rubbed his chin, like was pondering something. "But Kim Nash Clarke will be here tonight for the opening of the exhibit. I'll ask her about those. See if she has any."

"Clarke?" I caught what he said. "Kim remarried?"

"How should I know?" Roger was looking at me like I was crazy. "You had no interest in anything related to this museum. Why now?"

"Because it's all connected."

"I don't understand." Roger shifted in his seat and rubbed the armrests nervously. "Let me guess, you're a fan of Auguste Marchant as well now. If you tell me that, I'll pass out, right here."

"*Girl on Step* was actually painted in 1895, not 1896." I looked at him. In the dark, I could see the familiar composite profile of all of them—Marchant, Billy, Rick, and now Roger with their big green eyes—all so perfectly blended.

Those green eyes widened. "And how do you know that?"

"Because I was there."

He laughed and shook his head. "Stop kidding. I have a secret. Do you know that I have a new painting in the Marchant collection? I haven't shown it to anyone else. It came this week."

"What is it?" I was busy watching myself get murdered on the train. It occurred to me that I had no idea how the film ended because Nora had never actually watched the ending.

"It's called *Juliet*."

The name was like a punch to my gut. Quickly, I turned in my seat. "What?" Roger didn't understand the significance of the painting. Its role in all of this. It was the spark, the genesis, the reason for our marriage and this museum. "Can I see it?"

Roger looked thrilled. "Yes, it's in the vault. The appraisers need to look at it before I can hang it."

I followed him down the hallway, taking one last look over my shoulder as Nora acted dead on the floor. Roger was moving quickly to the door marked EMPLOYEES ONLY, which led to the main vault corridor. He scanned his access card, and we entered the basement vault. Roger didn't seem to remember that I'd had been here two days ago stealing Auguste Marchant's paintbrush.

Roger walked over to a crate and carefully pulled out a large canvas. Placing it on the table, he pulled the cover off to reveal *Juliet*. The drapes, the shadows, Juliet's skin, the look she gave the artist—one of desire and carnal knowledge, which for a girl of her age made up a pairing of doom. I touched the canvas. This was the painting that had been taken by Juliet's mother the night she stormed into Marchant's studio, not one of the sketch versions that Marielle Fournier had mentioned from the attic, the one with the burned edges that Michel Busson had taken. This was the real thing.

I'd thought the painting had been destroyed, but then Juliet's mother had gotten sick; perhaps she'd never gotten around to burning it. "Where did you get this?"

"It's the crown jewel of my collection," said Roger. "I am drawn to this painting more than any other. There is something about her." He waved his hand toward the canvas.

"Yes," I agreed. "There is."

"I can't imagine anyone looking at me like that." Roger cocked his head. "You know, she kind of resembles you."

I think I might have snorted out loud. "Really?"

He blinked. "Really."

While Roger didn't have the memories of his lives like I did, he was oddly drawn to different versions of himself.

"Anyway, most of my Marchant paintings have come to me through a Parisian broker."

I closed my eyes.

"Paul de Passe."

I smiled. "I see."

"Anyway, I've been begging him for this one for years, but the seller wouldn't budge until now. Remarkable, isn't it? You know, it's rumored that Juliet was the love of Marchant's life."

"She wasn't," I said. "She was only the muse. Only ever the muse."

"Marchant was lucky. Look at her."

"But she was very unlucky."

"I'm not sure," said Roger. "Nothing is really known about her." He lifted the painting and placed the cover over it. "But the muse is the creative genesis. Much more powerful than the lover or the wife. To the artists, it's the muse who is more important."

"Not at that time," I whispered to myself, studying *Juliet* one final time as the painting descended back into the crate. "It was a man's world then. Being a muse didn't get you very far."

"Well, can you imagine being the painter when the relationship ends?"

I didn't know where he was going with this. "I'm not sure I follow you."

"You're creating art where the muse is the centerpiece. Then, for whatever reason, the relationship ends. At that point, your art turns against you. Think about it. You can't look at your work anymore. Your own work becomes something distant, almost alien to you." Roger laughed. "I can't imagine."

But I knew that somewhere Roger could feel that emotion exactly... the betrayal of his own art.

As we were exiting the vault, I turned. "Any idea who the real owner was?"

"I think I know," said Roger. "There is a French art collector who contributed most of the money to fund the Hanover Collection."

"Let me guess. Varnier," I said. "Lucian Varnier."

"God, you are full of surprises today," said Roger. "How do you know Varnier?"

"I've read about him."

"Well, have you read that his interest in Marchant rivals my own? It wouldn't surprise me if he had scooped up the painting from a family member in France for a steal. He's been a big supporter over the years."

I remembered the envelope full of cash that Juliet's father had been given by Varnier. My guess was that the painting had always been with Luke. "I'm going to take one last walk through the Auguste Marchant installation," I said.

"Do you care if I join you?"

I looked at Roger. "I'd love for you to join me. It would be fitting." I touched his face and he let me.

But he looked at me puzzled. "Helen, you're awfully odd today."

"I loved you, Roger. Once... a long time ago."

"I loved you, too, Helen, but it didn't seem *that* long ago."

I smiled. This would be goodbye for Roger and me—one way or another. As we walked up the stairs through the main foyer and into the French painters' wing, I held his arm. The Marchant installation looked the same as it had a month ago when Luke had brought me here, but so much had changed since then. As I walked through the paintings, I saw Juliet as a younger girl; Juliet with Marcel; and then *Girl on Step (Barefoot)*. Roger led me through room after room, pointing out intimate things to me about each painting. The images of me—of my many lives with Marchant—were all captured within these walls. We had existed together. In our lives we had loved each other and created these things.

Roger's entire life's work—the Hanover Collection—had been a shrine to us. Contrary to the museum competing with me for his affection, it had been an offering to me from him—and I'd failed to see it.

And Luke. Luke had paid for it all.

29

Helen Lambert
Washington, DC, June 21–22, 2012

I made no pretense of going back to my house anymore. If tomorrow was the last day for me, I needed to spend it with Luke.

All of us—Juliet, Nora, Sandra, and I—were one again. It took a day for Sandra's story to meld with the others. From a span of 1895 to now, we'd all been such witnesses to history. And I felt humbled, as if I was the least worthy of all of them. They were all better women than me and struggled more than me against their own times. But their information was valuable if I was going to end the curse. And there was one thing about me that I knew: *I knew how to get things done.*

I thought of the knife in my purse, the one with Marielle Fournier's dried blood coating it. If Malique was right, it was my only hope of survival in this life. Could I stab him?

Luke was making dinner when I got to his house, whipping up something effortlessly, like we were a normal couple. It was endearing. "You okay?" he asked.

"Tell me about Sandra?"

He sighed. "I fucked that up—as usual. Seems I found a way to fuck up each of your lives. I was jealous of Rick Nash, and I caused her death as a result. She was strong and she asked the right questions.

She deserved better from me." He turned back to the stove, like he couldn't look at me.

"Speaking of Rick Nash, I went to the Hanover Collection today," I said, wondering why I even bothered to tell him, when he obviously knew what I'd done today. He knew everything.

"To see Roger." His voice was flat; there was a tinge of jealousy in it.

"Oh, I saw Roger, but I was more interested in the Richard Nash installation, the Billy Rapp film installation, and the newest painting in the Auguste Marchant collection. *Juliet*."

"Huh." He added wine to whatever he was making. It smelled fabulous once it hit the garlic.

"I know, Luke."

"Know what?"

"That the *Juliet* painting came from you. Didn't it? You bought it from Mr. LaCompte."

"Yes."

"And the funding for the Hanover Collection came from you?"

"Helen," said Luke. "I wasn't hiding it from you. My name is etched on the fucking wall in the foyer. You just never bothered to look."

It was true. I had gone through this life missing so many things. I walked over to him and placed my arms around him. "I realized something else today."

"What's that?"

"The love story…it isn't Marchant and me. It never was. I mean the first Juliet and Marchant. That was *real*, but it should have run its course. No, my love story. My real love story…is you."

He stopped chopping.

"We're the love that wasn't supposed to be and yet here we are. I keep coming back again and again going through the motions with Marchant, but it's you, isn't it?"

The room was silent. He put his hand over his face and I could see that he had tears in his eyes. "It took you this long to figure that out? Why on the last fucking day, Red. Why?"

I wrapped my arms around him harder. "I don't know. You are the great love of *all* my lives."

I considered that for a moment. "Maybe I don't have to die tomorrow."

He stared at the floor. "You cannot live past the age of your mother. Those are the rules; they are written in the curse, Helen. I can't change that, and you know I would if I could."

"Well then, let's not waste another minute of this life together, okay?"

We stayed up until morning came with the heavy knowledge of what the day brought. I also knew what I had to do. It had come down to today with either Luke dying or me. I wasn't sure which was worse. This was a decision of almost biblical proportions. My instinct was to protect the one I love, not kill him. Honestly, I wasn't sure I was wired for this, but I had no idea who I'd come back as next time.

The bed was empty beside me. I got up and walked out to the living room to find the French doors open. Luke was sitting on a black wrought-iron patio chair smoking a cigarette and staring at a honeysuckle bush that had invaded the nearby boxwood. I leaned down and kissed his forehead.

It was like waiting for the executioner to come to your door. I recalled the absurd story of Marie Antoinette, apologizing after stepping on the foot of the man who soon would cut off her head.

"What if I don't leave the house today?"

"It's no use. You know that. Don't even say it. I can't bear it." He put out the cigarette and walked into the house, leaving me. And I felt alone. Make no mistake, your own mortality is a lonely path that you walk alone. I felt the weight of it all. I don't know what I wanted from him. Maybe not to see so much of the struggle that he was going through? But in a way, he was dying, too, today. He'd begin waiting for me—a process that I knew was agonizing for him. At least after today, I'd have no memory of me for quite some time.

I reached for the pack of cigarettes on the table and slid one out. I lit it. The cigarette was far too strong for me, but the strangle in my throat made me feel alive, until I considered that it could be this very cigarette that killed me. I looked up. The trellis that hung over me could fall on me at any moment. All around me, household appliances lurked, drinks were potential choking hazards, and stairs...well, I had freely stepped down the stairs this morning, trusting the banister. I would not be so foolish again.

I put out the cigarette and walked into the kitchen, wary of Luke's silence. I stepped into the hallway to look for him. Finally I found him in his study, stuffing something in an envelope. "I'll be back, okay?"

"Okay," I said. It hadn't occurred to me that he'd leave me today of all days. If he knew what I planned, maybe he'd abandon me. He'd betrayed me before, never cruelly, but then I'd never plotted to kill him before. And Malique had cautioned me not to trust him.

He didn't even look at me as he passed me in the doorway. An unsettling feeling was forming in my stomach. Perhaps it was an aneurysm that would do me in while he was gone, leaving my innards bleeding out into my body.

I went back upstairs, carefully. Avoided windows. Checked the safety of the headboard and sat on the puffy duvet. I stared at my purse. Suddenly I had a strange desire to think of all my former selves: tragic Juliet, hopeful Nora, and wise Sandra. I felt an overwhelming sense of love for each of them, as if they were my own, flawed children.

I heard the door open and shut rather abruptly, then I heard footsteps that I knew to be Luke's. They were always the same, those footsteps. He stood in the doorway and I looked up at him. His eyes looked sunken and tired, a dark, dull blue that I hadn't seen in all my years of gazing into them. In that moment, I could see how much pain he was in and how much he loved me. He held something in his arms. It was in a box.

"Here." He placed it in my hands.

I opened it to find the familiar leather book with the goat symbol—Althacazur. Luke had kept it for me all these years.

"It's your power." He kissed my neck.

I stared down at the box with the book. Why was he giving this to me now? He'd given me more pieces of my story, and now the grimoire. Did he think that I could stop the curse? And if I didn't succeed, I would have all this information about Phillip Angier and the grimoire. If I failed, this would help me the next time. Was he helping me?

As we sat there next to each other, I was aware of everything about Luke: the blond hairs on his arms, the cut of his jeans, his breath. I reached over and pulled him toward me. If this was literally going to be my deathbed, then I was going out the way I wanted to. Nora and Sandra hadn't had the gift of that knowledge. I grabbed his face, probably more roughly than I'd ever done. There was such an appreciation, a finality to every kiss, every touch, like I was carving him with my own hands and I needed to remember the location of every muscle, every line, each hair and contour.

As my hands reached to slide his T-shirt over his head and then to unbutton his jeans, it wasn't just me; I felt Juliet, Nora, and Sandra—their desire and their disappointment. It was as if I had the energy, the emotions, and the senses of three different women within me—all of us focused on this one man. I remembered trying to make caramel sauce and ruining three batches because I'd scraped the sides of the pan. You had to let the ingredients sit together for a time, undisturbed. So that's what I did. I let each woman inside of me take her time—knowing it might be the last time we'd be together with him. I think he knew it, too—hell, he knew everything.

Although there were many incarnations of me, there was—and only has been—one of him. As I ran my hands over the curve of his back, I felt the familiar thin layer of sweat that always began to form before he came.

After, he held me in his arms. He took my hand and put it against his left rib. His voice was soft, and he held my hand there. "When you do it. You have to plunge upward. It's very important that it be upward. Do you hear me?"

I felt my insides swell. My breath left me. Tears welled in my eyes.

He took my chin with his hand. "Look at me." His voice was so soft, so patient. I recalled all of the versions of him: standing in the dining room, his hand on Juliet's shoulder; on the boat assuring Nora that Clint would never find her; and cradling a bleeding Sandra in his arms.

"I can't do it."

"You have to do it." He met my eyes. "I *need* you to do it."

I shook my head violently and sat up. "But I love you too much."

"Then you have to do it. I can't take this anymore, Red. You know I can't. This thing was all wrong. I think we made something beautiful out of it, but you might not come back as you again. This one was good, but it's done. You don't need me anymore."

I thought of the Hanover Collection. He'd gathered everything together under one roof for Roger and me. Proof of life. Our lives. His too.

"You need to do it now," he said. His fingers entwined with mine. "I can tell you don't have long."

I turned my head to look at him.

"I can't watch you die again."

I got up and opened my bag, finding the knife buried at the bottom of my purse, lurking innocently behind my iPhone. I held it in my hands. It was heavy, and I could smell the sweetness of the leather case. I sat on the edge of the bed.

"Take it out of the case, Helen." The use of my name jolted me. "You know that you have to do this."

"What will happen to you?"

"I don't know...and isn't that great, in a way? Maybe I'll be free again—we'll both be free."

"I can't accept that uncertain fate for you. If I die, at least I know what will happen in this curse. That script is already written. We just act it out again. I'll see you again."

He pulled me toward him and kissed me. His hand held my head for a moment. "Helen, you didn't need me in this life, but I can't take this anymore. *Please, Helen.*"

I took the knife out of the case. The red blood had dulled to something that looked like a Cabernet stain. I looked at the spot on his chest that he'd shown me.

"I love you." He smiled. "All of you."

With that, I began to sob, rather violently. "I love you, too."

"You have to hurry." He took my hand and put it exactly where it needed to go, even correcting the angle, never taking his eyes off me. I think he pushed my hand. I'd like to think he did. It's hard to accept that I did that of my own free will, plunged the knife into his chest. Like the pulling that Juliet felt when she went into the Seine, I thought I'd felt a tug on my wrist, right where he'd held it. Or perhaps I'd only imagined it and it had been my hand after all.

The entire room began to swirl. I wasn't sure if it was me or the room. Then the doors blew open and I heard windows begin to shatter one at a time, the sound coming closer.

At first, there was blood, lots of it. Oddly, Luke looked calm and peaceful, his torso slick with blood. I held him until he began to change. His skin became rigid like a smooth stone. I saw the bits of him hardening and for a moment, I could see that this was what he really looked like; this was the period of waiting for him when he was in limbo, his features now rubbed out like he was carved in marble. As I touched him, he began to disintegrate. I kept touching him, willing it to stop, until Luke's body was nothing but a pile of light gray ash. And then that dust began to morph, turning finer and finer until it was nothing but the particles that you sometimes catch swirling in sunlight. After several moments of watching, I looked down at the bedsheets.

They were pristine, white, empty. Like he'd never been there at all.

EPILOGUE

Helen Lambert
Maui, Hawaii, June 2013

Mickey's wedding wasn't until sunset, so I still had time. I drove to Hookipa Beach just beyond Paia to watch the surfers. I'd heard that you could see some of the pro surfers on this strip, catching some of the best waves at Peahi. After being an East Coaster for so long, I'd wanted to see real surfing. It had become a near obsession. My phone beeped—Mickey texted me that he needed me back by noon. Mickey was marrying the Rock look-alike, just as Madame Rincky had predicted.

In the year since Luke had died—and that's how I thought of it, Luke dying—my life had changed dramatically. A mysterious package appeared at my door a week after his death. It was from Paris—a lawyer—claiming that I was the heir to Lucian Varnier's estate. Two keys were enclosed. I felt the heavy weight of the first one in my hand and I knew what it was: the key to the old apartment in the Latin Quarter—our old apartment. The other one I didn't recognize, so I called the lawyer who recited an address he'd had on file for a house— Pangea Ranch in New Mexico. I laughed when I realized; I'd never actually used a key in Taos.

I sold *In Frame* for a good price and moved to the apartment in Paris. It had been Luke's, and I wanted him around me. I found the old painting of him that had hung over the mantel until it was replaced by the Auguste Marchant painting. I leaned it against the sofa and stared at Luke's canvas likeness for hours while I played my beloved Satie *Gnossiennes*. I think I was hoping for a conjuring of some sort, but nothing materialized. I'd gotten my wish—I was a dull mortal capable of dying now. I tried to draw on the collective wisdom of all my lives, Juliet, Nora, and Sandra, but we were all hopelessly in love with him as well so all four of us were like a family in mourning. With them near in my thoughts, I walked the streets of Paris looking for him, but he was never there.

My mother, Margie Connor, agreed to go with me over the winter to Pangea Ranch. She was skeptical about this fortune I'd inherited and even more skeptical when she realized I'd become a concert-level pianist overnight. There was no explaining what had happened to me, so I told her I'd secretly been taking piano lessons for years. She was my mother, so there was a part of her that wanted to believe me. I recalled Luke telling me that we'd be surprised at the illusions we allowed ourselves to believe.

The smells of Taos in winter—the smoke from fireplaces that hung over the town—brought back a flood of emotions for me. I teared up when I saw the old TV that Marie had loved so much. I half expected to see Paul and her at the old house, but their absence was more evidence that the curse was really gone. Unlike the time Hugh Markwell had gone to the house in the late 1970s, it wasn't empty. Call it magic, but everything was as it was when I'd last seen it, in March 1971. I uncovered the old Steinway M and sat in front of it for a long time before I played. In the bench, I found my old compositions. On the out-of-tune piano, I ran through them all.

I went down the hall toward what had been the studio and opened the door. It was there, just as I'd known it would be—the Neve console had sat sadly quiet for forty years; through the glass was Ezra's old drum kit with the microphones still in place, and next to that my Gibson G-101. I looked down at the Neve and saw that even the ashtrays were still in their places, although they were empty. In the closet, I pulled open the drawer and found them—the tapes from the No Exit recording sessions, the last one dated November 15, 1970. Since I had my recent Sandra memories, I knew how to move around the studio like it was yesterday. Placing the tape on the player, I fished it through the machine until it caught. Back on the Neve, I found the channel dedicated to the reel-to-reel machine and turned it up. No Exit hadn't been heard for forty years. Listening to the soundtrack from my past again after all this time reduced me to tears. It had been such a special moment. I placed the master tapes in a box and FedExed them to Hugh Markwell at the University of Texas, Austin, with a note. *It was real.*

Other than Luke, it is the piano and this music that has tied my lives together. Sometimes, after I play, I turn, expecting Luke to be standing there, the sound of his boots on the rough floor, but the hall is always empty. "I miss you," I say to the empty hall and there is an echo that carries.

Reconciling all of my lives has not been easy. I'm not sure that all of us were all meant to live together in one body like nesting dolls—I have their memories, but I also have their perspectives. I'm more a child of the 1970s these days, like Sandra. I question everything. I feel the weight of life more, like Juliet. Yet I'm more hopeful, like Nora—which has brought me here today to learn to surf. This is more Nora's wish than the rest of us. These are big waves. I won't start here at Hookipa Beach, but I want to watch the real surfers, artists in action.

And I'm not disappointed.

When I woke up the day after my thirty-fourth birthday and realized that the curse was broken for good, I felt an amazing sense of loss. I had made myself mortal, and though I didn't fear death, I'd gained a new understanding of my mortality, and for the first time, I felt vulnerable. There would be no other life—no restart like a video game. This life had to matter. It had come at such a cost.

There is still a darkness that hangs over me. Luke had retrieved Angier's grimoire—now mine—from my house in Challans and kept it with me all those years. I know now that the grimoire protects me, but it requires something from me for that protection. I've chosen to not use this power—not to summon the source that comes with it—not even to get Mickey a lifetime supply of free lattes at Starbucks. When I'm alone with my thoughts, though, I know in my soul that there is only *one thing that could tempt me* if the cost weren't so steep.

I took my flip-flops off and squished my toes in the sand. Finding a picnic table, I sat down and watched the waves slam into the rocks. There were two surfers—it was early, so there would be more coming.

"Do you surf?"

I turned to find a man standing there with a board hooked under his arm. He was in his late thirties with a ruddy, tanned face and hair that had begun to turn blond in places from the sun.

"No, but I want to. I'm imagining what could be."

"I give lessons if you decide to do more than just imagine."

"Hawaiian waves are too big for me." I rolled my eyes. "I'd probably kill myself."

"Well, you have to respect it, that's for sure." He smiled. "I had a pretty bad wipeout last year, myself. I was in a coma for a few weeks. I'm really just getting back into it. Teaching other people has been helpful."

"Oh," I said. "Be careful out there."

"It's okay," he said. "These waves today are pretty calm."

"Did it make you want to stop surfing? Your accident."

"No," he said, pushing the board into the sand. "The experience changed me. My family says I woke up a different man."

"Sometimes that can be a good thing." I stared out at the shoreline, thinking that I had some experience waking up being a different person.

As he turned his head to look at the other surfers, I caught something familiar about him—the mischievous look in his deep-blue eyes, the caramel tan and hair streaked from hours in the sun. Could it be?

I jumped up from the picnic table. "So where exactly do you give lessons?"

"Over at Lahaina," he said. "The water is calmer there for beginners."

"Okay," I said. "I'm trying new things. I warn you, though. I'm scared to death." I thought this sounded odd, and I regretted saying it immediately.

"Hey, they said I died last year. I don't remember it, but I woke up and I just got back out there. You just have to get out there." He pulled the board out of the sand. "Ninety-Nine Prison Street in Lahaina. Same time tomorrow?"

"Sure," I said. "Why not."

"I won't let anything happen to you."

"I'll hold you to that!"

"See you tomorrow, Red." He turned and headed toward the ocean.

I watched him walk away from me, then paddle out into the ocean, toward the horizon. He sat on the board for a moment, considering the incoming swell, before paddling deep into the thick of it. A big, violent wave picked him up and he stayed upright until the surf lost its torque, depositing him near the shore, like a stalled car. I could see the joy—the freedom—with his every movement, even as the board came to its final resting place. He idled while considering the vastness before him, then turned and paddled out again toward the horizon.

Acknowledgments

I want to thank my wonderful, tireless agent, Roz Foster, for believing in my writing. There is no one else I would have had by my side during this magical journey. And to my editor, Sarah Guan, whose insight into this book made it so much better than I ever imagined it could be! From our first phone call, she understood these characters so well. I'm so fortunate to have found a home with the great teams of Sandra Dijkstra Literary Agency and Orbit/Redhook.

To my sister, Lois Sayers, who is always my first reader. So powerful is her opinion that if she doesn't like something, it rarely makes it on the page. In Boston, she bought a painting that began this whole creative endeavor in the first place, and I'm so grateful to her beyond the words on this page.

Every book has a faithful group of first readers. I cannot express enough thanks to Amin Ahmad for his insights on both the book and the industry. He made this book far better with his critical eye and enduring friendship. Also, Laverne Murach who is such a faithful friend and devoted reader, Helle Huxley for her knowledge of Los Angeles and for introducing me to the Hollywood Museum in the Max Factor Building, Parthenon Huxley for his behind-the-scenes knowledge of the music industry and how records get made, and Daniela Fayer for the lovely Laurel Canyon details from her childhood. My gratitude to Daniel Joseph for always being there with a great cup of coffee, Karin Tanabe for always being so generous with her wisdom, and Mark for his support and inspiration though this process. Also thank you to my little best friend Butters who would be a great critic if only he could read!

I could not have written anything without the support of my colleagues at Atlantic Media. Thanks to David Bradley for changing the course of my life back in September 2000. In particular, I also want to thank Tim Hartman for his long friendship and for providing me with such an inspiring day job.

Writing a historical novel of any kind requires a good deal of primary research: *The Belle Epoque: Paris in the Nineties* by Raymond Rudorff; the marvelous Mark Walker article on William Bouguereau, "Bouguereau at Work" on the ARC (Art Renewal Center) website; *Bouguereau* by Fronia E. Wissman; and *Occult Paris: The Lost Magic of the Belle Époque* by Tobias Churton were essential reading for me for turn-of-the-century Paris. I'm grateful to Darrell Rooney and Mark A. Vieira for their beautiful book *Harlow in Hollywood*. Sadly, Agua Caliente does not exist anymore, but the book, *The Agua Caliente Story: Remembering Mexico's Legendary Racetrack* by David Jimenez Beltran provided most of the primary source material for the chapters on the Mexican racetrack. I'd encourage anyone to watch the film *In Caliente* (1935) to get a sense of this magnificent resort that is now lost to history.

I should add that this is a novel in which fictional characters mingle with historical figures. All incidents and dialogue are products of my imagination and are not to be construed as real.